DEATH
OF A UNION

ANDREW WOOD

Copyright © 2024

All rights reserved. No portion of this book may be reproduced, stored in a retrieval system, or transmitted in any form or by any means – electronic, mechanical, photocopy, recording, scanning, or other – except for brief quotations in reviews or articles, without the prior written permission of the author.

ISBN:

Table of Contents

PROLOGUE
1984 1

CHAPTER ONE
Present Day–The New Silk Road 7

CHAPTER TWO
1984–A Coal Miner's Daughter 13

CHAPTER THREE
George McDonald 19

CHAPTER FOUR
Rising Star 25

CHAPTER FIVE
2022–A Long Way Down 37

CHAPTER SIX
1982–NUM Headquarters, London 39

CHAPTER SEVEN
2024–Sir William Wallace Whisky 49

CHAPTER EIGHT
2022 Olive Green ... 55

CHAPTER NINE
Goodbye Robbie ... 59

CHAPTER TEN
2022–Local Knowledge ... 65

CHAPTER ELEVEN
Present Day–Career Change ... 69

CHAPTER TWELVE
Present Day–Meet the Press ... 75

CHAPTER THIRTEEN
March 1984 -The Miners' Strike ... 81

CHAPTER FOURTEEN
Present Day–Eat the Rich ... 93

CHAPTER FIFTEEN
Present Day–Election Day ... 101

CHAPTER SIXTEEN
1984–Koi Ponds, Gazebos, and Fancy Kitchens ... 107

CHAPTER SEVENTEEN
Present Day–Nicola's Bus ... 115

CHAPTER EIGHTEEN
17th April 1984–Yvonne Fletcher ... 125

CHAPTER NINETEEN
Present Day–Green Is the Color of Money ... 131

CHAPTER TWENTY
1984–Picket Line ... 135

CHAPTER TWENTY-ONE
Present Day–Gordonstoun ... 141

CHAPTER TWENTY-TWO
1984–Scabs ... 149

CHAPTER TWENTY-THREE
Present Day–Feed Her to the Lions ... 157

CHAPTER TWENTY-FOUR
June 18th, 1984–The Battle of Orgreave ... 165

CHAPTER TWENTY-FIVE
SNP Leadership Challenge ... 179

CHAPTER TWENTY-SIX
July 1984 Operation Halberd ... 187

CHAPTER TWENTY-SEVEN
1984–Strength in Numbers ... 197

CHAPTER TWENTY-EIGHT
2024–Rabbit's Head ... 199

CHAPTER TWENTY-NINE
1984–Desertion ... 203

CHAPTER THIRTY
Present Day–Rich Bitch ... 207

CHAPTER THIRTY-ONE
Present Day–Hospital ... 211

CHAPTER THIRTY-TWO
1984–Foreign Aid ... 215

CHAPTER THIRTY-THREE
1984–Red Tide November ... 223

CHAPTER THIRTY-FOUR
1984–Roxanne ... 231

CHAPTER THIRTY-FIVE
Present Day–Resignation ... 239

CHAPTER THIRTY- SIX
1984–The Enemy Within ... 243

CHAPTER THIRTY-SEVEN
Present Day–Change at the Top ... 247

CHAPTER THIRTY-EIGHT
1984–Suspicious Minds 253

CHAPTER THIRTY-NINE
1984–10 Downing Street 259

CHAPTER FORTY
Present Day–Referendum 2.0 265

CHAPTER FORTY-ONE
Present Day–Let the Games Begin 275

CHAPTER FORTY-TWO
Present Day–Leveling Up 287

CHAPTER FORTY-THREE
Present Day–Maggie, Queen of the Scots 291

CHAPTER FORTY-FOUR
Present Day–Independence Day 297

CHAPTER FORTY-FIVE
October 1984–140 Gower St., London 303

CHAPTER FORTY-SIX
1984–Kill Scargill 307

CHAPTER FORTY-SEVEN
Present Day–Beijing on the Clyde 311

CHAPTER FORTY-EIGHT
1984–Murder in Merthyr Vale 319

CHAPTER FORTY-NINE
1984–Deer in the Headlights 325

CHAPTER FIFTY
Present Day–An Offer You Can't Refuse 329

CHAPTER FIFTY-ONE
Present Day–The White House 337

CHAPTER FIFTY-TWO
1984–McMillan 339

CHAPTER FIFTY-THREE
Present Day–Trident 351

CHAPTER FIFTY-FOUR
1985–End of the Strike 357

CHAPTER FIFTY-FIVE
March 6th, 1990–The Cook Report 363

CHAPTER FIFTY-SIX
Present Day–Ghosts of the Past 367

CHAPTER FIFTY-SEVEN
Present Day–Data Breach at MI5 371

CHAPTER FIFTY-EIGHT
Present Day–The PM and the President ... 383

CHAPTER FIFTY-NINE
Present Day–Man on a Mission ... 389

CHAPTER SIXTY
Present Day–Retreat to the Highlands ... 399

CHAPTER SIXTY-ONE
Present Day–Confession ... 405

CHAPTER SIXTY-TWO
Present Day–A Message from the Grave ... 411

CHAPTER SIXTY-THREE
Present Day–Costa Del Crime ... 415

CHAPTER SIXTY-FOUR
Present Day – Rochester, Minnesota ... 421

CHAPTER SIXTY-FIVE
Present Day–Thomas and McGown ... 425

CHAPTER SIXTY -SIX
Present Day–Spain ... 429

CHAPTER SIXTY-SEVEN
Present Day–Sinatra's ... 435

CHAPTER SIXTY-EIGHT
Present Day–The Navy Bar ... 445

CHAPTER SIXTY-NINE
Present Day–Nicked ... 451

CHAPTER SEVENTY
Present Day –The Albanian ... 457

CHAPTER SEVENTY-ONE
Present Day–Nardini's ... 463

AFTERWORD
Where Did All the Money Go? ... 467

Notes: ... 477

ABOUT THE AUTHOR ... 479

PROLOGUE

1984

Ten-year-old Sarah McDonald sat in the back of her father's small car as it moved slowly around the narrow, bendy Scottish roads. It was a cold October's day; she was bundled up in jeans, a woolen sweater, and an army-green Parker jacket. The car's heating didn't work. As she looked out the window on to the splendor of Glen Coe, she could see her breath in front of her. When she got too close to the glass, it steamed up the window and she drew a smiley face on the clouded surface with her finger. She was happy.

Sarah was always happy up here. She loved the Scottish Highlands; it was a different world to the soot-filled air and the grimy streets of the small, terraced houses all the miners' families lived in near the colliery. On every trip north, Sarah drank in the rugged beauty of the mountains, the purple heather, and the yellow gorse. She picked the wildflowers, made faces at the shaggy Highland cattle, and swam in the beautiful cool lochs. The fresh smell of the air, the crystal-clear streams, and the exquisite taste of a freshly baked cake in one of the little tourist cafés was an entirely different life to the one she lived during the week.

Decades later, she would still longingly remember those Sunday outings in her father's tiny car. Few miners had a vehicle, but her father had inherited a small amount of money from an uncle who had emigrated to Australia and done well for himself. Her dad had used the money to make the family mobile by purchasing a four-year-old car. Sarah had such vivid memories of those times with her father, for she'd always been a daddy's girl. Her father doted on her and encouraged her to read, study, and think, making her an odd one out among her friends. Most were already resigned to their fate in the small Lanarkshire coal-mining town of Kendown. Few had plans for an escape. It was a grim, gritty place to grow up with little cause for optimism. That year, a heavier-than-usual gloom surrounded the adults in town. Talk of strikes was in the air everywhere you went.

Still, Sarah remembered one particular day. They were on Loch Lomond sailing on the paddle steamer, *The Maid of the Loch*. The water was still as glass, barely rippled by the passing boats, and the sun seemed to shine unusually brightly from the sky. Her father was snapping pictures of her like a Japanese tourist on his new Pentax camera. She recalled the steam train journey to Mallaig, where they enjoyed the best fish and chips ever, cod fresh from the boats. They learned to ski on the dry slopes at Aviemore. Sarah smiled at the memory that she'd picked up the sport faster than her father or mother, who kept falling over. There'd been a hike to the top of Ben Nevis, an idyllic weekend in a tent on the shores of Loch Mora. And her first knickerbocker glory at a café in Largs. A delicious combination of fruit, ice cream, and meringue served in a tall conical glass, eaten with a long spoon; it was a heavenly treat for a young girl. Life in a mining family was hard, but her father made the weekends special for her and her mother; they always went somewhere in that little car on the weekends until the miners' strike.

George McDonald, her father, was a handsome man in his mid-thirties, a natural-born leader. He had jet-black hair, worn long, with thick black sideburns. He was not a big man—trim, only five feet eight—but with his film star smile and easy demeanor he was popular with the other men. He'd always go down to the pub with them on Friday nights, but unlike most, it was two pints for him and then home. After years in the pits, George could tell coarse jokes and swear like a sailor, but he also played chess and loved reading. He knew how to be one of the boys, but first and foremost, he was a family man—albeit a family man with the drive and ambition to take the Union in a new direction.

The memories blurred. Sarah always came back to that day. The weather that day had been typical for November. She was eleven years old. The green grass at St. Michael's had been ruffled by a cold and grey wind from the North. It was not raining yet, but the rain would be coming soon. There were a lot of people gathered, at least two hundred miners. Her dad was a popular man, but there were also many people who should never have been there. People with cameras. It had come as a shock to Sarah to see his picture on the front page of the *Daily Record*. He was just her dad. Sarah did not understand why the men with cameras were there at all.

There was pushing and shoving, a few shouts, and threats of violence.

"Get the fuck out of here," one of the miners had yelled at a man with a camera. Small details stuck in Sarah's memory.

"Language!" yelled a miner's wife. "Remember where you are, Jock."

"We y'er no welcome here," yelled another miner to the man with the camera.

The reporter tried to take a shot of the family, but an unseen assailant pushed him to the ground from behind.

"Get out o' here before we put you in with him," the assailant spat.

The reporter scurried off with his broken camera, cursing as he left. The other press men moved slowly back, looking for a safe distance from which to continue their work. Cameras flashed. Lenses clicked. A prayer was muttered by a man in black. Sarah watched as her father's coffin was lowered on its final journey into the earth. She stood at the edge of the pit, looking in, feeling like the abyss had no bottom, like she would fall in and never get out.

At the graveside, her mother leaned down to whisper in her ear, "The bastards murdered him. Don't you forget it, my lassie."

Decades later, Sarah still wore a silver locket with his picture around her neck. But she could still hear the scrape of the shovel as the men covered the pine casket with spadefuls of dank, dark, musty Scottish earth, slowly layering soil on top.

They say time heals all wounds, but it's not true. Even at the age of eleven years old, Sarah knew that the pain would never, ever go away.

CHAPTER ONE

Present Day–The New Silk Road

President Anderson and his friend, Admiral James "Jim" Mitchell, were playing golf at the Greenbrier Resort in White Hot Springs, Virginia. The resort had been a favorite of presidents for decades, not least because underneath the historic hotel was a massive underground bunker with a command-and-control center. Built by Eisenhower in the late fifties and decommissioned after the *Washington Post* revealed its existence in 1992, still it was nice to know it was there when away from Washington just in case.

The president, who had just turned seventy, was in great shape for his age, tall, lean, with a full head of gray hair. His father had died young, and he'd been a health nut since his early forties.

Mitchell's face bore the weathered lines of a life spent at sea. He had a strong, square jaw, clean-shaven appearance, close-cropped grey hair, and steely blue eyes beneath a prominent brow.

As they teed off, with an army of Secret Service agents lining the fairways in golf carts, they made casual small talk for a while; then the president asked, "Jim, what do you know about BRI or the Belt and Road Initiative, also called the New Silk Road, envisioned by Chinese President Xi Jinping?"

"Good shot. Is that a never driver I see in your bag?" asked Mitchell as Anderson's tee shot sailed down the middle of the fairway.

"Yes, it the latest Calloway; I love it."

"As for your question, it's not my primary area of expertise, of course, but I know the Chinese have been heavily investing in Africa, South America, and Southeast Asia," said Mitchell. "They are building highways, seaports, power plants, and the like. Loaning money at reduced rates, providing know-how with obvious aims to increase its geopolitical influence globally."

Mitchell's tee shot was sliced off into the right rough and he gave an exasperated sigh.

"I see you've done nothing to fix your chronic slice," said Anderson.

"Not for lack of trying, I've taken a dozen lessons," groaned Mitchell.

"You should try my guy, Bobby Clampett. He's an X PGA Tour player who really helped my game. His stick is "It's all about impact." Nothing else matters; it's a much less complicated approach. I usually fly him up to DC, but I've got a campaign gig in Naples, Florida, next week, and we can go see him if you want to tag along," Anderson offered.

"I'm in," said Mitchell.

"That's correct," said Anderson. "The Belt and Road initiative consists of two main components: the Silk Road Economic Belt; this land-based component focuses on connecting China to Europe via Central Asia and the Middle East through a network of railways, highways, and pipelines. The 21st Century Maritime Silk Road; this sea-based component aims to link China to Southeast Asia, South Asia, Africa, and Europe through a network of ports and shipping lanes."

"I am familiar with their port-building activity, and we have been monitoring it closely," said Mitchell.

The two men were walking with caddies. "Golf is so much better when walking with a caddie," observed the president.

"That's a fact," said Mitchell. "I played at Galloway National last year at the end of May."

"Where is that?"

"It's on the salt marshes looking at Atlantic City, a great Tom Fazio course. Anyway, I had this guy caddying for me. He was about forty-five years old, five-six or seven, and one hundred and fifty pounds. He told me I'd be his last bag of the season until September and that he's going to spend the summer in Vietnam. I am like, 'Firstly, it's the beginning of the season in New Jersey. Why would you disappear all summer?' He tells me the marsh flies are as big as sparrows and will carry you away, so he prefers to wait until they are gone."

"And why Vietnam?" asked the president.

"That's the kicker," said Mitchell. "I asked the same question. The caddie says, 'Because here in the US, I'm a short, poor guy; over there, I'm a tall, rich guy.'"

The president burst out laughing as Mitchell chuckled.

"Do you also know about the '16+1' initiative, a platform established by China to enhance economic and cultural cooperation with sixteen countries in Central and Eastern Europe, which includes several EU countries?" asked the president.

"No, I was not aware of that, but if you'd asked me how many tanks Hungary has or the readiness of the Estonian army, I could have helped you," Mitchell said playfully.

When he got close to the area where his ball found the longer grass, a Secret Service agent pointed to it and Mitchell motioned to the agent to kick it back onto the close-cropped fairway grass.

"Hey that's executive privilege," said Anderson with a laugh. "But I tell you I'm very worried about China's increased presence in Europe, Jim, especially Western Europe. They have recently funded huge billion-dollar projects in Greece and Italy. We need to devise a sensible response to counteract them, or we will find ourselves beaten from within. It's a giant Trojan horse."

Both hit decent iron shots onto the green and continued walking down the pristine grass of the fairway. "I have a new putter too, Jim, check it out," said Anderson, taking it out of his large tour bag.

"Looks like a branding iron," said Mitchell.

"Well, it will beat your ass. How about we play the rest of a round for a hundred bucks and no kicking out of the rough either?"

"You're on. Now, what do you have in mind to counteract this China problem?" asked Mitchell.

"I am thinking of the old carrot-and-stick approach. We will earmark billions of low-interest loans to developing countries and help provide the know-how while taking tough sanctions on those countries that choose China's help over ours. The Brits have already blocked China General Nuclear from building their own plant near London, although they were dumb enough to let them partner with a French company on the last plant they built."

"Seems like a risky bet," agreed Mitchell, "putting a nuclear plan in the hands of a potential enemy." "It's beyond foolish and I don't intend to let anything like that happen again," said Anderson. "It's time to get tough and have people show us whose side they are really on or face the consequences."

Mitchell two-putted for his four while Anderson holed a twenty-foot putt for birdie and enthusiastically yelled out, "One down!" while brandishing his putter in the air. Mitchell smiled to himself; the leader of the free world and birdie could still make all your problems vanish, at least for a few moments.

CHAPTER TWO

1984–A Coal Miner's Daughter

Sarah McDonald stood staring blankly at her father's grave as the soil piled on top close to level with the ground. A miner Sarah barely knew as a friend of her father's grabbed her arm gently and whisked her away from the grave into the back of a large black car, where she sobbed alone. A few minutes later, her mother, eyes also wet with tears, joined them, and they hugged. Then they were whisked away on a fifteen-minute ride to a grey stone hotel built to look like a castle. It started to rain and kept on raining for days.

Once at the Lakeside Hotel, Sarah found someone had organized a big party to 'celebrate' her late father's life; she did not understand why. Death to Sarah was nothing to celebrate. Most of the men got drunk. She overheard a man from "the Union" telling her mother not to worry about the cost, that they would pick up the bill, and that she could look forward to more money once things were settled. Three agonizing hours later, she collapsed on the small bed in her tiny room clutching her Paddington Bear, physically, mentally, and emotionally drained. She was asleep almost at once.

Sarah woke early the next day; she had no clock in her room, but the daily newspaper always came right around seven a.m., and it came through the letter box as she descended the narrow stairs. She pulled it from the letter box and walked barefoot into the small, cold kitchen to put the kettle on. She was only eleven but an excellent reader, the best in her class. She opened the *Daily Record*; her father's picture was on page three. She gasped; she had almost forgotten, hoped perhaps it was just a nightmare, but it was all too real.

The article had more questions than answers. It described his death in a hit-and-run accident as suspicious. The paper questioned why the police could not find the vehicle that had pulverized his car as it must have been heavily damaged. Was a miner too low-born to warrant a better effort from the police? Or worse, was it just that the police were anti-miner because of all the troubles from the strike?

None of it made any sense to Sarah, and none of it mattered. Her father was dead. But it mattered to her mother; she heard her phone calls in hushed whispers to other miners' wives from the wall phone in the cramped hallway of their terraced house. The sound traveled up the narrow staircase to Sarah's tiny room, filled almost to capacity with a single bed and a small white chest of drawers.

"They killed my George," said her mother to someone on the other end of the line. "Those bastards in Westminster had him killed as a warning. Mark my words, Arthur Scargill will be next. They will stop at nothing to get our men back to work."

Someone on the other end of the line asked a question. "The police," said her mother loudly. "You think the police care about one less bloody miner? They would be happy to see the back of all of us. They are not going to do anything, and if they find out the truth, that Thatcher's government had something to do with it, they will only cover it up."

McDonald's death was considered a public relations opportunity at the Miners' Union Headquarters in Sheffield. "Look, this story is a gold mine," said Fred Working, head of communications for the Union. "Anything we can do that maintains the rank-and-file miners' hatred of Westminster and its Tory government is a big plus. We must spread some stories to Union-friendly media that there might have been government involvement in the crash. While we are at it, we can also shed doubt on the police's interest in solving the case. We can print flyers stating our beliefs and give them out on the picket lines for good measure. The story will spread and be embellished with each retelling until it becomes an urban legend."

"Yes," said one of the board members. "But is it true?"

"Well," replied Working, "as far as the police go, they have come up with nothing. There was no truck, no witnesses, no apparent motive. I don't think they are that interested."

"Maybe it was a drunk driver? Or a foreign driver heading back to Ireland on the ferry?" said the man who had objected.

"That's true," said Working, "but we won't be mentioning those options. We will accuse the police of not trying hard enough to solve the case. It will play well with the men. We must take advantage of this immediately before the news cycle moves on; McDonald has already had more than fifteen minutes of fame." There was a murmur of approval from those present.

Detective Inspector David McMillan, indeed, had no answers to the death of George McDonald, but it was not for lack of trying; he was pulling out all the stops despite the bad press, rumors, and outright lies he read in the newspapers. He was not the youngest detective on the force for nothing. He was very good at his job. He would get his man in the end.

From the day of the crash, life went downhill for Sarah's mother. There had never been much money; now there was almost none. The Union paid off the mortgage, and a lump sum of four thousand pounds in cash appeared in their bank account, and that was about it. There was a small insurance settlement, just over fifteen hundred pounds, but her mother had no job and the money quickly vanished, spent on cigarettes, booze, bingo, and helping other miners' families. She looked for work but only for a short time. The strike was still on. There was none.

The loss of her husband was more than she could bear. She loved her daughter dearly, but that did not remove the pain. She started drinking heavily. Previously only an occasional smoker, she quickly graduated to two packs a day and then three; but it was the stress that Sarah always thought caused the cancer, not the fags. His mother was obsessed with the cause of her husband's death; it ate away at her heart and soul. She lasted less than a year. That funeral was quiet; there were just a few miners' wives at it, and there was no party afterward. Sarah McDonald was now alone in the world, for she had no relations still alive and was not yet twelve.

Sarah's mind was blank; she wouldn't speak for several days. She just sat in the corner of a neighbor's house and cried while a dozen or so women from the funeral made tea and remarked how sad it was that the little girl had lost both her parents in less than a year. "What will become of her?" asked one.

"Wasn't that strange how her father was killed?" asked another.

Then all the voices seemed to merge. "They say it wasn't an accident." "Police cover-up, I heard from my brother-in-law." "The government was involved."

The women's chatter was lost on Sarah, but she knew that instead of talking about her mother, they were still talking about who killed her father; no one in her town believed his death was an accident. What did it matter? Sarah thought, he was dead; he'd been dead almost a year. Yet, even at eleven going on twelve, it did matter; it would always matter. But would she ever really learn the truth?

CHAPTER THREE

George McDonald

It was 1964, the world was young, and George McDonald would never forget his first day down the mine. He'd been just sixteen years of age. His father had glanced at him as they left their house and joined a parade of other men streaming from lines of identical row houses and walking towards the pit head. The great mounds of slag that surrounded Kendown Colliery were nothing new to him. He'd grown up with the sights, sounds, smells and soot that came from living in a mining town. But still, he felt a flutter in his stomach. After all, his grandfather and forty-six other miners had died in the pits in a horrific underground fire caused by a faulty fan.

"Don't worry about the butterflies," his father had said with a knowing look, ruffling his hair. "It happens to everyone."

The streets were colored black with coal dust as McDonald senior and junior had trudged through the iron pit gates with hundreds of other pitmen at seven-thirty in the morning. The endless ride down in the creaky lift shaft was like a journey to the center of the earth. He could recall the ribbing, rude jokes, and advice from the veterans on the trip down. The incredible noise of the machinery on the coal face and the frustration of not understanding the sign language the men used to communicate over the din. Then there was the constant coughing from the dust and the feeling of utter exhaustion at the end of a day that felt like weeks. He'd known from the first ten minutes deep underground that he did not belong there, but he stuck it out. The journey back to the surface seemed to take hours, but he could clearly remember his utter relief at seeing the blue sky and breathing fresh air again.

McDonald would go on to work on the coal face for the next ten years. While he grew to like the money and the tight camaraderie of the other men, he hated the soot and grime. No matter how much you scrubbed or bathed, you couldn't get all the blackness off your body. The coal dust hid in your nose, ears, and the crack of your arse. He loathed the extreme heat or cold, the artificial light, and the constant worry. The thought that one day he'd be crushed by falling rocks, blown up by a gas explosion, or drowned in a tomb a mile underground like a rat was never far from his mind. All the men in the pits had these thoughts. Some just hid them better than others.

On top of these fears, it was a brutal way to make a living and the life expectancy of a miner was just fifty-eight years old. McDonald wanted more from his life than forty years down the pits and a bang-up party on his retirement, after which he could expect to enjoy a couple more years, if lucky, before the black lung or cancer took him as it had done his father. Mining was a tough, dangerous, debilitating career. He knew he had to get out, and despite his youth, he quickly formulated a plan to make it happen. He'd disliked school, but the one teacher he'd bonded with was his English teacher, Mr.

Atkins. Mr. Atkins' favorite saying was, "The key to success in life is to read. You can learn anything and find out how to get anything you want if you only commit to reading." It was a lesson the young McDonald took to heart.

While the other lads played football, smoked cigarettes, and chased girls, McDonald spent his free time reading books he borrowed from the granite-faced library off the high street. He'd sit on one of the vinyl-covered chairs and trawl through pages and pages of whatever he'd picked up. It was a remarkably good library for a small coal town and had been funded by the industrial giant Andrew Carnegie—a poor Scottish lad who had gone to America and become the world's first billionaire around the beginning of the twentieth century. Carnegie's biography was one of the first books McDonald read, and his story of rags to riches enthralled and inspired him. His tale led him to read other books on success and achievement. He read Dale Carnegie's book *How to Win Friends and Influence People*, Napoleon Hill's *Think and Grow Rich*, and others on public speaking, management, and leadership. He'd read every damn book in the library if reading would get him out of the stinking pits.

In 1968, by the age of twenty, McDonald, when not down the mine, had begun to make himself useful to the local Union boss, Alan Cummings, running small errands, posting mail, making tea, collecting Union dues, and handwriting notes for him in meetings. As his usefulness grew, so did his stature among the other men. He set his sights on a career in the National Union of Mineworkers, for he had already noticed that all the top brass dressed in business suits, not boiler suits, had nice cars and sported Spanish tans from the weeks they spent in Torremolinos, Benidorm, or Magaluf. Most miners could only dream of those far-off places while they themselves were stuck spending their summer holidays in Blackpool, Morecambe, and Scarborough, hoping the rain might stop for at least a few days.

By 1972, at twenty-four, McDonald was getting paid a few quid a week working after his shift on the coal face as an assistant to the leader of the Lodge Committee. Lodges served as the primary point of contact for individual miners, providing representation, support, and coordination of activities within their respective collieries. McDonald quickly learned that lodges were the lifeblood of the unions—the men felt loyal to their lodge, not necessarily to the NUM.

McDonald worked hard at becoming indispensable. When Cummings retired with health problems, he was duly elected Union boss for the lodge at twenty-six years old. He rode up the shaft for the last time and dedicated his life to making things better all round for the miners. Safer working conditions, shorter hours, better pay, and benefits, not to mention increased retirement options, were all on his agenda.

The NUM was divided into different areas or regions, each covering a specific geographical location in Great Britain. By thirty, McDonald had graduated to leader of the Lanarkshire area. While his rise had been rapid, success had not come without a fight. The higher he got in the Union the dirtier he had to fight. And things had got downright nasty when he ran for the national executive office six years later, in 1982.

CHAPTER FOUR

Rising Star

McDonald's opponent for national representative from their area was Alex Craig. Craig was a pugnacious sixty-year-old Glaswegian; short, barrel-chested, red-haired, quick-tempered, and always ready for a fight. Alex Craig had been a Union man for thirty years and he figured it was high time he got national status. He reckoned he deserved it. He'd worked hard all his life. Then along came this young whippersnapper, McDonald. A prick who thought he was God's gift to miners. Well, Alex Craig would not give up a chance at a national Union post so easily. His speeches were laced with personal attacks on McDonald.

Craig stood on the small stage at a working men's club in Lanark holding yet another rally to build support for his candidacy among the local miners. The club was a large single-story building made of concrete with no windows and a metal roof. The air was thick with cigarette smoke, mingled with the smell of stale beer and male sweat. The sound system was bad and the rain pounding on the metal roof made it worse. Still, attendance was good, over a hundred and fifty men attracted by an open bar for an hour afterward, and Craig was picking up the tab.

The microphone crackled and Craig's voice boomed over the general din in the hall. "Thank you all for coming. We are here tonight to talk about who is your best choice for national office, a battle-tested veteran like me or this Jonnie-come-lately McDonald. This young McDonald isn't a real miner. The man barely spent a decade in the pits before he was up top in a suit. Then he brown-nosed his way up the Union. He's no tough negotiator like I am. He's no pit bull like I am. He's soft, Mr. 'Let's Compromise', and that's not how you get the attention of the National Coal Board or the bastards in the Tory government. I've heard from a little birdie that McDonald admires Margaret Thatcher so much that he has a picture of her in his bedroom." Craig made a brief wanking motion with his right hand in front of his groin as he rolled his eyes. There was a gasp from the crowd, followed by laughs, boos, and jeers.

Craig continued his assault. "I hear McDonald likes to read a great deal, a real bookworm so I'm told. If he wants to be a professor, I say do it. This Union needs men of action like me, not scholars."

There was a chorus of agreement. Craig could tell his anti-McDonald message was hitting home; he could see it on the audience's faces. Even though he knew many of the men thought McDonald was a decent guy, Craig was planting negative seeds in their heads and would keep on sowing them to get them thinking. Maybe McDonald wasn't a tough enough negotiator? Perhaps McDonald thought he was better than all of them by reading all those books? Two men, Buchanan and

Campbell, sat in the back row at opposite ends listening far more intensely than most to Craig's insults and innuendos for they were McDonald's men. When Craig's speech was finally over and everyone surged forward to the bar, Buchanan and Campbell slipped out the back of the crowded club unnoticed. They were off to report back on the evening's event at McDonald's small, terraced house. McDonald greeted them expectantly at the door. "Come in, come in," he said while glancing up and down the street to see if anyone was watching. He ushered them into his small living room and sat in the old armchair while both men took the small sofa. McDonald handed each a can of Tennent's lager already sitting on the coffee table, and they gladly took them. McDonald's wife Lorna busied herself in the kitchen making sandwiches.

McDonald looked at their faces. "So what did he say?"

"The usual crap," said Buchanan. "You were too young, didn't spend enough time in the pits."

"Read too much," chirped in Campbell. "Said you should go be a professor. I think you need to stop ignoring him and fight back, otherwise the men are going to think you are weak."

McDonald just shook his head. "Look, I hate the old bastard, but I refuse to be drawn into a mudslinging battle."

"You've got to do something, love," said Lorna from the kitchen.

McDonald frowned in her direction. "I vowed to take the high road in this contest and that's what I intend to do!"

Buchanan and Campbell looked at each other. "I hate to say it, but she's right," said Buchanan.

McDonald glared at them. "If you say so."

His wife came into the room. "He's walking all over you. You can make him look foolish and still take the high ground, you know. Just do it … I don't know … do it in a positive way."

"What if it was negative but he did it to himself?" Buchanan pondered aloud.

"Go on," said McDonald, and Buchanan explained his idea.

The next night, McDonald spoke in the St. Michael's church hall, a place the miners used as a get-together location once a week in Stirling. A potluck dinner from the wives and two cans of beer each. It was another in an endless stream of rec centers, social clubs and miners' lodges, but you had to get your message out. There were fewer people there than had been at Craig's event, but the turnout was still decent. At least some of the miners knew just how important this contest could be to their future, thought McDonald. He read out his notes on a ten-point agenda for why he should be the national representative. The audience looked bored.

McDonald put his notes down. "Look, I know what Craig is saying about me, but I come from three generations of miners. My grandfather died down the mines; my father died of black lung. I worked the pits for a decade and decided I could be far more useful to the membership up top than below ground."

He picked up his notes and brandished them at the faces of the pitmen. "I will not apologize to anyone for reading; the more I learn the more useful I am to the members."

"Bloody right!" shouted somebody from the back. McDonald didn't meet the man's gaze. He knew it was Buchanan. There was a small smattering of applause. "As for the picture in my bedroom, it's not Maggie Thatcher, it's a football player, Billy Bremner." The men started laughing. "No, not like that. Alright. Laugh. But Billy Bremner was a man whose leadership and work ethic on the pitch always inspired me." There were cheers for the former Scottish captain.

"I can't afford to buy you all beer after one of my events because I'm just a lodge leader on Union wages, but I can and I will be a fighter for your best interests at Union headquarters. And, unlike some, at least I can bloody well read!"

The crowd broke into shouts and whistles, and loud applause. And so it went every few days as they both spoke in the small smokey halls and working men's clubs.

As the campaign went on McDonald became increasingly curious about Craig's finances. Craig's campaign was not confined to speaking from the soap box. The man had an aggressive flyer campaign, frequently pushing his messages through letterboxes including McDonald's own. As McDonald walked around town, he could not help but notice Craig had signs plastered up everywhere, on telegraph poles, phone boxes, and fences. McDonald had run into Craig's canvassers at the corner shop and the newsagent and who knew where else they were lurking. *How the hell can he afford it?* McDonald wondered. Where was the money was coming from? There was no way Craig could spend the type of money he was spending on his Union pay. Either someone was financing him, or … or what?

A week later, Buchanan and Campbell attended another of Craig's rallies, at the Hamilton Miners' Club. This time they both stayed for the free beer and lingered until most of the men had left. As Buchanan had expected, Craig had downed five pints of beer, well over the legal limit. Buchanan walked out; he nodded at Campbell, there were only a few men left and the bar had shut.

Campbell left the venue and crossed the street to a red call box, which stank of piss, and made a call. "Hello, yes, I am very concerned about a man at the Hamilton Miners' Club; he's very drunk and I am afraid he might kill someone on his way home. He's about to leave and driving a blue Cortina. We tried to talk him out of driving, but he won't have it."

"Thank you, sir, I'll see if we have anyone in the area," came the reply from the police dispatcher.

Buchanan and Campbell sat in the parking lot in an old Ford Escort that had seen better days, its white paint lined with rust patches. After a few minutes they saw a police car pass by slowly twice in each direction. It was another ten minutes before Craig came out, yelling his last goodbyes and fumbling with his keys. It took him a couple of tries to open the door, but once inside he fired up the engine and headed out onto Green Lane. The two men knew what route he must take and so held back on following him but started the car and edged from the car park to the edge of the street. Before they had even started off in pursuit, the police car they had seen, which had been parked in an ally fifty yards up Green Lane, pulled out behind the Cortina, blue lights flashing.

"Fuck," said Craig who slowed at once and pulled over only two hundred yards from the club.

There was a short pause as the policemen called in the license plate. Then two officers got out of the car and approached the blue Ford on the driver's side to find Alex Craig at the wheel. Craig looked up at them through the open window.

Buchanan edged his car out into the road at once, slowly past the police car, and turned into the next street, Marston Way. There he made a U-turn out of sight, parking facing the action. He killed the engine and opened the windows; the two men had a perfect view. "Good evening, sir," said one of the officers.

"Yes, officers, is there a problem?" asked Craig, trying to be pleasant but sounding annoyed.

"Have you been drinking, sir?" asked the first officer, Alistair Dorland, a large man sporting the build of a rugby player with a shock of red hair poking out from beneath his flat cap.

"Yeah, I had two pints at the social club," Craig said. "I'm fine. Hey, don't I know you? Aren't you Peter Welling's boy?" Craig said, grinning at the second constable who had the lean, athletic build of a runner.

"I am, but at this point, I'm going to have to ask you to step out of the car, sir," said Welling.

"Do you know who I am?" Craig growled back.

Constable Welling looked down at him with a pained smile. "Get out of the car, please, sir."

"Why don't you go catch some crooks instead of hard-working people like me?" snapped Craig.

"Since you have an NUM sticker on the back of your car, you are most likely not working all that hard since your lot are always on strike. Get out of the car now, sir, and I do mean now," said Welling in a commanding tone.

Craig lumbered out of his car, suddenly not feeling as sober as he had felt when leaving the club. Welling put a breathalyzer bag in front of his face and Craig batted it away casually with the back of his left hand. "Some bastard put you up to this didn't they?" he snarled.

Welling looked at his partner, Dorland, with a questioning look, and he nodded. Welling went to cuff him. Craig struggled and lashed out, punching Welling in the face; there was an audible crack as his nose broke.

Then Craig became a punching bag for two very pissed-off Glasgow cops. Welling smashed his truncheon into Craig's solar plexus. Dorland grabbed Craig from behind as he doubled up in pain gasping for air. Then Welling punched Craig in the face a dozen times. Craig's head swung from side to side and he grunted with each blow.

"Enough Welling!" barked Dorland, letting Craig crumple onto the pavement. "You don't want to kill him. It's too much fucking paperwork." Welling reluctantly stopped and headed back towards the police car to attend to his nose while Dorland proceed to cuff the semi-conscious Craig.

Buchanan and Campbell watched in fascinated horror at the beating from their vantage point fifty yards away. All they had expected was an embarrassing night in jail for Craig; this was indeed a bonus. Despite the late hour they excitedly headed off to McDonald's home to brief him on their mission.

The next day, Craig's mugshot, his face black and blue from the beating, made all the papers.

McDonald quickly reworked his speech for that evening to an Edinburgh miners' club to take advantage of these latest developments. "I am not sure who Mr. Craig's PR company are, but he must be paying them big money to get him on the front page of every newspaper in Scotland on the same day."

The crowd roared with laughter as McDonald held up a copy of the *Scotsman* and the *Daily Record*. "Mr. Craig says he has no intention of dropping out of the Union race, while the newspapers say he's looking at a lengthy prison term. While I am sure, brothers, we all offer him the best with his current legal woes, black and white stripes are not a good look for a member of the NUM executive committee. More laughter from the crowd. "It seems clear to me that in the highly unlikely event our situations were reversed I'd be much more worried about staying out of jail than the day-to-day running of the Union."

The men in the crowd called out "Aye" and "Hear, hear!" The tide had turned quickly in McDonald's favor. He knew the first battle was won.

The day after the election, McDonald made the trip into Glasgow to buy a new suit, only the second he had ever owned. It was a stylish light gray pinstripe that cost way more than he wanted to spend, but you had to look the part, didn't you? He was on the NUM executive committee now he had won, and they all wore suits. He proudly put a small Union pin in the lapel and admired himself in the mirror; he was thirty-six years old and in his prime. He'd need new shoes and a briefcase as well for those long eight-hour train rides once a month to London where the NUM had its headquarters. There, McDonald would take his place among a handful of others who formulated the policies and strategies for the Union. He had always wanted this position, a place at the table where he could make a difference for the working men.

CHAPTER FIVE

2022–A Long Way Down

THE SMALL MAN IN ARMY FATIGUES HAD OLIVE SKIN AND close-cropped black hair; his eyes were dark and his mood was foul. He sat on the top of the cliff looking out to sea. The damn boat was late again; engine trouble coupled with communication problems, it was a bad combination. It was time to ditch that old trawler for something better. It was dusk now and would be dark soon. He scanned the sea's horizon with his field glasses. Then, out of boredom more than anything, he turned them inland. There was a car coming down the dirt road, a white SUV; that was unusual. He'd been to this spot many times and had never seen a car. It was a remote part of the island, one the locals called smugglers' cove, a very apt name he thought.

The car must have stopped at the old man's croft for he lost sight of it and it never reappeared. Suddenly his radio came alive and a voice not in English told him they had put the boat in for repairs in Ireland and it would be delayed two, maybe three, days. *Fuck it*, he thought. At least he had brought a couple of books and his fishing rod; he would have to make the best of it. He started to read until the light grew too dim, finishing his chapter with the aid of a flashlight.

It was dark now and, suddenly, in the distance, he saw the car's break lights go on as they went very slowly down the dirt road to the edge of the cliff, but they had no headlight lights on. That was strange. He went into the tent and grabbed his binoculars. It drove close to the cliff edge; two large men got out and together unloaded something heavy from the back of the white SUV. He could not make out what it was, the men were just shadows. The two men took a few lumbering steps to the cliff's edge and threw it off the cliff to the rocks below.

One of the men went back to the car, came back with something small and threw it off the cliff as well. Then they got back in the car and drove, lights off, back up the dirt road to the B road. Then they turned right onto the tarmac and switched on their lights as they headed towards the mainland.

He thought about going down to see what it was they had dumped but quickly dismissed the thought as he was hungry. He'd go look in the morning, probably nothing. The man made a meal of French bread, cheese, and salami washed down with a cheap Spanish wine he drank from the bottle. Then he got into his sleeping bag and read for an hour or more before drifting into a restless sleep.

CHAPTER SIX

1982–NUM Headquarters, London

It was May, 1982 when McDonald took the train from Glasgow to London in his new grey pinstripe suit to assume his place on the NUM executive committee. Just as he joined the committee the pragmatic Joe Gormley was stepping down from his eleven years as Union president. Yorkshire firebrand Arthur Scargill was taking over. Scargill's politics were left. They were all left-wing in the NUM leadership in that period, but Scargill was left of left, a militant Marxist with no room for negotiation.

In theory, under Union rules the executive committee was the government of the NUM between conferences, whose policy decisions it was charged with executing. Years of unchallenged authority had emboldened the group into becoming a power of its own. It was a cozy old boy men's club with surroundings to match.

The twenty-six-man executive committee met the second Thursday of every month, at a purpose-built three-story concrete building in London, located at 222 Euston Road, conveniently close to the Euston railway station. McDonald had expected the meeting room would have a low ceiling with no windows, cheap furniture and fluorescent lights that flickered; after all, they were just working-class miners. About that he was dead wrong. The group met in a high-ceilinged chamber with wood-paneled walls around a huge mahogany conference table covered in green leather. This was surrounded with heavy wooden easy chairs and plush leather cushions, watched over by a giant two-story mural of a miners' gathering etched on the floor-to-ceiling windows at the back of the hall. It felt more like the Houses of Parliament or a tory gentlemen's club complete with the smell of stale cigarettes and cigar smoke. The opulence of the surroundings was the first of many signs that made McDonald uneasy. Why spend all those precious Union dues on creating a palace like this, he wondered.

Arthur Scargill sat at the head of the table. Scargill was forty-two years of age, of average height and build. With his fuzzy brownish hair, already greying at the temples, long sideburns and bright blue eyes that seemed to bulge out of their sockets when he got animated, Scargill spoke in his thick Yorkshire accent.

"We cannot let this conservative government get away with their plans to close more pits. We must declare all-out war with them. We must take a stand and shut the country down until they give in to our demands."

McDonald, at the farthest end of the table from Scargill, spoke up. "Mr. Scargill, I think we would do better in continuing Mr. Gormley's more pragmatic approach to this government. I have researched the economic realities of mining and the National Coal Board's position. The Union's stance on looming issues like pit closures for uneconomic mines has to be negotiated; that cannot be done by flat-out ignoring the fundamental economic reality."

"The economic realities they quote are lies," replied Scargill loudly. "No pit should close no matter how unprofitable they say it is. If they close any, we go on strike and bring the government to its knees just like we did in 1974 by starving the power stations of fuel. No fuel, no electricity. It has worked before and it will work again."

There was a loud murmur of approval from the room. Someone yelled out, "Right you are, Arthur." Another, "Bring 'em to their knees." A few clapped while Arthur smiled like a Cheshire cat at the appreciative audience.

McDonald waited for the noise to evaporate then replied in a serious tone, "With all due respect for your previous achievements, Mr. Scargill, we now live in different times. Margaret Thatcher is not Edward Heath. She is not called the 'Iron Lady' by chance."

Scargill glared at him while the other executives in the room gave McDonald a curious glance; perhaps the new kid didn't know what happened to people who didn't think the same way as King Arthur. They knew it was his way or the highway, and people who disagreed with him instantly became the enemy or a traitor. There was no middle ground. Suddenly, Scargill changed the topic.

"London is a prostituting place. We need to move Union Headquarters to a more politically friendly place. I have done some research and propose we temporarily move our offices to Yorkshire, specifically Sheffield, pending the construction of our new NUM headquarters there."

"An excellent idea," said Ken Miller, the pugnacious Yorkshire leader.

"Anywhere's better than London," chipped in Garth Evans, the diminutive and always jovial representative from Wales.

"I don't agree," said Peter Noad, the representative from Kent. "I like it here, and not just because it's close to me. London is the easiest place in Britain for everyone to travel to."

McDonald, realizing he might have offended Scargill, offered his partial support. "Well, at least Yorkshire is closer to Scotland." He looked down at the green of the inlaid leather on the table and drummed his fingers on it. *Christ.* What the hell was wrong with this place? The rank and file did not care where their headquarters were located, they just wanted quality representation. But he knew he'd already said enough for one day. He had to pick his battles and this one sounded far enough along Arthur's road to be a done deal anyway. He wouldn't have been at all surprised if Scargill already had plans for the new building, even though it was the first anyone on the executive committee had heard of the idea.

Still, McDonald did not want to make waves right away. He was young, new to the executive club, and tried his best to bite his tongue. So much so that he often tasted his blood. He had many great ideas he wanted to implement, the energy of youth, and an entrepreneur's vision.

When the meeting adjourned, several men retired to the Dog and Gun pub and invited McDonald to join them. "How was Spain?" Miller asked Evans.

"Oh, very nice, boyo," replied Evans in his strong Welsh accent. "I came back looking like a Paki." He rolled up his sleeves to show off his dark tan. "Have you been over to Portugal yet this year?"

"No, but we are going for a couple of weeks in September when it's a little cooler," replied Miller warmly.

"Ah, that will be nice," said Evans. "And where are you going for your summer holidays, then, George?"

"Err, we might get a weekend in St. Helens or a couple of days in the Highlands," he said, rather embarrassed.

"Ah well, I hope the weather's fine for you, you can never be sure of getting any sun in Britain no matter when or where you go. That's why me and the Mrs. prefer Spain."

McDonald had never left Britain, although he longed to travel. He just didn't have the money for it. How the rest of them seemed to afford it all was puzzling. The conversation turned to football. Two of the men present had been to the previous cup final at Wembley.

After two pints everyone left for their respective trains home. McDonald spent his trip back to Glasgow lost in deep thought. Trips to Spain, cup final tickets. Something was fishy. Something didn't add up.

January 1983

As the weeks gave way to months, like so many people who enter politics of any kind, McDonald was quickly confronted with the realities of fostering change in a behemoth of an organization.

About the office move, McDonald had been right. Shortly after his first meeting he had found out that the lease for temporary offices had already been signed by the time Scargill had first mentioned it. It was obvious that Scargill ran a dictatorship, not a democratic union. He'd only tell the executive committee what they should do after he'd already done it.

McDonald was visiting the Union's new temporary headquarters, located at St. James House on Vicar Lane in Sheffield, for the first time. The building was a square, unassuming eleven-story 1960s office block. A secretary gave him a short tour. She told him it had been completely refurbished on Scargill's instructions. McDonald shook his head. *Why?* Scargill had already started construction of a giant new glass-and-steel palace nearby. So what was the point of the refurbishment? The organization occupied floors from eight to eleven and half of the seventh floor for storage. That Scargill designed the office layout himself McDonald didn't doubt. His managerial views were firmly stamped on the design. It was an office design straight out of the 1950s with the best offices dished out in a clear hierarchy. Scargill's, of course, was the largest on the top floor.

McDonald entered Scargill's lavish private office and was immediately struck by the fact it was decorated with multiple paintings of the man himself. One in particular struck him, Scargill in a gray flat cap, pointing at the head of a large group of men holding banners.

Scargill stood up to greet him.

"I'd like to discuss a few things with you," said McDonald.

"What's on your mind?" asked Scargill as the two men shook hands and sat opposite each other at Scargill's huge desk.

"Three things. Mine safety issues; rethinking our position on unprofitable mines; and Spanish holidays," McDonald stated flatly.

"Spanish holidays? What has that got to do with anything?"

"I don't know," said McDonald. "But it seems a lot of the Union leaders go on holiday there."

Arthur Scargill smiled. "Why not? The weather's great. The food and wine are cheap."

"Cheap compared to what? A miner's holiday in Blackpool?"

"What are you saying?" asked Scargill, eyes bulging slightly.

"Where does the money come from for all these exotic holidays and new cars?" McDonald asked.

Scargill chuckled to himself. "I'm sure there is a perfectly logical reason. A lot of the guys are pretty tight with their wallets. They're savers not spenders."

"Well, I'm careful with my money and yet there is no way on my Union salary I could afford all these holidays," said McDonald.

Scargill put his hands flat on the big desk. "Look, George. They all work hard, so why shouldn't they enjoy a holiday in the sun? Anyway, it's not important compared to the other challenges we face. The government is still threating to close over twenty pits and we can't have it. That's the real problem we're facing. Not your so-called Spanish holidays."

McDonald paused before speaking again. "We need to re-think our position there."

"That's not going to happen," said Scargill flatly. "We are ready for a fight with the coal board the Tory government. It's not just about the mines." He slapped his hand on the table. "They're screwing the working man. It's about the entire country's political future."

McDonald gritted his teeth. Scargill's bloody-mindedness was infuriating. He seemed far more interested in pushing the country towards communism than he was in the everyday plight of the miners. McDonald knew he had to try to change the man's mind on certain issues. He couldn't just let Scargill steamroll over everything he held dear.

"Mine safety, then. Surely that's something everybody can agree on."

Scargill nodded. "Of course. That's a very important issue." But he suddenly announced he had to leave for a previously scheduled meeting.

"I have heard a lot of good things about you, George. You have a bright future in this Union." Scargill's smile suddenly looked less than friendly. "Don't let your enthusiasm mix up your priorities. Right now, those priorities are stopping any pits from closing. We've got to kick out the Tory government. There's no time or resources for anything else. What's the point of mine safety discussion if the pits are closing down? Once we've put the Tories back in their place, we can get back to improving safety and pay increases so *everyone* can holiday in Spain. Even you! Now, if you'll excuse me, I have to run."

The two men rose and shook hands. As Scargill ushered McDonald through the door, McDonald noticed Scargill was wearing a gold watch he'd not noticed in their previous encounters. He glanced back to see Scargill going back into his office. There was no other meeting he had to rush off to. Something was not right in the Union. McDonald determined he was going to find out what it was.

CHAPTER SEVEN

2024–Sir William Wallace Whisky

Maggie McGown stared out from the pulpit at the rows and rows of ancient wooden pews. Over three hundred people were in attendance, a who's who of businessmen, movie stars, and politicians. She was having a tough time holding it together, never mind speaking. She was short, only five feet four inches tall, but she was pretty, with a shapely figure, bright red hair, and large green eyes that shone like emeralds. At forty-nine, she worked out daily with a rigorous routine to keep that nice figure and the muscle definition in her arms and legs. She wore a form-fitting, long-sleeved black dress, black heels, gloves, oversized sunglasses, and a black pillbox hat.

Maggie hated black. She looked around the church. Well, not exactly a church—it was St. Giles Cathedral, an imposing dark twelfth-century building in Scotland's capital city, Edinburgh. The memories came spooling back, like snippets of an old film. It had been fifteen years.

Maggie had been born into a coal-mining family. They'd been poor but had a passion for education, so she had done well in school. In her twenties, after graduating from Edinburgh University with degrees in history and economics, she had been a model for a Scottish whisky company. After modeling, in her late twenties, she'd worked in sales for a large beverage company and excelled at it. She'd become head of their European sales division and spoke French, Spanish, and German, albeit with a strong trace of her thick Scottish accent. After a decade of disastrous relationships with men who could not handle her, she'd finally met the special someone.

"Robbie," she said. Her voice carried throughout the cathedral's cavernous chamber. "I was married to Robbie Gordon for fifteen years."

She looked out at the faces. "I see the crowd in the church today is not unlike the one at our wedding. Many of you were there, at Skibo Castle." The memories took her back to that day. The Beckhams had been there somewhere, and so was the author Ken Follet, actor David Tennant, golfer Colin Montgomery, and a bunch of Rangers football players whose names she didn't remember. Duran Duran was the wedding band.

"We spent our honeymoon on Santorini, we had safaris in Kenya, balloon rides over the Namibian desert, sailed yachts in Sardinia, and spent weekends in the famous capitals of Europe. I had fifteen glorious years with Robbie. Robbie Gordon showed me the world."

Suddenly Maggie couldn't see the faces anymore. Her eyes were full of tears. Her voice was unsteady, echoing around the cathedral's great walls. "But that's all over now, since last Tuesday. He'd been out riding his bike with a couple of friends; he'd seemed in perfect health. He'd passed a physical with flying colors only four weeks before. Then boom, a giant heart attack out of the blue."

Maggie's voice broke. She choked back tears. "Robbie wasn't overweight; he ate well, never smoked, and only occasionally overindulged, but when you owned Scotland's most popular brand of whisky, that was an occupational hazard." There was a small ripple of laughter around the hall.

Maggie carried on. "But none of that matters now. Robbie's dead, at sixty-nine. Life can be sweet, life can be good, but it can also be terribly unfair. To give you a true soul mate and then snatch everything away in seconds.…"

She tried to focus on the stained-glass window at the back of the great hall to push away all the images that clouded her mind. She glanced down at her text. "Robbie was not just a successful businessman but a generous philanthropist. He helped build hospitals, playing fields, and community centers. He sponsored Highland games all over Scotland and.…"

Her voice read out the words of the eulogy she'd prepared, but her mind stretched back to think of him, her voice catching as she held back the emotion. One of the choirboys broke ranks nervously, looking around at the priest, who nodded almost imperceptibly as he strode over and handed her a bottle of water, which she gratefully accepted.

Maggie took a gulp. "Thank you all so much for coming. I hope to see all of you at the celebration of Robbie's life right after this service at the Lakeside Hotel. Let's throw him the kind of party he would have loved." She glanced once at the coffin as she passed, decorated with white lilies. The next time she saw it, nothing would be left but ashes in an urn. "Robbie…" she said, "Robbie…" but she could not finish the sentence. She had held it together well, but now the floodgates opened.

She staggered away from the lectern and back towards her front row pew until Max, her chauffeur-cum-minder, grabbed her by the arm and helped her half walk, half stumble out a side entrance. Max was the strong silent type, tall lean, ex-military, but when he did speak people listened. He bundled her into the black Range Rover and headed for the hotel. She wished her parents could have been there, but they were halfway between San Francisco and Australia on a cruise and she hadn't wanted to ruin it for them by even telling them.

Maggie sat in the back in silence, lost in her memories. Why had she never taken his last name? She wasn't sure. There was nothing wrong with Gordon, but she was a modern woman. He could have taken hers just as easily. Anyway, it was never a big deal, just like it was never a big deal to fall in love with a man twenty years her senior. Maggie had been thirty-three, him fifty-three when they'd met at a beverage industry event at the Old Course Hotel in St Andrews. He'd never looked his age. He'd been fit and vibrant. Strong and handsome, he loved hiking, skiing, cycling, and golf, all activities she enjoyed.

He was good in bed, always making sure she took her pleasure before he did. He was also wealthy, but she loved his mind the most. They could talk for hours about history, politics, books, movies, and business. It started as a friendship that slowly became an office romance: the older boss, the young, bright star. *What a cliché.* Maggie smiled.

CHAPTER EIGHT

2022 Olive Green

Reporter Duncan Frasier was tall and fit with broad shoulders, curly black hair, and bright blue eyes. He loved his job as a reporter but wondered with all the newspapers going out of business and the curse of AI if he would ever finish his career doing the same job as his father had done all his life. He was staying in a small pub, up in Skye, doing a story on Scotland's distilleries and Talisker was first on his list. His mobile rang as he ate breakfast and the voice from the office told him a man had fallen or perhaps jumped off a cliff on the island and that he should investigate this current news first.

It was a short drive to the pin spot on the map the office texted him. When he arrived, there was a police car and an ambulance. An officer and a medic were discussing how to get the body from the beach to the ambulance for the path down was very steep and narrow. It was decided they would call for a helicopter and airlift the body.

Frasier waited patiently for the right moment. "Do you know who the victim was?" he asked the policeman, who was short and fat. *Far too fat to catch anyone not on crutches*, thought Frasier.

"Aye, Magnus Baird, an old crofter who looked after the sheep, probably drunk as a skunk and stumbled off the edge," replied the policeman. "Anyway, who are you?"

"Duncan Frasier, I'm a reporter for the *Record*."

The policeman grunted, "I should have known."

"So that's it then, death by misadventure?"

"Not for me to say; that's up to the coroner, but I don't see how it could be anything else. Now, if you'll excuse me, I've got work to do." The policeman wandered over to his car while Frasier snapped pictures of the tarpaulin-covered body below from the cliff's edge.

Frasier got back in his car and headed up the dirt road that connected with the B road towards Talisker; he saw the old man's croft over on his left a few hundred yards away. He thought about stopping there, but with the police still on the scene, that seemed like a bad idea. He took a picture without getting out of his car; the zoom on his new iPhone was amazing. He got to the B road and turned left; then, suddenly, he stopped. Up beyond the croft, in a small enclave in the hill, was a tent. It was a one-man tent, very small; in fact barely visible so well did its olive-green fabric blend in with the grass. Nonetheless, he wanted to check something.

Frasier made a three-point turn on the B road and entered the dirt road again as if going to the croft. As he suspected, the croft's outline covered the tent entirely. It could not be seen when approaching the home down the dirt road. It could be seen clearly only if you knew to look for it if you turned left on the B road but not at all if you turned right, which was the way you would turn for the bridge to the mainland.

Frasier parked in front of the croft and started walking back to the tent. It was meant to blend into the environment, just like the man who slept there. He was making coffee over a tiny gas burner, a small man, wearing olive-green fatigues, who was very surprised to see him.

CHAPTER NINE

Goodbye Robbie

WHEN THEY ARRIVED AT THE LAKESIDE HOTEL, MAX helped Maggie out of the car and walked her arm-in-arm to the banquet room. This event would be even more challenging than the church, reliving his life on the big screen. She grabbed a glass of champagne from a tray, downing it in one, and picked up another. She looked up at the giant screen, a picture of Robbie outside the distillery, the narrator's deep voice telling his story.

When his father died in 1994, Robbie Gordon took his family's ailing distillery business and turned it around. The movie Braveheart *was a huge smash the following year, and, thinking quickly, Robbie changed the name of the brand to that of the famous Scottish hero Sir William Wallace. Over the next decade, he turned the Sir William Wallace brand into hot property, first in Scotland and then the world….*

The trial run of the video presentation finished with a picture of Robbie glass in hand. Maggie smiled at the image. She'd put on her large square sunglasses, but they couldn't hide the tears.

Robbie's two sons were among the first to enter the banquet hall. Robbie's first wife, Ann, had succumbed to breast cancer while still in her forties leaving Robbie with two boys: Paul and Iain. The elder boy, Paul, had emigrated to America and made it big in a series of business ventures. Gordon should have had so much in common with him, but, strangely, his son's success without his father's help bothered him—that and his lack of interest in his Scottish heritage or involvement in the family business. Maggie had met Paul just once and liked him a lot, which was less than could be said for Iain, aka the Mooch. Maggie just rolled her eyes; better not to say anything. But she could think it. She suppressed a smile. Iain aka the Mooch was dumb as a rock and was rarely gainfully employed. But somehow, despite his failings, Gordon had doted on him, giving him the attention he craved.

Maggie set aside her thoughts and greeted both boys warmly. She thought of them as "the boys" even though they were closer in age than she liked to think. She was braced for unpleasantness. There had been no prenuptials in her marriage to Robbie and she would be getting most of his extensive wealth. Almost immediately after Robbie's death, Maggie had been contacted by the grey men, his solicitors, Turcan & Harper LLP, although money or the business was the furthest thing from her mind. But they'd insisted. Because of his sudden departure and the complexities of running a multinational business, there were things that simply had to be done.

Maggie knew that, despite Robbie's ambivalent feelings towards his first son, her husband had done the right thing by both boys, leaving them five million pounds each, more than enough to live a very comfortable life. Maggie would get the rest, more than ten million in investments managed by a discreet private bank. But the real gold was in the magic of the distillery. Sir William Wallace whisky, and associated businesses, were worth hundreds of millions of pounds. Robbie had told her all about the arrangements a very long time ago, the paperwork long signed, *T*s crossed, *I*s dotted. It had all seemed so dry and theoretical. Robbie was still a young man—young-ish, anyway—back then. Maggie was his true soul mate and Robbie Gordon knew it. And now he was gone.

Paul gave her a formal embrace. "Maggie. Good to see you. Sorry, of course, about the circumstances." Paul was handsome, outgoing, and with a strong resemblance to his father.

Maggie tried her best to sound cheerful. "He was so vibrant. So alive. Just days ago. I really can't believe he's gone."

"I don't think it's right," grunted Iain. The Mooch was a big, brooding lad with a pug nose and a receding hairline. Maggie reckoned he looked like a night club bouncer.

"I take it you heard from Turcan & Harper, then?" Maggie replied.

"I'm taking it under legal advice," said Iain. "You had him tied up in knots. It's not legal, it's not right, and it's not fair."

The elder brother looked at the younger. "Why's that, then? All you've ever done your entire life is mooch off the family tit."

The Mooch glared at his brother and stated, "I might have to challenge the will."

Paul smiled. "Your lawyers will be delighted. They'll take your inheritance off you in fees and you'll be left with nothing but a nasty grudge. If I were you, I'd take the generous amount that Dad left you and thank the good Lord that he remembered you at all."

The Mooch stomped off.

"Thank you," Maggie said. "I didn't expect him to take it well."

"He'll not give you any trouble, Maggie. He's far too lazy and it would be a lot of work."

Maggie had been so distracted by Iain's performance that she hadn't noticed that the room had filled. She looked around. The chatter was loud and the champagne flowed. She turned back to Paul. "Did your father tell you he was going to sell the business?"

"No," Paul said, looking surprised. "We rarely talked, but I didn't think Dad would ever retire."

"Oh, he wasn't planning on retiring," said Maggie. She took a sip of champagne. "Ever since Donald Trump's remarkable—if lamentable—term as president, Gordon had the idea that a successful Scottish entrepreneur like himself might make a great first minister. He had the money and the wealthy friends to fund a campaign. He was going to run for an SNP seat in the Highlands as a first step and take things further assuming he won a seat. It was to have been his legacy. He reckoned he had the business and life experience to make a real difference to the country and to finally gain independence for Scotland."

Paul laughed, "Well, well! That sounds just like Dad. Aim for the stars and maybe you'll hit the ceiling." He grabbed two glasses of champagne from a passing waiter and handed one to Maggie. "Well, here's to Dad, and here's to Scotland! It's just a shame he never got the chance to get it off the ground."

"It might fly yet," said Maggie.

"Oh. How's that? Strange things have happened in Scottish politics, but I don't even think the Scots would vote for the dead."

"I'm going to do it." It was the first time she'd spoken the thought out loud. "I'm going to run."

Paul's eyebrows shot up and he almost choked on his champagne. "You're not serious?"

Maggie gave him a deadpan look. "I am, and I have a plan. You're looking at Scotland's next first minister."

"Good God. Well, here's to the next first minister!" Paul drained his glass and set it down empty. "Dad always said you had a mind of your own. I see he was not wrong."

CHAPTER TEN

2022–Local Knowledge

"Hi," said Frasier to the startled man who had obviously not heard him approaching his tent.

"Hello," he said in heavily accented English, glancing around nervously as he did so.

"Been up here long?"

"No, no, I just came this morning to go fishing," he replied.

Frasier looked at the empty wine bottle, an empty can of stew, a discarded can of beans, and a bite-sized piece of a baguette then looked back at the man with a quizzical look and said, "Really?"

"Look, I don't want any trouble; I just want to fish," said the man.

"But you were fishing last night as well?" asked Frasier.

"Are you a policeman?" asked the man.

"No, I'm a reporter, and if you tell me what I want to know, I won't have to tell the police what you tell me," said Frasier with authority.

He hesitated for a moment then said, "Nothing really. Two men in a white truck came to the house at dusk. Later, they drove away."

"Where are you from?"

"Albania, and maybe I have overstayed my visa, so I cannot tell the police what I told you, you understand?"

"Perfectly. Did the truck go near the cliff at all?"

"Yes, it made a big circle on its way out down away from the house then turned and went back to the road."

"And you saw nothing else?" pressed Frasier.

"No, you see, it was getting dark," said the man, almost pleading.

Frasier handed him a card. "Please call me if you think of anything else. There may be a few quid in it for you." But he knew the man wouldn't.

Frasier walked back to his car and drove to the nearest village. There, he found a small coffee shop open. There were old men at a large table in the back and two couples who looked like tourists. He sat near the men and, as he'd suspected, word of Magnus's death had already hit town. Frasier ordered a cappuccino and buried his head in that morning's newspaper so no one could see how intently he was listening to the old men. But the men clammed up when he sat down. Frasier sipped his coffee patiently and the chatter started again.

"Bloody fool should have taken the money," said one.

"Aye, you're right about that, but Magnus was a stubborn old dog," said another.

"I'm glad he didn't," said a third. "Those dammed turbines are a blight on the countryside."

"It was an awful lot of money; can't say I'd have turned it down." Frasier put some pound coins on the table and left.

CHAPTER ELEVEN

Present Day– Career Change

MAGGIE SAT NEXT TO HIM IN THE SMALL CONFERENCE room at Sir William Wallace Whisky headquarters. Brian Harmon was one of Robbie Gordon's closest friends. He had been with him on the fateful bike ride the day Robbie died. Harmon had a Scottish father and English mother. He had been born and educated at Oxford before a successful career in banking. That was followed by a decade as a Conservative MP before retiring to the Highlands to golf and fish. Brain Harmon was Robbie's financial advisor and political guru and he had now inherited Maggie.

Maggie was fond of Harmon. He was a larger-than-life personality; six feet tall with a full head of silver hair and an athletic—if a little overweight—build. He was close to seventy now but could easily have passed for ten years younger. He had a great deal of energy and an infectious personality. There were two other people present: John Lawton, the company's chief financial officer, and Sheila Benson, their corporate lawyer.

Benson was a tall brunette in her early forties. She was dressed in an expensive red trouser suit with seventies-style flares. Maggie reckoned she looked more like one of Charlie's Angels than a corporate lawyer, but she was good. Lawton, on the other hand, was a stoic Scott with a ruddy face and round glasses. He looked every bit the accountant he was.

Lawton started cheerily, "All the paperwork is done, the official transfer of the business to InBev will happen tomorrow at noon. The press will be there, statements are prepared, and the final price is two hundred and fifty million pounds."

Maggie nodded quietly. It was an eye watering sum. Even now, after over a decade of success, she had a hard time comprehending the numbers. Some part of her was still the coal miner's daughter who had grown up living in real poverty. Now she was a multimillionaire, Robbie was the sole shareholder. She was a simple Scottish lass; she would pay the capital gains taxes, put twenty-five million in trust.

Benson continued, "InBev have guaranteed everyone's continued employment for the next two years while they evaluate the existing people. I see no reason why they won't keep most of them on far beyond that, why break up a winning team?"

"Indeed," said Maggie.

"That's it," said Benson. "Short and sweet. I just need you and John to sign here; I will sign as the witness." She tapped a finger on a single sheet on top of a mountainous contract.

They both took turns signing. It was bittersweet for Maggie without Robbie.

"Do you need a moment, Maggie?" Benson asked. "Are you alright?"

Maggie shook her head and forced a smile. "I'm fine.'"

Benson and Lawton left, with the usual formalities. Brian Harmon stayed behind.

"I'd like to go through some political strategy if you are up for it, Maggie."

"Sure, why not? I just lost my job," she said with a rueful smile.

She had expected to feel something—anything—but not this. Just a great emptiness inside. Robbie's death had left a gaping hole in her life that great mountains of money simply couldn't fill.

Benson cleared his throat before he spoke again. "As you know, Robbie was planning to run for the local seat near your Highland estate when the current candidate retires in September. As the local laird Robbie was well-liked in the community. He funded the town's Highland games, built a small playground and a football pitch. He'd kept a local pub from closing and was a soft touch for a generous donation to any local cause. I think his popularity will transfer over to you as you have been seen by his side at almost every event. It should be an easy win for you, but the seat has little political clout."

There were a few moments of silence as he let the words hang; then Maggie asked, "You have a better idea?"

"I might," Harmon responded, "and I might not. An MP in Edinburgh has been diagnosed with Alzheimer's and he is now also planning to give up his seat in September. It's in an area where you happened to own a townhome. Winning will be a far more significant task as the powerful district will be hotly contested, but it is much closer to Holyrood and a far bolder, more powerful play for your plans down the road."

Maggie narrowed her eyes. "Interesting," she said.

"You'd be trading an almost guaranteed win for a possible win," said Harmon. "You will face stiff opposition from several candidates, but you'd also be interacting with the Edinburgh elite, who can help you politically in the future."

Maggie drummed her fingers on the conference table for a full five seconds before deciding. "I'm in. Let's make it happen. Get a team together. Oh, and one other thing—I want to set up a charitable foundation in Robbie's name. Can you see to the paperwork? The first project will be a home for battered women. I've found two beautiful loss-making hotels in the Highlands I want to purchase and will set up an endowment of twenty million pounds to run them."

Harmon raised his craggy eyebrows. "You don't mess around, do you, Maggie? Of course I'd be delighted to help. I'd be happy to be an unpaid executive director of the foundation." He put his palms down on the table then flipped them over. "I have way too much idle time on my hands."

"Done," replied Maggie. "Make it so."

Robbie had planned to follow in the footsteps of Andrew Carnegie, or more recently people like Bill Gates and Warren Buffet, by promising to give most of his wealth away; Maggie was committed to doing the same. She suppressed a smile. The lawyers and accountants would have a heart attack if they knew.

CHAPTER TWELVE

Present Day– Meet the Press

Four weeks later, Maggie McGown announced her surprise candidacy for the soon-to-be-vacant Edinburgh seat at a press conference in the Balmoral Hotel. She was surprised by the number of media in attendance as she stood on the dais and read a prepared statement. The questions rained down on her fast and furiously. Fortunately, she had prepared thoroughly. She'd found that throwing herself into her work 24/7 was the only thing that took her mind off Robbie's absence, and her grief.

A reporter raised a hand. "Sam Johnstone, the *Scotsman*. Are ye no worried about your lack of political experience?"

"Given what we have seen from those with experience in Holyrood I'd say that lack of experience might be one of my major assets. I'm used to actually getting things done!"

A titter of laugher went around the room.

Another hand went up. "Joe Pellegrini, BBC. You're a multimillionaire business owner; what do you have in common with the average voter?"

"If the average voter is unhappy with the progress that's been made in the last decade on health, crime, education, and independence then I'd say I have a lot in common with the average voter. And in case anyone forgot, I was a poor lass from a Scottish coal town before I became an entrepreneur."

"The Labour candidate is quoted as saying you are, 'A rich upstart intent on collecting a trophy of power rather than helping the poor or working-class Scots," said Pellegrini.

"Well, I find that a little rich from an Eton-educated man who spent half his life south of the border and was once a Conservative MP who then suddenly switched to Labour to keep his job."

There was laughter among the audience. Points had been scored.

Another hand shot up. "Anne Langford, The *Times*. There is a fear among the financial community here that while many of your ideas appeal to them now, you'll suddenly turn left once you're elected."

"The only turn I intend to make is to turn this country around and make it the hotbed of science, ideas and discovery in which we once led the world."

Maggie noticed Sean Robertson, the SNL first minister, had slipped into the room and was sitting quietly in the back. She knew exactly what he must be thinking. Maggie McGown made him nervous. While the party was excited by her wealth, which could come in handy for a chronically underfunded party, they were very fearful of her stated agenda. She was a wealthy entrepreneur, not exactly their core voter; she stood a good chance of turning voters off for no reason other than being rich. But what they didn't understand, and Trump had shown very plainly, was that the uneducated and the poor hero-worshiped the powerful and the rich if they thought they were their friends.

After thirty minutes Maggie called time on the press conference. The reporters all shuffled out, checking their phones or muttering to their colleagues. All except Duncan Frasier. Frasier was tall and lean with broad shoulders, a shock of curly black hair and a pleasant smile.

"Duncan Frasier, the *Daily Record*, any chance of a quick interview?" he said. He glanced around as his competitors left the room. "In private?"

Maggie broke off her conversation with an aid. She glanced at Frasier and smiled. "Sure. There's an alcove with two chairs at the end of the second floor. Meet me there in five minutes. I'm sure we won't be disturbed."

Four minutes and fifty-nine seconds later, Frasier rose from his seat in the alcove as Maggie arrived.

"You don't mind if I record this, do you?" asked Frasier. "I always record important interviews."

"No, but thanks for asking," said Maggie.

Frasier hit record on his mini recorder and glanced at the notes on his iPad. "You said you grew up in a mining town and your father was a miner?"

"That's right."

"So it's really true what you said about growing up poor?"

"Well, we had a wee car but no heating in the house. I don't know if that's poor, but it sure as hell wasn't rich."

Frasier gave her a slight smile. "So you married into money?"

Maggie looked at him hard and paused before answering. "Mr. Frasier, I was head of European sales for one of the UK's largest beverage companies. I was making a six-figure salary long before I met Robbie Gordon. I had my own house, a 550 SL Mercedes, and a decent pension pot. I didn't need a penny from Robbie. But he was my true soul mate, and I was his."

Frasier smiled. "You went to university here in Edinburgh? To take—" He paused as he consulted his notes again.

"History and economics," Maggie said.

"Is that not a strange combination?"

"You tell me. History teaches us about mankind's—and womankind's—successes and mistakes from time immemorial. Economics is what makes the world go round today. Two important aspects of human life on Earth, would you not say?" replied Maggie.

"Indeed, thank you for your time, Mrs. McGown," said Frasier.

"And yours," said Maggie with a warm smile as Frasier got up and left.

She stayed seated watching him walk down the hall replaying the interview in her mind. It had gone well she thought. He had come into it with a negative view of her and her policies, but he had left knowing there was far more depth to her than he or her critics had imagined.

CHAPTER THIRTEEN

March 1984 -The Miners' Strike

It was the first week of March 1984. German singer Nena was number one on Top of the Pops with her song "99 Red Balloons." Footloose was the top-grossing movie. Manchester United was leading the English football Division One, and the Soviets announced they would boycott the LA Olympics. Although no one except the juiced-up Soviet athletes really cared. The Labour government of James Callahan had been swept from power five years earlier, in 1979, leaving behind the dour days of strikes, power cuts, and disruptive industrial action: The Winter of Discontent. McDonald was aware that the public mood in Britain had changed; all you had to do was read most of the newspapers or watch the TV news. Margaret Thatcher's vision of a revitalized, entrepreneurial Britain had created a new mood of optimism in most parts of the country. Most parts, but not the coal-mining counties.

McDonald stared at the Six O'Clock News program on the black-and-white TV in the corner of his living room, a mug of tea in his hand. The newscaster spoke. "Today, March the sixth, after weeks of rumors, the National Coal Board, backed by Margaret's Thatcher's Conservative government, announced the immediate closing of twenty money-losing pits. This will result in the loss of twenty thousand jobs. Yorkshire miners have gone on strike in protest." McDonald rubbed his chin. "Shit!"

He stuffed several of the day's newspapers in his leather briefcase and headed for the station. The train journey to Sheffield was not easy and took over five hours, often with two or three changes depending on the time of day, which always meant a very early start. Thankfully the emergency meeting of the NUM executive committee at Union headquarters in Sheffield on March 9 was scheduled for 1:00 p.m. All twenty-six executive committee members were there; the general mood was one of excitement, but it was not a mood McDonald shared.

NUM President Arthur Scargill spoke his words like a fire-and-brimstone preacher. "If they want a war, it's a war they shall have. We will defy the National Coal Board, ignore Ian McGregor, and bring down Margaret Thatcher's Tory government. We will bring the country to its knees if we must. This not just a fight for the pits or the miners, it's a fight for every working-class man in this country. This is not only about the future of mining; it's about the future of our country. We will all stay out until they agree to keep every pit open!"

There was a murmur of approval from several in the room. "You've got my support!" called out Evans.

McDonald listened thinking that lighting up the crowd was what Scargill did best. Negotiation was not his strong point, and yet he would be the point man on any negotiation. McDonald tried to make a case for reason. "Look, it makes no sense to strike to stop pits losing millions of pounds from closing. Instead, it would be far better to negotiate for generous redundancy packages and retraining for the miners in other professions. As you well know, most of our members know nothing but mining. Or we could push for comprehensive relocation packages to other communities."

"No mine will close," stated Scargill emphatically. "We will bring the country and the government to its knees just like we did in 1974."

McDonald shook his head. "You can't get blood out of a stone, Arthur. My beef with the Tory government is not the closing of money-losing pits, it's the fact that they don't seem to care what will happen to the men. There is a total lack of empathy from the government and the NCB. We all know what happens when a pit closes in a mining town, the devastation and ripple effect the closings will have on the communities. Every business in town will fail. Compensation, retraining, and relocation are what we should focus on! That and reinvestment in new, more profitable mines."

Scargill slapped his hand onto the table. "We need to support the Yorkshire miners and call a national strike!"

McDonald glanced around the room then shrugged. "Then why not have a national vote on the issue and let the workers decide? Don't you think you'd win?"

"Of course we'd win. That's why there's no need. We'll just let the local areas go on strike and we'll support them."

"The lack of a national vote will come back to haunt us, and if we were to go on strike, surely it would have been better to do it in January or February in the middle of winter when demand for coal was at its peak, not now with spring just around the corner."

Scargill looked exasperated. "Timing doesn't matter, right is right."

Nightingale, a short, fat executive from Lancashire with a round face that always seemed to be halfway through a Mars bar, chipped in. "McDonald has a point," he said. "Would it not be better to wait until later in the year?"

"No," yelled Scargill. "We must support the Yorkshire miners, not to mention the other nineteen pits slated for closure."

"Arthur, I understand how you feel, and of course we all want to support Yorkshire, but Thatcher has been stockpiling coal for months and she had the foresight to change several of the power stations from coal to oil. Her battle plan is all in the Ridley report. You know the one that Tory MP wrote after we were victorious in the 1974 strike. We can't be using the same old tactics," said Martin Green, a tall, thin executive from Cheshire with the weathered face of a cowboy whose suits always seemed too big for him. "It's been in the newspapers. All you have to do is read them. It's basic intelligence we shouldn't overlook before acting."

"The newspapers are full of Tory propaganda," spat Scargill. "You shouldn't believe a word of it."

What should we believe, thought McDonald, the communist Morning Star and the working-class Sun?

Nothing George McDonald said could change Scargill's mind. While it was clear from the muted reactions that not everyone on the executive committee agreed with Scargill, it was also clear no one was going to stand in his way. Even the seven or eight more conservative voices stayed quiet. McDonald's anger was rising, but what could he do if only a handful of men were willing to support the voice of reason? Scargill's force of personality was just too great.

The meeting ended late on Friday, March 9, so Scargill waited until Monday, March 12, before he declared the NUM's support for the regional strikes in Yorkshire and now Scotland while calling for supporting strike action from NUM members across Britain.

For the next two weeks McDonald had the unhappy task of presenting the Union's position to large groups of miners at pits across Lanarkshire, trying to do it with an enthusiasm he did not feel, before attending the next executive meeting.

***

McDonald circled a paragraph with his biro and folded up the newspaper he was carefully reading and placed it with several others in his briefcase as he readied himself to exit the taxi parked outside Union headquarters. He entered the building took a lift to the sixth floor, grabbed a coffee from the pot inside the door and headed for his place at the table nodding, shaking hands and offering the occasional "Hello," "Alright," and "Morning," as he went.

In the large sterile meeting room at Union headquarters the show began promptly for once at 11:30 a.m. A battle map on an A-frame at the end of the table showed all the regions supporting the strike. The map showed that the strike was almost universally observed, but McDonald saw far less support across the Midlands, North Wales, and Nottinghamshire. And he knew why: the miners enjoyed better pay in these areas and worked in pits unlikely to close anytime soon. They had little to gain and plenty to lose: weeks or months without a paycheck if they went on strike.

"As you can see, most of the men support the strike except for those bastards in Nottingham," announced Scargill. "But we will be taking care of the scabs in the Midlands the same way we took care of them in '74. Starting tomorrow, we will be busing flying pickets from all over the country into their area to stop miners who want to work from going through the colliery gates. This tactic will be our trump card."

"Apparently, the government has recruited an army of lorry drivers to move coal stockpiles to the power station," said Martin Green from Cheshire, now sporting a new pair of steel-rimmed spectacles.

"We will just call our friends at the Transport and General Workers Union and tell them to blacklist any driver who participates," said Gareth Evans.

"I doubt that will work," said McDonald. "Drivers who refused to break the picket lines in the steelworkers' strike of 1980 were all backlisted by haulage companies. Most are still out of work. It's too big a risk for them to observe a strike that has nothing to do with their interests."

"It has everything to do with their interests," yelled Scargill. "And the interest of any working man who wants to see the back of this government."

McDonald waited a second for silence then continued. "And there is something else I read in the Times today."

"Why the fuck are you reading that Tory rag?" scoffed Evans, a short, stocky guy with a barrel chest and a thick mane of long brown hair, in his heavy Welsh accent.

"Because" replied McDonald, "it's full of useful information about the enemy."

"Like what?" demanded Miller aggressively as if reading the Times alone made McDonald a traitor to his class.

McDonald took a copy of the Times from his leather briefcase, holding it up by two hands with a sardonic smile, rotating it slightly for all to see, then opening it at the business section. He started to read aloud from an article entitled, "Thatcher Aims to Clip Union's Wings."

In February 1981, less than two years into her premiership, Margaret Thatcher's Conservative government *was forced to accept the National Union of Miners' (NUM) pay demands, aware that her government was unprepared to withstand a prolonged conflict.* Mrs. Thatcher also withdrew plans to close twenty-three pits in her first major U-turn since she had come to power. *A secret group was also established in Whitehall, codenamed MISC 57. Its goal was establishing a rock-solid plan to defeat the miners when they chose to strike again, which Thatcher saw as an ideological battle between a meritocracy and communism.*

Learning from the previous Tory government's mistakes in the 1974 dispute, Thatcher's team has set up mobile police units so that forty-three forces from outside the strike areas can be moved quickly and in large numbers to neutralize the efforts of the flying pickets trying to stop the legal transport of coal to power stations or steel works. In extreme cases, police plan to set up roadside checkpoints several miles from the pits on all major roads and turn back picketers before they reach their destination.

"They can't do that!" said Scargill indignantly. "That's like having a national police force. This isn't Chile. It's Britain. I don't even think it's legal."

"Well, legal or not, they plan on doing it," said McDonald flatly. "Which means flying pickets won't be as effective as in '74."

"We will see about that," barked Scargill. "This strike is not just about pit closures. It's a social class struggle. It's the working man against the Tory elite."

McDonald watched Scargill's hands as he went flying off into a political rant. A fist, a short chop, a pointed finger. McDonald blocked out the words. They were meaningless to him. When Scargill had finished, seeming to have exhausted his spleen, and looked at him, expecting a rejoinder, McDonald merely shrugged.

The meeting dragged on until after five, tea and sandwiches arriving at some point midafternoon to keep the men appeased. When it finally ended, McDonald decided it was too late to do the train and taxi shuffle back home and walked instead to a small pub he had discovered nearby on a canal, making a reservation at a chain hotel on his way past. He ordered a pint of local ale and steak and kidney pie with chips and mushy peas. It was delightful. After a second pint he took a walk down the towpath until he came to a bridge then crossed it and circled back, pitch black now save for the bright light of the moon. Not that darkness ever bothered a miner thought McDonald.

McDonald grabbed his key at the front desk and opened his room with its faint smell of disinfectant, cheap furniture, sagging bed, and orange carpet; he turned on first the light and then the Nine O' Clock News.

Margaret Thatcher was on the screen speaking in that infuriatingly posh clipped accent: "This strike has nothing to do with a class war, as Mr. Scargill is so fond of saying. It is a straightforward business decision. The government cannot keep pouring money into losing pits; the coal costs twenty-five percent more to mine than the Coal Board can sell it for on the open market. If Britain is ever going to get out of the downward economic cycle left by the previous Labour government, it must make better, more entrepreneurial business decisions. If you ran a butcher's shop and sold steak for twenty percent less than it cost you to buy, how long would you stay in business? Unprofitable pit closures are a simple economic necessity."

McDonald turned the TV off. There was so much about her he didn't like, but her simple logic was hard to refute. So why did Scargill not turn his attention to winnable wars? McDonald was resigned to the fate of all the poor decisions Scargill had made and, for appearances' sake, had cautiously thrown his support behind him while trying to stay in the background, biding his time for a change in Union leadership. He knew he could do much better for the men if he were in charge. He had no subversive political agenda. He only had the pitmen's best interests at heart.

He tried to think instead about where he might take his daughter that weekend, maybe a nice hike in the Cairngorms or a trip to a hidden white sand beach he knew near Arisaig. But ominous thoughts about the strike kept creeping back into his mind and he couldn't keep them out. The strike had only just started, but he knew it would last a long time. Thatcher had no intention of caving in to any of Scargill's demands. It had already become personal between the two of them. Something told him that things would never be the same when it was all over. Not for him, Scargill, the Union, the men, and maybe even the country itself. McDonald had a gnawing sense of dread in his gut, which told him that the strike was a monster, already out of control. It needed feeding, and in the end, it would consume them all.

CHAPTER FOURTEEN

Present Day –Eat the Rich

Edinburgh's iconic Waldorf Astoria Hotel was located on its most famous road, Princes Street. The ballroom had stunning castle views and combined Victorian style with modern luxury. High above the room's polished wooden floors, majestic chandeliers hung like suspended galaxies, casting a warm glow upon the room. Each crystal pendant refracted the light into a myriad of colors, bathing the space in a gentle radiance. The ballroom's décor blended classic sophistication with a contemporary flair. Rich, velvety hues adorned the walls, interspersed with intricately crafted panels that bore the mark of skilled artisans, while gilded frames showcased the oil works of Scottish artists old and new. It was the perfect venue for Maggie McGown's first event. With only three months before the election, she needed to make every presentation count.

She peeked at the crowd from behind a curtain at the side of the stage. There were about two hundred people. The men were all in suits or sports coats; the women were dressed to the nines. It was the Edinburgh elite: power couples, bankers, lawyers, stockbrokers, CEOs and entrepreneurs. Maggie was used to presenting to crowds, but this was different and she still had a few butterflies in her stomach. The room was alive with conversation over the Muzak.

The music suddenly stopped. A man in a tuxedo took to the stage and the chatter turned to silence. He gave a brief introduction to Maggie McGown.

"She was born a coal miner's daughter. Graduated from Edinburgh University, had a career as a model before becoming a very successful sales and marketing executive in the beverage industry. Despite her own success she married well." The entire audience laughed. "Many of you knew Maggie's late husband Robbie." There was a mummer as people in the crowd remembered him. A nodding of heads. "What you might not know is that Robbie was planning to sell his business and run for public office." The crowd hushed. You could have heard a pin drop. "He wanted a better future for Scotland; a future that Maggie McGown is now determined to deliver on his behalf."

The crowd applauded politely and the announcer exited to the left. Maggie took a deep breath then walked quickly to the center of the stage. She was dressed in her signature navy-blue pinstripe jacket and matching skirt. As he began to speak, she took instant command of the event.

"Ladies and gentlemen, thank you for coming. I know many of you must be very skeptical of any SNP candidate after some of our previous leaders and their disastrous policies. So, let me come right out and say it: I do not want to eat the rich. I do not want to drive them out of Scotland with higher taxes or more rules and regulations for their factories or employees. I want them to stay and invite their friends. I want business owners and entrepreneurs to be the bedrock of a new Scotland."

There was a pleasing murmur of approval from the crowd. Maggie had expected it, but it was still nice to hear it. She did not think she would have much problem attracting wealthy voters to her agenda. A bigger problem for her was to convince the working class and poor voters that she also had their best interests at heart. Her stump speech was short, to the point and designed to connect with any audience. She would start with the "Damaging Disclosure," the topic all her enemies used to attack her credibility. She was too rich, was not one of them, didn't know the price of bread or milk, lived in a castle, not a row house, and so on. Once she admitted to the charge, it took it away as ammunition for her enemies. She would then counter the accusations and gain the audience's trust. Now to put it to the test, for among the wealthy audience were a few hand-picked members of the press, none of whom was pro-Maggie.

Maggie looked out at the ballroom. She began to speak again.

"There is no doubt I now live a charmed life, as many of my detractors will tell you. You have all seen the headlines in the news about my lavish lifestyle. And it's true, at least some of it. I have experienced the travel and luxuries of the good life that many never have.

"Churchill came from one of Britain's wealthiest families and yet championed many causes that helped the poor. Roosevelt was a very wealthy man yet invented the modern social system in America and got them through the Great Depression. You don't have to be poor to achieve notable public service. Nor should you think that wealth provides immunity from corruption. Unlike many, I am not entering politics to profit from it in anyway.

"But make no mistake about it. I also know what it's like to be poor because my family was poor."

The speech came with a carefully crafted slideshow. Behind her, a slide appeared on screen: a picture of her as a teenager outside their grim Lanarkshire row house. It was followed by a picture of her soot-covered father, fresh back from the mine.

"My pa, Cameron, was a Lanarkshire coal miner, and my ma, Morag, was a miner's wife living on just a few hundred pounds a month. I know what it is to be hungry, for we went hungry many times during the miners' strike, which lasted twelve long months."

There was a photo of pickets standing in line for bacon sandwiches being cooked on a makeshift grill outside the colliery gates.

"I know what it's like when the people around you have lost all hope, lost faith in the government as the pits, steel mills, and shipyards vanished. I have witnessed entire communities condemned to live lives of quiet desperation.

"I know what it's like to struggle with a failing family business, with banks and creditors breathing down your neck, threatening to take away your home and livelihood. Yet, I also know the power of education and the opportunity it provides.

"I know what it's like to enjoy good health and how it feels to taste the fruits of success.

To be from a country that once boasted the world's greatest inventors, scientists, and businessmen.

"As your next SMP, my quest will be to share those fruits with you and foster a culture of success and innovation in Scotland again, a culture that's been missing for a very long time."

Multiple pictures appeared of happy people of differing sexes and ethnicities, though mainly young white Scots, working in restaurants, in electric car factories, installing solar panels, and working on computers at coffee shops.

On the ballroom stage, Maggie continued. "Last year, 28% of all UK taxes were paid by just 1% of the population. At the same time, Britain ranked third in the world behind only Russia and China in the tables of wealthy people leaving the country.

"Good riddance, you may say, but it does not take many people paying two hundred thousand pounds in income tax to leave before the numbers start to hurt. And that's just the tax side of the equation; we also lose their spending power.

"Wealthy people buy the goods and services you make and sell—cars, boats, ATVs, solar panels, and air-conditioners. Wealthy people hire gardeners, nannies, drivers, cooks, and cleaners. Wealthy people use their capital to start businesses and employ hundreds, sometimes thousands, of people. Scotland needs to attract wealthy people; do not drive them out. As Abraham Lincoln so aptly said, 'You cannot help the poor by becoming one of them.'"

Maggie looked out at the tables of Edinburgh's wealthy. She saw heads coming together as people talked. She continued over the quiet murmurings of the crowd. "If there is no money in the till from the government for an appropriate program, then I'll spend the money myself."

There was a sudden, shocked silence from the crowd.

Maggie looked out through the bright stage lighting. "My late husband was a man who built a worldwide brand out of a failing family business, a business burdened by red tape and over-taxation. Yes, he managed to prosper despite the odds, but he saw no future and was preparing to sell out when he died. His legacy will be a free and prosperous Scotland, a Scotland teeming with jobs, opportunity, and hope. And I will spend every hour I'm awake and every penny I have to make it happen!"

Suddenly, as if possessed, Maggie put down her carefully prepared script and looked out directly at the audience. "I shared Robbie's dream of economic growth for Scotland, but I also have a passion he did not share, at least not to the same degree—a complete and utter disgust with the powers that be in Westminster."

She paused for a second, wanting to say something but holding back from doing it. The leaches and snakes of the Tory government and the dark puppet masters behind the scenes who craft their policies of subversion and control; Scotland must be rid of them and their influence in our lives. The thought passed and she gave a quick, forced chuckle, regrouped, and went back to her prepared script.

"But on a lighter note, all I need is your help getting me into the game, for it's a game many people don't want to let me play, as you'll read about in the news. I hope I can count on your vote!"

The final slide was a smiling photo of her late husband Robbie in a kilt with a bottle of Sir William Wallace in his hand left hand and a raised glass in his right.

"Now enjoy yourselves. I'll be here to take your questions and your selfies."

Amidst moderate applause, Maggie walked to the left of the stage where a giant banner with a picture of the famous Eilean Donan Castle, perched on a small island at the edge of a loch, would be the backdrop for the photo ops.

Three suited men took to the stage to organize the crowd who swarmed onto the riser into a single-file line so they could all get their "Moment with Maggie." An aide with an iPad took everyone's email, while a professional photographer took one picture of each person and promised to forward it to their email address. The picture was taken in such a way as to make people believe there was no one else in the room and make the voter feel that extra bit special.

Once the photo line was exhausted, Maggie took to the floor and walked the room. The wine was flowing and no one seemed in a rush to leave. She moved from group to group trying to pick up on the chatter; several of her aids were doing the same thing, taking notes on casual conversations to see what the people really thought.

Coffee mornings were organized in the poorer parts of town in social clubs and church halls to reach grassroots voters, but for the most part she carried out her campaign online tailoring her message for each different demographic and hitting them on multiple channels. No one had seen a campaign quite like it.

CHAPTER FIFTEEN

Present Day
–Election Day

THE NEXT DAY, MAGGIE SKIMMED THROUGH THE MEDIA soundbites. Most of them were very positive.

A populist candidate with a business mind.
Someone who could get the job done for once.
Understands basic economics.
A straightforward common sense business approach.
Short and to the point, a breath of fresh air.
Shares all Scots' disgust with Westminster.

There were a few skeptics of course, and she noted issues she might have to deal with.

Too good to be true.

Scots like to despise success.

Money started pouring into her coffers, building a war chest of funds never before seen in Scottish politics. Not that she needed it, but it all helped; the less she had to spend of her own money the more of it she could use to help good causes.

There was of course some staunch opposition to her candidacy. She had three primary challengers for the seat plus a host of—as her campaign manager put it—inconsequential numpties running as independents who would rarely be mentioned during the campaign and would disappear without a trace.

Maggie had no doubt that the three main challengers had quickly obtained a copy of her speech.

She watched with amusement as the veteran Labour candidate David Johnstone was very vocal in attacking her on TV the following day with his pointed soundbites in answer to a reporter's questions on what he thought of her. "She will cut social funding for everything. She wants tax breaks for the rich. She has no experience in how things get done in Holyrood. She's on a power grab. The seat is nothing more than a trophy to her."

Maggie smiled as she listened to the Green candidate, Sally Claxton, who took to the radio. It seemed she thought Maggie was the devil's reincarnation. "Sure, Maggie McGown says she believed in climate change and taking action to halt it, but where was the proof? McGown has a jet, a helicopter, and at least two large cars that we know of. She has a massive Highlands estate and a swanky Edinburgh townhome. How many homes or cars does a person need? As if that's not enough for Scottish voters, McGown is championing the addition of two nuclear power plants. There is also a rumor she is in favor of fracking, raping our beautiful Highland landscape. I for one will not sit idle. I will organize protests, marches, and sit-ins to stand up against Maggie McGown and her wasteful policies."

The young Conservative candidate, Gavin Neilson, was notably absent from the media frenzy. Maggie reckoned she knew why. Her policies were more progressive and entrepreneurial than anything the Conservative Party had come up with in decades. He could not attack her inexperience as he had little himself. He could find little fault with her ideas on business or taxation. What did that leave him? Attacking her because she was a woman? That would go down like a lead balloon these days. She'd stolen the wind from his sails.

Nor was Maggie safe from attack from within her own party. There were plenty of SNP MPs in Holyrood openly criticizing her stance on a wide range of issues. Her aids frequented the Members' Restaurant in the Parliament building, which was open to the public, daily listening to the scuttlebutt from other MPs. These comments were typed up and handed to Maggie for review each morning. Some made her smile; some made her frown; others made her think of what the correct soundbite answer should be to any question or charge. "She may be Scottish, but she's not one of us with these ridiculous policies." "She might be a great public speaker but is there any substance to her?" "How can a woman with her own jet even begin to think she had anything in common with the average Scot?"

Maggie McGown was new to politics but was very familiar with a hostile male-dominated world. There she had learned speaking, negotiating, selling, and managing a team like a well-oiled machine. Something Scottish politics had lacked from the very start of the SNP way back in 1934. She spoke at multiple events over the next few weeks, sometimes in church halls or social clubs and other times in top-notch hotels. Either way, she worked the crowd of working class citizens or professionals with good-natured ease.

Two months into her campaign Maggie was scanning her way through the newspapers in the early hours of the morning as usual when she took an interest a story in the Scotsman. They had a front-page story on the rapid decline in performance of the Scottish education system while noting that two of the SNP cabinet ministers had boys at the forty-five-thousand-pound-a-year private boys' school Gordonstoun. A third cabinet member had a girl at the equally posh and expensive St. George's girls' school. Maggie thought that was interesting, not that there was anything wrong with sending your kids to posh private schools, she would have done the same thing herself, but then she was not on a salary of sixty-seven thousand pounds a year either.

A week later, the Herald ran a story on SNP members padding their expenses. Maggie added one more important aspect to her speech: ETHICS. She would stamp out corruption and cronyism and treating the tax players' money like your own personal piggy bank. She would push for a "one strike and you are out" policy. It was a message that resonated well with the average hard-working Scot.

When Election Day arrived, Maggie was waiting nervously in a private meeting room at the Waldorf Astoria Hotel, watching the local results on television with her team. There were bottles of Dom Perignon on ice around the room, waiting for the final result. The polls had predicted a very close race, but polls could be wrong.

The television showed lines of people at the polling stations in what BBC Scotland said was a larger than usual turn out. The results seemed to come in agonizingly slowly and for a while there was little difference in the projected result between any of the candidates.

Maggie was confident but edgy and paced about the room, looking at her Fitbit as she passed the first twelve thousand and then thirteen thousand steps. Finally, there was a loud murmur in the room as a reporter took the screen live and the results were announced. The chatter in the ballroom stopped at once and Maggie's heart pounded. She was not superstitious but crossed both her fingers just in case it helped this once. The announcer looked dead at the camera. "The winner is Maggie McGown with an impressive 68% of the vote."

The announcement was followed by a thunderous cheer, immediately followed by the popping of champagne corks. Maggie McGown had won by a near landslide and would take her seat in Holyrood at the Scottish Parliament. The party lasted into the small hours.

Finally Maggie escaped and was in the back of her Mercedes on the way home. But despite her elation at victory, she also felt a profound sadness. She took two pictures from her handbag; both were on her mobile phone, but there was something tactile about holding them in her hands. A feeling that somehow got you closer to the person you loved. She stared at the one in her left hand that was of Robbie. She had taken the picture the year before on holiday in Santorini and had preserved the print in a plastic coating. How she wished he had been here to share this moment with her, and she smiled at him. The other picture was old and faded, a Polaroid taken long before Robbie, the plastic coating fraying around its edges. Maggie looked at it and burst into tears.

CHAPTER SIXTEEN

1984–Koi Ponds, Gazebos, and Fancy Kitchens

THE WHITE HORSE WAS A STANDALONE BUILDING whitewashed with its stone window frames painted black. A traditional English pub, it served cask ales in a bar and a lounge, both served by the same L-shaped bar, by a rotund barman with a shaved head. A large stone fire blazed in the lounge, forcing out the dreary weather, and the smell of fried sausages and chips wafted in from the kitchen.

Gareth Evans, a district Union leader from Wales, sipped at his pint. "I don't like this McDonald kid, he's way too puritan for my taste and he asks way too many questions. The prick even asked me the other day how I can afford to take my family to Mallorca for a week."

Ken Miller was the Union's second-in-command, a hard-nosed Yorkshire man, a short, stocky man, in his late thirties with broad shoulders and a large pug-nosed face. "What did you tell him?"

"I told him to mind his own fucking business," said Evans. "Then I told him that if he must know, my wife's aunt died and left us a little cash for a holiday."

"That was smart." Miller rubbed his chin. "McDonald's been making a lot of noise about the Union's finances for the last few weeks. If he doesn't stop it could become a problem with the rank and file. There's at least two hundred thousand quid missing from the strike fund and no one seems to know where the fuck it's gone."

"When you say no one," said Evans in his thick Welsh accent, "you mean no one outside the inner circle?"

Miller nodded. "McDonald's on his way here now."

"In that case," said Evans, downing his pint of beer. "I'll be off. See you later, Ken."

It was ten more minutes before McDonald appeared dripping wet from the rain that had been falling all morning. He greeted Miller, sat down at the battered old table, and ordered fish and chips. Miller was already eating a tasty-looking pie with a huge helping of chips. They had both spent the morning on the picket line but had sneaked off for a pub lunch while the miners stood in line for a plate of questionable beef stew. Miller had invited McDonald or he would not have been there; as he was, he thought he might as well take advantage of some decent grub.

"What do you do when you are not picketing, Ken?" asked McDonald. He knew that outwardly Ken Miller had a jovial fat man persona but behind the facade he was a hard-nosed bastard who would stop at nothing to get what he wanted.

"Oh, with all this time on my hands, I've been doing a lot of gardening," said Miller. He did not mention he had just put in a koi pond, stone pavers, and a new gazebo, but he added, "The wife just got a nice bonus, so we are doing some minor home improvements; you know, fixing stuff that should have been fixed a long time ago."

McDonald knew Miller's wife was a secretary. *How large a bonus could she have got?* He smiled and nodded.

Miller smiled back and drank from his pint, glad to have dismissed his new kitchen as a minor home improvement. But driving up and down the country for rallies, picketing, and begging other unions for help and money was exhausting work. So what if he padded his travel expenses a little—okay, a lot? Everyone did it. Well, everyone except snow-white George McDonald here.

McDonald dropped it and changed the subject. "How is the lovely Sally?" he asked.

"Oh, she's fine, busy with her job and helps with food on the picket lines at the weekends."

They talked shop for a while, but McDonald stopped talking when his fish and chips arrived. He ate while Miller spoke interminably about the strike.

Miller didn't say what he really thought. He didn't like McDonald; he was too good-looking, intelligent, and bloody strait-laced for his taste. Miller knew McDonald had his eye on the NUM leadership that should rightfully be his—Miller's—after twenty years in the Union, a half dozen of those as Scargill's number two. He also knew dammed well that McDonald had a good chance of snatching it from him; he had charisma and charm, while Miller was just a craggy old Yorkshire bulldog. It wasn't right; it wasn't fair; he'd put his time in. If Scargill faltered or, heaven forbid, died, Miller should be head of the NUM, not some Scottish usurper. He watched McDonald finish his fish and chips.

"Okay," said McDonald as he got up to leave the pub. "I'm going back down to the picket line."

"Aye," said Miller. "I'll see you down there when I've finished my chips," which he was picking at slowly. *And when it stops fucking raining,* he thought. The he added silently to himself as he smiled, *And what a self-righteous Scottish prick you are.*

McDonald put on his tartan cap and military-green raincoat then headed back out to the car park and the rain. He was amazed at how blatant these guys were. The previous week, he had seen one of the Union leaders, Peter Simpson from down south, driving a gold XJS Jaguar. He had at least made a point of not parking it in the hotel parking lot, where they were all to meet, but down a side street nearby.

McDonald had come by train and had been walking down the road towards the hotel when by chance he saw the Union man from Kent get out of the gold car. It was brand new, beautiful, and would have cost more than a year's wages for the average miner, possibly two with the right options. Cars were to get from A to B and meant nothing to McDonald, but he could not help but be impressed with this one. It had such beautiful lines, wire wheels, and the leaping animal hood ornament. He stopped to peek inside, looking up the street quickly first to make sure the driver was still heading towards the hotel. McDonald took in the wood-paneled dashboard and the beautiful black leather interior with gold piping. This was the type of car movie stars drove, not miners.

McDonald sat patiently in the meeting and waited for the first coffee break before he approached the driver standing alone in a corner.

"That's a mighty fancy car you've got there, Simpson," said McDonald, trying to feign sounding in awe.

"Sorry?" said Simpson, feigning confusion.

"The gold Jag you showed up in, is it the V12?" asked McDonald.

"Err, yes, actually it is. It belongs to a friend of mine who's overseas and he asked me to look after it for him. He likes to keep her running. You know, better for the engine. Lucky me."

Boy, this guy's fucking stupid, thought McDonald. "Do you think I just fell off the banana boat going up the Clyde?"

"I don't know what you mean."

"Does your friend have the same name as you?" asked McDonald. "The number plate was PAS 1950. Peter Alan Simpson, is it?"

"Yes," Simpson said, embarrassed to be caught in the lie. "But look, you understand I just inherited a large amount of money, and with everything that's going on with the strike and all, obviously, I don't want to flaunt it."

"Obviously," said McDonald. "It's funny how many people in the Union have suddenly inherited money from a long-lost relation. In fact, it happened to me a few years ago as well."

"Did it?" said Simpson in surprise, eager to change the subject away from himself.

"Yes, I bought four-year-old car with the eight hundred quid I was left from an uncle in Australia," said McDonald with a smile.

"Oh," said Simpson, trying to make light of the obvious sarcasm. "Well, very economical, at least, right?"

"Right," said McDonald. "And if you really don't want to flaunt it, I wouldn't show up at the next meeting with a two-week Marbella suntan either. It's been very cold and damp here in the UK."

He smiled, nodded, and moved away, leaving Simpson to stew in his own juices.

God, these guys are so arrogant and so stupid. It's only a matter of time until they're all in jail, thought McDonald. He slipped out of the hotel with his small backpack. He walked back to the side street, made sure no one was around, took out his camera and took several shots of the Jag.

A week later, when the developed film came back in the mail, he added three photographs to his growing file on Union corruption. It was snowballing. The men on the take were so flagrant; it was not something he could just ignore. The cars, the holidays, the home improvements; the math didn't add up, especially when families were going hungry from the strike. They had to be skimming thousands from strike funds and expense accounts. The whole thing was a giant house of cards, and when it fell, McDonald intended to pick up the pieces and run the Union the way it should be run, for the workers. He'd still be driving that old car he had a decade from now and there would be home improvements in his future, but they wouldn't cost vast amounts of money, although Lorna had a list as long as his arm.

McDonald could see how easy it was to cheat for there was plenty of cash coming into the Lanarkshire Union as well. The difference was McDonald kept meticulous records and always had two witnesses in the room when they counted out the five-pound notes, tenners and twenties mailed in by supporting workers from a hundred other trades. They opened the mail twice a week together and he had receipts made at the end of each counting. Then he would match them with each bank deposit the following day. McDonald could not be sure if any of the mail went missing before it was opened, but he had hand-picked Denton and MacKay for the accounting and banking tasks and he did not think they would ever dream of it.

But these days could you ever be sure.

CHAPTER SEVENTEEN

Present Day –Nicola's Bus

Maggie McGown was all business today, dressed, as usual, in a navy-blue pinstripe jacket and matching skirt. While she wanted to wear sensible shoes, she gave up too much height in flats and so she opted for two-inch heels in matching navy patent leather. As she entered the building, she picked up a glossy brochure from the table in the foyer and read it as she walked down the hall to her new office:

In the heart of Edinburgh, the Scottish Parliament Building stands as a testament to architectural ingenuity and modernity. With a harmonious blend of innovative design and a deep-rooted connection to Scotland's history, the building's striking exterior features a series of interlocking geometric forms that evoke the nation's rugged landscapes and ancient rock formations. As sunlight dances upon the intricate panels, the façade seems to shift in hue, mirroring the ever-changing Scottish skies.

The building's interior spaces reflect the country's democratic ideals, fostering transparency and inclusivity. Vast halls adorned with local materials pay homage to the land's natural beauty, while contemporary chambers equipped with cutting-edge technology speak to the progressive spirit of the nation. The Scottish Parliament Building stands not just as a center of governance but as a living embodiment of Scotland's identity, a symbol of its proud past and forward-looking aspirations.

Maggie laughed out loud; she thought the Parliament building's design was hideous and massively out of place with the city's historical surroundings. She also knew there had been bitter complaints about the building's lousy acoustics, functionality, and management's ability to maintain the funky design. Of course, all those things paled into insignificance compared to the main issue. The forty-million-pound price tag given to the project in 1997 had risen to an eye-watering four hundred and thirty-one million when it was finally opened three years behind schedule. *How is that for government efficiency?* she thought. *These people couldn't run a piss-up in a brewery,* but she aimed to change that and the stench of corruption that surrounded it.

Maggie's Holyrood office was stark with a cheap modern desk, an ergonomic black leather swivel chair, and two plain steel-framed chairs facing the desk. There was a large stock art picture of Ben Nevis behind the desk. Maggie had not had time to customize the office to her taste yet, and, anyway, she did not expect to be spending much time there; her home office in her nearby townhouse was far more agreeable. She did have a solitary picture of her and Robbie. It had been taken on the famous small bridge on the 18th hole at St Andrews golf course and it sat in a small glass frame on the right side of her desk. She picked up the picture and her mind wandered back to that day, a special day a decade ago. They had both birdied the final hole; she had chipped in while he had holed a short putt to match. God, she missed him so much.

There was a knock on the door; she put the picture down on the desk and looked up.

"Come on in," Maggie said, although the door was half open, and a young woman entered.

"Hi, my name is Abby St. Clair," said the young woman cheerfully. She was in her mid-thirties, tall and skinny, with long jet-black hair and large green eyes. She was wearing a red dress and white Reeboks.

"Hello, I'm Maggie McGown."

"Yes, I know," said Abby. "Welcome." She paused for a moment. "Look, I know you are just settling in here, but I have been asked to invite you to join a special committee investigating possible ethics violations. The media recently published allegations involving the misuse of expenses and contract rigging. One of the whistleblowers is an engineer for one of the wind farm companies."

"Why me? I've only just got here."

"I think that's the point," said Abby. "You don't have any long-term friendships or political debts. You're far more likely to be impartial." She gave Maggie a shrewd look. "That and the fact that you are so rich you don't need to steal from anyone and that makes you probably unbribable too."

Maggie laughed out loud. "I'm sure there are plenty of crooked rich people, but I'm glad you don't count me among the wicked."

St. Clair laughed nervously, a little embarrassed. "Sorry." She paused and looked expectantly. "So you'll do it then?"

"Yes, of course," said Maggie. "Anything I can do to make a positive difference. How many people are on the committee?"

"Five, including you and me," said St. Clair. "I'll have a file on the information we have gathered so far sent over; our next meeting is this Friday at eleven a.m."

After Abby had gone, Maggie settled down to look at the other matters she had lined up. There were the turbine purchases, hundreds of them with a cost overrun of twenty-five million pounds. While Maggie was sympathetic to the Green agenda, she figured there must be a way to do it without these giant windmills interrupting the world-famous beauty of the Highlands and its coastline. Getting permission from the local council to put a Sky dish on your home was nearly impossible, but these turbines popped up everywhere and anywhere and seemed to breed like rabbits.

The nuclear plant at Torness generated enough clean electricity to meet the needs of every single home in Scotland for nine months. Maggie did not understand why the government had not already committed to build another one and become a net energy exporter, one without all the turbines, which, amazingly enough, only worked when it was windy.

An assistant turned up with Abby's corruption file two hours later and Maggie flipped it open immediately. She had hoped to get to work on far more important issues, but she wanted to be seen as a team player and corruption had dogged the party for far too long. It needed stamping out. Fast.

The dossier started with a bit of history. In the grand scheme of things, the charges that were leveled at the SNP over the years were laughable. Nicola Sturgeon's so-called "Battle Bus" was an RV costing one hundred thousand pounds that was never used. Heck, a proper rock star tour bus costs ten times that amount. Then there was the missing six hundred thousand pounds that had gone into an account specifically for Scottish independence and had vanished. Not that six hundred thousand was a little money, but it was a laughably small amount in the grand scheme of government over-spending or grand-scale corruption.

The ferry fiasco was another matter; while it had started two leaderships ago, the current first minister, Sean Robertson, was still taking the heat. During Nicola Sturgeon's reign, two ferries to serve the *Highlands'* island communities had been ordered at the cost of ninety-three million pounds. That cost had since risen to three hundred million. The first boat was six years behind schedule when it launched and the second was yet to be put in the water. The company had gone bankrupt and the SNP had been forced to bail them out. It was a never-ending saga of incompetence and corruption and Maggie wasn't sure which was worse.

This, of course, was all ancient history and could not be changed, but more alarming was a recent string of sweetheart government contracts that had been given out with little or no bidding process; in some cases none. A couple of SMPs had already resigned amid a string of allegations of financial impropriety, but several who were implicated in various shenanigans remained in office. It would be a good start to show the Scottish people that their government officials would be held accountable. Maggie hated cheats of all kinds and cheating the people who elected you was the worst possible deceit. The SNP needed a clean sweep.

Maggie checked the time. She decided to clear her afternoon schedule. She carried on reading the file. It was getting interesting now. It was covering current issues. Several MPs under suspicion had recently founded companies that appeared to do nothing. This was not particularly unusual, but the fact that they were all done within two months of one another seemed highly suspicious.

Maggie flicked through the printed records from Companies House. Haggis Investments sounded like a joke, Highlander International, Celtic Holdings, and Brown Industries seemed deliberately generic. As she turned over the pages, one name caught Maggie's attention: Bonny Bridge Land Company. Bonny Bridge, she knew, was a small town four or five miles west of Falkirk and about the same distance northeast of Cumberland. It should have been of no particular interest to anyone other than those seeking the best-preserved Roman fort on the Antonine Wall. The town's best days had been during the Industrial Revolution when it had boasted a thriving paper mill, sawmill, brick plant, and several foundries, now all closed. Maggie doubted many people were considering investing in local real estate; maybe it was nothing. Or was it?

She called in one of her staffers; Julie was on her personal payroll, not the country's. She was just a couple of years out of university with mousey hair, a small, freckled face, and plenty of enthusiasm. She handed her a list of company names with instructions to do a little digging. Julie had already shown great aptitude for computer research. She grabbed the paper and rushed off in the direction of her small office.

She came back to Maggie's office within an hour. "Found something," she said with a smile, waving several sheets of paper in her right hand.

"Do tell," said Maggie.

"All of the companies on the list have recently purchased farmland a couple of miles south of Bonny Bridge," stated Julie.

"Did they now?" said Maggie. "I wonder why."

Julie shrugged, smiled, handed Maggie the papers and left.

Maggie tapped her pen on her desk as she thought. Someone obviously knew something that most people didn't. She would bring it up at the Friday committee meeting and see what the others thought.

When Friday came around, the ethics meeting was in a large conference room in Holyrood with floor-to-ceiling windows. There was a long white table with twelve leather swivel chairs around it. The four of them sat close together at the sunny end.

Abby St. Clair stood. "Maggie, allow me to introduce you to the rest of the members. This is David Hartman and Sandra Denning, both SMPs. This is Darin Harding, he's an independent lawyer." Maggie acknowledged each with a smile and a wave of her hand.

St. Clair continued, "While the committee's main focus was to follow up on reports that had been in the media, it is also tasked with some general investigation and there are plenty of issues swirling in the wind."

Denning was a large woman, in her late forties, at least thirty pounds overweight, with a bright green cotton dress and large square glasses. She started with a report on the excessive expenses claimed by the five SMPs. Five-star hotels, first-class train travel to London, expensive restaurants, personal trainers, and doggy daycare services. Maggie thought it stupid that they would be so blatant but also that it was a hill of beans, a few thousand pounds in the grand scheme of things.

Hartman had a stocky, powerful build and his tattoos peeked out from under the sleeves of his casual attire. His shaved head and a pair of aviator sunglasses perched on his brow lent him a cool and rugged appearance. He reported on funds missing from public donations to the party coffers; over one hundred and fifty thousand pounds needed to be accounted for. He was going through all the recipients with a bookkeeper, trying to find where the money had gone. Maggie just shook her head that this type of thing could continue to happen.

Harding was a striking figure, standing tall with an air of confidence. His auburn hair was just beginning to grey at the temples and his piercing green eyes exuded a mix of wisdom and charm. He had nothing to report on his task but had set up appointments with the headmaster and headmistress at Gordonstoun and St. George's schools the following week. He intended to inquire how an SMP with a salary of £67,662 might afford to pay forty-five thousand pounds a year to send his son or daughter to private school. In the case of Gordonstoun, it was the same school attended by King Charles, his father, and a long list of other royals from multiple countries. Maggie found it a bit depressing that they were chasing their own colleagues for such small sins. But a sin was still a sin.

"Right," said Maggie. "What about this business in Bonny Bridge?"

Abby nodded and pulled out a file, but the other members looked at one another in confusion.

"What business in Bonny Bridge?"

Abby handed a sheet of paper to each of the members present. "I spoke to the four SNP members who have bought land south of Bonny Bridge through shell companies. They had nothing to say, except that they'd done nothing wrong."

David Hartman laughed. "There's naught in Bonny Bridge but sheep!"

Maggie drummed her fingers on the table. "So why are they all setting up companies and buying land in the same place? Smells fishy to me."

The other members looked at one another. "Aye, so it does."

"Keep looking, Abby," Maggie said. "See what you can find out." Even though Maggie was the newest one there, she took it for granted that the others would do as she requested.

As the meeting broke up, and everybody scraped back their chairs, Abby St. Clair spoke quietly.

"By the way, Sean Robertson admitted to losing a considerable amount of money in a failed Bitcoin company."

Everybody stopped and looked at her, and Maggie smiled. "Did he now?" she said. "How very interesting."

CHAPTER EIGHTEEN

17th April 1984 –Yvonne Fletcher

George McDonald was at Kendown Colliery when the news of the killing broke on BBC radio through transistor radios on the picket line around 11:00 a.m. Initially, some picketers cheered at the news that a policewoman had been gunned down, but as the indiscriminate nature of the crime and the number of victims unfolded, the mood changed. The men grew restless and angry, but now their talk changed to "Arab bastards," not "scabs" or "pigs." Eleven people were machine-gunned down in broad daylight in England. It was unimaginable, another bewildering chapter in an increasingly violent world. The men lost interest in their task and, by lunchtime, had begun to drift back home to watch the news on the telly. It was one of those days in life, thought McDonald, when you always remembered where you were when you heard the news.

McDonald, like most other people, was appalled and fascinated by the events in equal measure. He had a treasured daughter of his own and could not image how the father of Fletcher must have felt.

McDonald watched the TV as they pieced together the story. It had been a chilly morning on April 17, 1984. Tensions were running high. Outside the Libyan Embassy in London's St. James's Square, a crowd of seventy people had gathered to protest the murderous regime of Libyan strongman Muammar Gaddafi. Their voices had echoed through the air as they demanded justice and freedom. The embassy building was an attractive four-story Georgian-style building in white stone, with five large windows across each floor.

The protesters had been kept well back from the embassy building behind a barricade, where they traded shouts with a small number of pro-Gaddafi demonstrators across the street. Everything was peaceful as around thirty police officers looked on. One of those officers was a twenty-five-year-old Metropolitan police constable. She stood with her back to the embassy among a group of her fellow police officers some fifty yards away. She was a young, well-liked woman with an infectious smile. Little did she know that this day would mark the end of her life and ignite a diplomatic crisis that would grip the nation for years to come.

Suddenly, around 10.14 a.m., two gunmen with Sterling submachine guns had opened fire from the first-story windows on the west side of the embassy building. Eleven people, including protesters and police officers, were wounded. Panic ensued as people scattered in all directions, seeking cover from the hail of bullets. The young policewoman was struck in the back; the impact sent her crashing to the ground. Shootings of any kind were almost unheard of in the UK, but the shooting of a police officer was unthinkable.

Her fellow officers rushed to her side, their faces etched with concern, shock, and total disbelief. They desperately called for medical assistance, hoping against hope that her injuries were not fatal. She was rushed to a nearby hospital, where a team of doctors and nurses fought valiantly to save her life. But despite their best efforts, her internal injuries proved too severe and she succumbed to her wounds. She was the first female police officer to die in the line of duty in Britain. Her name was Yvonne Fletcher.

The following day, McDonald sat at the small wooden table in his cramped kitchen and started his morning as he did daily, reviewing the major newspapers. He knew how the media covered the strike played an increasingly important part in gaining and maintaining public support, at least from the left-leaning papers. They would never get a fair shake in the right-leaning *Times*, *Telegraph*, or *Daily Mail*. But they could count on support from the *Star*, *Mirror*, and the *Morning Star*, a newspaper founded by the British Communist Party. The miners' strike was front-page news almost daily, but not on April 18, 1984; every paper in the country ran a picture of PC Fletcher and the strike was nowhere to be found.

That day on the picket lines, the mood was somber. Although anger at the police was a daily occurrence for the miners, this was different. A young female copper doing nothing but standing on the pavement was shot through the chest by an Arab gunman. Usually, on the picket lines, McDonald marveled at the spirits of the men and the army of women who supported them. There were brass bands, sing-a-longs, football chants, and bagpipes. The women washed and mended clothes, cooked and served meals, and often stood arm-in-arm with one another on the picket lines. It was a brotherhood, a community like battle-hardened soldiers in a foxhole. McDonald reckoned that in years to come, these men would never forget the days they'd spent together.

The miners' strike was relegated to the inside pages for the next two weeks as the murder of Yvonne Fletcher continued to be front-page news and caused a significant diplomatic crisis between the United Kingdom and Libya. The police surrounded the embassy and an eleven-day diplomatic standoff ensued as the calls for justice mounted. Eventually, all inside the embassy were allowed to leave, including the two gunmen, and were expelled from the UK as Britain severed diplomatic relations with Libya.

The British public was incensed that no one had been brought to justice and the incident stayed in the news for weeks. George McDonald was dismayed by the loss of her life, as he was sure was most of Britain. She was a pretty young lass with her whole future ahead of her; it was tragic.

It was well over a week before the miners' strike made the top of the BBC's Nine O'Clock News again. When it did, McDonald could not help but notice that Arthur Scargill's Ford was gone. He was now riding around in the back of a brand-new Silver Daimler Sovereign 4.2. McDonald noted that it was the same model of car the queen drove. He had seen a picture of her receiving the vehicle from Jaguar in the newspaper. He guessed that the car cost what a miner might earn in a year. The funny thing was in the second picture of the queen's story there was a picture of her actually driving the car herself while "King Arthur" as some of the Tory press had begun to call him had a chauffeur-cum-minder at the wheel of his car. It was getting harder and harder for McDonald to disguise his disgust with everything he saw. But he knew he would have to be careful. Making an enemy of Arthur Scargill would be a dangerous thing to do.

CHAPTER NINETEEN

Present Day–Green Is the Color of Money

MAGGIE SAT IN THE BACK OF THE RANGE ROVER watching the hills roll past as her driver, Max, guided the car up into the countryside northwest of Edinburgh. After an hour they came to the town of Bonny Bridge. From there, they headed south again to High Bonny Bridge. The road quickly gave way to wide open fields. Maggie had the coordinates from the land registry in her iPhone. She watched as they approached along a narrow road peppered with bends. "Pull over here," she said.

Max eased the Range Rover onto the grass verge. Maggie got out of the car, not waiting for Max to open the door. She was dressed in black leggings, a white polo shirt, her favorite ScotteVest windbreaker, a pair of Hoka hiking sneakers, and she held a small set of binoculars in her right hand. She felt a little surge of excitement.

"Hey, you have your remote?" Max called out. Maggie gave him the thumbs up.

There was a thick hedge bordering the lane. She walked for a hundred yards, following the turns, until she came to a wooden gate. She looked back over her shoulder. The Range Rover was out of sight now. She stood at the gate, using it for support as she scanned the fields with her binoculars. Three hundred yards away was a static group of vehicles: two white vans with green trim, a small yellow JCB, and the tractor-trailer that had brought it; next to the vehicles stood a bunch of men.

Maggie watched the men for a couple of minutes. It was clear that they were in the process of surveying the area. *Interesting.* She put her iPhone on maximum magnification to snap a few pictures; even from this distance, she knew they would be good enough—she was constantly surprised how good phone cameras were these days. As she put her phone away, she turned and almost walked into a man who was standing behind her. She let out a small shriek of surprise. The man was dressed in black sneakers, slacks, and a turtleneck sweater.

"You scared me," she said.

The man glared at her. "What do you think you are doing?" His tone was less than friendly, the accent Glaswegian.

"It's a free country," she said with an air of confidence she did not feel. "I'm just doing a little bird watching. I got a great shot of a kestrel."

"Let me see," the man said, putting a big hand out, waiting for her to give him the phone.

"You don't look like the bird-watching type," she said, slipping her right hand into the pocket of her leggings. She pushed the button on her remote panic alarm.

"Give me the phone," the man repeated, stepping towards her with an air of menace.

"Have you, by any chance, seen any woodpeckers?" Maggie asked him. She could hear the engine of the Range Rover, the sound of tires on gravel. "I'm dying to get a picture for my collection."

The man stared at her then jerked his head around as the Range Rover roared up behind him. Max jumped out, giving Maggie a look to see if she was alright. The man in black looked Max up and down then turned towards Maggie and grunted, "Who the fuck is he?"

Maggie snapped at him, "He's my guardian fucking angel. And I'm betting they don't pay you enough to find out if he can take you down, which, I promise you, he can and he will."

"Aye," said Max. "It would be my pleasure."

"Then who the fuck are you?" the man said, glaring again at Maggie as she moved towards the car.

Maggie got in the back of the Range Rover, closed the door, then powered down the window. "You'll find out, soon enough, sonny. Now, you can either tell your boss you saw me here and that you were too frightened to take on my bodyguard or you can keep your mouth shut and keep your job. I really don't care which path you choose."

The man in black watched them through narrowed eyes as Max drove the Range Rover down the road, expertly spun it around on the narrow road and went back the way they had come.

In the rear seat, Maggie slowly exhaled; while she had tried not to show it, that had been quite a frightening experience.

"Well, Max, that was interesting," she said, which was what she always said in a challenging situation.

"You really must be more careful. That could have turned nasty," Max replied.

Maggie laughed. "Maybe I'm just coming out of my shell. Home, James," she said mockingly. "But thank you."

As the Range Rover glided back along the narrow lanes, Maggie reviewed the photos. She zoomed in on the white vans to maximum magnification until she could clearly see the logos on both of them.

CHAPTER TWENTY

1984–Picket Line

Tom Brodie woke up in his cramped row house; it was Monday, May 7 and unseasonably cold. His house was dark; it was always dark these days because they had turned the electricity off two weeks ago. He was two months behind on his rent and the council, despite saying they were sympathetic to the miners' cause, were threatening his entire family with eviction. He had a horrible headache and his throat was raw. He had the flu, as did the rest of the family—Sally, his wife, and the two boys. Sam was three and David was six. They had no medicine to give the kids, the doctor hadn't come, and the only food left in the house was what they'd been donated: a large bag of rice and some cans of manky-looking tinned stew. Tom stared at the bedroom ceiling, anger growing inside him. They'd had to give Winston away, their beloved Golden Labrador, when they ran out of money. They couldn't afford to feed him. The boys had wept, and he'd remember the look on his boys' faces for as long as he lived. And it had broken Sally's heart.

Tom Brodie was only twenty-eight, but he felt much older since the strike. He'd been a big man once, broad-shouldered and muscular, with a shaggy mane of curly brown hair, but now he felt like he was wasting away. He'd lost a stone since the start of the strike; his blue eyes once bright and alert, seemed to have shrunk back into their sockets rendering them dull and lifeless. He'd had a part-time job as a bouncer in Legends, a local nightclub. He didn't think of himself as a tough guy, but he knew how to take care of people who got out of hand after a few drinks. But Legends had closed a few months ago. Nobody had any money to throw around anymore. If there was one thing he could take from it, he knew that he wasn't alone in his misery. Everybody was suffering. With thousands of miners on strike, whole towns were closing, shutting their doors, many of the businesses for good.

Brodie forced himself out of bed, cursing. It was cold in the house—there was no coal for the fire, no money for the electric heater. He pulled on a black T-shirt with a red Rolling Stones tongue logo and a pair of faded Levi jeans. He tightened his old brown leather belt. Sally had put two new notches in the leather to keep it in place. God, he could do with a proper meal.

Brodie sneezed, coughed up some phlegm, and slugged down a glass of cold water at the sink to relieve his burning throat. He donned his tattered denim jacket—too loose now—and worn-out brown work boots. He blew Sally and the boys a kiss and walked out his front door into the bitter, cold dawn. As if on cue, miners up and down the street began to emerge from their row homes one by one into the grey dawn light, a look of grim determination on their faces. They set off with nods and muttered greetings, resolved to stake their claim for another tedious day on the picket line.

How many days was it now? Tom had lost count. He called each man by name as their ranks grew, marching towards the colliery gates. "You alright, Harold, Joe, Frank?"

The pitmen had always had good camaraderie, but the picket line took it to a new level, almost like sharing a foxhole must be, thought Tom. They all knew the fight was not just about pits closing, wages, and working conditions—it was about preserving a way of life, a proud tradition, and a shared heritage, one that the government was all too eager to flush away.

"What do you call a person with a briefcase in a tree?" asked Harold, a short, fat miner who always seemed to wear clothes that were two sizes too small for him, but he was often good for a laugh. "A branch manager."

Some of the men laughed. Others groaned.

He tried another. "Two fish are in a tank. One says, 'How do you drive this thing'?"

More groans.

"Harold thinks he's Tommy fucking Cooper," shouted Frank, who was wearing two days of stubble and black satin bomber jacket that looked strangely out of place on the picket line.

Tom rolled his eyes; the longer the strike went on the worse the jokes got.

Harold was about to tell another joke, but thankfully somebody turned the ghetto blaster up. Queen's "Bohemian Rhapsody" came up on Radio One and Freddie Mercury's voice rang out. The whole gang started singing along in fake soprano voices. Tom joined in despite his sore throat and aching head and he almost smiled. Brodie briefly remembered a line from his English class in school that seemed to sum up the moment. *It was the best of times; it was the worst of times.* Somehow that summed it up. What was it? Shakespeare? No, maybe some other long-dead poet, it didn't matter. His breath was visible in the frigid temperatures as he sang.

Brodie couldn't wait to get to the colliery gates, where he knew he could count on a hot cup of tea and a bacon butty. Despite his heavy cold and blocked nose, he was sure he could already smell the bacon grilling outside the gates. Some new banners fluttered in the wind on the mine's fences.

Coal Not Dole.

Save Our Pits.

Victory to the Miners!

It sounded good, but it didn't feed his kids. He wondered what the boys were having for breakfast; then he pushed that thought from his mind as he queued for his bacon butty.

There were around twenty policemen at the gates, bobbies in traditional uniforms with their tall Centurion helmets that made them look like saps, he thought. The sergeant, hoping for a trouble-free day, greeted the approaching miners with a shout of, "Morning, lads!"

"Fuck off!" came a shout back from someone at the back of the line. Tom saw no reason to antagonize them. All it did was make them more ready for a fight. Tensions between both sides were already high and the slightest thing could lead to a violent clash. It was a David-versus-Goliath struggle. The sticks and stones the miners wielded were no match for truncheons or the seemingly unlimited reserves of riot police.

Yet, as much as Brodie wanted to avoid violence, the occasional battles with the police were almost a welcome distraction from the daily boredom of the picket line. When the scabs showed up, there would be pushing and shoving, shouting, and jeering as the bobbies tried to form a shield around them to let them in. Some days, it amounted to nothing more. Other days, anger flared and emotions spilled over. Sometimes it was too much to watch the scabs go in to take the strikers' wages while their wives and kids were hungry at home. Frustration built up and the men couldn't take it anymore. Someone would knock off a copper's helmet or accidentally elbow him in the face in a struggle, and after that, the truncheons would fly.

It had got into a kind of routine. The next day, the pickets would all proudly show their cuts and bruises, black eyes, and broken noses. The physical wounds would heal. What would never heal was their anger at the scabs. They were now returning to work in small groups, not just ones and twos. It made life on the picket line harder than ever as brothers turned on brothers. And as the strike had grown from days to weeks to months, deep divisions had emerged within the mining community. Some, fed up, chose to defy the strike and return to work, igniting a fierce debate about loyalty and solidarity. Brodie knew today would be no different. It would be another day of broken friendships and festering hatred. The only thing he just didn't know yet was which of the men he knew as brothers would choose today to return to work.

Tom knew he would rather die than break the picket lines, but if something didn't change soon, that was a growing possibility. He'd been beaten and arrested twice already, knocked about by the old bill, a police truncheon leaving a small dent in the back of his skull. Food was scarce, money nonexistent, and with the threat of eviction hanging over them, his family dreaded hearing any knock on the door. It would happen sooner or later. They'd get kicked out of their house. Then what? What the bloody hell was a man supposed to do?

CHAPTER TWENTY-ONE

Present Day –Gordonstoun

WHEN FRIDAY CAME AROUND, THE ETHICS COMMITTEE meeting was once again in the large Holyrood conference room with the floor-to-ceiling windows, although this time rain lashed against the glass, erasing any view of the castle. It looked set to continue all day.

It was Maggie's turn to speak. "Can anyone tell me why Bonny Bridge is suddenly such a hot spot for land speculation?"

The other members looked at her nonplussed. Then they looked at one another, puzzled, shaking their heads and murmuring. "Yes, why Bonny Bridge?" asked St. Clair.

Maggie picked a large manila envelope from her briefcase. "That's the very question I was asking myself. So, I went up there to have a look."

"And?" said St Clair, looking at the envelope.

Maggie pulled out five large photographs and dished them out to eager hands. She kept one for herself. The pictures showed the two white vans, the JCB, and the people milling around.

"So, what are we looking at?" asked St Clair. "Looks like a survey crew."

"A survey crew that works for Green Energy Industries," said Maggie, "surveying land owned by Haggis Investments."

The other members all looked at one another. "Then that would be Andy Hamilton," said St. Clair.

"Bingo," said Maggie. "Andy Hamilton, our very own minister of energy. But that was last month. Now, Haggis Investments is owned by a trust company based on the island of Jersey, and Mr. Hamilton's name is nowhere to be found."

There was a general murmur of disapproval, broken by St. Clair. "So. What steps can we take?"

Maggie liked St Clair. She had real leadership potential and was intelligent, quick, and action-orientated.

"We do nothing," said Maggie. "We watch, we wait, and not a word of this leaves this office. And in the meantime, Darin Harding here is going to get himself an education."

The other members all looked at Harding. "Aye," he said. "The finest money can buy."

*

Gordonstoun School was set in a 150-acre estate owned by Robert Gordon in the 17th century. His mansion served as the center piece of the magnificent property that had welcomed the children of royalty and the social elites since 1934 when the school was founded. Harding had attended the school himself and had bittersweet memories of his time there, a time when his bottom had frequent contact with a master's cane. Still, he'd forged some lifelong friends there and that was priceless.

Harding was greeted warmly by the headmaster, Derick Johnstone. Harding didn't know him but was sure he was ex-army from his posture, mannerisms, and crisply pressed red trousers.

"Always happy to welcome an old boy back," Johnstone said, standing up from behind his oak desk. He stepped around to shake Harding's hand. The headmaster had large, strong hands and shook vigorously. "You must have been before my time."

He motioned to an oversized green leather couch studded with brass rivets, which sat in front of a wall-to-wall bookcase lined with antique volumes.

The two men sat facing each other and the silence was just beginning to become awkward when Harding spoke. "Mr. Johnstone," he began.

"Derick, please," said Johnstone.

"Okay then, Derick. I have a couple of questions to ask you, which I know will be a little touchy, and I apologize in advance, but I do need answers."

"Alright," said Johnstone in a cautious tone. "I'll try to help, of course, but what's this all about? My secretary said you were rather vague."

"I am part of a team looking into a possible breach of ethics at the SNP."

Johnstone blurted out a half chuckle, half grunt, then mumbled, "Sorry, it's just that … well, you know better than I do what's gone on with that sorry bunch."

"I know some, but I'm one of them and I want to know more. I want to put a stop to it once and for all." Harding pulled a sheet of paper from his attaché case. He tapped the paper where two names were printed in in large type. "I need to know who paid the tuition for these two boys."

Johnstone took the paper and stared at it, but Harding could see he was already mulling over his refusal in his head. He passed the paper back. Held out his hands. "Look, you know I can't give you that information. Privacy. Data protection. You know how it is these days."

"Somebody has been ripping off the Scottish taxpayer. My God, don't you know that people are getting ripped off nine ways till Sunday?"

"Look, the trustees would fire me at once, and rightly so, if I gave you that information," Johnstone said, almost pleading. "My hands are tied."

"I understand," said Harding. "In fact, that's what I expected you to say, which is why we are organizing a police investigation into the matter. I'm sure it will take several days and will be highly inconvenient and I cannot guarantee there will be no negative press coverage. In fact, I'm sure it will make the headlines, for all the wrong reasons."

"Now look here—" Johnstone said, but Harding interrupted him.

"I appreciate the dilemma, Derick. You can't tell me, even if you wanted to. It's very unfortunate."

Johnstone shook his head. He went back around his desk and pulled a file from a filing cabinet and put it down on his desk. "Now, I'll go and see about that tea you asked for." He walked unhappily towards the door.

"Milk and two sugars, Derick. Thank you," said Harding.

Johnstone left and Harding got to his feet to scan the volumes of books on the shelves. All the classics were there, *Treasure Island*, *The Three Musketeers*, *The Canterbury Tales*, *Moby Dick*, *The Old Man and the Sea*, and *Huckleberry Fin*. Then he walked to the desk, opened the file, and looked inside. He took photographs with the camera on his phone.

When Johnstone returned, Harding was already back in his seat. Johnstone handed him a cup of tea then returned the file to the filing cabinet.

Harding sipped the tea. "There's no sugar in this."

Johnstone grunted. "You're a Gordonstoun old boy. You're used to privations."

"Touché." Harding smiled. "Both boys are on scholarships paid for by Green Energy Industries. Are they outstanding students?"

"I don't know," said Johnstone honestly. "I don't interact with either of the boys up here in my ivory tower. But I've heard nothing extraordinary."

"And do you know why Green Energy Industries paid for both boys?"

"As you just said, both boys won scholarships," said Johnstone.

"Tell me about these scholarships," said Harding.

Johnstone exhaled through his nose. "They both entered and won an essay contest about the energy benefits of wind power and sustainability in Scotland."

"Did they indeed?" Harding raised his eyebrows. "Did you, by any chance, ever see these essays?"

Johnstone looked at his watch. "The contest was run by Green Energy Industries, not the school. We had just agreed to reserve two places."

"And how many winners were there?"

"I don't know. Other schools might have been involved. I read in the paper that a girl had also won a place somewhere. Look, I really have to be in a staff meeting now."

Harding nodded and got to his feet. "You've been very helpful, and I'll do all I can to minimize any bad publicity about the school. Oh, and thanks for the tea."

Johnstone gave a tired smile as Harding left.

As Harding drove back towards Edinburgh, he dialed Maggie's office.

"Maggie McGown."

Harding flicked the indicator stem as he turned onto the A125 southbound. He jammed the mobile phone under his chin as he drove. "Maggie. I've got a math problem for you. If a wind turbine costs two and half million pounds and Green Energy Industries has stuck more than a hundred of them up across Scotland, then how much is their contract worth?"

Maggie's voice came over the airwaves. "Quarter of a billion pounds, at least."

"Interesting," said Harding. "We don't yet have any cast-iron proof of wrongdoing, but it is beginning to look mightily suspicious."

Maggie paused for a moment before responding. "As my dear father used to say: If it looks like a duck, swims like a duck, and quacks like a duck, then it probably is a bloody duck."

"Yes," said Harding drawing out the word, "and I wonder what else we might find if we keep digging."

CHAPTER TWENTY-TWO

1984–Scabs

Tom Brodie stood and looked around him. He was thinking about his future and that of the men around him. It was late afternoon outside the colliery gates, almost time for the night shift to appear—if they were going to appear. Some lads had taken their shirts off, their skin red as lobsters. It had been a scorcher of a day and they would pay for it later. Some hundred or so men stood in small groups smoking or chatting. Radio One played on a small transistor radio and some sang along to Billy Idol's "Rebel Yell."

There was a group playing cards and another playing dominoes, the men sitting on wooden crates. They told jokes, related stories, sang football songs, and kicked a ball about; anything they could to do to relieve the boredom. The day-after-day tedium of standing around twelve hours a day waiting for someone to attempt to cross the picket lines was mind-numbingly boring. It was also a place where tempers flared and lifelong friends became mortal enemies in moments.

Everyone on the picket line knew that large groups of miners in Nottinghamshire and Derbyshire had no interest in striking. Their pits were unlikely to close. Their output was higher—which made their pay higher—so they never joined the strike. Others had supported the strike early on but now, four months in, were wavering in their commitment. He knew the decision to break the picket line was never made easily. Like Brodie, those men had wives, kids, mortgages, car payments, and electricity bills, which were now all in arrears. Worse still, there was no end in sight to the strike. It could go on for weeks or months, and then what? How long would it take to catch up on their bills? How many holidays would they have to forgo to build back even a tiny amount of savings?

Brodie stuck his hands in his pockets and kicked away a small stone. It bounced across the road. He shook his head. Shit. Was the strike more important than feeding their families? Were their brothers on the picket line more important than their children? Brodie watched the faces around him. He could tell some of them were thinking the exact same thing. No matter what anyone said to the contrary, these thoughts were never far from anyone's mind. A murmur of disquiet swept across the picket line. The activities stopped, and heads turned.

"Scabs!" somebody shouted. There was a chorus of booing. A dozen men appeared on the horizon, flanked by as many policemen on either side. Twelve. Twice as many as yesterday. Brodie squinted to see who had broken the solidarity today.

With each step closer to the gates, the dissenting miners faced a barrage of insults, admonishments, and pleas. He could see their faces contorted with conflicting emotions—defiance mingled with regret. He could almost feel the weight of their decision upon their shoulders. It was a stark reminder of the anguish that accompanied every miner's choice to break the picket line.

The tension in the air was palpable as the picketers fixed their gazes upon their fellow miners.

"Bloody scabs!" somebody shouted again.

"Shame on you!" called out another voice.

The atmosphere crackled and Brodie felt caught up in a blend of anger, betrayal, and confusion. He knew them all, by sight, most by name, but this was worse. And two of them were friends. Or ex-friends. John Davis and Ralf Stanton. It was a moment that would forever change their relationship. Brodie knew things would never be the same between them again.

As the scabs approached the gate, their eyes met the searing glares of Brodie and his comrades.

"Turncoats!" somebody shouted.

A man next to Brodie bellowed, "Traitors!"

The picket line began to chant in unison, pointing their figures or shaking their fists: "Scabs! Scabs! Scabs!"

The chants drowned out the sounds of boots trudging along the road. Jeering, swearing, and threatening followed, and the picketers' mood was now dark with anger.

This was not Brodie's first strike. He knew that the weight of the scabs' decision to return to work would haunt them in the weeks and months that followed. They would be ostracized, abused, overlooked. But he also knew that all that mattered was feeding their families and keeping a roof over their heads. Everyone was in a bad way, but some were worse than others, looking after babies, aging parents, or kids with problems. Many of the pickets knew that the scabs' decision was not born from malice or defiance but from desperation, and it was an unwelcome reminder of the growing chasm between principles and the grim reality of life with no money.

Someone behind Brodie threw an apple core. It flew through the air and hit a policeman on the helmet. The policeman turned and glared at Brodie. Brodie laughed. The policeman grabbed for his truncheon then thought the better of it and marched on.

Brodie raised his fist in the air and joined in the raucous shouting: "Scabs! Scabs! Scabs!"

The scabs looked away, eyes cast down at the tarmac or staring straight ahead. They seemed to walk with steps made hurriedly from guilt, betrayal, and regret. But they'd have money in the bank again this Friday for the first time in months.

"Scabs! Scabs! Scabs!" The chants continued and Brodie shouted with them. But he knew there was a nice bonus for going back to work. The threat of foreclosure would disappear. The car they'd hidden would not be repossessed. Their families would find food in the larder again.

"Scabs, scabs, scabs!" Brodie shouted. "Bastard scabs!"

Brodie stepped out of the picket line and picked up a stone the size of a golf ball. On a whim, he threw it. It hit a policeman on the side of his helmet. *Shit.* Brodie retreated into the crowd, but it was too late—they'd clocked him. The scabs marched on and the remaining police turned to face the picketers. Two of the cops immediately broke rank and came towards Brodie. Two more followed. Brodie turned to run and skidded on an apple core. The picket line broke apart as two of the coppers pounced on him. Brodie heard shouting, a woman's scream, and then a flash of white light as a truncheon came down onto his head.

He was only vaguely aware of the rest of it; a scuffle and brawl broke out as they belted him with their truncheons repeatedly.

"That will fucking teach you, you dozy bastard," said one of the policemen as he retreated into the procession.

"Get back to work, you arseholes," said another copper.

When it had stopped, the picketers lifted Brodie and began to pull him away. It was his third beating at the hands of the increasingly violent police. He was not sure he could survive another. His head ached worse than ever, but at least he'd socked one of the cops in the face. You had to try to focus on the positive, thought Brodie, but it was getting harder and harder to do.

It would be a week before Brodie took his place on the picket line again, bruises still visible on his face, the lads giving him a good-natured ribbing about his absence.

There was another brief commotion among the picket line; one of the Union bigwigs had arrived to show his support. It was Ken Miller, the vice president from Yorkshire. He stepped onto a makeshift stage of three wooden crates and addressed the men with a megaphone. He gave a fire-and-brimstone speech like a demonic preacher, and the men all ate it up with a spoon.

"Brothers, we stand here today as a symbol of solidarity. We fight not only for ourselves but for every miner and every working-class family in this country. Those who choose to cross this line betray the very essence of our struggle. Let us remember that our fight is not against one another but against those who seek to dismantle our livelihoods.

"Prime Minister Margaret Thatcher has called us miners the 'Enemy Within.' But I can tell you today that the enemy within is not us, brothers. It is Thatcher's spies in our Union at the highest levels, planted there to sow distrust among the men, to pit family against family, to offer large bribes to motivate men through our picket lines. Let us stand strong, united, and resolute."

Miller ended, and there were deafening cheers. After ten minutes of shaking hands, he headed back towards his car. Tom ran after him, burning with passion and indignation. "Mr. Miller, I am in a desperate situation financially. Is there anything I could do to help?"

Miller looked at him thoughtfully. "What was your job?"

"I was down the mine, but I had recently switched to driving a truck," said Brodie, "before the strike, I mean. Oh, and I was a part-time bouncer at the local nightclub before it closed."

"Is that where you got those bruises?" asked Miller.

"No," said Brodie with a laugh. "You should have seen what the copper's face looked like."

"So, you can drive and know how to handle yourself?" asked Miller.

"Yes," said Tom.

"There just might be," said Miller thoughtfully. Scargill had his own chauffer-cum-bodyguard and it made him look much more important than he already thought he was. Miller thought it was about time he had one, especially since he intended to replace Scargill as head of the Union soon. He might as well hire as if he was already in the position. It was not like the money would come out of his pocket, he thought with a laugh, and he'd be helping the lad out.

He pulled a wad of notes from his pocket and, counting out five twenties, handed them to a grateful Brodie. "There, this will keep you going for a while, lad. I'll send someone to pick you up from the picket line tomorrow."

He got into his large, green Jaguar XJ6 and drove off. It was a B number plate, which Brodie knew meant it was new. Every August, there was a big rush in Britain to be the first on the road with a new letter. *Maybe it was a friend's,* thought Brodie, *who has the money for new cars in these challenging times?* His wife would be happy, but he wondered what he'd have to do to earn the money. Scabs were approaching the picket line. *Bring it on,* he thought as he went back to join the others, trying to keep a big smile off his face.

CHAPTER TWENTY-THREE

Present Day–Feed Her to the Lions

The following week, Darin Harding was stricken with flu and it fell on Maggie as a last-minute stand-in to fulfill his appointment with the CEO of Green Energy Industries, Harold Janssen. Green Energy Industries' corporate office was located just outside of Aberdeen. It was a large, modern, glass-and-steel building, its roof lined with solar panels and two giant wind turbines on a strip of closely mown grass on either side of the building made it look like it might take off at any minute. The interior walls of the building were decorated with colorful modern art. At least, Maggie supposed, someone thought it was art. She could have done art like this from about the time she was three or four years old.

She was shown into a glass conference room by a Barbie doll secretary with a squeaky voice, a skintight black leather mini skirt, and four-inch heels. The room had a rectangular glass desk and the typical twelve-wheeled leather chairs of a corporate boardroom. She sat down at the head of the table and glanced at her watch. She was five minutes early, or, in her opinion, on time. The secretary returned with a coffee, gave her a strange look at her choice of seat, and disappeared.

Maggie had a bet with herself on how long they would keep her waiting. She settled on thirteen minutes. She got out her Kindle and started reading; she was halfway through Golda Meir's biography and enjoying it immensely.

After ten minutes, two men showed up; one introduced himself as CFO James Jackson and the other as legal counsel Mark Goldstein. Maggie nodded politely, gave her name, and ignored wasting time on small talk by turning her attention back to her reading until the CEO came. At fifteen minutes past the hour on the dot, Janssen breezed in. He was a tall, athletic-looking man in his early forties, dressed in designer jeans, a black T-shirt, and a turquoise sports coat. *Very Miami Beach*, thought Maggie. It was no surprise when he spoke that he was not Scottish; his accent was Dutch.

"Sorry for keeping you," he said with a smile.

"No, you are not," said Maggie, smiling back at him.

Janssen stood there momentarily taken aback by her response and realized for the first time that she was sitting at the head of the table. "Have a seat," said Maggie, pointing at the seat to her left rather than right.

Janssen looked at her, confused and trying hard to control his displeasure. He managed a fake smile and said, "Yes, of course, Miss McGown."

"This is a fact-finding meeting, Mr. Janssen. There was no need to bring counsel," said Maggie, gesturing at the lawyer further down the table.

"You can never be too careful these days; the board insists on legal counsel for almost every meeting," said Janssen, opening his hands in a gesture of surrender.

"Can you tell me about your sponsorship of an essay writing contest for teens?" asked Maggie.

"I'm sorry, but that's a bit below my pay grade, some kind of small community marketing program, I suppose," said Janssen condescendingly.

"So, you knew nothing about it?" persisted Maggie.

"Oh, it may have been mentioned in one of our staff meetings, but if it was, I had other far more important things on my mind," said Janssen, opening his hands again. The other two men sat silently, one playing nervously with his steel-rimmed glasses, polishing the lens with his handkerchief, the other making notes on his iPhone.

"But you know who the three winners are?" Maggie asked.

"Why would I know that?" said Janssen, offering a confused expression.

"Because their surnames happen to be the same as three of the SNPs responsible for Scotland's energy policy and the purchase of millions of pounds of wind turbines," said Maggie flatly.

"Is that a fact?" said Janssen in mock astonishment. "What an amazing coincidence, are they actually related?"

Was he serious, Maggie wondered, or did he think she was that gullible? She decided to play it straight. "I've no idea if they are related," she said. "But if they were related and if the press decided to dig a bit further below the surface, I don't think your board of directors would be too happy with the results. This would include, and of course I'm just guessing here, no more contracts from the Scottish government for Green Energy Industries, your immediate resignation, and three or four SNPs going to jail on bribery charges. But then again, maybe it's just a coincidence these kids have the same name."

Janssen's annoying arrogance was clearly rattled. "Jim"—he addressed the CFO—"do you have any information on this essay contest we apparently ran?"

James hesitated. "No, but I'm sure if Rebecda from marketing was here, we could get some quick answers."

"Okay," said Maggie, "but I bet Rebecca is on holiday this week and maybe next, am I right?"

James blushed, "Err … yes, that's correct."

"Miss McGown," said the lawyer, "I think we are all getting a little excited over nothing."

"The only thing I'm excited about is finding out the truth," said Maggie with a smile, which she froze on her face for a few extra seconds.

The men look nervously at one another.

Janssen went on the offensive. "Miss McGown, are you aware of the critical importance Green Energy's wind farms play in generating clean, renewable energy? It helps reduce our dependence on fossil fuels and mitigates the environmental impact associated with conventional energy sources. We contribute greatly to the reduction of greenhouse gas emissions. This aligns with global efforts to combat climate change and meet targets set in international agreements like the Paris Agreement. Plus, the development, construction, and maintenance of our wind farms create employment opportunities. This benefits local communities by stimulating economic growth and supporting a skilled workforce in the renewable energy sector."

"I am sure I am more aware of the benefits of wind power than you appear to be with the workings of your own company," Maggie retorted.

"Look," said an exasperated Janssen. "Green Energy is not just for Scotland but for the world, for the children. A cleaner future. Why are you wasting your valuable time on some essay contest? We have far more important things we should be working on."

"I am sure something can be worked out," the lawyer cut in.

"I'm not interested in something being worked out," said Maggie. "I'm interested in the truth, and if the truth is people in the SNP are taking bribes from your company, however cleverly disguised they may be, then we've got a problem. If you have someone else on site who might give me more details of the contest, I'd love to meet them. If not, I think we are done."

No one said anything until Maggie broke the silence. "In that case, I am going to recommend that all contracts with Green Energy Industries be placed on hold until this matter is resolved. I can't say for sure if the first minister will agree with me, but I guess we will all know the answer to that soon enough. Good day, gentlemen." She got up and left the room.

"Well, that went well," said Janssen sarcastically.

"NO, I don't think it did," said the Jackson solemnly. "She just put the kibosh on an eighty-million-pound contract. She could be a real problem and she can't be bought. She's richer than the Ramesses."

"Who the hell is Ramesses?" Said Janssen irritably.

"He was a Pharaoh," said the Goldstein.

"And what would a Pharaoh do with a problem like this?" asked Janssen. "Hypothetically, of course".

"Feed her to the lions, I expect," said Jackson.

Janssen nodded slowly.

CHAPTER TWENTY-FOUR

June 18th, 1984–The Battle of Orgreave

George McDonald was heading south from Glasgow with five coachloads of Scottish miners towards the Orgreave coking plant in Rotherham, South Yorkshire. It was a plant that turned coal into coke, critical to the nation's steel production. McDonald looked out the window from a seat near the back, lost in thought as the coach lumbered down the M74 motorway south of Hamilton. It was pitch black outside, so there was nothing to see; most of the other men were asleep. It was far too early to be awake, but the man awake next to him was Fred Scranton, a miner originally from the Midlands. He was a thin man in his mid-forties with an aquiline nose and thinning hair who looked more like an accountant than a miner. He had married a Scots girl he'd met while they were both on holiday in Blackpool and was now working at Kendown.

"I was there, you know," he said, "with Arthur Scargill, at the Salty Gate coke plant in Birmingham back in seventy-two."

"Were you?" said McDonald, interested to hear a firsthand account.

"Aye, I was, me and fifteen thousand other lads bused in from all over the country. There were lots of coppers, too, maybe a thousand of them, and I remember it was mid-February, cold as fuck it was. The picketing was generally nothing more than spirited pushing and shoving; there was no violence, but the chief constable got cold feet because there were so many of us. We were like a fucking army and he ordered the plant closed in the interest of public safety, so we could all go home. Then Arthur borrowed the police chief's megaphone he was broken and gave us a victory speech and told him we could all go home 'cause we'd won. He was magnificent."

McDonald nodded and said quietly, "If only history would repeat itself."

"I hope it does," said Scranton enthusiastically. "We got a substantial pay rise and Arthur brought down the Tory government of Edward Heath."

"So, I've heard," said McDonald sarcastically, having had the story from Scargill's own mouth multiple times already. Scranton didn't seem to notice he was still lost in the memory of that glorious winter's day. *It's a wonder they didn't write poems about it,* thought McDonald. *Men will curse the day they were not here with us or something like that.*

"Maybe the police will shut down the coke plant and we'll all be home by lunch," said Scranton absentmindedly.

"Times have changed, Fred," said McDonald flatly. "The public doesn't like the strike. Thatcher's painted us as public enemy number one and the Nottingham miners are all working."

"Scab bastards!" spat Scranton.

"We are already three months into the strike and neither the National Coal Board nor the government has shown any interest in backing down. I don't see how this action will change much," said McDonald.

"Then why are we doing it?" questioned Scranton, somewhat taken aback by McDonald's pessimistic statement.

"Because British Steel plants had been receiving dispensations from the Union for 16,000 tons of coal to prevent damage to their furnaces; however, a little bird told us there were plans to deliver 5,000 tons of Polish coal to the Orgreave plant, which was outside our agreement. So, Mr. Scargill insisted action be taken."

"Too right," said Scranton.

"Well, Fred, that's as maybe, but there is a good deal of opposition among the Union leadership to the picketing of steel plants as closures in the steel industry could reduce demand for coal and lead to job losses in the coal industry. Still, as usual, Mr. Scargill pushed ahead with his own agenda anyway," said McDonald.

McDonald thought Scargill seemed more personally motivated by bringing down Margaret Thatcher's Tory government than he did by achieving victory for the miners' cause. In McDonald's opinion, Scargill was beginning to resemble a caricature of Captain Ahab of *Moby Dick* fame. He seemed possessed with the desire for vengeance, and it was that vengeance that was increasingly clouding his judgment.

"Well, I hope you are wrong," said Scranton. "I'm almost through all my savings."

"I hear you," replied McDonald.

The coach pulled into a motorway service area and lurched to a stop. Those sleeping were given a shake and everyone got off so they could take a piss and grab a cup of tea—well, those men who actually had fifty pence in their pockets anyway McDonald thought as he followed them down the aisle.

"I'm leaving in fifteen minutes, boys, so be back on the bus. It's a long walk home, and I'll not be waiting for any of youse," barked the driver behind them.

As they all walked into the service area, a dozen policemen were sitting at a large table, tucking into a hearty English breakfast of eggs, bacon, beans, black pudding, a large tomato, and some field mushrooms. On seeing the miners, they stopped eating and all stood up, pulling ten- and twenty-pound notes from their pockets. They waved them over their heads, jeering at the miners.

"Thanks to you, mate, I'm taking the wife to Tenerife instead of Morecambe," said one, pointing at McDonald.

"Keep it going, boys. I never made such money in my life," yelled another.

It was humiliating, but McDonald just kept walking as the taunts continued. Several of the men stole longing glances at the cooked breakfasts, but most just took a pee and got back on the bus. McDonald bought a cup of tea for himself and Scranton. The coppers left, perhaps heading to the same place they were.

As dawn broke and the coach finally drew close to the Orgreave plant, McDonald wiped the condensation off the window and was astonished by what he saw. "Christ, there are coppers everywhere," he exclaimed. There were thousands of grim-faced officers in full riot gear with a shield in one hand and a truncheon in the other. The sheer numbers indicated they had been brought in from other forces in the area. Their ranks included a significant amount of mounted police standing in disciplined order like soldiers. They stood on their horses like the cavalry battalion preparing for a Napoleonic War reenactment.

"Look at all the fucking police dogs, too," said Scranton. "There must be fifty of 'em."

McDonald didn't like it; it was predicted to be a scorching day, and most of the lads wore jeans, T-shirts, and trainers.

They were dressed for a day out at Blackpool, not for a battle. Another thing made him uneasy. Over the past few months, the police had gotten increasingly aggressive in stopping flying pickets on the roads leading toward plants and turning them back, but that had not happened today. It felt like they were walking into a trap, or was he just paranoid?

There were rows of cars and buses parked in a field and their bus took its place among them. McDonald noticed Scargill's new Daimler Sovereign off to the side so knew he must already be there. There were cheers as the Scottish miners got off the buses and their brothers greeted them warmly with accents from around the country. There were Scousers, Geordies, Taffs, Cockneys, and a bunch more regions McDonald could not place. McDonald's crew was rewarded for their travel with hot tea, coffee, and a bacon butty, which they all ate greedily before taking their spot arm in arm on the picket line. McDonald took his and a second cup and wandered over to chat with Ted Watson, sitting behind the wheel of the Daimler.

"How's it going, Ted?" asked McDonald.

"Aye, alright," he said in a thick Yorkshire accent.

"Here, I brought you a coffee," said McDonald, holding out a paper cup.

"Oh, thanks, that's kind of you," Watson replied, reaching for it.

"I see you've got some nice new wheels, must of cost a pretty penny," said McDonald casually.

"Aye, I reckon so," said Watson.

"I'll be off then. Take care," said McDonald and walked over to the bus.

Several thousand men were already on site and the numbers were swelling rapidly. The plant was out in the countryside, but miners were streaming in from the small village behind him like the gates of a football match had just opened. There must have been ten thousand or more.

On the picket line, the atmosphere crackled with anticipation. Thousands of miners, their faces etched with steely resolve, united in their determination to defend their livelihoods, assembled near the entrance to the Orgreave coking plant. The police faced them with their backs to the plant.

McDonald took his place a few feet from the police and the pickets engaged in the usual trading of insults, a little pushing and shoving of the regular police force.

"Where you from, pig?" yelled the picketer next to McDonald at the copper in front of him. "You're not from around here, are you?" The copper just looked at him.

"I wonder who's banging your missus tonight while you are all the way up here in Yorkshire?" said the picket.

"Fuck off, you worthless cunt," sneered the officer. "At least she's not working the streets like yours is to feed the kids. I'm on double time babysitting you cunts. If you stay out another few months, I'll be able to take early retirement."

Suddenly, McDonald was distracted from the verbal warfare before him by a deafening noise to his right. He turned his head to a narrow side road. What he saw shocked and worried him. "This cannot be happening." Hundreds of policemen marched in tight formation, advancing on the pickets like an army. All were dressed in full riot gear with shiny blue helmets, thick plastic face masks, and large Roman-shaped riot shields, which they banged relentlessly with their truncheons, creating an almighty noise. As they marched toward the miners, the picketers started throwing rocks, bottles, cans, and anything they could find at them. They bounced off the hard plastic shields with a thud, smash, or a clang. It was surreal, thought McDonald, who wanted no part of the violence.

The numbers had continued to swell. There was a massive crowd behind him now. Suddenly, without warning, the police line opened and the mounted police behind them charged into the crowd, batons raised. "What the fuck?" screamed McDonald. Men scattered in every direction, but they were so tightly packed together many could not get out of the way of a two-ton horse with a truncheon-wielding rider. Into the crowd they rode indiscriminately, belting people on their heads, shoulders, and backs, felling men running away like skittles. McDonald pushed and shoved his way from the front of the picket line to the side, away from the melee in the middle of the crowd. He made it a couple hundred yards from the gates and stood on a small ridge next to a solid-looking tree to survey the scene.

A young skinny picketer, maybe twenty, in sneakers, jeans, and a T-shirt, scrambled up the ridge towards McDonald, chased by mounted copper. The copper swung his truncheon and clocked the picketer on the back of the head with an audible thud. He went down face first like a felled pine. The horse reared up and almost trampled him. The rider spat at the unconscious man on the ground, got his animal under control, then took a step towards McDonald swinging his truncheon wildly at his head, narrowly missing as McDonald quickly ducked and moved back around the tree. The copper sneered at him and headed off in search of new quarry.

McDonald grabbed the young man by the arms and pulled him a few yards to the relative safety of the tree. The smell of the horse in his nostrils was overpowering as he breathed deeply with the exertion of the man's dead weight despite his small frame. He tried to revive the man to no avail; there was nothing he could do for him. Hopefully, he would come around eventually.

McDonald decided he would try to find some of his men and retreat to the village as the riot police waded into the fight on the open ground in front of the factory. He broke into a run along a dry-stone wall offering some protection towards the village, scanning the crowd for any of his men and finding none. As he ran, he saw a group of men overturn a parked car to form a barricade into the village. Others piled on wood, an old oil drum and an abandoned sofa; then they punctured the fuel tank and set the whole thing on fire. Thick, acrid smoke drifted back towards the plant and the oncoming police slowly advancing towards the village.

There was another car on the plant side of the barrier. McDonald saw two young lads siphon some petrol from the Ford Escort into a Coke bottle. Then they smashed the driver's window with a brick and threw the petrol into the car. Then one opened the door, let off the hand brake, and both began to push it down the road towards the plant. It gained speed quickly as it was downhill; they both threw cigarettes into the cab and the petrol lit at once. They let go as the ball of flame careened toward the advancing battalion of cops several hundred yards away.

Fortunately, they had plenty of time to get out of the way and it crashed harmlessly into the plant fence, but it had upped the ante, thought McDonald. It could just have easily killed fleeing miners as cops. McDonald finally found Scranton, who was bleeding badly from his right thigh. "I fucking hate German shepherd," he spat.

"We need to find our boys and get the hell outta here before someone gets killed," shouted McDonald over the din of the noise around him. Thundering hooves, beating truncheons, shouts, screams, and obscenities. This was not the sound of picketing; it was the sound of war.

The stench of tear gas permeated the atmosphere, stinging McDonald's eyes and choking the breath of all caught in its grip. Smoke billowed from barricades set ablaze, casting an eerie haze over the battlefield, for that was now the only way McDonald could describe the events, as a battle. Looking for his men, he finally locked on Scargill just fifty yards away. Seconds later, he saw him slip and fall down an embankment, hitting his head hard on what looked like a railway sleeper. Two coppers watching picked him up and took him, dazed, to a nearby ambulance.

McDonald walked over to the ambulance. "Are you alright?" he asked.

"Two coppers hit me from behind with a shield on the back of the head," said Scargill.

McDonald had seen the whole thing, as had another policeman standing by the ambulance.

"That's not what happened," said the cop emphatically.

Scargill protested that he'd be fine, but he was obviously concussed, and the police insisted he be taken to Rotherham Hospital for observation. McDonald concurred it was for the best, and Scargill grudgingly agreed.

McDonald walked away and moments later came upon four coppers beating a man flat on the ground with their truncheons. "Stop, you'll kill him," he screamed at them as he tried to drag one of the coppers away. The copper spun fast and punched McDonald in his right eye so hard it sent him sprawling dizzily to the ground. But luckily for McDonald he just left him there and went back to beating the other man. It took McDonald a couple of minutes to regain his equilibrium by which time the coppers had been called away to drag some arrested miners into paddy wagons. He got up groggily and walked unsteadily towards the village.

Eventually, McDonald connected with a handful of his crew and they walked to the far end of the village, away from the advancing police battalions. The bloody skirmishes went on all afternoon until both police and miners were exhausted. Eventually, everyone headed back to their coaches.

"Anyone know what happened to these men?" asked McDonald as he read out a list of ten missing people from the front of the bus.

"Most likely arrested," yelled Templeton from the back. "They arrested hundreds for doing naught."

"Yea, I saw Davis and Ratcliffe thrown in a paddy wagon," added Charlton.

"Bell and Pickering were both taken to hospital," said Atkins. "They'd been beaten bloody."

"Aye and there were plenty of coppers in those ambulances too," yelled Young, a big lad from the Gorbals. "I put two or three of them there meself."

McDonald could see that many on the bus sported bandages, black eyes, and broken noses. But what he noticed most was the mood on the bus; it was decidedly mixed. While some were still fueled by the adrenaline of battle and boasted of their martial exploits like Young, others like Scranton were quiet, heads down, lost in thought. The bus started moving slowly across the field where it was packed.

His thigh now sporting a bloody bandage, Scranton finally said, "George, is it all worth it? All the hardships at home, the picketing, and the violence. Shouldn't we just go back to work? It not our pit that is closing. Pits closed all the time when the seams ran dry or the mines flooded."

"Fred, it's not for me to say, I just do what I'm told. Union man till I die," he said evasively. Inside, McDonald boiled with anger and not just at the police. Hundreds injured, hundreds more arrested, and for what? This was another avoidable debacle, a battle of Scargill's choosing, yet the miners had been soundly whipped. He could imagine the stories he would read in tomorrow morning's papers. And he could not imagine any of them would be pro-miner no matter who was to blame for the battle. It would sap away what little public support they had left.

Suddenly there was a banging on the side of the bus; McDonald peered out. Two men, Harris and Fredricks, were carrying a third man, one with each arm over their shoulders. McDonald could not tell who it was, his head was slumped forward, a blood-soaked bandage on his head.

"Stop the bus," yelled someone at the back to the driver who slammed on the brakes and caused everyone to lurch forward, which was immediately followed by a stream of profanity. Two men up front jumped off to help the injured minor onto the bus.

CHAPTER TWENTY-FIVE

SNP Leadership Challenge

After six weeks to acclimate to Holyrood's nuances, Maggie McGown started her campaign for SNP leadership in earnest. She did not intend to sit in the back of the room and wait for her turn to inch up the political ladder. She minced no words with the current first minister, Sean Robertson; in her opinion, he was an idealistic left-wing moron who had never had a real job. He wasted far too much time pandering to the Greens, the trans community and woke brigades. It was not that she had no sympathy for some of the causes. It was just that focusing on those issues would do nothing to turn around Scotland's economy. If the Scottish government could not offer the people better economic prospects, they would never gain independence. It was really that simple: fix that and you could fix everything, thought Maggie.

She used the very same Win Friends and Influence People tactics she had used successfully in the beverage business to secure multimillion-pound deals. She quickly went through the Scottish Parliament, inviting two or three members to lunch or dinner each day at Edinburgh's better restaurants. No one refused, even those she knew might be political enemies, because she was paying and they wanted a chance to find out about her as much as she wanted to know about them.

Today, Maggie sat opposite Vicky Parker at a table in Heron, a relatively new Michelin-star restaurant she had always wanted to try. Parker was a short, heavy woman with a plain oval face and blonde hair cut tight so that from a distance, it was hard to tell her gender. "All your policies are about helping the rich get richer," she almost spat while chewing happily on her filet mignon.

"Well, Vicky, I'm not sure what you call rich, but most wealthy Scots have already left the building, taking their wallets and wages elsewhere," replied Maggie. "We must attract companies back to provide high-paying jobs. If companies and individuals can get a substantially better deal in another country, like Ireland, they leave and take their tax revenues with them."

"Let them go," said Parker. "The SNP should be all about helping the working class, not the rich."

"It doesn't help the working class if there are no jobs," Maggie explained patiently as if talking to a five-year-old. "I want Scotland to attract entrepreneurs to create more jobs."

"All you are going to attract is tax dodgers," said Parker dismissively.

Some people you just can't reach, thought Maggie, although Parker seemed eager enough to run up the lunch tab on this 'rich bitch' with a three-course lunch and two glasses of champagne. Another X on Maggie's list.

Andrew Murphy was a sixty-four-year-old veteran of the SNP, dressed in a nice Savile Row suit and arriving at Baba's ahead of Maggie in a white Bentley. He'd been a successful property developer in his early forties and gone into politics. Murphy was handsome with a full head of slicked-back silver hair and a well-tanned face. No wonder they called him the Silver Fox, for he was also charming. He greeted her warmly and they sat. He ordered a beer and she a Pino Grigio.

"Maggie, I'll get straight to the point. I like you. I think you have a lot of spunk, but I simply don't think you are qualified to be the party leader," said Murphy.

Maggie gave him a big smile and said, "And why would you think a thing like that, because I'm a woman?"

"Give me a little more credit than that," he replied, theatrically shaking his head. "I just don't think you have the experience. Yes, you were a roaring success in the business world, but politics is totally different. Look, it took me over a decade to figure out how to get anything done around Holyrood."

"And you think Sean Robertson has the experience?" asked Maggie incredulously.

"Of course not, he's an idiot," replied Murphy.

"Then why did you vote for him?" Maggie challenged.

"Because with all the bullshit about buses, ferries, and missing funds, I wanted someone else to clean up the mess first before I threw my hat in the ring," he said with a smile.

"Ah," said Maggie. "So now would be the right time?"

"It might be, I haven't decided yet," he said coyly. "What I have decided, though, is I'm going to have the sole. It's delicious here."

Charlie Lang was young, fit and charming. He'd been a high-flying corporate lawyer but after winning a controversial high-profile case had bailed before he was forty and switched to politics. He asked Maggie if she would mind if they met in his favorite gastro pub and Maggie agreed. After the normal pleasantries were out of the way and food was ordered they got down to business. "Maggie, I think you can count on my support on just about every issue, but...." said Lang.

"Ah there is always a but," said Maggie.

"I think you should back off Green Energy."

"Why?" asked Maggie with an amused smile.

Lang knocked back a slug of beer. "Because we need the clean energy and they make the most efficient turbines."

Maggie smiled. "Why them in particular?"

Lang blew out his cheeks and exhaled. "I dealt with them when I was a lawyer. You have more important things on your agenda than fighting with them and they do make a good product."

Maggie watched his face. "And?"

Lang toyed with his empty beer glass. "Be careful," he said. "They sometimes play rough."

"I'll bear that in mind," said Maggie with a tight smile as her bacon-wrapped scallops arrived.

"There is something else you should see." Lang pulled an iPad from his backpack. He pulled something up on the screen and handed it to Maggie. It was a blog post with a picture of Maggie with the headline "McGown to Empty Mental Hospitals to Save Millions."

"What?" she said in disbelief, staring at the iPad.

Lang closed the article and opened another window. This headline was on Facebook: "McGown to Move Drink Driving Needle to Zero Tolerance." "For Christ's sake, I ran a whisky company. Why the hell would I propose something like that?"

"You should see the video interview explaining why you made the dramatic U-turn," said Lang.

"There is no such video," stated Maggie.

"There most certainly is and I don't think even you could tell the difference between the real Maggie and the fake one," said Lang. "AI is scary stuff."

Wow, thought Maggie. How did you deal with that? She would need to develop a strategy, but for now, she had to press on with her meetings.

Maggie met Sharon Carter and Michelle Lafferty at L'Escargot Bleu, a little French bistro Maggie loved on Broughton Street. While she had not known beforehand, it seemed likely they were partners.

"The SNP has to champion the voice of diversity," stated Carter.

"I do champion diversity," protested Maggie.

"The SNP must do more to protect gay rights," said Lafferty.

"Five percent of the population is gay, lesbian or bisexual with another one percent transgender, which is just six percent in total. That leaves ninety-four percent who most likely never think to mention their sexual orientation. What percentage of them do you think is more interested in improving their economic future than debating which bathrooms one percent of the population should be allowed to use?" asked Maggie.

"I don't think you are hearing us," protested Lafferty.

"Don't you want an independent Scotland?" asked McGown.

"Of course we do," they said in unison. "But we want one that protects the rights of everyone," said Carter.

"To gain independence, we must prioritize. God only knows how many different issues there are to address, but we have to start with the economy," stated Maggie.

Carter folded her arms and looked at Lafferty. "Well, we've told you where our priorities lie," said Lafferty with a closed-mouth smile and a nod.

And so it went week after week as she uncovered far more causes, issues, and agendas than she could ever have imagined. Maggie made it through all 129 SNP members in three months of lunch, dinner and coffee meetings; as she suspected, most were not fit for purpose. She scanned her printed list; she had identified twelve as very competent, eight as capable, five as maybe, and the rest a waste of space. Your basic eight-twenty rule, thought Maggie.

She had one of her growing team compile basic files on all of them using their Facebook, Instagram, and LinkedIn profiles backed up by Google searches for any mention of them in the news. It was surprisingly easy to find and advantageous to know such simple things as their kids' or dogs' names, hobbies, and favorite sports teams. The info was uploaded into a Customer Relations Management program for easy access anytime she needed the information.

She studied the bios and, with her excellent memory, instantly bonded with almost all of them when she met them in person or on the phone, using scraps of information from her files. She greeted everyone by name and had staff send each member birthday cards and small gifts on their special day. She worked the crowd like a carnival barker, and most of them bought it hook, line, and sinker. Even people in the party with whom she had serious political differences had a hard time disliking her. It was the same talent people said Bill Clinton had and it was a master class in How to Win Friends and Influence People. It was influence she fully intended to use to fulfill Robbie's and her dream of a free and prosperous Scotland, but there was another reason why she needed to be first minister; she needed access to some files. The type of access only prime ministers and first ministers got.

CHAPTER TWENTY-SIX

July 1984
Operation Halberd

McDONALD SAT IN HIS SMALL SITTING ROOM EXCITED, waiting for the Six O'Clock news to appear on the small black-and-white TV in the corner. Sarah sat on the floor near the TV watching The Magic Roundabout, which always came on ahead of the news to signal the end of kids programming for the day. He smiled just watching her as she giggled at the show; he and his wife were so lucky she was such a great kid.

McDonald had just gotten an interesting phone call from Union headquarters; the dockers were with them. The presenter's familiar face filled the TV screen and quickly faded to a group of dock workers leaving the quayside and closing the gates with a large padlock. The interviewer swept in and started to pepper the men with questions.

McDonald took his place at 11:00 a.m. with the other twenty-five executive committee members in the NUM's temporary headquarters at St. James House, Sheffield. All were chatting, drinking coffee, and smoking cigarettes under the harsh florescent lights of the stuffy conference room, waiting for the president to arrive. McDonald had had to leave his home in Scotland at 5:00 a.m. and take a series of trains and taxis to arrive on time. Yet they all had to wait an extra ten minutes past eleven before Arthur Scargill made his entrance. When he did, everyone in the room could tell he was excited. You could see it all over his face. The chatter died down and he stood at the head of the long table to speak.

"Gentlemen, finally, I see the tide of this historic strike turning in our favor. We are now getting the support we deserve from some of the other powerful unions. We have sadly failed to gain the endorsement of the Steel Workers' Union or the Electrical Workers' Union, but yesterday, as you all know, the dock workers came out on strike. Better still, I have it on good information that the rail workers are seriously considering the same action. With the mines closed, the ports closed, and the trains not running, we will surely bring Thatcher to her knees."

Scargill was on a roll now, his voice high pitched, his words brimming with passion and conviction, his eyes bulging out slightly as a bead of sweat ran down the right side of his face. It was hot in the room now as the summer sun streaked through the street-facing windows.

"The Tory government has threatened to rule the strike illegal and sequester the Union's funds. They have created a quasi-state police by busing thousands of coppers from all over Britain to specific locations well beyond their borders. They have tapped my phone lines, placed agent provocateurs in the picket lines, and had me followed by police and government agents. They have planned fake stories about me in the news, brought nuisance suits against our Union in the courts, and arrested thousands of our members on trumped-up charges. Now we will make them pay. We will make them squirm and sweep Thatcher from power just like we did with Edward Heath." He thumped his fist on the table as he stood there with a glazed look in his eyes, clearly caught up in the moment; he smelled victory.

There was a genuine buzz of excitement around the executives in the room as they started chatting about what this new development might mean. "How long do you think they will last?" someone yelled.

"No more than a couple of weeks," replied Scargill.

McDonald was lost in his thoughts, thinking for the very first time that they could actually win this strike, even if it was through the aid of other unions rather than any strategy Scargill had employed. The whole strike had been called far too quickly and planned far too poorly in his mind. Still, a renewed sense of hope was in the air and McDonald embraced it.

***

At the same time, at the opposite end of the country, Prime Minister Margaret Thatcher opened a Special Cabinet meeting of a dozen ministers in a wood-paneled room at 10 Downing Street. She rose from her heavy leather chair, dressed in a royal-blue tweed skirt and jacket with a white shirt, all perfectly complementing her coiffed red hair. She began to speak slowly in her strained middle-class tone.

"The violence at Orgreave last month has positively affected public opinion against the miners. Even some of the left-wing papers are now condemning their actions. However, the Association of Chief Police Officers has told me that the miners, 'frustrated by the failure of mass picketing,' are taking to 'guerrilla warfare' based on the intimidation of individuals and companies. There are hundreds of incidents of criminal vandalism where the property of those choosing to work has been damaged with the intent of intimidating them. Miners who have gone to work in defiance of the strike have had their tires slashed, cars overturned, windows in their homes smashed, and garden sheds set on fire."

There was a general murmur of disapproval from those in the room.

"Leon, I think you have some examples."

"Yes," said Leon Brittan, the Home Secretary. He was young for a Cabinet post, his slicked-black hair parted at the side, his mouth a little crooked in his boyish face. "The National Coal Board and associated suppliers have also been targeted. Five buses used to transport working miners were torched at a private coach company depot. At a colliery in Derbyshire, sabotage machinery caused one hundred thousand pounds in damage. In South Yorkshire, picketers seized some bulldozers and used them to destroy several NCB offices. And I could go on with this list for another ten minutes," he said, gesturing at the list he held in his hands.

"It's outrageous," commented Norman Tebbit, minister of employment, his long oval face nowadays seeming longer as his scalp had already lost much of his hair.

"Needless to say, this sort of behavior cannot be allowed to continue," said Thatcher.

"Hear, hear," came the collective response.

Brittan continued. "We also have a serious new problem on the horizon: the opening of a second front. As I am sure you all know, the dockers went on strike to support the miners. The strike began yesterday when dockers at the British Steel Corporation port at Hunterston decided not to handle coal imports. Members of another union declared their willingness to unload it and things rapidly degenerated from there.

"The rail workers are also threatening to strike. This industrial action will cut off our coal imports quite quickly and lead to shortages of food and industrial materials, if not from the delayed delivery then from panic buying in the supermarkets. I am afraid that time is not on our side; at best, we can hope existing coal stocks will last until mid-January. It is essential for Britain that we end this strike by October.

"We have drawn up a list of worst-case scenarios to consider. These include rolling power cuts and a return to a three-day work week."

"I don't need to tell anyone here what a disaster that was for the country, the Party, and Mr. Heath in particular," said Thatcher.

"Not an option," came the strong voice of Michael Heseltine. He was the minister of defense, a very handsome man with a thick mane of wavy blond hair and dense eyebrows to match. His tanned face was in perfect proportion.

Thatcher continued, "I have asked the minister of defense to draw up plans for a state of emergency. Let me be clear. We will bring in the troops to keep the country moving if necessary. Michael," she said with an open hand in his direction giving him the floor.

"Yes, Prime Minister. The plan involves 4,500 service drivers and 1,650 tipper lorries capable of carrying 100 kilotons daily of coal to the power stations," said Heseltine. "A separate contingency plan, codenamed Operation Halberd, has also been devised to use troops if the dock strike continues too long. It involves using 2,800 soldiers in thirteen specialist teams that could be used to unload 1,000 tons a day at the docks. This plan would also require a state of emergency declaration to ensure they can access port equipment, such as cranes, if needed."

"Won't that be seen as a sign of weakness and encourage the strikers to continue?" asked Peter Walker. The minister for energy was another good-looking man with a strong square jaw and a fine head of greying hair.

"Bringing in the army may be pouring fuel on the fire and might encourage even greater violence and lawlessness," stated Tom King, secretary of transport.

"Both those arguments have merit," replied Thatcher. "But when and if I need to use troops to keep this country going, I will not hesitate to do so and take full responsibility for the consequences, whatever they might be." There was a murmur of support from the room.

"Politically, the stakes in the miners' strike are far higher, so we should focus on ending the dockers' strike first. They need the complete support of their members since 25% of the ports continue to operate. If both the dockers and the rail workers join the strike and continue for several weeks or even months, it will put this government in a very precarious position and undermine all the great work we have done over the last five years.

"This situation will play right into Scargill's hands and we must not allow that to happen. We have tamed inflation, unemployment is finally in check, and we have dramatically increased government efficiency. We must not let the militant unions take us back to another Winter of Discontent."

There were cries of "Hear, hear," and a smattering of applause as Thatcher ended her short speech and sat down with a slight nod of appreciation to her audience. Heseltine turned to King and quietly whispered to him, "You really do have to admire her composure and confidence in such difficult situations."

"Maggie strikes again," said King.

"Yes quite," replied Heseltine.

The PM adjourned the meeting and moved to her private offices, reading quickly through a new stack of paperwork at her desk. After fifteen minutes, the phone on her desk rang and she picked it up. "Yes?" A pause. "Thank you. Send him in."

A heavyset man with thick, slicked-back grey hair and an immaculate pinstripe suit entered the room. He smiled.

"Yes, Sir John?"

"You are considering calling in the army to break the strike, ma'am?"

"Yes, that's right. How do you know?"

"It's my job to know, ma'am." Thatcher nodded. The man went on. "That makes it a matter of national security."

"Indeed, it does."

Sir John smiled. "You have my full support."

There was a moment of silence. "What is the reason for your visit?" the PM finally asked.

Sir John put his hands together and made a steeple of his fingers. "There might be a ... how should I say, more pragmatic solution."

Thatcher put the lid on her pen and set it down. "Go on."

CHAPTER TWENTY-SEVEN

1984–Strength in Numbers

Bruce Springsteen was on the radio, "Dancing in the Dark." Some of the men, mostly dressed in jeans and a T-shirt, were dancing around, the ghetto blaster sitting on top of an oil drum at the colliery gates. Others played air guitars or sang into fists, mimicking mics. The mood was buoyant the men laughing and joking.

With the dock workers now on strike, McDonald felt the same renewed sense of optimism as the men on the picket lines; they were no longer alone in their fight with the government.

"Aye, there is strength in numbers, George," said Sullivan, a large man in his mid-forties, now sporting a thick black beard McDonald had not seen before. "If the rail workers do come out as well, I'm thinking we will wrap this strike up pretty quickly."

"I hope so. What's with the beard, Mac?" asked McDonald.

"No money for razors. I might keep it, though the missus says it makes me look like a pirate," said Sullivan with a wink and a smile.

McDonald noticed, too, that in the morning's papers there were growing calls for the government to offer something to the miners to avoid a national crisis, although since Scargill refused to talk unless the government promised no pit closures, McDonald could not see how that was possible; it was a Mexican standoff with both sides waiting for the other to blink. But if the rail workers came out, it truly would grind the country to a halt and the government would be forced to give. Surely now victory was within their grasp.

CHAPTER TWENTY-EIGHT

2024–Rabbit's Head

MAGGIE WAS GIVING A SPEECH ABOUT THE FUTURE OF Scotland at the posh Chester Hotel in Aberdeen for around a hundred people. The event was sponsored by a friend of Maggie's in the beverage industry, but in reality, it was more of a campaign event designed to test future platform ideas. It was the usual format: cocktails and canapés followed by a short speech, then more cocktails and canapés. Some attendees would donate money, others influence; for Maggie it was all about building a powerful base of supporters in the right industries.

It was a typical windowless ballroom with large brass chandeliers adorned with fake crystal hanging from the bulbs. The tables were small, round stand-up types, and a stage was set up at one end of the room. The buzz of chatter hummed loudly and Maggie waltzed quickly from one group to the next for the obligatory handshakes and selfies. There were only a couple more tables to go when she approached table eighteen. There stood two middle-aged women with their husbands and a lone man in his late sixties or early seventies with broad shoulders, white hair, and a white beard. Maggie immediately thought of an old sea captain.

He wore a large dark overcoat with a highly polished wooden cane in his right hand topped with a silver rabbit's head. He smiled at her and she smiled back. One of the two women at the table stepped before her and introduced herself as Morag, her husband as Peter. Maggie posed for a selfie with the couple and Morag gushed, "We love what you're doing for Scotland."

Maggie turned back to the captain and was shocked to see the rabbit's head had vanished from the walking cane and was replaced with a gleaming six-inch dagger. The captain held the walking stick with two hands just below the dagger's blade and lunged at her belly with surprising speed for an older man. It had been years since she had taken taekwondo, but instinctively, she parried the cane downward and outward away from her gut with her left hand. The dagger plunged into her left thigh and she screamed in pain as she instinctively punched the man in the face with her right fist with all her might. Blood spurted from her wound like a fountain. The room erupted in screams and confusion; she heard someone yell in a shrill female voice, "My God, he's got a knife." Then she fell to the floor, the dagger and walking stick still embedded in her thigh, causing another round of nauseating pain as it hit the floor and moved upward in her flesh.

The captain grabbed for the weapon, yanked out the walking stick dagger from Maggie's leg, and was poised to strike again when a quick-thinking young waiter banged him over the head from behind with a bottle of Dom Perignon. A half second later, Max her chauffer-cum-bodyguard arrived from a few steps away and side-kicked the woozy man violently in the chest sending him sprawling backwards. The cane, already loose in his hand from the blow on the head, slid across the ballroom, and the man crumpled to the floor six feet away. Several men in the crowd immediately subdued him. Three doctors were in the room and all instantly attended to Maggie, applying a napkin tourniquet to stem the bleeding—another called for an ambulance. Within ten minutes, the place was swarming with police and the room was cleared save for the doctors and an unconscious man , now handcuffed on the floor with two large officers standing over him.

Paramedics arrived, applied a rubber tourniquet, removed the blood-soaked napkin, and put on fresh bandages. Maggie was sweating and in pain; they took her away on a gurney to a waiting ambulance accompanied by Max.

CHAPTER TWENTY-NINE

1984–Desertion

Outside the Kendown colliery most of the picketers stood around a large ghetto blaster set on top of an oil drum. It was a blistering hot day and many men already had their shirts off. Radio One DJ Simon Bates had just revealed the answer to what almost everyone on the picket line had already guessed as 10cc's "Dreadlock Holiday" played out its final notes on the Golden Hour. "See, I fucking told you the Golden Year was 1978 you wanker," said Campbell to Skywalker.

"Shush," said McDonald as the news headline grabbed his attention. "Turn it up, Mac." The chatter stopped at once.

"Today, at a meeting in London, delegates representing members of the Transport and General Workers Union in eighty-five British ports voted overwhelmingly, seventy-six votes to eight, with six abstentions, to end the dock strike. Ports that have been affected will reopen for business tonight or Wednesday morning. From the outset, the strike got only patchy support, with Dover and other passenger ferries operating normally. According to the employers, about seventy-five percent of regular trade was maintained. However, the ports of London, Liverpool, and Bristol are estimated to have lost about $18 million over the last three weeks. John Connolly, the union's national docks officer, conceded that the lack of solidarity was one of the reasons for the end of the walkout, the second maritime strike in support of the miners. The end of the strike will no doubt be seen as a victory for Mrs. Thatcher in her ongoing battle with the Miners' Union and a defeat for Union boss Mr. Arthur Scargill," announced the BBC newscaster.

"The weak-minded bastards!" yelled Buchanan.

"Traitors!" came the cry from another.

"Scabs, scabs, scabs," came a chorus from a dozen or more at once.

The men's deflation was palpable, hunched shoulders, grim faces, clenched jaws, a couple even looked close to tears. McDonald saw a mixture of emotions on their faces—fear, anger, frustration, and betrayal. They had all come to the realization that without the backing of other unions, the bargaining power of the NUM was diminished. McDonald just shook his head in despair not wishing to voice his true feelings. It was a heavy blow after enjoying a few weeks of hope. Now it was back to fighting their cause alone again—a lost cause at that.

Everyone knocked off the picket line a little early that day as a result of the news. McDonald decided to go meet Sarah as she left school. He was waiting for her at the gate and she gave a look of surprise when she saw him and ran to him, leather satchel bouncing up and down on her back. "Hi Daddy," she exclaimed, excited to see him.

"How about an ice cream?" he asked.

"Sure," she said then added suspiciously, "but how come? It's the middle of the week, we never have treats in the middle of the week." "Well, today we got some good news and we think the strike will be over soon, so you and I are going to have a mini celebration and we will take a choc ice home for Mum as well," said McDonald.

"Yippie," said Sarah. "I hate this stupid strike!"

CHAPTER THIRTY

Present Day– Rich Bitch

The day after the attack in Aberdeen, Scottish police offered a short-term protection officer to Maggie. Max had other ideas and called a friend he had at Global Protection in London. They suggested he engaged a highly trained team of four from their database of security professionals. Two ex-SAS, one ex-Marine, and a Scots Guard were recommended. They would work as a rotating team so nothing like this would happen again. Maggie gave her blessing to the idea.

Back at police headquarters in Edinburgh, a gritty detective named Jack Thomas was about to interview the suspect. Thomas was a veteran of the force and something of a legend. It was rare for officers in Scotland ever to be shot at, but Thomas had been shot three times, hence his nickname name Bullet Proof Jack, or just Bullet for short. He was short with a small round head and a crew cut but with a large barrel chest busting out of his cheap suit.

Thomas entered the cold, windowless interrogation room with a small steel table and two steel chairs in the middle of it, lit by a center strip of fluorescent lighting. The suspect's name had been established as Cameron Mackintosh.

A uniformed officer stood in the corner of the stark room looking on. Thomas took his seat with a small file in his right hand, which he placed on the desk. It detailed Mackintosh's short history: drunk and disorderly at a football match, a drunk driving conviction, and a criminal vandalism case brought by his neighbor, which was later dropped; nothing out of the ordinary. Thomas had seen a thousand such files and certainly there was nothing in this one to suggest an assassination attempt on Scotland's most famous political candidate. Macintosh was ex-army with a twenty-year stint, but that was ancient history now.

"Why did you do it, Mackintosh?" asked Thomas, it was always best to try a straightforward line of questioning first.

"I don't like rich bitches," said Mackintosh in reply. "I especially don't like rich bitches that think they are better than anyone else. They need to be brought down a peg or two. When it comes down to it, rich bitches bleed like everyone else, don't they? All the elite should get what's due to them for ignoring the ordinary people."

Thomas rolled his eyes and shook his head slowly from side to side. It was not the professional thing to do, but it just happened. Thomas stared at Mackintosh for a few seconds; he was disheveled and sported a shiner of a black eye from one of Thomas's boys. That made him smile just a little. It was always nice when they could get one in before putting them in the cells.

"So, you have had girl problems in the past, have you?" said Thomas with a knowing smirk.

"What?" roared Mackintosh, angry at the attack on his manhood.

"Well, it's just when I hear shite like that, it usually tells me a woman has dumped the guy. In your case, obviously, a woman who made a lot more money than a cockroach like you," said Thomas.

Mackintosh went to rise but was cuffed to the chair and quickly sat back down.

"There's a good boy," said Thomas as if talking to a dog. He needed little more from this prick; he had his newspaper quote. Now it was just a question of whether Mackintosh's lawyers would talk him into an insanity plea. He had already turned down the chance to have one present for the interview, but Thomas knew that could quickly change as the reality of twenty years behind bars became a little more real for him. Macintosh had enjoyed his fifteen minutes of fame, his picture on the front page of every newspaper in the country; the rest of his life was downhill from here.

Thomas left the room and bumped into Metcalf in the hallway. "Anything political?" he asked, n nodding at the interview room.

"Naw, just some mad wanker," replied Thomas.

CHAPTER THIRTY-ONE

Present Day–Hospital

The next day, Detective Thomas visited with Maggie in her hospital bed, she was sitting up reading from an iPad when he arrived.

"How are you?" he asked. "I'm ok, twelve stitches, and a pint or two of someone else's blood, but I'll be fine." Said Maggie.

Then Thomas told her the details of the interview he had had with her assailant.

"I am flabbergasted," she exclaimed. "Making things better for ordinary people is exactly what I am trying to do. You must focus on economic growth to make that happen. How can people get it so wrong and harbor such hatred?"

Thomas shrugged and shook his head. "The world is full of psychos and crazy people. Did you know there were over 10,000 dangerous weapons crimes in Scotland last year alone?"

"No," said Maggie, shocked at the number. "I thought Scotland was a pretty safe country."

After two days of rest Maggie's leg was stiff and sore, once she had the stitches out she would have a battle scar for the rest of her life. Nonetheless she got out of her wheelchair and opened the door to the makeshift press room set up in the hospital's staff cafeteria. She walked stiffly to the podium with the aid of crutches. There was some clapping, a few cheers, and lots of flashing cameras. She read her prepared remarks before being discharged, thanking the hospital staff, police, and public for their support. She ad-libbed a little about how she would stamp out crime in Scotland, specifically knife crime, and vowed to make Scotland's streets safe again, then took questions.

"What have you got to say to your assailant?" yelled one reporter.

Maggie answered, "I'd tell him I got his point." There was a titter of laughter.

"How are you feeling?" yelled another.

"I feel Like Captain Ahab right now, but my team tells me I'll be just fine in a few weeks," replied Maggie. More titters from the crowd.

"The assailant was quoted as saying you are only out to help the rich, and that's a sentiment echoed by many of your critics. What have you got to say about that?"

"I'd say if my critics saw me walking barefoot over the river Clyde, they would say it was because I couldn't swim." Another burst of muffled amusement.... It was vintage Maggie, ready to give the perfect answer to any question.

The next day, her leg was as stiff as a flagpole, but she was pleasantly surprised at the news headlines and read the *Scotsman* aloud.

"McGown Shows True Grit After Attack

"Feisty female Maggie McGown is beginning to win the hearts and minds of many Scots who had been on the fence about her, and even some who have been totally against her progressive agenda. One has to admire her courage, determination, and optimism." Maggie smiled; she would take the week off to recover. It would be another three before she wore high heels again. Security measures at all events were tripled, but she wondered if that would be enough. It was a crazy world that she could not make better if she were dead.

CHAPTER THIRTY-TWO

1984–Foreign Aid

MONDAY, OCTOBER 1ST SAW ANOTHER MAJOR SETBACK in the miners' struggle and another emergency meeting in Sheffield's Union headquarters. McDonald was in the room early as always and the mood was somber as the other executives slowly made their way in one by one. Heads down, shoulders slumped, frowns on their faces. Not so Arthur Scargill. He came into the room in a fighting mood, practically shouting from the start of the meeting.

"Good morning, gentlemen. As you all know, two days ago, the High Court in London ruled against us. Judge Sir Donald Nicholls accused us of 'riding roughshod' over the Union's members and failing to observe the Union's rules by not calling for a national ballot on the strike action. I did not believe a national ballot was necessary, and I still don't.

"In ruling the strike illegal, the judge has instantly denied any of our members from receiving social benefits, thus cutting them off from their last financial lifeline. As far as the government and the law are concerned, we can return to work or starve. It is our choice."

There was a loud murmur of disapproval along with a liberal sprinkling of expletives from the assembled men. "Fucking arseholes," yelled Ken Miller, banging his fist on the table.

"Cowards," yelled a round, red-headed guy from Manchester whose name McDonald could not recall.

Scargill continued raising his voice even higher. "The judge also fined me personally one thousand pounds and the Union two hundred thousand pounds. This ruling is another attempt by an unelected judge to interfere in the Union's affairs. Obviously, we have no intention of paying this outrageous fine. We need to take immediate action to transfer funds to bank accounts overseas to stop the courts from seizing the Union's assets."

To George McDonald that did not sound like a good idea for the members; in fact, it sounded terrible, yet what else could they do? The courts would sequester the Union's funds if they did not act. This situation was all Scargill's fault. None of this would have happened if he had only held a national vote. But that might have been a vote he did not win. There was little discussion and the meeting ended with no one objecting. Things were getting desperate—and desperate times called for desperate measures.

***

For George McDonald the next month, as the weather grew colder and colder, was another month of mundane duty on the picket lines at Kendown Colliery. Old oil drums were filled with debris to keep them warm and the arid smoke rose in several places around the colliery gates. The picketers' denim jackets were replaced with parkas now, their fake-fur-lined hoods up against the wind.

"Anyone go to the match this weekend?" asked McDonald, trying to keep spirits up.

"Which one?" asked Wallace, a young freckle-faced lad of eighteen, who looked even younger.

"Which one?" asked McDonald incredulously. "Which one? The local derby Hearts against Hibernian."

"I went," said Ferris, a skinny blonde lad in his twenties. "My brother works on the gate and lets me in free. It was shite, a nil-nil draw; my school team could have beat either of them. They are both lucky to mid of the table."

"Hey, turn that one up!" yelled Wallace as the Clash boomed out "Rock the Casbah" from a nearby radio and a few of them sang along. Some danced. Anything to relive the boredom, thought McDonald as he sang along.

Then, the next day, on October 29th, a bombshell dropped. McDonald sat at his kitchen table with a cup of tea and piece of toast with marmalade. He stared wide eyed and open mouthed at the headlines of the multiple morning newspapers to which the Union had subscribed for him. Over a dozen now came through his letter box every day so he could monitor how the strike was being covered by the media and report back. He could not believe what he was reading and shook his head in disgust. "You've got to be fucking kidding me," he yelled, quickly looking around to make sure his daughter was not in the room; his wife was just pushing her out the door to school and turned with a scowl.

"What is it, George, that you need to be swearing at the top of your voice at eight in the morning," she asked with a disapproving look.

"Yea sorry, luv," said McDonald, embarrassed by his outburst. "But look," he said, pointing at the paper. He began to read. "After weeks of denial that he had been seeking financial support from Libyan dictator Muammar Gaddafi, NUM President Arthur Scargill today finally admitted to the press that Union officials had in fact met with the dictator and Libyan government officials but only to 'explain the strike,' he claimed."

"Oh," said his wife and walked into the kitchen.

McDonald continued reading. "According to the *Times*, Mr. Scargill and Roger Windsor, the Union's chief executive, had traveled recently under assumed names to Paris and met with Salem Ibrahim, who the newspaper said had been identified by French intelligence officials as a 'bagman' used by Col.

Muammar Gaddafi to arrange financial support for various activities backed by the Libyan leader, including international terrorism. That meeting was followed by a five-day visit to Tripoli by Mr. Windsor. That included a meeting on Thursday with Colonel Gaddafi and senior officials, which was broadcast on Libyan television and reported widely by the Libyan press agency, showing Mr. Windsor hugging the dictator.

"Mr. Scargill went on to say that the miners had not received 'a single penny' from Libya, but when pressed by a reporter, he refused to condemn the regime of Colonel Gaddafi. He also left the door open for Libyan aid for the miners, provided it came from unions and not the government." McDonald rolled his eyes; who in their right mind would believe that statement?

He wondered how much money they had got and guessed it went straight into the Union's Swiss bank account. He threw the paper down in disgust but then picked it up again and reread the story, rubbing his chin in thought. Surely this would be the beginning of the end for Scargill, begging for money from terrorists?

On the picket line that day the men were all asking the same question. John Lampson, an old miner near retirement with a well-worn face, was the first to confront McDonald, "Did the Union really take money from Gaddafi?" he said, the disgust clear in his tone.

"I don't know," said McDonald. "But I sure as hell mean to find out."

"Don't be so hasty now. If it feeds my family, I don't care where it comes from and I'm not about to ask," said Luke Dodington, although everyone just called him Skywalker, a young miner with three little uns.

"Well I can tell you this, if they spent a week out there in Libya and have not, as Mr. Scargill claims, '"taken a single penny', I'd say that was a pretty poor result," said Lampson, his anger rising as he spoke. "Those Arab bastards shot that young lass Fletcher in cold blood outside their embassy. I say we should have nothing to do with them. Nothing. It will drive people away from our cause mark my words."

"Indeed it will," said McDonald, nodding slowly in agreement, his lips pressed tightly together.

The talk on the picket line was of nothing else that day and while some agreed with Skywalker the ends justified the means, most did not.

As McDonald he sat eating his tea on his sofa that night Scargill was on the Six O'Clock News still denying he had done anything wrong. The next morning, as McDonald scanned the daily papers, the public backlash was even worse than he had feared. The Libyan meeting was now front-page news across the UK. All were predictably brutal in condemning the Libyan visit. Even Neil Kinnock, leader of the Labour

Party and one of the miners' biggest supporters despite his qualms about violence on the picket lines and a personal dislike for Scargill, had harsh words for the Union. *Why, oh, why has Scargill been so stupid?* wondered McDonald.

Each morning for the next few days as McDonald read the papers the story was still in the news. A story in the Russian news was picked up across the UK. McDonald shook his head as he read. The Russian miners had donated over a million dollars to the Welsh miners' strike fund to support them. Only the Welsh miners' strike fund had never actually seen any of the money. McDonald banged his fist on the table; he was going to find that money.

CHAPTER THIRTY-THREE

1984–Red Tide November

THE FIRST WEEK OF NOVEMBER, MCDONALD WAS CALLED to London for a meeting with the Kent miners, many of whom wanted to return to work. It took place at the Hilton Hotel on Park Lane, a huge concrete and glass tower with a meeting room overlooking Hyde Park. For McDonald, it was the latest in an endless stream of worthless meetings where nothing was accomplished other than listening to the same old rhetoric spewing from an increasingly militant Scargill in response to any challenge.

There was one interesting thing, however; Ted Watson, Scargill's minder, standing at the back of the meeting room, had a sour look on his face. He was of average height but had wide shoulders, meaty hands, and a pleasant face. His thick black hair, sideburns and dark square sunglasses made him look like one of Elvis's Memphis mafia. Watson was normally jovial, but McDonald had seen him and Scargill in a heated debate in the hotel lobby before the meeting and he guessed that must be the reason why Watson looked glum.

The meeting broke up early for once, Scargill had another appointment and was staying overnight for a meeting the next day. He talked briefly to Watson on his way out of the room, dismissing him for the afternoon, thought McDonald.

Watson slunk off and McDonald decided to follow him at a discreet distance. McDonald had always gone out of his way to greet Watson and treat him with a little respect while the rest of the executives just ignored him. Watson stopped at the Rose and Crown pub on Park Lane, just a few minutes' walk from the hotel. McDonald walked past the pub, continued around the block, and then went in. He went to the bar ,ordered a pint and looked around; Watson was sitting in the back corner alone, his pint half empty already. McDonald walked over to Watson who seemed lost in thought. "Well, fancy meeting you here," said McDonald cheerfully.

Watson looked up, startled.

"Mind if I join you?" McDonald asked.

"Sure," mumbled Watson with little enthusiasm.

"Cheers then," said McDonald, holding up his glass. Watson raised his glass half-heartedly. "Who took the jam out of your doughnut?" asked McDonald good-naturedly.

Watson just grunted and the two men fell into an uneasy silence, but McDonald felt if he gave him time Watson wanted to get something off his chest.

Finally, Watson spoke. "I was down the pits for fifteen years, you know."

"I had ten," said McDonald.

Watson nodded and continued. "I know a lot of these men on the picket line. They are good men, hardworking, salt-of-the-earth types. "I hate to see them getting fucked."

"What do you mean?" asked McDonald.

Watson went cagey. "Are you still driving that little white car?"

"Yes," said McDonald, puzzled.

"You are the only one then, said Watson sadly, shaking his head. "I figured you were not like the others when I saw you in that piece of shit," he continued without any malice.

"I don't understand," said McDonald. "It's just a car that gets me from A to B. I only paid eight hundred quid for it."

"The rest of the Union guys all have brand-new cars. Together they are worth more than my fucking house. And talking of houses, they are all buying new ones. Bigger ones. You are not on the take, are you?" said Watson, clear by his tone there might yet be doubt in his mind.

"No," said McDonald with conviction, but conviction could be faked. Watson saw it daily.

"And you still live in the same home you lived in as a miner?" asked Watson.

"Yes," said McDonald, opening his hands in a nothing-to-hide gesture. "It was four thousand pounds and I have ten years left on the mortgage."

"And you don't have a second home in Marbella?" continued Watson.

"No," said McDonald emphatically. "Do you?"

"Chance would be a fine thing," said Watson ruefully.

He finally seemed satisfied, rubbed his chin with his right hand, and nodded. McDonald had been patient, and he had been right, there was plenty Watson wanted to get off his chest. "There is a lot of shit going on I don't like and I get to see it every day up close and personal. I'm just a driver, a minder to be there when needed. They act like I'm not even in the car half the time, like I'm the invisible man or something. There is a lot of money changing hands in brown paper bags, briefcases, and backpacks, and I don't like the smell of it. The Arab money is especially smelly. Direct from that fucking asshole whose people killed that young female copper in London.

"Then there is the Russian money. There was so much of it that it came in grain sacks. But my real problem is not where the money is coming from. It's where it's going, and large chunks are not going where they should be. They are fucking the very people they are supposed to represent and I can't be part of it anymore. They don't know it yet, but I just quit."

McDonald nodded and stayed silent, waiting for him to continue. Watson took a swig of his beer, wiped his mouth with his beefy right hand, and continued. "They had me pick up this Arab fellow. The guy had a briefcase full of twenty-pound notes; there must have been fifty grand in there, maybe more. I took it to the Union office and then it all went up to Scargill's office along with all the mail-in money to be counted. The last lot he took out was twenty-nine thousand pounds to pay off Windsor's home loan.

"Our car is being followed. I don't know if it's Special Branch, MI5, or the fucking KGB, but someone is always tailing us. I can shake them sometimes, but not always; they work in teams. I know they are watching us and I no longer want to go down with the ship for money laundering or embezzlement or whatever the heck you call it when you skim money off the top meant for someone else."

This guy is a goldmine, thought McDonald and he quickly bought him another drink.

"There is a guy you need to watch out for; he's a district leader in Yorkshire with an English name, but he's a go-between for the Union and the Soviet miners. I've heard him speaking Russian and barking down the phone what sounded to me like orders," said Watson. "He never saw me or I'm sure he'd have been more careful, but the whole thing is getting too political and too big. It's not just about the miners anymore. It's about ousting the government.

"I went to Russia once, they invited a bunch of us miners on holiday, and communism is all one big red lie. I saw it for myself; there is nothing in the shops, the people are half-starved, and there are police and soldiers on every corner to make sure no one complains about anything. It was horrible."

"Is there anyone else at headquarters who feels the way you do?" asked McDonald.

Watson thought for a moment then said, "There is a woman called Joan, a bookkeeper, we've had a couple of chats."

The conversation lasted over an hour as Watson spilled the beans on all he knew. McDonald was going to miss his train, but that didn't matter, although he had to call home and let his wife and Sarah know.

The phone rang only twice before Sarah snatched it up. "Hello, McDonald residence," she said breathlessly.

"HI darling, it's Daddy," said McDonald.

"I knew it would be you. Guess what; I got an A on my English test today!" she said excitedly.

"Good girl," said McDonald encouragingly. "Listen, I won't be home tonight."

"But you said you would," she protested.

"I know, honey, but I missed my train. I'll be up in the morning and I'll bring you a little present from London."

"How little?" she asked jovially.

"Very little. Is Mommy there?" he asked.

"No, she just went down the street to help Mrs. Akins with something."

"Okay. Well, tell her I called and was delayed. Love you."

"Love you too, Daddy."

McDonald smiled and hung up. He left the pub and went outside to flag down a taxi; it was still before rush hour and only three cabs passed before one stopped.

"Where to, mate?" asked the cabbie in his thick Cockney accent.

"140 Grower St," said McDonald as he got in.

The cabbie glanced back at him with a questioning look but said nothing. Once at the location, McDonald looked left and right, took a deep breath, and walked in. He felt a strange, misplaced sense of betrayal, and yet he also knew it was the right thing to do.

CHAPTER THIRTY-FOUR

1984–Roxanne

Union number two, Vice-President Ken Miller, had organized a trip to the Netherlands to seek funds for the Yorkshire miners' relief fund from their brothers in Holland. Tom Brodie was driving Miller's British racing green Jaguar XJ6 down the M6. It was an amazingly smooth and luxurious ride; the smell of the new Connolly leather was still strong in Brodie's nostrils. *How does anyone afford a car like this?* thought Brodie.

They drove from Barnsley to Birmingham, where Miller had a short meeting, and then on to Dover where they took the ferry across to Calais. It was the first time Brodie had ever left the United Kingdom and there had been a mad rush to get him a passport for the occasion. He was excited. From Calais, they had driven four hours north through France and Belgium to Amsterdam. It was a very flat and boring drive Brodie had thought. Also, he was a little nervous at driving on the other side of the road, with such an expensive car, and had to mentally check himself whenever he came to a junction or roundabout.

In Amsterdam, Miller checked into the plush Tivoli Doelen Hotel. On the hotel steps, he handed Brodie a hundred quid in twenties. "Go find yourself a place to crash and have some fun while you are at it. We are only here for one night," Miller said and winked at him. "You only live once," he added. Then he turned again and added, pointing at Brodie with his finger as he did, "Make sure you park the car somewhere safe." Brodie nodded his assent and pulled the car away from the hotel.

It had been a long day for Brodie. He found a quiet street, a leafy avenue of lovely four-story town homes bordering a canal, in which to park Miller's Jaguar. It looked as safe as anywhere he thought. He walked a couple of blocks and found a small neighborhood bar, with only enough room for twenty people, with four battered wooden tables and chairs. He ordered a peperoni pizza, which he assumed came from the joint next door, and washed down two well-deserved pints of Heineken beer. When he was finished, Brodie walked around the city for a while, marveling at the architecture, canals, and bridges. It sure didn't look anything like Hamilton, where he lived, or even a big city like Glasgow. It was so beautiful. He returned to the Jag two hours later and slept in the backseat of the car. The ninety-two pounds he had left in his wallet would be far better spent on his family in Scotland than with whores in Amsterdam. He'd seen them in the windows but was never tempted to part with his hard-earned cash.

The next day, Miller met Johan Claasen, leader of the Netherlands Miners' Union, for lunch. He was fortyish, six feet four, with a square face and long hair. They met at a high-end restaurant on one of the main canals several hundred yards from the hotel. "Good to see you, my friend. I have a gift for you," said Claasen as he handed Miller a new black Puma sports bag with a picture of football legend Johan Cruyff in an orange Dutch national kit on one side, Cruyff's signature in large white letters on the other. "I apologize that there is not more for our striking brothers in England, but 10,000 guilders was all we could muster at this time."

"We appreciate all the help we can get," said Miller as he took the bag with his left hand and shook hands with his right. As he smiled broadly at Van Der Pelt, Miller wondered how much the giant, sneaky Dutch bastard had skimmed from the bag full of cash. Not that it mattered; Miller's take was eighty percent anyway. Didn't they say the 80/20 rule was the rule of the world since time began?

They dined on fresh fish, cabbage, Lyonnaise potatoes, and a perfect bottle of French champagne to celebrate their solidarity. Brodie arrived at the hotel at 2.30 p.m. as arranged, his neck stiff and his back sore from his night in the car. Miller got into the car and opened the bag to give Brodie a quick peek at the contents. "Mission accomplished," said Miller proudly.

"I'm sure the lads back home will be very thankful," said Brodie.

As they drove back south towards Calais, Brodie said, "A man in the pub told me we could have sailed from Rotterdam instead of Calais."

"That's true," said Miller. "In fact we could have sailed from Hull, but the dumb bitch of a travel agent I have apparently didn't know that. She said I should have been more specific on how I wanted to go to Amsterdam. Anyway, the Calais ferry was twenty quid cheaper, a penny saved is a penny earned.

"I hope you had a good time, son. I certainly did," said Miller, smiling.

"Oh yeah," said Brodie, trying to sound enthusiastic.

"I hit the red-light district and fucked my brains out, not once but three times with three different window girls, each more beautiful than the next: Roxanne, a blonde, Trixie, a redhead, and Katrine, a brunette; after all, don't they say variety is the spice of life?"

"They do," said Brodie.

"The first was a girl called Roxanne, dumb as a fucking rock. So I say to her, 'Your name, Roxanne, is like the girl in the Police song.' She said, 'Police? I want nothing to do with the police,' in heavily accented English. 'No,' I say, "I mean the group the Police.' 'I don't like one policeman, never mind a group of them,' she replies. I rolled my fucking eyes and thought, *Why the hell doesn't this dumb bitch speak English? Everyone knows English is the language of money.*

"'You know Sting?' I say in a last-ditch effort at communication. 'No, what is that?' she says. 'Okay, never mind, just suck my fucking cock,' and she duly obliged."

Brodie gave a forced chuckle.

"I didn't bother trying to communicate with the next two girls. I simply told 'em them the physical positions I wanted them to assume. Anyway, what could they possibly have to say that would have interested me? Talking to women is a mug's game," announced Miller.

"Yeah," said Brodie.

"The fatter my wife Sally got the more challenging time I had getting excited, you know. At first, I thought it was me, but not anymore; this trip has shown me the truth—that there is nothing wrong with the Yorkshire blood that flows through these veins. Those young girls in Amsterdam made me horny as a toad. I had never been so stiff in my life, even in my twenties, and this old bull taught them a thing or two!" Miller laughed.

As Brodie drove south Miller changed from boasting about his sexual prowess to ranting about Thatcher. "Did you know Thatcher has placed MI5 spies in the Union?"

"No," said Brodie, astonished by this revelation.

"If they are not rooted out, the strike will fail and we will all work in Tory chains for the rest of our lives," stated Miller.

"Agent provocateurs as well," he continued. "Off-duty coppers posing as picketers. Throwing stones at the scabs and coppers to start some agro. Then the media can write about the violent miners who are really fucking pigs in disguise."

"Are you kidding me?" said Brodie. "Cops dressed as picketers."

"You bet your life they are," said Miller.

"Fucking bastards," muttered Brodie.

"Tory bastards, every fucking one of them," spat Miller.

A car cut Brodie up and he jammed on the brakes.

"Fucking frogs!" yelled Miller shaking his fists, although they were passing through Brussels at the time.

It was 9:00 p.m. before they returned to Dover and they checked into a cheap hotel for the night. They got up early and made the long six-hour drive back to a small village near Barnsley. Miller slept most of the way, snoring loudly. Brodie dropped him off at his large bungalow and headed to the bus stop on foot to get a bus back to his bedsit in the town center. Oh, how he missed his wife and kids back in Scotland, but at least now they were not starving.

The next day, an excited Miller called a meeting of his colleagues and handed the Yorkshire Union bookkeeper two thousand guilders in cash. There were congratulations on his successful trip.

After the office it was back to the picket line to tell the boys the good news about his latest venture.

Miller was greeted enthusiastically as he handed out a few five-pound notes to some of the lads while he held court among them. "I hate going abroad—foreign food, no real ale and nobody talks fucking English. They don't know how to drive, we were almost run off the road, then they try to trick you when they give you change 'cause the numbers are so big. I tell you, lads, I'd rather stay home in Yorkshire any day, but you've got to do what you've got to do to help the cause."

"Too right," said a couple of lads in unison.

You had to know your audience, thought Miller; they thrived on tales of hardship, not glamour.

CHAPTER THIRTY-FIVE

Present Day– Resignation

Scotland's First Minister Sean Robertson sat at his glass desk. He stared at the headlines of the Scotsman on his twenty-inch flat screen monitor. Even the 'friendly' newspapers were making fun of him now, saying his quotes were meme-worthy, his gaffes prolific, and his business decisions baffling. On top of his failings, he was still haunted by sins of the past. Today, he was pictured in a luminous life jacket aboard the unfinished hull of one of the infamous island ferries.

A Sinking Ship ran the headline.

He closed the tab. A similar image replaced it.

First Minister out of His Depth, said the Daily Record.

He glanced at the editorial.

Sean Robertson's career will be finished long before the ferries ever will.…

He didn't bother to read the rest. His head sank into his hands.

The job was now beginning to affect his mental health; his Cabinet support was waning fast, his relationships were suffering, and his finances were in shambles after a disastrous Bitcoin scheme had gone wrong. While helpful, the hundred-thousand-pound book deal arranged by Janssen was not enough to solve all his problems. He had mortgaged his house to buy Bitcoin as it dropped like a rock.

"I'm fucking fucked," he muttered into his sweat-greased palms. His phone rang. "Fuck off," he barked at it.

The phone kept ringing. Eventually, Robinson picked it up. "What?"

He stared at the screen, his eyes no longer seeing the image. His forehead creased into a frown. "Who?" A pause. "You're fucking joking." Another pause. "Of course you should bloody well put him through."

The first minister waited until he heard a beep on the line as the call was connected. His face cracked into a boyish grin. "Jimmy! Hi!"

There was a long pause as he listened. "I would be very fucking interested. Lunch? No, no, affairs of state can wait. I'll see you there." Robertson put down the phone. He put his feet up on the desk then suddenly lashed out with one foot and kicked the flat screen monitor to the floor.

He picked up the phone once more. "Fiona. Cancel everything." A pause. "Read my lips. Every- fucking-thing." He stood up, took off his suit jacket, and hung it on the back of his chair. From a discreet closet at the edge of the room, he took out an extra-large Hibs shirt and tugged it on over his formal shirt and tie. He sauntered out of the office and passed Maggie McGown and Abby St. Clair, who were coming in the opposite direction. The first minister raised a single digit in their direction then sang at the top of his voice, "We hate jam tarts, and we hate Dundee...." before skipping down the stairs.

Abby stared after him. "What the hell…? Has he finally lost his mind?"

Maggie shrugged. "I believe he's just been offered a post as a non-executive director at Hibernian FC."

Abby frowned. "Well, he can't take it. He's first minister, for Christ's sake," she said, shaking her head.

"Unless he resigns," said Maggie.

"Resigns? But that would throw the leadership of the SNP wide open.…"

Maggie put a hand on her arm. "Indeed."

Abby looked at Robinson's back then slowly turned to look at Maggie. Her jaw dropped two inches as her mouth hung open before she could get a single word out. "You?"

Maggie smiled for half a second before glancing at her watch.

"I'm announcing on the lunchtime news. No time to waste. Come on."

CHAPTER THIRTY-SIX

1984–The Enemy Within

McDONALD WAS NEW TO ALL THIS CLOAK-AND-DAGGER stuff, but he had already stopped using his home phone weeks ago and instead used the payphone at the end of his street. The red phone box stank of urine, stale beer, and cigarettes, but thankfully, none of his calls were long. "Alright, I can do tomorrow but it will have to be the afternoon," he said and hung up.

As the train rattled south towards London McDonald looked out the window watching the countryside slide by lost in his thoughts. He was beginning to feel the pressure; he was walking on dangerous ground and knew it. On the one hand, he wanted to be the Union's next president, stamp out the endemic corruption, and do the right thing for the members. On the other hand, he was working with an instrument of the Tory government most men professed to hate. In a way, he was the "Enemy within"—the very same charge Thatcher made against the miners. He did not like Thatcher, but if it came to organizing a piss-up in a brewery, he would choose her to lead the event over Scargill. Moreover, he thought it highly unlikely she could be bought by anyone, at any price, least of all the Soviets or the Libyans.

The ticket collector came down the aisle yelling, "Tickets please," and McDonald searched his trouser pockets in vain before remembering he'd put the ticket in his jacket. "Sorry," he said and as he handed it over to the unsmiling agent who punched it and scurried off.

McDonald glanced up at the unassuming concrete-clad, six-story building sat on the corner of Grower Street in the posh Bloomsbury section of London. The concrete was covered in streaks of black soot and a power wash was long overdue. He went in and was walked by an elderly secretary to a small windowless corner office on the sixth floor sparsely finished with a metal desk and two swivel chairs. John Elliot was a small, well-dressed man with a round face, short-cropped brown hair, and a friendly, concerned air about him. He spoke with a hint of a private schoolboy accent. "The person or persons unknown who are supporting the strike financially are intent on pursuing a political agenda."

"You mean they are pushing Britain towards communism? That would suit King Arthur down to the ground. He's already got miners going on paid holidays to the Soviet Union," said McDonald.

Elliot's lip twitched as he contained a smile. "King Arthur? Is that what they call him?"

McDonald shrugged. "That's what some of the papers are calling him and it is what he is. King of the bloody unions. He can do what the hell he likes."

"And that is why he must be stopped," said Elliot. "We are actively monitoring union leaders' phone calls and suspect that the KGB might be doing the same."

McDonald raised his eyebrows but said nothing.

"You need to be extremely careful as the Soviets will not want their involvement revealed and may go to great lengths to keep it that way. I suggest you do not use your home phone for sensitive calls and be alert to those around you," Elliot said.

McDonald nodded.

"We have identified the bank accounts in Poland and Switzerland where Russian funds have been deposited. In the meantime, I suggest you stay quiet until we can positively identify all the agents in this cell. ."

"So, you want me to sit on my hands while the miners and their families starve and the fat cats steal their money?" asked McDonald.

"I'm afraid so," said Elliot.

McDonald nodded but was unconvinced. He handed Elliot a sheet of paper with some details he had managed to find about how funds might have been funneled through the IMO, a trade union organization set up in Paris with Arthur Scargill as its president and one of his cronies as the only other employee. "I managed to get a couple of photocopies from one of the Union bookkeepers who shares some of my concerns. "

"Okay, great, we will look into this," said Elliot. "If you see or hear anything suspicious on your patch, I'd like to know at once.'

CHAPTER THIRTY-SEVEN

Present Day –Change at the Top

Back in her Spartan office with Abby St. Clair, Maggie launched her campaign for the vacant position before Robertson had left the car park. It started with a flurry of prewritten emails, videos, and special reports to every SNP member stating her claim.

"Nobody even knows Robertson's gone yet," said St. Clair.

"They do now." Maggie smiled.

St. Clair began writing notes. "You won't be the only candidate. Most of them are 'special interest' cases and can't get more than three to five percent of the vote. But there will be a serious challenger."

Maggie's phone started to vibrate. "Speak of the devil," she said, glancing at the number. "Andrew," she said with a smile, as she answered. She knew Andrew Murphy would be her biggest rival, that handsome old silver fox.

"I don't suppose you had anything to do with Robertson's sudden departure," came his charming Edinburgh brogue down the line. "How the devil did you do it?"

Maggie looked up at St. Clair as she spoke and pulled a face. "I really don't know what you mean."

"Come, come, Maggie. You and I enjoy a good working relationship. There will be a place for a smart worker like you in my cabinet; I give you my word on that. Agreed?"

"What makes you think you'll be in any position to offer me that?" Maggie said carefully.

Murphy chuckled softly down the line. "I've been with the party for over two decades. I've seen our successes and faced numerous challenges. My approach is grounded in experience and pragmatism. I believe in continuity, building on what works, and ensuring a stable transition of power. I'm the natural choice for the leadership."

"You sound like a true politician, Andrew. I respect your service and dedication, but nothing the SNP have done in the two decades you have been a member has worked. The party needs a fresh perspective, a passionate new voice that can invigorate our members and resonate with the broader public. We need to evolve with the times, addressing the concerns of a new generation and offering them a bright economic future."

"You don't have the experience for the job," Murphy countered.

Maggie smiled. "And you have too much experience."

"There is no such thing as too much experience." Murphy laughed.

"Oh," said Maggie, "is there not? Well, not everyone likes me, I admit, but I haven't made many enemies or voted against causes that are dear to people's hearts. I haven't got into public spats with any members. However, your position on every issue is well documented. You'll never get a majority. The problem with being around politics as long as you have is you've accumulated more enemies than friends."

There was a pause on the line. Maggie could tell that he was trying to do the mental arithmetic. People he'd voted down, lambasted, or ridiculed in his long career.

"I think I have more than enough support," he eventually said.

Maggie glanced up at St. Clair, who was watching her intently, trying to gauge the tone of the call. "I have more passion, ideas, and energy than you do. I like you, but you sound tired, Andrew. Politics has worn you out."

"Everybody knows I'm the favourite," he said. "Listen Maggie. I've waited two decades for an opening like this. It's my time."

Maggie responded quickly. "It's time you were enjoying life. Your credentials are impeccable; you're an experienced statesman and a great raconteur. I have the perfect job for you. Ambassador to the US, when we gain independence, which we will."

"Washington?" he said dismissively. "I'd rather hang out in a pit of vipers. Yeuch."

"Paris then," she said.

"You are in no position to offer either, Maggie. You are not first minister, and we don't have our independence. Forget it. I'm running, and you know I'll win."

"Are you certain?" Maggie said.

"I am."

Maggie rubbed at her forehead for a moment. He was slipping off the hook, and she knew it. She had to think. Fast.

"Look, Andrew. I don't play dirty, but if we run for independence with you as leader, the English press will go for your throat."

"What's that supposed to mean?"

"You know as well as I do. The first minister job comes with far more scrutiny, and once the press starts digging, they may find things about your personal life that you prefer to keep private."

"I've absolutely nothing to hide," he said angrily.

"Oh really," Maggie responded quickly. "No skeletons in your closet? Because that's not what I've heard. It appears—" and she paused for effect "—not everybody's as discreet as you'd hope."

There was silence on the line for a good ten seconds. "Are you trying to blackmail me, Maggie?"

Maggie laughed. "Of course not. Don't be ridiculous. I'm just trying to help. The press can be awfully tenacious, you know, once they get a promising lead."

Murphy was silent again.

Maggie knew she had him then. "Endorse my bid, Andrew. Save yourself the humiliation, and then help me gain independence. The ambassador's job in Paris will be yours. At least tell me you'll think about it?"

She waited.

"I'll think about it," he eventually said.

As Maggie hung up, she blew out a long breath then laughed. "Who knew?"

Abby St. Clair looked at her expectantly. "He folded?"

"Yes. He folded."

St. Clair clapped her hands together. "So, what's the dirt? What do you have on him?"

"Nothing," Maggie said, turning up her hands. "That is, I had nothing on him until now."

Abby threw her head back and laughed. "The leadership is as good as yours. All you have to do now is not throw it away." Then she wagged an admonishing finger at her. "Maggie McGown! You play rough!"

CHAPTER THIRTY-EIGHT

1984–Suspicious Minds

Back on the picket line later that week, McDonald had become a little paranoid, looking at all his fellow workers in a new light; who was the Judas among them? He glanced a few yards to his left. Was it that red-bearded Sean Fitzpatrick in the dirty denim jacket he always wore on top of a Celtic shirt? He always stank of sweat, was as left as they came politically, and usually among the first to start trouble, throwing missiles and yelling insults. Or looking across the street, maybe it was Mick Jones; he was small, quiet, and introverted, but he always seemed to watch everything carefully, as if he was taking mental notes. Sometimes it was the quiet ones that surprised you, wasn't it? *Christ, it could be anybody.*

McDonald lit a cigarette and took a long drag, offering the pack to the man next to him as he did. The endless Union meetings, constant travel, and daily stints on the picket line were taking their toll. He'd taken up smoking again, although not at home. His wife hated it. Picketing had become insanely boring, standing around all day for ten minutes or so when scabs or lorries tried to break the line. Despite the adrenalin rush of the shouting and screaming, pushing, and shoving, the sheer dullness of the rest of the day doing nothing but standing there week after week was exhausting.

Peterson sported a shiny new black eye. "Been in a fight with the rozzers, then?" asked McDonald.

"I wish. The bloody missus hit me with a tin of soup. Threw it at me from across the room."

McDonald smiled. "Why?"

"That was our Sunday lunch. A tin of fucking soup." He grabbed McDonald's sleeve. "Listen, you're on the Union. Things are getting bad, do you see any end to this?" asked Peterson, a man in his late twenties with bleached blond hair, black jeans, and a T-shirt with a picture of Sid Vicious standing atop the words No Future in a bold red type, as he took a cigarette from McDonald's packet.

"It will have to end sometime," said McDonald noncommittally.

"It's wrecking homes, tempers are short, food is scarce, and marriages are fraying under the strain. We are all in desperate financial circumstances, and despite the sacrifices, we don't seem to be getting anywhere. I hate to say it, George, and don't share it with any of the lads, but to be honest, I'd like to go back to work," Peterson muttered quietly. "I've got three small bairns, you know."

"Aye, I know, and I hear you. It's gone on too long," said McDonald. There was an uneasy silence.

McDonald's own savings were nearly exhausted and were it not for his legitimate Union travel allowance his precious little car would have been long gone. With all the turmoil around him, he looked forward to his weekend trips with his family more than ever as they escaped to the peace and splendor of the Highlands. It seemed a million miles away, not just a couple of hours.

On Sunday, McDonald's wife was busy with a Miners' Wives support event, so he took his young daughter Sarah alone on a trip up to Glen Coe. They left at 7:00 a.m., with no traffic on the roads. It was such a beautiful drive. The weather was great for that time of year. By mid-morning, it was in the mid-fifties and bright sunshine. The two of them went on a three-hour hike amid the brilliant splendor of the Highlands. That day's colors were vibrant: purple heather, yellow gorse, blue waters, white sands, and dark mountains.

Sometime after noon, they stopped by a small stream and he took off his backpack filled with goodies for lunch. Cheese and Branston Pickle sandwiches on hearty brown bread, two slices of Battenberg cake, an apple each, and two cans of Iron Brew. He loved spending time with his daughter; she was so pretty, so smart, and so full of energy. Like him, she had an inquisitive mind and a love of reading. She had already torn through Enid Blyton's catalog of *Famous Five* and *Secret Seven* books.

McDonald was so proud of her reading; he smiled at her. Reading had opened his mind to the endless possibilities life offered beyond the pits, the town, and even the country. He wanted his daughter to go to college, to have a career beyond making babies, and see the world, not rot away in the arse of some soot-filled Scottish mining town. Mining was a dying industry that would take down everything around it, just like cancer. He could see why the Union men were skimming off the funds. They'd given up. Lost all hope. But it was the wrong choice to make. No good would come of it. They were robbing not from the rich but from the poor.

All McDonald could do now was get the men he represented large redundancy packages, retraining, and relocation. That's why he wanted to lead the Union, to change the direction of their efforts from militant attempts to keep open money-losing pits to something more practical for the men, a direction that would give the younger men a real future and the older men enough money for a comfortable retirement.

"I wish we could stay up here forever," said Sarah.

"That would be nice but there's no work here, darling," said McDonald.

She saw a rabbit, got up and slowly crept closer to have a better look.

McDonald watched her, smiling, but his thoughts drifted. Things were coming to a head; he now had a large enough corruption file to publish. Some of it was painfully obvious, like the cash payments for houses and cars. Other stuff like the bank accounts would need substantiation from the authorities. But he had statements from Union insiders that would point them in the right direction. The entire Union's house of cards would fall from there. If things played out the way he thought they would, he'd be there to pick up the pieces.

He was sure the boys at MI5 would not be happy he was going to the newspapers. They would much rather he continued to feed them information, but he had no intention of telling them his plan. The time to act was now, and he'd already set up a meeting with Angus Frasier, a reporter from the *Daily Record*, at the end of the coming week. A few more days and all the clandestine spy work would be over. Publication of the information would no doubt end the strike as Scargill and his cronies lost the respect of the miners they were supposed to represent. He could focus his efforts on supporting the men.

The rabbit dashed off and Sarah turned her attention to the stream dropping sticks in it and watching them being whisked away downstream. She was singing, smiling, and splashing in the shallow water with the innocence of youth. She had not a care in the world. He pulled out his Pentax camera and snapped a couple of beautiful candid pictures. He tried to picture what her future would look like, after mining was gone. Through the lens, against the backdrop of the mountains, she looked so small, so beautiful, so alone.

CHAPTER THIRTY-NINE

1984–10 Downing Street

Prime Minister Nigel Preston glanced up at the large flat screen TV playing the BBC News and scowled as he ran his hands through his perfectly styled black hair as he was prone to do when thinking. "Why does the BBC give that Scottish bitch so much fucking airtime?" he asked in an irritated tone to no one in particular.

"Because," said Simon Morton, the foreign secretary Preston's closest political ally and friend. Like Preston an Eton and Oxford man, he was short and fit with a small round head shaved clean. "She's attractive, articulate, intelligent, has just survived an assassination attempt, and unlike the last three pretenders at the SNP, she appears to be delivering on her campaign promises of improving Scotland's lot dramatically without any help from Whitehall. She just announced a billion-dollar overseas investment for an electric car and battery plant in Glasgow."

"From whom?" demanded Preston.

"Well, on the surface, it's a group of investors from Singapore, but we think it's just a front for the Chinese government," said Morton, making a what can you do gesture with his hands as he spoke.

"Can't we stop them?" asked Preston.

"What and kill the four thousand high-paying jobs they are offering? It would be political suicide across the border, and we are not exactly popular to begin with. What's more, proving it could take months," said Morton.

"And what about that massive Indonesian investment in reopening a ship-building plant on the Clyde?" asked Preston.

"Also suspected to be funded by the Chinese," replied Morton.

"Maybe you could get them to rebuild Heathrow Airport for us?" said Preston sarcastically.

"Not a good idea," said Morton. "You remember what a political stink was raised when they invested in that nuclear plant in Somerset."

"It wouldn't have happened on my watch I can tell you that. It seems like they are buying this little Scottish bitch, right under our noses, the same way they bought up most of Africa and half of South America."

"Well, it's not just Third World countries anymore. They are also investing heavily in most European countries with their Belt and Road initiative, and they are buying up technology companies in Germany left and right," said Morton.

"In a way, I quite admire their strategy, but what the hell are we going to do about it?" said Preston, banging his hand on the table, his bright blue eyes flashing with anger.

"For a start you should be more careful with your language, PM; one slipup on a live mic calling her a bitch and you'll be spending six weeks making apologies while the wolves chant for your head," said Morton sternly.

"You are right, of course, but I hate the bitch, all she does is cause me problems," said Preston, clearly agitated. "I can't believe anyone is dumb enough to fall for her shit. Although she is rather hot.... I've never had a redhead. Have you, Morton?"

Morton ignored the question and said, "They fall for her because she is actually delivering on most of her promises. The SNP is no longer broke; their membership is rising rapidly, and if she doesn't get her Scottish independence vote in the next few months, there will be trouble. They have more fanatics than ever. There is an excellent chance of an independent Scotland this year if you give her the referendum she demands. A recent poll shows seventy percent of Scots now favor the idea, and, as you know, most English voters are so sick of the eternal sideshow that they will be happy to let them go."

"That's a fact," said Preston. "If the Scots want independence, all they have to do is let the English vote."

"On top of that, she is anything but dumb; the way she ousted Robertson was proof of that and she doesn't seem too particular about what she might burn down to get what she wants."

"Okay, okay, let's get her down here and have a chat," said Preston reluctantly.

"She's not interested in coming down here to chat with you. She doesn't like you," announced Morton.

The PM gave an overdramatized look of mock offense as he ran his hands through his hair again. "Moi?" he said, pointing at himself.

"Yes, she thinks you are a twat, and she wants you to go to her," said Morton. "I already proposed a meeting, and she turned me down flat."

"Oh, damn it. Well, check the long-range weather forecast and pick a couple of nice days on the west coast of Scotland next week, if there are any. Then propose we meet at Turnberry, and at least I might get a round of golf in," replied Preston thoughtfully.

"She might not agree to that either," said Morton. "She not exactly a fan of the ex-US president either; I doubt she'll be up for spending taxpayers' money there."

The PM sighed. "Then suggest Loch Lomond but check the weather in Glasgow first; you know how changeable it is up there. Oh, and ask her for an agenda."

"She only has one. When does she get another independence vote?" replied Morton.

"I'm so tired of it all. If it were up to me, I'd just let the damn Jocks go and be done with it," said the PM exasperatedly. "What do we really know about her anyway? It seems like she appeared from nowhere. Have you got any dirt on her? She must have done something wrong, somewhere, sometime."

Morton opened a note on his iPhone. "Her father was a miner. He worked in the Lanarkshire pits all his life until they finally closed in 2002. After he took redundancy, he didn't do much until the daughter hit it big in the beverage business. Then, to thank her parents for all their sacrifices on her behalf, she kindly bought them a two-bedroom apartment in Benidorm where they are no doubt still enjoying fish and chips, bacon sandwiches, and retirement in the Spanish sun."

"Sounds lovey," said Preston sarcastically. "Find something more interesting and useful. Something we can use against her as leverage. In the meantime, set something up so we can at least have a chat, we need to be clear on what she is doing with all these Asian investors and make sure it does not compromise our national security," said Preston.

CHAPTER FORTY

Present Day –Referendum 2.0

Prime Minister Nigel Preston flew to Inverness on a small private jet with his bodyguard, an overnight bag, and his Ping golf clubs. One of Maggie's minders, Max, picked them up in an army-green Range Rover. It was a short drive to Maggie's baronial-style mansion, and the PM could not help but be impressed as they drove through the gates, as he was a lover of architecture. The distinctive Scottish baronial style that emerged in the 19th century, drawing inspiration from medieval Scottish castles and tower houses, was one of his favorite styles.

Standing proudly amidst sprawling green landscapes, hedges, and flowerbeds, the mansion commanded attention with its majestic presence. Its exterior was adorned with a symphony of turrets, battlements, and crow-stepped gables punctuating the skyline. The somber grey hues of the granite lent a sense of timelessness to the structure.

Maggie greeted him in the foyer, which was adorned with a magnificent chandelier suspended from a soaring ceiling. Polished marble stretched ahead, leading to the heart of the mansion. Ornate tapestries lined the walls, depicting scenes from Scottish history, while a suit of armor stood as a silent guardian. "I say, this is all very nice," said Preston in his posh Eton accent. He wished he had something like this for himself.

"Thank you, Prime Minister," said Maggie with a smile. "Let's go into the library." She led the way into a beautiful wood-paneled room with towering ceilings, large windows, and plush velvet drapes. There they chatted amenably for a couple of hours feeling each other out.

"You were captain of the rugby team at Eton I understand?" said Maggie.

"Yes," said the PM with obvious pride.

"I understand you are also a fine golfer?" said Maggie.

"Oh, I have my days," replied Preston modestly.

Maggie asked most of the questions, Preston did most of the talking, which was exactly as Maggie wished.

"We need to talk about your relationship with China, it's not healthy," said Preston.

"No, we need to talk about independence for Scotland," Countered Maggie.

"Well, I want to talk about China," responded the PM indignantly.

"Go ahead."

"China is our enemy, you should not be getting into bed with them."

"I'm not in bed with anyone, but Scotland is open to overseas investment, unless Westminster has plans to offer us a few billion more to help us grow our economy?"

"What about this new battery plant?"

"The investors are from Singapore."

"Are they really?"

"Well, that's where they live."

They took a short break strolling in Maggie's magnificent grounds and Preston marveled at the manicured gardens, picturesque ponds, and meandering pathways. They walked through her large walled garden with its delightful assortment of vibrant flowers and fragrant herbs.

That night, she wined and dined him with local fare in a banquet room adorned with carved wooden panels, clan crests, and shields.

"Is that what I think it is?" asked Preston as his appetizer was served.

"I guess that depends on what you think it is," Maggie answered. "But if you think it is haggis, yes."

He prodded at it with his fork then put a bit in his mouth and smiled. "You know it's not that bad."

"I'll take that as a compliment, from an Englishman," said Maggie.

There was a starter of haggis bon bons followed by a main course of smoked salmon, and fresh veggies from her garden. This was followed by crème brulée, and a superb plate of Scottish cheeses. Preston's body language had relaxed; he was smiling and joking long before they retired to the library for whisky or brandy or, in the PM's case, both. After all, his hero Winston Churchill pickled himself daily with a bottle of champagne and brandy.

"But the referendum was supposed to be once in a generation," protested the PM for the umpteenth time.

"It's a new generation," said Maggie patiently.

"It's only been twelve years," said Preston. "That's not a generation; a generation is twenty or thirty years."

"A generation is defined as however long it takes for a child to grow up; these days, kids grow up fast. They are computer geniuses by the time they are twelve," said Maggie. "If you won't grant us a referendum, I'll have one anyway."

The PM shook his head wearily. "Do you remember what they did in Catalonia? They had an illegal referendum, which voted for independence from Spain. The leaders of the independence party were all tracked down and arrested then put on trial for sedition. Is that what you want?"

"I want a referendum for the Scottish people."

So, they went back and forward for a final hour; she had won many concessions from the visit but not the prize she needed most: another referendum. With Preston in his weakened state, having had at least two drinks too many, she made her move. "If you won't agree to a referendum for the Scottish people how about one for the entire UK? After all, the outcome will affect everyone; let all the countries vote."

Preston raised an eyebrow, that was clever he thought, for he well knew that if the English were asked if Scotland could leave the answer might well be yes. He was also getting tired of this game; truth be known he thought Westminster would be far better off without Scotland.

"Did you ever see those two American CEOs who arm-wrestled for control of the company or the two billionaires who cage-fought to settle an argument?" asked Maggie casually.

"They never went through with it. Anyway, I hardly think cage fighting you would be fair," said Preston.

"I tell you what; how about we play golf? I win, I get my referendum; if you win, I drop it for a decade."

"What's your handicap?" asked Preston suspiciously.

"It's nine, what's yours?" she asked, although she already knew the answer. Preston was a four, although her research found it was a vanity handicap and that, in truth, he rarely broke eighty.

"It's a four, but how do I know you are not sandbagging me? I'd have to give you five shots," said Preston drowsily.

"I'll make it easy," said Maggie. "I'll play you straight up, no shots."

Preston looked at her in disbelief. "You'll play me even up?" he scoffed, his manhood being challenged if not insulted. Men were so easy and so predictable, thought Maggie; challenge their ego and they lose all reason.

"Yes," said Maggie.

"You're on," said Preston, "but for one hundred pounds cash, not for something I can't deliver."

"Okay," said Maggie a little deflated. They shook on it, and Maggie suggested one more for the road. She gave Preston his whisky and poured herself a drink from another decanter she had been drinking from all night. It looked like whisky but was, in fact, colored water.

Preston was groggy when they left the next day for Dornoch at 7.30 a.m. Maggie had been up since 5:00 a.m. as usual. She never overindulged. It clouded your judgment. The day was bright and sunny, and the course played hard and fast. Dornoch had a major tournament coming up, and they had let the rough grow up and narrowed the fairways to protect the course from the long-ball hitters eating up the old links. Preston, even nursing a hangover, was a long hitter. Still, he was not a straight hitter, and the bouncy conditions had his balls disappearing with frequent regularity.

"Oh dammit," yelled Preston as another wayward tee shoot careened off a mound in the fairway and into a gorse bush. "These damn links courses are so unfair, that ball landed in the fairway."

Maggie was not a long hitter, but she was a very straight hitter, and with the hard fairway conditions, she was getting an extra twenty-five yards from her tee shots, which was always welcome.

"That's the fifth ball I've lost today, and you couldn't even see that stream from the tee," protested Preston.

"It's a burn," corrected Maggie, enjoying his growing agitation.

"What is?" questioned Preston.

"In Scotland we call streams burns," she said.

"Whatever," he said as pulled another ball from his bag and dropped it into play.

The match was over by the fifteenth, Maggie having won four and three. They played in with Maggie carding seventy-nine-two shots better than her handicap and Preston having lost too many balls to care. Maggie had the caddie take a picture of Preston handing over the hundred pounds for posterity. A chastened Preston returned with Maggie in her Range Rover to her baronial castle for lunch. They dined on fresh trout, wild asparagus, and delicious new potatoes washed down with some excellent champagne.

Maggie handed Preston a brief. "What's this?" he asked.

"It's a brief to help you sell the new UK-wide referendum to any of your colleagues who may not all be in favor of the idea. It's full of useful bullet points about how an independent Scotland would be better for England and the other two countries in the United Kingdom," said Maggie.

Preston could not tell if she was joking or not, but he agreed. He would raise it with the Cabinet. The problem was that after the nightmare of Brexit, with so much lost and little if anything gained, not everyone in his Cabinet agreed. There would be work to do to sell it to his political advisers, but he knew Maggie was right about one thing: Scotland would be independent at once if they let the English voters vote on the issue. The English public had tired of the SNP a long time ago. "Who cares? Let them go," was the attitude of a large majority.

Four weeks later, after much-heated discussion, the Cabinet finally agreed to a new referendum date during the second week of September the following year, thus giving both sides of the debate ample time to campaign and settle the issue once and for all. But there was a difference; Maggie had been waiting for this moment for all of her short political life. She was already well-organized, well-funded, and ready for action. The AI-aided social media campaigns were triggered at once. Blog posts, newsletters, emails, and planted stories in what was left of the mainstream media.

Whitehall was slow to act in defense of the Union and far more ambivalent as to the result than they had been in 2014. So many other things were going on in the world; it was tiresome to keep fighting the same battle with your closest neighbor. It was like living with someone who wanted a divorce, and Preston knew thing or two about divorce; sooner or later the will to stay together simply collapsed.

CHAPTER FORTY-ONE

Present Day–Let the Games Begin

MAGGIE SAW NO NEED TO WASTE TIME OR MONEY RENTing an office for campaign headquarters and instead used the two large en suite bedrooms in her four-bedroomed townhouse. Her government would be lean and practical. As she saw it, her biggest problem was not getting the Scots to believe they would be better off without England, which she thought she could do with ease. Her biggest challenge was convincing the Scottish people that after decades of mismanagement, incompetence, and scandal, the SNP could be trusted to do anything!

Maggie had been heavily involved in the marketing of the whisky company and was confident in her ability to put together her own virtual marketing team rather than outsource the job to an ad agency. She lured the talented Frank Morris away from his position as marketing manager of her former beverage business to be her new independence campaign manager. Morris was that rare combination of a computer whiz, graphics guy, and salesman. He was the whole package. Young at twenty-nine, he looked much younger, had a tiny waist and a small round face that tried unsuccessfully to grow a beard and look like it never saw sunlight.

Within a week, they had a virtual team comprised of an SEO expert from India, a pay-per-click genius from Aberdeen, a talented copywriter from Glasgow, a social media girl from St. Andrews, and an AI expert from Los Angeles transplanted to Dundee. Plus a team of six aides in various flavors to help execute.

Frank Morris took charge of their first virtual meeting. "The Scottish government spent 2.5 million pounds trying to persuade the Scottish people to vote yes in the 2014 Independence Referendum, which resulted in 1,617,989—45%—voting Yes and 2,001,926 people—55%—voting No. I suggest we add a zero to the advertising budget, a nice round twenty-five million, and turn those numbers on their heads. This figure is still seven million less than was spent on Brexit advertising but more than enough to get the job done, even with inflation."

"Okay," agreed Maggie.

Morris continued, "I have gone back and studied all the US presidential campaigns since 1960 and came up with the following observations regarding their marketing tactics. John F. Kennedy won the US presidency by harnessing the new power of TV; Obama did it by exploiting the power of email. Trump did it on the power of Twitter and Celebrity.

"We will do it by harnessing AI's power and running a US-style shock and awe marketing campaign the likes of which dreary Scottish politics has never seen before." Although the sound was muted on the screens, there was excitement on everyone's faces. "We will not use all the tools at our disposal, but we must realize all those tools will be used against us by multiple people in and outside the UK."

"Duncan, can you go over a few of these so we are all on the same page?" asked Maggie.

"Yes, I've prepared a short slide show." He began.

1. Disinformation Campaigns:

AI algorithms can be used to generate and spread false information or deepfakes. Deepfakes use AI to create realistic-looking videos of individuals saying or doing things they never did. This can be exploited to spread misinformation and influence public opinion.

2. Social Media Manipulation:

AI algorithms are used to analyze user data on social media platforms and identify patterns, preferences, and vulnerabilities. This information can be exploited to target individuals with personalized political content, advertisements, or fake news, amplifying echo chambers and reinforcing existing beliefs.

3. Automated Bots:

AI-powered bots can be deployed to create the illusion of widespread support or opposition on social media. Bots can automate the generation of posts, comments, and likes, influencing public discourse and trending topics.

4. Microtargeting:

AI is employed to analyze vast amounts of data to create highly targeted political advertisements. This practice, known as microtargeting, tailors political messages to specific demographics, maximizing the impact of the content on individuals.

5. Manipulation of Online Discussions:

AI algorithms can be used to manipulate online discussions by flooding platforms with certain types of content or by amplifying specific viewpoints. This can distort public opinion and create a false sense of consensus or controversy.

6. Deepfake Audio and Video:

This can be a powerful tool for spreading false information and damaging the reputations of individuals.

"We have already seen all of these tactics in use to discredit Maggie and we have only just got started," Morris continued. "On a more positive note we will use Maggie's rags-to-riches story in the beverage business as proof of her competence and compassion. This will be her back story, or her creation myth as they call it in the business. It's a subtle blend of fact and fiction merged into a compelling story that will check all the boxes without the voter ever noticing the subtle way in which it was done.

7. Born into a poor Lanarkshire coal-mining family, her father worked down the pits for thirty years. – She knew what it was like to be poor.
8. But her father stressed the need for education. – It was one of her priorities.
9. She was among the few miners' daughters to attend college.
10. Became a model. – She knew how women felt to be objectified.
11. Worked in sales and marketing in a male-dominated industry. – Learned to negotiate and spoke several languages.
12. After a successful career, she moved to manage a famous worldwide brand. – She knew the challenges of a global operation and the excessive restrictions on many industries that stunted growth.
13. Her husband had died. – She knew what it was to experience a profound personal loss.
14. But he had a dream. – She would pick up the mantle and make that dream come true. His dream, her dream, was a prosperous and independent Scotland."

"Awesome!" Maggie smiled. She was going to enjoy the fight. "Let's get this rolling at once."

The following day, SNP communications director Stephen Walker walked into Maggie's Holyrood office; the door was seldom closed. He was holding a tabloid newspaper.

"Did you see the headline in the *Record*?" he asked, holding it up for her to see.

"Aye, I did." Maggie glanced at it without much interest.

"Well, is it true?" He slowly read the headline out loud. "'Scottish North Sea Oil Money Used to Fund Luxury Holidays for Tory MPs.' It's also all over social media, and several of the English Tory-hating rags like the *Daily Mirror* are running with it."

"Tomorrow is better," she said with a sly smile.

"And what might that be?" asked Walker, always put out when her Independence campaign team put out something without running it by him.

"Tories Try to Kill 4,000 Scottish Jobs from Singapore Investment Group."

"That's inflammatory, I agree, but is it true?" asked Walker.

"Does it matter? All is fair in love, war, and politics," said Maggie with a flick of her hands.

"It matters to me," said Walker indignantly.

"I am sorry to hear that, Stephen," said Maggie with a frown. "Have you seen the shit they put up about me? How I'm some evil, power-hungry witch from *Game of Thrones*. Or the fake porn images of me having sex with some black man whose willy is the size of a stallion."

Walker blushed. "Oh, you have seen that one then?" she asked, smiling at his discomfort. He blushed some more. "Man, would I like to find a real guy hung like that," she mused, enjoying his embarrassment after chastening her for doing whatever one had to do to win. "They are killing me online and I won't have it. I'm going to fight fire with fire."

"Who is writing that shit?" asked Walker.

"The computer," she replied. "Here, watch this. It's amazing." She typed into Open Chat AI, "Give me ten negative Tory headlines."

"In seconds, the computer just spits them out," she explained to Walker.

"I know how it works," said Walker.

"Which ones do you like?" asked Maggie as she read them off.

"Power Corrupts: Tory Agenda Exposed"

"Dark Secrets Unveiled: The Sinister Machinations of the Tory Elite Revealed"

"A Nation Betrayed: New Book Chronicles Tory Betrayals"

"Tory Tyranny Unmasked: Gripping Inside Account Exposes their Authoritarian Tactics"

"Infiltrating the Shadows: Political Thriller Exposes the Tory Cabal"

"Behind Closed Doors: New Video Sheds Light on Tory Manipulation"

"Unleashing Chaos: The Dystopian Vision of Tory Rule"

"Deception and Desperation: Podcast Exposes Tory Lies and Desperate Measures"

"A Broken Promise: Tory U-turns and Broken Dreams"

"Democracy at Stake: Threats Posed by the Tory Regime"

Walker glanced at them. "I don't like any of them. I may be old-fashioned, but I prefer real news to fake news," he stated crossly.

"So do I and there, my friend, is our problem. Who can tell the difference when anyone can have the computer spit out plausible fictional stories promoting their agenda or version of events in seconds?" said Maggie as she showed him screenshots of outrageously false stories about Maggie, the SNP, and the Independence campaign.

"This one says I am hiding the fact that I have contracted AIDS from a male prostitute.

This one says I will double the corporate tax on all companies with over a hundred employees. Another says that I am a power-hungry bitch and that my real goal is to be prime minister of Britain, not the first minister of an independent Scotland. It's really quite good. You should read it; they make a very plausible case." She made a mock thinking gesture then added, "Maybe I'm not thinking big enough, Stephen. Maybe I should run for UK prime minister instead of just our little corner of paradise. What do you think?"

He grunted in response.

"And it's not just the Scots and the English playing this game. The Russians want to see Scotland win independence as they know we want to eliminate the nuclear sub-bases. And they are spending millions to help without us even having to ask. The French and the Germans want to keep Britain together. It's kind of funny, really; the UK has been at war with both on and off for as long as it has existed as a country, but now they are very anxious to keep it together. Then, of course, the US outspends all other countries and uses even dirtier tricks to keep us together. Then the Chinese—"

Walker cut Maggie off mid-sentence as he raised his hand. "Okay, okay, I get it."

But Maggie wasn't yet through with her ethics lecture. "The fact is politics is and always has been a dirty business. Taking the high road simply doesn't work anymore. It has never been easier for foreign governments to mess with internal politics, and the only way to stop them is to fight fire with fire; I will not apologize to anyone for taking the fight back to them. You stick to everyday SNP communications and let the Independence team stick to theirs."

"Can you at least have them give me a heads-up so I'm not blindsided by anything?" pleaded Walker.

"Yes, of course, you'll see everything in advance," said Maggie. "Just don't try to change it."

"You are spending a fortune on advertising," observed Walker.

"Don't worry; we are going to auction off Nicola Sturgeon's famous battle bus as a vital piece of Scottish memorabilia," she said with a laugh. Walker frowned and left.

He was good at his job, but for a communications guy, he was a bit of a stiff, thought Maggie. It would get a lot worse over the coming months as both factions ramped up their PR machines. There would be claims and counterclaims, leaks and denials, statistics that showed one view and statistics that showed the opposite. Teams would dig for dirt on both sides and invent it when they found none. Ultimately, it would be almost impossible to tell fact from fiction, so voters would vote with their hearts. They would vote for the person they felt had their best interests at heart. This time around, she would leave little doubt as to who that person was.

CHAPTER FORTY-TWO

Present Day –Leveling Up

Prime Minister Nigel Preston had much more on his mind than the pesky Scottish referendum. He couldn't care how the vote went; although he didn't dare say so, his party was in trouble. He was chairing an emergency strategy meeting with a close circle of advisors after another round of dismal poll results for his Tory government had hit the newspapers that morning.

"Look, it's obvious there needs to be a significant change in our policies or Labour will trounce us in the next election; we need to convert votes from the northern cities that are Labour strongholds," said Preston.

"That was the whole point of investing five billion in our leveling up scheme to win votes beyond the home counties by supporting various local initiatives," said Chancellor Alex Morton, a well-respected old-school Conservative with a bald head and pronounced nose on which sat turtle-framed bifocals. Glasses he constantly played with, taking them on and off, chewing on the end, or using them to point.

"Well, it's not enough," protested Preston. "We are losing hands down in the polls, especially up north."

"We don't have any more to give, the NHS is crumbling, and our infrastructure is in decay. In the wake of Russian aggression, our depleted military budget needs tripled, and due to the recent inflation, everybody and his brother wants a twenty to thirty percent pay raise. On top of that, taxes are at their highest level in decades," pleaded Morton.

"We are giving far too much money to Scotland, forty-five billion pounds last year," said PM Nigel Preston.

"True, but to be fair, they did generate eighty-one billion pounds in tax, including North Sea oil revenue, up seventeen percent from the previous year. We won't see any of that if we let them have independence," said Morton.

"Yes, but we are spending 11,549 pounds per head on English voters and 13,881 on Scottish voters. That's almost twenty percent more, and none of the bastards ever vote Tory. We'd be a dammed sight better off spending that extra two thousand pounds per head in Leeds, Liverpool, and Manchester and getting some fucking votes out of Labour instead! The truth be known, I think we'd be a dammed sight better off without Scotland, no matter what the rest of the party thinks. All I hear is constant whining for independence and bullshit about leveling up. How can we level up in North England when the Scots get free college tuition and free prescriptions? The average youngster in England has to pay ten thousand pounds a year in tuition. If the Scots did away with free tuition, they could spend all that money on fixing the NHS. We should do away with it on the grounds of leveling up for the English."

"It would be political suicide in Scotland if you wouldn't get a Conservative vote in the next hundred years," said Sheila Weston, the secretary of state, a middle-aged moderate dressed in a white summer dress decorated with sunflowers, her blonde hair in a bun.

"What does it matter? We haven't had one in the last hundred years either. That's the point. The Jocks all hate us. I think it's time we returned the love and do what's best for England," said Preston. "And what's this I hear about Scotland wanting to overturn the fracking ban?"

"There is a large amount of oil on the mainland in the Central Valley area. This we knew, but using traditional mining made the extraction too costly. However, with the lower cost and higher yield of fracking, not to mention the higher oil price, it's beginning to look like a very profitable idea. According to my counterpart in Edinburgh, while Scotland has committed to wind, hydro, and nuclear power, it sees no reason to let its greatest cash asset sit buried in the ground. Quite Frankly, I agree with them," said Nick Revson, the energy secretary. He was young, fit, aggressive, and ambitious. His muscles bulged from his deliberately snug-fitting, custom-tailored bright blue suit. A suit that matched his eyes and went well with his blond hair, even if it was dyed.

"You realize what a political hot potato this is?" asked Preston. "The Greens will go ballistic."

"Of course, it's a sensitive subject both here and in Scotland, but they are threatening to go ahead whether licenses are granted or not, and then what?" replied Revson.

"Then we will sanction any firm that helps them. Find them, threaten the ministers with jail, or tell them to proceed. Hell, I don't know why they are always such a pain in the ass," whined Preston shaking his head in despair.

"Given the referendum vote looks to be close again, I'd say it's a terrible time to do anything that upsets the apple cart," stated Weston and the other two members concurred. The PM nodded silently, but that did not mean he agreed. The meeting dragged on for another fifteen minutes with different ideas to boost their flagging poll numbers and ended without a consensus.

Preston, as petulant as ever, decided that despite the advice to the contrary, he'd float a couple of trial balloons in the media and see what the public's reactions were. Stories were placed to trusted reporters from unnamed government sources stating the Scottish government's desire to restart fracking. The second story discussed the possibility that Scots might lose their free college education to fund the NHS; after all, English kids did not enjoy such a luxury.

CHAPTER FORTY-THREE

Present Day–Maggie, Queen of the Scots

The sun shone on the imposing silhouette of Stirling Castle set high on a cliff with vertical drops on three sides and granite stone buildings dating back to the fourteenth century. Many Scottish kings and queens had been crowned there, including Mary Queen of Scotts, thus making it the perfect dramatic setting for an independence event. The hostile English papers had already taken to calling McGown "Maggie Queen of Scots." A name she did not mind one bit, although few people knew what a sad historical figure Mary was, as was the Bonnie Prince. Yet somehow, they both remained romantic figures in the hearts and minds of the Scots, and that was all that mattered to Maggie's campaign.

A large stage had been set up in a field below the castle. There were a lot of people tonight, the largest crowd yet. Maggie was used to speaking in boardrooms and even to a few hundred people at conventions, but tonight, there were a few thousand. It felt more like a rock concert. What difference should it make? A few hundred or a few thousand thought Maggie, but it did, and the number unnerved her. As did the setting, she was used to a ballroom, not open fields, but at least the weather was nice. It could have been raining. There were a lot of policemen and that unnerved her as well. *Why so many?* she wondered. She glanced at Max who read her mind and gave her a reassuring nod.

After a brief introduction, Maggie took the stage in a tartan skirt and white ruffled blouse to thunderous applause. She started right into her speech. "We will have our independence from the tyrannical government in Whitehall, and we will have it sooner rather than later," yelled Margaret "Maggie" McGown to a crescendo of cheers and applause from the rabid Scottish crowd.

Behind her, the big screen was playing a montage of film and still pictures of famous Scottish heroes like William Wallace, Rob Roy, and Robert the Bruce. These were followed by the images of famous Scottish inventors like James Watt, inventor of the steam engine, Alexander Graham Bell, the telephone, John Dunlop, the pneumatic tire, and Alexander Fleming, who discovered penicillin.

Then there were images of Scottish authors and poet—Sir Walter Scott, Robert Burns, Robert Louis Stevenson, and Sir Arthur Conan Doyle. There were sports stars Like Kenny Dalglish, Jackie Stewart, Sandy Lye, Alex Ferguson, and Andy Murray. Finally, there was a montage of singers, actors, and entertainers, including Ewan McGregor, David Tennant, Billy Connolly, Susan Boyle, Annie Lennox, and Sean Connery. It was ironic, thought Maggie. He had been a staunch supporter of Scottish independence for decades despite living in the Bahamas for the last forty years of his life.

Maggie McGown succinctly summed up her main points, pausing after each to let them sink in and allow the clapping and cheering to die down so the next point would not be lost in the din. The images stirred the crowds' emotions and her words sealed the deal.

What have the English done for us?

They took billions of barrels of our North Sea oil and gave us back pennies in the pound.

They took away our access to Europe when we in Scotland voted overwhelmingly to stay in the European community.

We have no say in our own immigration policy.

And they make Scotland a target for nuclear war by keeping their Trident subs in OUR lochs.

Maggie reached under the podium and took a quick slug of Iron Brew from one of the two open cans. It hit her dry throat with its burnt citrus taste that she always found refreshing. She continued.

This week, we learn from unnamed sources that the Tories want to take away our children's free university education.

There was a roar of disapproval from the crowd, the loudest Maggie had heard yet.

And dictate how we best use our vast energy resources. We have millions of barrels of untapped oil on the Scottish mainland that, with new techniques, can be tapped and used for a better Scotland that Westminster won't let us touch!

Another roar of disapproval.

Did you know the king owns all of Scotland's shoreline until twelve miles out at sea?

There was a roar of astonishment and disapproval.

I know, amazing, right? How do you ever get a deal like that? asked Maggie, egging on the crowd. *Anyway, once we get independence, we want it all back! I mean, how can you have an English king owning all of Scotland's shoreline?*

"Yea, he's noo our king," yelled someone in the audience to a chorus of cheers.

It's time for change. It is time for Scotland for the Scots!

Suddenly, in the middle of the crowd, a group of maybe forty or fifty people took off their outer clothing to reveal orange T-shirts with a slogan printed on them. Maggie could not read them from the stage but got the message a second later when they unfurled a large white banner with "Just Stop

Oil" in black. She stopped speaking as the protesters started chanting. Security personnel moved in from each side, pushing and shoving through the crowd. Many in the crowd howled in protest as their feet were trodden on or they were rudely manhandled aside. The security personnel wrestled some protesters to the ground, and their approach was none too gentle. Protesters lashed out with their feet, and punches were thrown in the tumultuous confrontation.

Maggie glanced to the side of the stage to make sure Max was there. He nodded, telling her he thought the situation was in hand. That lasted only a few seconds as a red smoke canister arched through the air and landed twenty feet to Maggie's right on the stage. The popping sound of muffled gunfire followed it. Maggie was hit in the chest, a red patch spread across her white blouse as if she had spilled ketchup on it. She looked at it in disbelief, clutching her chest in shock and gasping for breath. There were screams from the people at the front of the crowd, now turning to run in panic.

Max rushed onto the stage, smothering Maggie to the ground to shield her from further attack. Maggie hoped dearly that Max's Kevlar suit would protect them both. With Max's hands over her head, Maggie could see very little, but she felt him twitch twice and suspected he'd been hit. Still Max started to crawl along the stage pulling Maggie with him. A single loud gunshot echoed from the back of the crowd, triggering more screams and utter panic as the crowd stamped like a herd of buffalo. One of the two SAS minders joined them on the stage, pulling Max and Maggie to exit to the left. The other minder stood over them, sidearm drawn, scanning the crowd for the remaining members of the security team or a second shooter. A second shot from the back of the crowd indicated that someone had neutralized the first threat.

Finally Max and Maggie scrambled to the safety of the stage wings. Maggie's chest ached. "Lie on your back," commanded Max, who tore open her blouse to tend to her wound. There was none, just a large red spot that would be a whopper of a bruise in a couple of hours. Max rubbed his fingers in the red liquid on her blouse. It had been a paintball gun. Maggie was wide-eyed and still panting for breath, trying to process what had happened. Was she dying? "Breathe," said Max. "You are going to be fine. Just breathe, slowly."

CHAPTER FORTY-FOUR

Present Day
–Independence Day

MAGGIE WAS SHAKEN UP BY THE INCIDENT AND KEPT personal appearance after it to a minimum choosing instead to step up her online presence with a barrage of videos and emails. Her talented marketing team was relentless in the creative ways they shared Maggie's vision using celebrities, influencers, and technology to connect with the Scottish people.

When referendum day finally came, the atmosphere in the banquet room at the Scotsman Hotel was electric. It was a four-story sandstone hotel, located in the heart of Edinburgh, built in 1905 that Maggie loved for it had kept many of its original features, including luxurious floor-to-ceiling wood paneled rooms, a grandiose marble staircase, and stained-glass windows.

The polls predicted a slim majority for leaving the Union, but polls were often wrong. There were four TV screens in the room on BBC, ITV, and Skype; pundits were all talking at once, plus they had CNN on mute who offered occasional updates from US perspective. The champagne was on ice and Maggie's victory speech written, but so was the magnanimous defeat speech, just in case. It was one speech Maggie prayed to a God she did not believe in she would never have to give.

Maggie gnawed nervously on a nail. She paced up and down; she had already done thirteen thousand steps today on her Fitbit. She glanced at the constant stream of text on her iPhone. Voting had stopped at :00 p.m.; it was already 11:30 p.m. The early results looked good, but most were from the Highlands and islands, and they never felt any connection to Westminster. Trickier would be winning votes from Glasgow's economic hub and Edinburgh's financial hub, both of whom relied heavily on south-of-the-border trade.

The bat phone rang, and the chatter in the room stopped as all eyes turned to look at it. An old-style red phone with the receiver cradled on top, nicknamed the Bat phone, had been placed on a side table so Maggie could take the first few congratulations calls if she won. Abby St. Clair picked it up. "Hello," she said and listened to the voice on the other end. She hung up, and the crowd of two hundred people looked at her expectantly. "Wrong number," she said. "It happens." The crowd erupted in laughter and groans, but it relieved some tension.

Maggie glanced up at the BBC TV, where a report stood on Princes Street with the castle behind him. "It's nail-biting time for both camps as much of the financial district in Edinburgh seems to know which side its bread is buttered on and is voting to remain. This large block of votes has pretty much evened things up. Looks like we will be in for a long night."

"Shit," said Maggie under her breath.

"Don't worry," said Harmon. "Glasgow will be ours by a wide margin."

"I don't know," said Maggie. "A lot of the unions seemed to be against us."

"Well, the unions ain't what they used to be, thanks to Margaret Thatcher," said Harmon.

"Did you know her?" asked Maggie rather more sharply than she had meant to.

"I did," said Harmon. "She was a lot like you."

"Like me?" asked Maggie in astonishment.

"Yes, very intelligent, very principled, and passionate about doing what she truly believed was in the country's best interest. I take it by your tone you were not a fan?"

"I don't know. I was only a child," said Maggie dismissively. It was no time to be arguing with her chief advisor.

As the Glasgow votes slowly trickled in, the gap began to widen. At first, it was just a crack, but then it became a canyon. At 2:00 a.m., the BBC announced, "While Westminster had not declared defeat, as usual, the polls were dead wrong. Instead of the super thin margin predicted for leave, 71% of the UK voted for independence this time under a vibrant new government led by Maggie McGown, a coal miner's daughter from Lanarkshire."

The banquet hall at The Scotsman erupted in euphoria, and the champagne corks flew around the room. The emotion was too much for many now crying tears of joy. The bat phone rang, and Abby St. Clair answered it, trying hard to hear against the din. A bell rang, and the crowd became quiet. Maggie picked up the phone cameras flashed, but it was not Prime Minister Nigel Preston as she had expected but Mr. Wang, the Chinese foreign minister.

"Congratulations on your historic victory. I hope our two countries can work together in a new spirit of cooperation that is lacking in our relationship with Westminster. I look forward to discussing trade and investment opportunities with you at another time," said Wang in perfect but heavily accented English.

"Thank You, Mr. Wang," responded Maggie excitedly. "I look forward to discussing trade opportunities at your earliest convince."

"It will be my pleasure. Good evening to you," said Mr. Wang and hung up.

The crowd erupted again with chatter, cheers, and toasts.

Maggie's parents, Cameron and Morag, had been flown in from Spain the day before for the historic occasion and stood beside her, beaming for the television cameras. It was a joyous occasion for everyone, yet despite the exhilaration of the evening Maggie once again felt melancholy on her ride home. She sat in the back of her chauffeur-driven Mercedes and pulled out the plastic-covered picture of Robbie. Looking at it longingly she shook her head and smiled. "Can you believe it?' she whispered to him. Then she pulled out the other picture of a much younger man, a handsome man; she stared at him for a long time then clutched it to her chest, and silent tears streamed down her face.

CHAPTER FORTY-FIVE

October 1984–140 Gower St., London

On the sixth floor, in a corner office, the director general of MI5, was sitting at the small round teak table, with a protective glass top, adjacent to his large desk in an office too small for both pieces. There were six chairs, although only one was occupied by Alan Ainsley, the deputy director general.

"Who knows about this?" asked the director.

"The prime minister, the home secretary, Mr. Lawson, the minister of defense, Mr. Heseltine, yourself, myself, and the agent involved; it's the smallest circle of knowledge I could get away with," stated Ainsley.

"And they are all okay with this action?" asked the director.

"Yes, I don't think all of them like it, but the PM feels the strike could end in nationwide anarchy if we don't stop it now. Scargill is more interested in removing the government than stopping pits from closing. Even some of his people are voicing that opinion now," replied Ainsley.

"And the agent involved is?" questioned the director.

"Lee Collins, sir. He's been with us for fifteen years, infiltrated the Union five years ago in Yorkshire, and he's been a solid source of information on their activities. He's even got us a little dirt on the Soviets."

"Has he now?" said the director, his interest piqued.

There was a knock at the door and both men fell silent. "Come," said the director and a middle-aged secretary brought in tea and biscuits on a wooden tray. "Thanks Margie," said the director who poured tea into two china mugs with images of Buckingham Palace. "Go on," he prompted.

"Scargill's phones are tapped. We have operatives in the Union at almost every level, including the Executive Committee. We have a good idea of when and where Scargill is going. Even though he seems to know he is under surveillance, he's either too stupid or arrogant to care," said Ainsley.

"Or maybe he's as smart as a fox and feeding you false information," said the director and he paused for thought before continuing. "You know what a disaster this will be if Collins fucks up or word of this ever gets out?" said the director.

Ainsley did not speak but gave a nod and a grim smile. The business was dirty, but the country was on the verge of chaos. If Thatcher went ahead and called in the army, who knew what would happen? It could result in a civil war or something close. Hundreds could be killed if the miners fought to keep the army out of the pits or tried to stop them from transporting coal to the power stations. Or maybe the miners would back down in the face of such drastic peacetime measures. Who really knew? Hindsight was always twenty-twenty. Who would have thought it would already have come to a pitched battle with riot police?

"Okay," said the director. "Keep me informed of the outcome."

CHAPTER FORTY-SIX

1984–Kill Scargill

THERE WAS A KNOCK AT THE DOOR OF MILLER'S BUNGAlow, a lovely modern three-bedroom with a large garden in a small village near Barnsley. It was 6:00 p.m., and Miller was not expecting anyone. He opened the door cautiously and vaguely recognized the man standing before him, a Yorkshire miner in the Union. He was a large man, six foot one or two, in his early forties. He was fit too, but his face was not handsome, his nose too small, his ears too big, his short, cropped hair already receding. Miller looked at him with suspicion. Miners did not come to his home. Miners did not even know where he lived.

"I have some important information for you," volunteered the man smiling and speaking in a Yorkshire accent.

"How did you know where I lived?" asked Miller cautiously, still trying to size up the situation.

"It's not hard. I work for MI5," said the man.

Miller's face showed surprise and suspicion as he fought hard to remember the man's name. He'd chatted with him on the picket line once or twice. "Collins?" Miller inquired.

"Collins if you like, but my given name was Petrov. I grew up in Hull, the bastard son of a sailor," said Collins, trying to gain Miller's trust.

"Did you now?" said Miller, who had still not moved from the door as he considered this new titbit of information. "Well, you'd better come in then." He led Collins into a well-appointed lounge.

"As I am sure you know, there are several MI5 agents active in the Union, but I don't know who they are as I am working on a different mission reporting to different people," said Collins. "Anyway, what I must tell you is far more important: MI5 intends to kill Arthur Scargill, which, in their minds, will end the strike. Moscow does not want that to happen."

It sounded incredible to Miller, but why not? Thatcher's bastards could do anything they pleased with impunity. He listened to Collins spell out more of the details. Miller gave Collins a stern look. "Are you sure that everything you have told me is true?"

"Yes, my orders from MI5 are to kill him myself," he said flatly. "But Moscow does not want him dead; he's too valuable to their cause, creating economic chaos in the UK."

Miller thought how convenient it would be to have Scargill gone "just like that," as his favorite comedian, Tommy Copper, would have said. He briefly considered paying Collins to go through with it, but he thought he was unlikely to do it after exposing himself to Miller as a double agent. Besides, Miller had a less complicated plan. He had discovered the million pounds from the Soviets had gone into a Polish bank account belonging to the Paris-based IEMO organization whose president was none other than one Arthur Scargill. He planned to blackmail Scargill into resigning.

Miller went to the safe and pulled two huge wads of twenty-pound notes from it. "Thank you, Collins," he said. "The Union owes you a great deal of gratitude for this information. Do not breathe a word of this to anyone. I'll tell Arthur, and we will take immediate security precautions."

Collins nodded.

"What will you do now?" asked Miller.

"I'm going on a fishing holiday and retiring from MI5." Collins got up and headed for the door. "One more thing that might interest you."

"Aye, and what's that?" asked Miller curiously in his thick Yorkshire accent.

CHAPTER FORTY-SEVEN

Present Day–Beijing on the Clyde

MAGGIE ADDRESSED THE SCOTTISH CABINET AT THEIR Monday meeting in the Holyrood government building. She had worked fast and furiously over the last couple of months, regularly putting in twelve and fourteen-hour days.

"As you all know, our priority has been to find countries that might invest or do trade deals with us. Westminster is offering as little money as possible to get rid of us without a total collapse of our systems. The EU has their hands tied unless they let us back into their club, Shaun."

Shaun Talbot, foreign secretary, took over. He was a barrel-chested man in his mid-forties with a shock of red hair. "The EU's cooperation seems like a long shot given the opposition to our membership from Spain and others who have regions of their own that want to break away. The USA is stubbornly quiet, no doubt influenced by Westminster, but the reality is they are and always have been a protectionist country. Canada and India are both possibilities, but neither seems interested in moving quickly."

Maggie continued, "This brings me to our most promising but somewhat controversial option, China."

There was a murmur of discontent in the room.

Maggie continued, "Yes, I know this won't please everyone, but I remind you that China owns almost 900 million dollars of US government bonds. The US may brand them as a totalitarian state and complain about their human rights record, but they are happy to take their money. The Hinkley Point nuclear power station in Somerset was financed to the tune of almost forty billion by EDF Energy, a French company, and China General Nuclear Power Group."

There was another murmur.

"China recently rebuilt the port of Athens as part of their Belt and Road Initiative, which is investing heavily in infrastructure projects in Italy and the sixteen former Eastern Bloc countries. So it's not like we are the only one in Europe looking for help. We either look to forge a working partnership with the Chinese or return to begging from Westminster, and there is very little guarantee they will give us anything," said Maggie.

"But what about China's human rights record?" said Abby St. Clair.

"It's terrible, so is Saudi Arabia's, and we do business with them on multiple fronts. In Qatar, hundreds, some say thousands of migrant workers died building their World Cup stadiums, but European fans still went. Many of our citizens enjoy a holiday in Thailand and love it, yet it's run by a military dictatorship. The world of geopolitics is not so black and white as anyone wishes.

"There are goals and principles we must strive for, and then there is the reality of the world as it is. Scotland needs trade, capital, and jobs, and we need them now!"

"Is this not selling out?" asked Abby St. Clair again.

"No, it's not; the investment and trade deals will be on our terms, and if we don't get them soon, the project we know as an independent Scotland will fail. We knew this going in, we had a budget deficit last year of over ten billion dollars, and the forty plus billion we get from Westminster will of course be going away. China is investing all over the world, especially in the former Eastern Bloc countries and are even 50/50 partners in the nuclear power plant in Somerset, so why not let them invest in Scotland? Westminster had no problem taking their money for that!"

"Okay, let's hear the deal," said Sandra Peters, education secretary.

"Certainly, I am sure all of you know, Glasgow Prestwick Airport is, in fact, one mile north of Prestwick, on Scotland's west coast, thirty-two miles from Glasgow. Passenger traffic peaked in 2007 at 2.4 million. Sadly, traffic has declined to less than 500,000 passengers in recent years.

The struggling airport has been bought and sold many times over the years. In 1992, to Canadian entrepreneur Matthew Hudson. The airport was sold again in 1998 again in 2001 to a New Zealand enterprise. In 2012, they announced they would sell, having incurred annual losses of £2,000,000. Having been threatened with closure, the Scottish government bought the airport in November 2013 for £1.

"Then the deputy first minister, Nicola Sturgeon, told BBC Scotland, 'Work will now begin for turning Prestwick around and making it a viable enterprise.' As you might imagine, they went up the Clyde in a banana boat, the same way as her disastrous ferry deal. In 2021, the Scottish government announced it was selling the airport. In a U-turn two months later, the government announced the airport would remain in public ownership. Still, Sturgeon stated that the government was committed to 'returning it to the private sector at the appropriate time and opportunity.'

"As of today, surprise, surprise, no private investor has been found for the money-losing business. The government has pumped in around sixty million pounds in loans to the unviable airport. The USA currently has short-term agreements to use the airport as a refueling base for its military and has done so for decades. And for all you pub quiz buffs, Prestwick Airport is the only place in the United Kingdom where Elvis Presley was known to have set foot when a transport plane carrying him home to the United States stopped to refuel in 1960, en route from West Germany.

"Thank you, thank very much," said Maggie in a mock Elvis voice.

There was applause and some laughter.

"So, in a nutshell, we have an airport that no one wants to buy that's been owned by multiple companies, some foreign. It is a money pit for the Scottish taxpayer, with rapidly declining passenger counts and aging infrastructure that is primarily used by the US military as a petrol station. However, we have an exciting solution to these multiple challenges.

"As I mentioned earlier, the home secretary, Martin Shaw, foreign secretary, Shaun Talbot, and I have been in discussions for the last few weeks with the Chinese foreign minister Mr. Wang and his team. His government is very interested in a long-term lease of Prestwick Airport. This would include a substantial up-front payment, which would go into our sovereign wealth fund, followed by annual payments at a very favorable rate. What's more, they are willing to make a massive investment in the airport's infrastructure. In addition, their national carrier, Air China, will lay on several direct flights a week from Shanghai in an effort to spur mutual tourism."

"How long is that flight?" someone asked.

"Around thirteen hours," Maggie replied. "This will guarantee future employment for the airport staff, which is currently in doubt, and create hundreds, perhaps thousands of construction jobs," she added. "Also, with the upgraded facilities, we expect to attract other European airlines to fly there, especially since it's the only airport in Scotland with its own rail station. Thus, making it the most convenient to travel to and from."

"Sounds good, almost too good," said Abby St. Clair. "What's the catch?"

"Well," said Maggie, pausing. "The Chinese want us NOT to renew our contracts with the various US military branches that currently use the base. They also want the Royal Navy nuclear subs out of the Clyde, which we at the SNP have wanted for decades anyway."

There was a hushed silence while the room considered the enormity of the proposal.

"Why would we let a foreign country have control of an airport in Scotland?" someone asked.

"We have sold it twice to foreigners and we let the US rent it, why not the Chinese?" said Maggie with a smile. "It would only be a minimal presence. If the US can have bases all over the globe, I see no reason why the Chinese can't do the same." There was a mixed response to this statement from the Cabinet.

"How many bases does the US have outside the USA?" asked Peters.

Maggie had done her homework. "The USA operates 750 military bases in eighty countries and territories outside the USA." There was another murmur in the room. Maggie ignored it and continued, raising her voice slightly to regain command of the room. "We still have to work out many of the details, but we do have an excellent framework for a working partnership with the Chinese on multiple fronts."

"Westminster is not going to like it," said Abby.

"Neither are the Yanks," chimed in Peters.

"Yes, I am sure you are both right, but I'm not interested in playing worldwide geopolitics with two countries uninterested in helping us. I'm only interested in what's best for Scotland," snapped Maggie, a little more forcibly than she had intended. "Anyway, it's not a done deal yet. I'm going to meet with the EU first and see what they have to offer, although given how they typically drag their feet, I'm not optimistic. Nor did our initial phone conversations go well. If nothing else we can perhaps use the framework agreement with China as a negotiation strategy."

CHAPTER FORTY-EIGHT

1984–Murder in Merthyr Vale

THE PHONE RANG IN THE HALL; IT WAS PAST EIGHT o'clock. McDonald picked it up and asked for the man's name. "Okay, call me back on this number in five minutes." He grabbed his jacket off its peg and yelled, "I'll just be a few minutes, luv." As he headed to the phone booth at the end of his street he realized it was chilly tonight. The conversation with a miner called Smith, if that was his real name, was short. He claimed to have specific information on where the Russian money had gone if McDonald was interested. McDonald was skeptical but the pay phone rang when it should and the brief details he gave were indeed interesting.

Smith, like McDonald, said he was disgusted by what he saw going on at the Union and wanted to end it as soon as possible along with the strike. If his information would help, he'd be glad to provide more details, but not over the phone, and just to be clear, he was not looking for any money. They were indeed kindred spirits, thought McDonald. Smith had suggested meeting at a small layby on the Dalry Road, which worked nicely as McDonald could then take that road straight into West Kilbride, where he was to meet Frasier.

The next afternoon George McDonald glanced up at the small black-and-white TV in the corner of the small café where he was having a cheese and onion sandwich. It was unusual to see news on television during the afternoon. There was a picture of a crashed car on an embankment just past a bridge. It was half-covered with a tarpaulin and surrounded by tape, but you could clearly see the car's windshield had a massive hole in it. Behind the reporter with the microphone were police cars blocking the road with cones and policemen milling about. McDonald had a bad feeling in the bottom of his stomach for the words underneath the reporter said, "Merthyr Vale, Wales." McDonald knew that it was a coal town.

The grave-looking reporter started to speak from the screen in a very solemn tone. "Today, November 30th, 1984, was a workday like any other for the thirty-five-year-old father of three, David James Wilkie. He left his house where he lived with his fiancée Janice Reed at 5:00 a.m. this morning. She was the mother of his two-year-old daughter and is pregnant with a second baby due in six weeks. He also had a twelve-year-old daughter and a five-year-old son with a previous partner.

"Wilkie was a hard-working taxi driver for City Center Cars, based in the Welsh capital of Cardiff. He had just picked up David Williams, a miner who, despite the ongoing strike and the pickets, had opted to go to work at the Merthyr Vale mine just six miles away. Because of the threat of violence from picketing miners, Wilkie's Ford Cortina was accompanied on the short journey by two police cars and a motorcycle outrider. Wilkie was driving the same route as he had for ten days. He had just turned onto the A465 north of Rhymney Bridge when two striking miners dropped a forty-six-pound concrete block from the bridge you can see behind me"—he turned and pointed—"twenty-seven feet above the road. The block smashed through the windshield and trapped Wilkie at the wheel. He lost control of his car and crashed into an embankment. Firemen fought to cut him from the wreckage, but he died at the scene from multiple injuries. Mr. Williams was described as traumatized by the incident but escaped with minor injuries.

"The chief constable of South Wales, Mr. David East, later told a press conference at Merthyr Police Station, 'This is not industrial action. This is not picketing. This is murder. Whoever threw those things down must have known the likely consequences. Prime Minister Margaret Thatcher said, 'My reaction is one of anger at what this has done to a family of a person only doing his duty and taking someone to work who wanted to go to work.' Labour's Neil Kinnock, leader of the opposition, called it an 'atrocity.'

"Today was the latest incident in an increasingly violent strike that has gripped the country for the last eight months and split communities apart. One can only hope it will be the last. John Hutchins, ITV News, Merthyr Vale, Wales."

McDonald felt sick to his stomach; Scargill's continued talk of fighting, wars, and class struggle had finally boiled over he thought. This was Arthur Scargill's fault. The sooner McDonald could replace Scargill the sooner this insanity would stop. He was going to put the final nail in Scargill's coffin today when he met with Angus Frasier. He had wanted to do it sooner, but Frasier had been out of town. Maybe he could have saved the man.

Killing this taxi driver would erode what little public and political support the miners had left; it was all over now but the shouting. It would be front-page news in tomorrow morning's newspapers, and everyone, including their traditional supporters, would condemn the miners. McDonald shook his head in disgust, left some money on the table, and walked to his car. There was no going back now. He looked around, scanning the area; it was one of the paranoid habits he had developed since walking into Grower Street. There was no one there. *Stupid,* he thought.

McDonald left the café's car park and headed towards his meeting. It was twenty minutes before he reached the Dalry Road. There was a long-deserted stretch of road in front of him with nobody on it. The drivers saw each other for the first time two hundred yards away as they rounded a series of S bends in view, then out of view as they maneuvered around the winding road. A huge MAN diesel truck was heading downhill, loaded with more than two tons of coal. The VW was slowly heading uphill, with its 48-horsepower motor laboring against the climb. McDonald wondered with dismay which scab was driving a truck full of coal to the power station down the coast in Ardrossan. He knew at once it was a scab truck, for it had a steel mesh fitted over the windows so the bricks and stones the striking miners threw at it wouldn't cause any damage.

McDonald did not want to be on strike, but once the Union was on strike, like it or not, you had to support your brothers no matter what. He hated scabs almost as much as the corruption he had found at the highest levels of the Miners' Union. It was endemic; they were just as corrupt as the pompous Tory government trying to crush them. At least it was Friday; he was going to take Sarah up to Oban this weekend, the forecast looked great for a change. She would love McCaig's Tower, a mock Colosseum of Rome, standing conspicuously on a hill looking over the town, for she had been learning about Rome in school.

CHAPTER FORTY-NINE

1984–Deer in the Headlights

Tom Brodie was nervous, sweating in his truck cab; he'd only get one shot at this opportunity. The VW rounded a bend at fifty yards and faced the truck on a short, straight section. There was a dry-stone wall to the right and a bank with a drop of some twenty feet to the left. Brodie, already doing 40 MPH, hit the gas.

McDonald's eyes opened wide. Had this idiot fallen asleep at the wheel? No, he was staring right at him through the mesh. There was a maniacal grimace on his face. In a hundredth of a second, McDonald glanced left then right; there was nowhere to go. The forty ton truck hit the car slightly off-center, hoping to send it off the road down the embankment. McDonald was not wearing his safety belt. He was thrown with astonishing force into the windshield, breaking his neck on impact. His legs were crushed and pinned below. He was clinically dead a few seconds later as blood flowed in torrents from multiple wounds sustained from the managed wreckage. The car plunged down the embankment, flipping three times before coming to a rest upside down.

Brodie stopped the truck but left the engine running. Then he got out to survey the damage to his truck, glancing up and down the road to ensure nothing was coming. The enormous front metal bumper had only minor dents and bruises, but one of the lights was damaged. He quickly retrieved a Polaroid camera from the cab and walked over to the embankment's edge to take a few quick snaps of the wreck as instructed. McDonald had to be dead, he thought; fuck him, he was a traitor and deserved to die at least according to Miller!

That thought did not stop the Brodie's stomach from protesting at what he had done and the image of McDonald with his neck in a very unnatural position halfway through the windshield, looking at the sky with his mouth wide open. Brodie vomited his steak and kidney pie, the best meal he'd had in weeks. Then he saw something out of the corner of his eye. He turned quickly in panic; a deer stood on the right-hand side of the road looking down at him from fifty yards away. It was a buck with an impressive rack of antlers, maybe the best he had ever seen. It was only a deer watching him, but it unnerved him further.

He was supposed to check McDonald was dead. He was supposed to drag the body from the car as if he had come to McDonald's aid. He was supposed to retrieve his briefcase and set the car on fire. Then he was supposed to wait until a car passed, wave them down, and ask them to get help. But as Robert Burns said, "The best-laid plans of mice and men." So, instead, he panicked, ran for the cab, and could not flee the scene fast enough.

Brodie quickly drove the truck down towards Blackshaw Farm; he did not see another car until he had turned south on the A78, and by then, it didn't matter; by tomorrow, the truck would be a different color and wearing different number plates, just in case. He headed towards an industrial estate in Irvine. He drove the tuck into the open bay and someone closed the steel doors behind him quickly. He grabbed his small workman's rucksack, stuffed the camera in, and let himself out by the side door without seeing or speaking to anyone. The estate was quiet, no one around; in fact, it looked half empty. He walked the few hundred yards to the railway station and took the train home, wrestling with his actions as he did but ultimately deciding that the Union was at war, the man was a traitor, and traitors should be hanged.

CHAPTER FIFTY

Present Day–An Offer You Can't Refuse

Maggie McGown, the recently minted first minister of an independent Scotland, met for the first time with the French president, Gaston Dumont, the German chancellor, Hans Meyer, and the head of the European Union, Dirk Van Der Veen, at a private meeting in Zurich. They gathered at a beautiful stone hotel built on top of a steep hill with a spectacular view of the simmering blue waters of Lake Zurich below. It was a charming location furnished in Renaissance style where its $500-a-plate dinners had once been a favorite of FIFA executives. Maggie had chosen the location herself. She had stayed there once but got in a day early with a bodyguard and a secretary to re-familiarize herself with the hotel, room setup, and general area. This simple familiarity gave her an extra edge and confidence. She did not need to ask where the bathrooms were, where dinner was served, or which corridor led to the lawn overlooking the lake. They would all follow her lead, a simple and subtle power grab.

The next day, after the briefest of cordial introductions where they all appraised her in detail, she outlined her plans to turn Scotland around quickly and asked those present to fast-track the country back to EU membership. She knew it was a long shot, but she had to be seen by the Scottish voters to be asking to get back in even though the answer would almost certainly be no. Then she could point the finger at the EU, giving her license with the spurned Scottish voters to pursue some of her more radical economic ideas.

There was a long silence as those present reviewed her carefully crafted bullet points. She had kept them to a minimum for clarity, and none would be a surprise since all were part of her campaign promises and had been well documented in the media. Maggie watched them intently. Dumont played with his expensive Mont Blanc pen, occasionally sticking it in his mouth and nibbling on the tip. Meyer kept flexing his right shoulder while he read as if trying to get a knot out of his muscle. Van Der Veen leaned his head on his left hand, looking bored as he went through the motions. They all wore expensive tailored suits; the Frenchman's a rather bright but fashionable shade of blue, the German's a light grey, and the Dutchman's a dark pinstripe. All had power ties, blue, red, and orange, and although Maggie could not see them now under the table, she had noticed their shoes before they took their seats. All three had highly polished Oxfords, the Frenchman's in a dark blue, the other two in black.

Chancellor Meyer spoke first in his deliberate but heavily accented English: "Many of your ideas, such as cutting taxes and VAT, would give Scotland a clear competitive advantage and not fit in with EEU philosophies."

"Ireland has been doing that for years. Their corporate tax rate is half what others in Europe are charging, so why not Scotland?" asked McGown pointedly.

"It was an experiment we permitted that we now regret," said the president of the EEU, Van Der Veen.

"An experiment that worked out extremely well for Ireland," said McGown . "Look, Scotland is in the exact same place Ireland was in the 1980s. We are an economically depressed country with poor production and a declining birth rate; we need a serious injection of outside capital to reboot. It cannot be business as usual; we all know there need to be some incentives to make that happen and a free market to sell those goods in."

"These things take time, First Minister," said Van Der Veen.

"I don't have time to dick around. I need to produce results for my people, and I need to do it now, not three years from now or even three months from now. Like now, now!"

"As you well know, First Minister McGown, there is a lengthy process for any state to join, and there will be opposition," said Van Der Veen.

"From who?" asked McGown, although she already knew the answer.

"Spain, for sure, they don't want anyone thinking that if Catalonia tries to break away from Spain and form a new country, they will get membership," replied the Van Der Veen in a rather condescending tone.

"But there might be others," replied Dumont in support.

"Well, I have some interesting options from India and China on the table to fast-forward Scotland's growth plans. If the EU is not interested in helping Scotland, one of France's strongest historical alliances…?" She left her sentence hanging.

There were nervous glances around the room. Maggie knew exactly what they were all thinking. *What does this upstart populist mean?* Was she so naive that she thought they would roll out the red carpet for her because she was an attractive redhead in a tartan skirt?

"What kind of options?" asked the chancellor.

"Options that are quite frankly far better than anything I expect to get from the EU. Still, we live on each other's doorstep, and you are my preferred option. Provided, of course, we can come to a speedy agreement and take Scotland back into the club. A club I will remind you that we were in before our English masters took us out of it without our permission," said McGown forcefully, but she ended with a smile to take the sting out.

There was an uneasy silence. Then President Van Der Veen asked if they might have fifteen minutes alone.

"Fifteen it is," said McGown cheerfully, pointing at her watch as she got up quickly and left. She went to her room, made a cup of tea, checked her email briefly, and the alarm on her iPhone went off before she knew it. It had been thirteen and a half minutes since she had left the room, and it would take her precisely ninety seconds to walk back downstairs to it.

She entered the meeting room without knocking, striding confidently, and retook her place at the table; the conversation between the three leaders stopped mid-sentence. "Well," she said, smiling. "What did you three boys decide?" There was something in the way she said "boys" that was sexy, charming, and demeaning all at once. What's more, they all knew it.

She looked at them, three of the most powerful men in Europe, if not the world. There was something about power that just amped the sexual tension a notch. Power created sexual electricity that was always lingering in the air. She wondered if they thought about fucking her. Of course they did. The French guy was dreaming about it right now; she could see it on his face.

Durant coughed loudly, and everyone returned to business, stating in his sophisticated bureaucratic style, "All twenty-nine countries would have to be contacted and agree to Scottish membership. There would have to be changes made to some of her key economic policies regarding lower taxation, and we could reconvene at the same time next year to see how things are going."

About exactly what she had expected from the gang of three. Still, the two-day break was lovely. She had managed a massage at the spa, slipped out for a quick shopping trip, and the food was terrific. But none of this was what she came for, and she was far from done yet.

"Gentlemen, thank you for your time. You have six months to fast-track Scottish membership in the EU or I will pick one of the two deals I have on the table from India or China. Both include several billion dollars invested in Scottish infrastructure." She got up and headed slowly for the door. As she did, the dumb fucks actually chuckled behind her back. She knew why; she was a woman, new to politics, and was unfamiliar with the workings of the European Parliament or the old boys' club that ran it. They thought she was an upstart, a political idiot, but they were wrong. She had also had a twenty-year career selling and negotiating deals with strong men in the beverage industry. These three were amateur bureaucratic hacks that couldn't sell a dog a bone.

She paused at the door, half opened it, then turned slowly; they all looked at her smiling, waiting for a clever parting jibe. But, instead, they got a kick in the balls so hard it would be a long time before any of them had sexual fantasies about Maggie McGown again. "Oh, and one more thing," she said with a smile, pausing for a few seconds for effect so they were waiting in anticipation. "China is interested in buying and expanding Prestwick Airport."

CHAPTER FIFTY-ONE

Present Day–The White House

ADMIRAL JAMES "JIM" MITCHELL ENTERED THE WEST Wing of the White House, walked quickly down the hall, and stepped through the imposing mahogany doors into the Oval Office. The president was seated at the iconic Resolute Desk in the center of the room. Sunlight streamed through the large windows overlooking the manicured South Lawn and the White House Rose Garden. The office walls were lined with portraits of past leaders, watching over the room like silent observers. Eyes of long-dead presidents seemed to follow every step, a reminder of the weighty decisions that the office had demanded. The faint scent of polished wood and leather permeated the air. Mitchell noted that the bust of Churchill had been replaced by one of Aristotle. The presidents always made subtle changes to reflect their taste. Mitchell had served a few of them.

Mitchell stood before the president in his deep blue jacket adorned with an array of gold-braided insignia. A cluster of medals was displayed on his chest, each representing a chapter of his storied career. The president greeted him warmly and motioned to one of the plush, high-backed leather armchairs surrounding the desk. Mitchell took a seat.

"Mr. President, we have a serious situation developing in Scotland that needs your immediate attention," said Mitchell.

CHAPTER FIFTY-TWO

1984–McMillan

DAVID MCMILLAN HAD SHORT-CROPPED HAIR LIKE A US Marine. He was only five foot six but was built solid and kept in shape. He had played center half for Glasgow Rangers before his knee went out at twenty-one. He'd just been promoted to detective inspector, young for the title in his mid-thirties, but McMillan had a blistering career that demanded a rapid rise.

He stood on the Dalry Road, looking down at the mangled wreckage of the white VW Beetle, mulling over the possibilities. It had taken the firefighters over an hour to extract the body, which was now strapped to a stretcher for his penultimate road trip to the morgue. It was a strange one, a single car on the scene, but it had obviously been hit by something, and that something was big. Why had the driver of the other vehicle not stopped? Drunk? No License? Banned from driving already? Illegal worker? Drugs? Who had thrown up at the side of the road and was it related? There were hundreds of possible reasons. Maybe it was not an accident, but that was a far-fetched idea at this stage. Perhaps the other guy just got scared and was in shock; it happened all the time; people freaked out after an accident. Maybe he'd call into the station in an hour or two and admit to the accident.

Where the hell was his accident scene team, he wondered. His resources were stretched beyond his limits, with this fucking miners' strike taking every available man and then some. What was it now, eight months? Eight months of policing pickets, stopping grown men throwing bricks while in the real-world women were raped, pensioners murdered for fifty quid, and kids got addicted to drugs earlier than ever in their teens. No, there were a million better things he and his men could be doing than making sure a bunch of striking miners did not tear apart the working miners or the drivers that took the coal away, but c'est la vie, this was the world he lived in.

A world in which he'd collared the Glasgow rapist, nailed two mafia bosses' intent on burning each other's businesses to the ground, and closed a sex trafficking route run by the Triads. Once he got a case, he seldom let it go without result.

McMillan nodded his recognition at Angus Frasier; he was tall for a Scot, six feet, with broad shoulders, and an unruly mop of curly black hair. He had just walked down the road from fifty yards above where McMillan now stood. He had watched Frasier take a few pictures of the wreck. McMillan wondered how a *Daily Record* reporter always made it to the scene before the police.

"Care to comment on what we have here, inspector?" asked Frasier politely.

"Detective inspector," McMillan said with a smile.

"Is it now? My apologies: I must not have gotten the press release on that one; congratulations and well deserved, no doubt," said Frasier enthusiastically.

"Now, don't try to sweet talk me into an unauthorized statement," said McMillan. "What we appear to have here is a hit-and-run accident. I'll be releasing a statement later today, Angus. And how the hell did you get here so fast?"

"I was playing golf down the road at West Kilbride. Have you got a name for me?" asked Frasier.

"George McDonald," said McMillan.

"The Union man?" asked Frasier, in shocked surprise. This story had suddenly gotten a whole lot bigger.

"The same," said McMillan, who eyed the reporter suspiciously.

"Is there something you are not telling me, Angus?" asked McMillan quietly.

"Aye," said Frasier. "And I'll share if you promise to keep me in the loop on this one; it's personal."

McMillan eyed him coolly, he didn't like making these kinds of pacts, but he'd dealt with Frasier before and he'd always been as good as his word. "Okay."

"That man was on the way to meet me at the golf club," said Frasier.

"Was he now?" inquired McMillan who waited patiently for Frasier to say more.

There was a long pause before Frasier continued. "The office called the club and told me to get up here. I'd left word for McDonald at the club for that I'd be right back after appearing at this accident. I wasn't meeting him until five, so I figured I could run up here and still return there in time. He was coming to see me with proof of widespread corruption in the Miners' Union."

McMillan said nothing but rubbed his chin thoughtfully. "Any ideas?" asked Frasier.

McMillan pursed his lips tight and shook his head. "Not a one at the moment, Angus."

Frasier nodded in an "I see" gesture, then said, "Well, if there is nothing to add, I'll be off."

"Nothing to add, Angus," said McMillan as the reporter returned to his car and left.

Finally, his crime team arrived, blue lights blazing from a navy-blue Ford van. The crash site was already roped off with yellow tape and the forensic examination, already tainted by firemen, began.

On the passenger's side floor was a well-worn brown leather briefcase; the crime scene technician tagged it and removed it from the car, holding it up and pointing at it. McMillan motioned for him to bring it up, and he donned some plastic gloves. He laid the briefcase on the bonnet of his police car and opened it; inside was a large manila envelope. McMillan motioned at the technician to return to the crashed car and continue his search.

The first page was a spreadsheet. The next few were names and notes accompanied by pictures of expensive vehicles and nice-looking homes. But it was the two pages on the Soviet Union that caught his interest. Details of how they were financing political unrest. This stuff he knew at once was well beyond his pay grade. He also knew that in the last the last few minutes this crash had gone from a hit-and-run accident to something more. He would announce to the press that it appeared to be a hit-and-run accident and appeal for witnesses. McMillan would send the manila envelope to London as soon as he had time to read through the whole thing. He quickly returned everything to the case.

The following day, McMillan began visiting every repair garage along the Ayrshire coast with paint samples from McDonald's car. His first visit was a sign of things to come. He walked into a small, cluttered office that stank of oil. A small, bald man in his fifties, in dirty overalls, was handwriting a receipt sitting at a steel desk.

"Morning," said McMillan. "Are you the gaffer?"

"Who wants to know?" said the man flatly.

"Detective Inspector David McMillan, I'd like to ask you a few questions."

"McMillan, eh," said the man thoughtfully. "Fuck off!"

"That's no way to address a police officer," said McMillan with a smile, trying to make light of the insult.

"Yeah, but it's the right way to address a Rangers player," said the man with a forced smile and a nod at the poster of the Celtic team behind McMillan.

McMillan glanced at it. "Ah, well, former Rangers player. I'm sure the man who was killed was a Celtic supporter, so that ought to make helping me alright. Has anyone brought a large truck to you in the last couple of days with damage to the front?"

"No," said the man. "This about that guy McDonald?"

"Any idea where the best place would be to take a large truck for repair?" McMillan asked.

"Buchanan's in Irvine specializes in commercial vehicles, but I'd guess I was some drunk Irish bastard, and the truck made it back to Dublin on the ferry the following morning."

McMillan nodded, said, "Thanks," and strolled back to his car.

He let a few days pass before visiting McDonald's widow. She let him into the modest row home, and they both sat on the sofa in the lounge.

"First, my deepest condolences to you and your daughter, Mrs. McDonald," he said.

"Thank you," she mumbled quietly.

"I know this is difficult, but do you know of anyone in the Union who might have wanted to harm your husband?" asked McMillan.

A young girl wandered into the room looking lost and sad. "Go make us a cup of tea, Sarah," said Mrs. McDonald. The girl nodded and went into the kitchen. "No one in the Union had any reason to kill my husband, but I know who did," she said defiantly.

McMillan had not expected this and looked at her, waiting for more.

"That bitch Thatcher; that's who done my George in. It was a warning to Scargill: he'll be next, you mark my words. The Tory government will stop at nothing to break this strike," she said with passion.

McMillan was disappointed. "Do you know what kind of work your husband did as an executive in the Union?"

"No, but I can tell you this: the miners in this region could not have had a better man to fight for them," she replied.

"We think it was most likely a hit-and-run accident, Mrs. McDonald, but I want you to know we will run down all the leads," said McMillan.

Sarah returned with a tray containing a pot of tea, two cups of milk, and sugar. She was a pretty girl but obviously still distraught at her father's death.

McMillan went back to the house a couple more times to try different angles of questioning. On his second visit, he had taken the young girl an Enid Blyton book to try to cheer her up. "Mrs. McDonald did your husband ever say anything about any of the other members of the executive committee?" asked McMillan.

"No, not that I recall," she said absentmindedly.

"Do you remember anything he said about them?" questioned McMillan.

She thought for a moment looking up. "He said they all had nice cars and Spanish tans."

"And what do you think he meant by that?" probed McMillan.

"He wasn't jealous if that's what you are thinking," came her retort.

"No, no," said McMillan who could see it was going nowhere.

It took him a week to visit all the garages on the coast, and then he expanded to Glasgow, which took two more. His men canvased all the junkyards and scrap metal dealers to see if the truck had just been ditched and contacted all the haulage companies to see if a truck had gone missing or had returned damaged. Everywhere they looked, they came up blank; of course, the vehicle could have been driven anywhere, but it seemed unlikely to McMillan that it had gone far. After all it was a huge fucking truck, it couldn't have just disappeared; somebody had to be hiding it.

Several weeks later, he finally secured an interview with Arthur Scargill, at the Union's Yorkshire headquarters. "Did you know McDonald was concerned about corruption in the Union?" asked McMillan.

"No," Scargill said angrily. "You lot should be far more concerned with police brutality than what's going on in the Union."

"Did you know McDonald well?" asked McMillan.

"No," replied Scargill.

"And I don't suppose you know why anyone would want him dead?"

"NO, but it wouldn't surprise me if Thatcher's thugs had a plan to take me out. Wouldn't surprise me at all."

McMillan could see this was going nowhere.

He tried to set up interviews with several of the Union leaders who, according to McDonald's notes, all of which he photocopied, were on the take. He had set up three interviews the following week when he got the phone call.

"McMillan, special branch on line three, and, McMillan, be nice, sounds like a big wig," called Parker across the open-plan office filled with cheap desks at the station.

"This is Chief Inspector Simon Wilkins," said a commanding voice on the other end of the phone.

"To what do I owe the pleasure?" replied McMillan pensively.

"It's about your inquiries into the death of George McDonald," said Wilkins.

"Aye," said McMillan, already not liking the sound of this.

"I need you to back off all inquiries among the Miners' Union executives," said Wilkins, who added sternly, "At once."

McMillan was silent for five seconds or more before responding. "And why would that be?"

"Look, I am sorry I can't go into details, but we have our own people in the Union, you need to drop it," said Wilkins more cordially, then added more forcefully, "It's a matter of national security."

"Ah," said McMillan, although what he wanted to say was, "Go fuck yourself … sir."

"Are we clear, McMillan?" asked Wilkins.

"Crystal," said McMillan. The line went dead, and he smashed the receiver back into its cradle so hard the rest of the chatter in the office stopped and everyone looked at him.

The newspapers asked for answers, the public wanted answers, and rumors of McDonald's supposed assassination were rife in the mining communities. Everyone demanded progress, and yet McMillan was being stonewalled at every turn. The weeks turned to months, and any real chance of solving the crime, if indeed it was a crime, seemed to vanish. After all, just because McDonald was investigating Union corruption did not mean anyone knew or, if they did, would be willing to kill for the information; it could have been an accident. The problem was that the timing was too much of a coincidence, and McMillan did not believe in coincidences.

CHAPTER FIFTY-THREE

Present Day–Trident

Admiral Mitchell spoke to President Anderson with a note of gravity in his voice. "We have a man inside at the Faslane Naval Base and have it on solid information that the Scottish government is about to get a major influx of investment capital from the Chinese. One of the conditions of this investment is that they kick out the nuclear subs. They have talked about this for so long we have ignored it, but now it looks like it will actually happen."

"Wait," said the president. "We closed our base in Holy Loch in the nineties, didn't we? When the idiots in the Democratic Party thought the threat of war had vanished from the earth."

"That is correct, sir," said Mitchell. "I am referring to the UK's fleet of four nuclear subs armed with Trident missiles based at the Faslane Naval Base, located on Gare Loch, near Helensburgh, Scotland. They form a large part of our NATO defense strategy." He handed the president a brief.

DEPARTMENT OF THE NAVY

Trident Brief

The Trident program is the UK's nuclear weapons system, consisting of submarines armed with Trident ballistic missiles. Here are some critical details about the Trident program:

1. **Nuclear Deterrence:** The primary purpose of the Trident program is to provide the UK with a nuclear deterrent capability.
2. **Components:** The Trident program consists of three main components:
3. **Submarines:** The UK currently operates four Vanguard-class submarines carrying Trident missiles. These submarines are designed to remain undetected and can launch ballistic missiles from underwater.
4. **Ballistic Missiles:** The Trident system uses submarine-launched ballistic missiles (SLBMs). The missiles are equipped with multiple independently targetable re-entry vehicles (MIRVs), which means that a single missile can carry multiple warheads capable of targeting separate locations.
5. **Warheads:** The UK maintains a stockpile of nuclear warheads that can be fitted onto the Trident missiles. The exact number of warheads and their yield is classified information, but it is believed to be a few hundred warheads.
6. **Continuous At-Sea Deterrence (CASD):** The UK follows a policy of Continuous At-Sea Deterrence, which means that at least one Trident submarine is on patrol at any given time, ensuring a continuous nuclear deterrent capability. This policy aims to maintain an element of unpredictability and ensure that potential

adversaries cannot know the exact location of the submarines at any given moment.
7. **Sovereign Control:** The UK government maintains complete operational control over the Trident program. The decision to use nuclear weapons rests with the prime minister, who can authorize their deployment if deemed necessary.
8. **Replacement Program:** The UK government has initiated a program to replace the current Vanguard-class submarines with a new class of submarines known as the Dreadnought class. This program, known as the Successor program, aims to ensure the UK's nuclear deterrent capability beyond the lifespan of the current submarines.

The president put the brief down with a frown and shook his head. "Can the Scots do that?" he asked. "Kick out the English subs?"

"The base is leased, and the lease comes up next year. The Scots have been campaigning for decades for Whitehall not to renew it for various reasons. There have been many protests, but they have become much stronger in the last six months. There have been hundreds of people a day showing up. There is a lot of anti-English graffiti in the area and a good deal of anti-American sentiment, as they see us as puppet masters. Sometimes, they burn tires in the street just like their French cousins."

"There has also been a massive increase in AI-generated anti-American sentiment on social media. Plus, a significant increase in violence at local pubs. Things have gotten so bad that all personnel are confined to the base."

"What are the Brits—I keep calling them Brits, I mean the English—going to do about it?"

"It's the perfect base with deep water and ocean access. As for what they are doing, vacillating as usual. The prime minister says it's just the Scots being the Scots and it will go away, but I don't think it will," said Adams.

"Is there somewhere else they can station them?" asked the president.

"Yes, there is a deep water harbor in Falmouth, on the very south coast of England but it's not as good a location strategically and there would be no support infrastructure for a long time. Also, they are not as strategically located. But channels have been opened to discuss the matter."

"Doesn't McGown realize that getting in bed with the Chinese is like inviting a wolf to dinner?" asked the president, exasperated.

"The first minister is of the opinion that being in bed with anyone but the English is preferable," replied Mitchell.

"There is something else, sir," said Mitchell gravely. "She is also talking of ending our military use of Prestwick Airport and leasing it to the Chinese, starting next month."

"What!" exclaimed the president in alarm. "Has she gone mad?"

CHAPTER FIFTY-FOUR

1985–End of the Strike

KEN MILLER AND ARTHUR SCARGILL WERE AT THE Horse and Hound pub near the NUM's Sheffield headquarters. Miller had waited a couple of weeks for all the fuss about McDonald's death to die down before he approached Scargill with his knowledge of the missing million. They both had pints and an order in for pie and chips. Miller hoped that Scargill would resign to stop the information from becoming public.

"Arthur, what's all this I keep hearing about the Russians giving the Welsh miners relief fund a million dollars?" asked Miller casually.

"What about it?" replied Scargill.

"Well, I've heard it never got there," said Miller with a smug look, but to his astonishment, Scargill simply blew him off.

"Of course it never got there, you idiot. If we'd brought it into the UK accounts, the government would have sequestered it," replied Scargill.

Miller was taken aback. "Well, where did it go?"

"I kept it offshore," said an increasingly irritated Scargill.

"Offshore where?" asked Miller.

"The money is in a bank account for the International Union of Energy and Mine Workers, and they will transfer it to the miners when appropriate," replied Scargill.

Miller wondered when that might be. "Have you shared this information with the executive committee?" he asked.

"You can share it with whomever you like. I make no apology for my actions, which are in the members' best interests," said Scargill defiantly.

To Miller, Scargill's defense seemed like an alternative reality of the facts, but if he took the gamble, pushed the issue, and failed, he'd be out on his ear. It was a good job. He'd brought it up casually and not as the threat it was in disguise. He would have to bide his time and find more dirt on Scargill before he moved to oust him. Besides, it was beginning to look like the strike gravy train might be ending, and he'd have to rely on his Union salary again. The National Coal Board had offered cash incentives to any miners returning to work. More than a few were taking the offer.

The two steak and kidney pies appeared, and they ate silently.

***

By January 1985, the strike was beginning to disintegrate as miners facing increasing financial hardship returned to work in more significant numbers each day. Despite Scargill's tireless efforts, the NUM had failed to gain support from other key industrial trade unions. Nottinghamshire men still working were threatening to form a separate breakaway union, the Union of Democratic Mineworkers.

On March 3rd, 1985, all the NUM executives met at the Trade Union Congress conference in London.

"As of tomorrow, we have been on strike for a fucking year. Men have lost their cars, homes, and wives over this dammed strike. Families are near starvation, living, if you can call it that, on charity. It's time to admit defeat and go back to work," shouted Evans from South Wales. "It's time to end the strike."

Cheers and jeers, yeas and nays greeted his statement.

"We must never surrender. We have lasted this long; why not another week or month? We must show solidarity and fight until the end," stated Mark Green, a short, pudgy veteran miner from Manchester.

Cheers and jeers greeted his statement.

Scargill started talking in a normal voice, which rose with each sentence until he ended up shouting. "We have come too far and suffered too long to quit now. They have attacked us in the press and jailed thousands of our members on trumped-up charges. Turned local police forces into a brutal state police and have sent MI5 agents into the Union. No, my brothers, now is not the time to quit. The government is running scared. The government will quit before we do!"

About that, he was wrong. When the vote was finally taken, after the passionate pleas from both sides went back and forth for over three hours, the vote to end the strike passed 98 to 91.

Scargill was livid when confronted by reports. He left the building, his face flushed in anger. "This strike was brought down by the very people it sought to protect, the working men and women of this country. If the other unions and the Labour government had supported us, we would have had the change we sought. I am shocked and saddened by these organizations not rising to the occasion when it mattered by supporting the miners."

Two days later, on March 5th, 1985, Ken Miller joined a large crowd in South Yorkshire and watched grim-faced as the men of Grimethorpe Colliery marched back to work. It was a sight none of them had seen in a year. Miller could see the mood was mixed. Some men laughed and joked, relieved to be earning a paycheck again. Others looked shell-shocked.

They and their families had endured a year of severe hardship and it had all been for nothing. There was no settlement, and Thatcher's government hadn't made a single concession. The miners had lost the strike first called on March 6th, 1984. At its height, 142,000 mineworkers were involved. By the end of the strike, over 11,000 people had been arrested. Three had died; hundreds were injured. Many were asking, "Was it worth it?" It certainly was for Miller; the truth is he was sorry to see it end, for the gravy train would never be that good again.

As the miners strode down the street like a marching army towards the colliery gates, they were accompanied by the village's world-famous brass band, dressed in fresh one-piece overalls, white helmets, and work boots. As the music played, the band was followed by a parade of women, family, and friends who lined the street. They held banners and placards with messages of support, many of them in tears, cheering and clapping. Together, they all shared the emotional weight of returning to work and bracing themselves for the uncertain future that lay ahead.

Miller smiled, nodded, clapped men on the back, and offered words of encouragement. Surely, this crushing defeat would usher in new leadership at the NUM. His leadership. After all, there were still 140,000 dues-paying members, and that was nothing to sneeze at. Or maybe it was time to take the money and run. Somewhere warm.

CHAPTER FIFTY-FIVE

March 6th, 1990 –The Cook Report

THE NEWSROOM OF THE *DAILY RECORD* IN GLASGOW WAS a typical newsroom of cheap furniture, phones, pens, notepads, and noise. Angus Frasier sat at his desk with a cup of tea and a bacon sandwich, studying an article from that morning's edition of the rival *Daily Mirror*, with a serious look on his face.

"That Peter Cook Report on last night on TV was something, eh?" said Roy Clark, a newsroom veteran with a deep baritone voice and an equally large frame to match, topped with a mop of flat grey hair.

"It was," said Frasier gravely as he took a satisfying bite of his sandwich.

"It's got to be bullshit. Those NUM lot taking the money from Libya."

Frasier took a swig of tea before answering, "Five million quid. Never made it to the miners' pockets. Wouldn't surprise me one bit." He shook his head sadly.

"Another million from Russia," added Clark. "And did you see the size of Scargill's new house? That's some upgrade, eh? Must have cost a few quid."

"He claimed not to be taking a paycheck during the strike," said Frasier. He crumpled up the wrapper of his bacon sandwich, tossing it towards a wastepaper bin twenty feet away. "My money says he was getting paid hand over fist. By himself." The wrapped went into the bin. "Bingo!"

"We're in the wrong bloody game," said Clark. "Aye, so, you think it's true then?"

Frasier held up the copy of the *Daily Mirror*. "It's right here in black and white. The *Mirror* wouldn't print without knowing the sources. Scargill is awful quick with his lawsuits."

"Can't wait for part two next week," Clark said.

"Bugger that," said Frasier. "I'm calling David McMillan. He was the detective on the McDonald case. See what he makes of all this."

"McDonald? The car crash bloke? That's old history. Everybody said it was MI5. You'd better watch your back or you might be having an accident yourself."

Frasier snorted out a laugh. "MI5 my arse. There are three things you cannot hide for long."

"I've got a horrible feeling you're going to tell me what they are," said Clark with an expectant look.

"The sun, the moon and the truth!" said Frasier slowly and clearly. "Follow the money, my son. Follow the money."

Clark nodded thoughtfully and started towards his desk. "Good luck, then. Let me know how it goes with McMillan."

CHAPTER FIFTY-SIX

Present Day –Ghosts of the Past

Tom Brodie woke in the middle of the night in a cold sweat, gasping for air. His heart pounded furiously. The nightmares had started immediately after the killing but had grown less frequent over the years. Years when he could not hold a job drank heavily and fell into a deep depression. His wife left, taking the kids with her, and moved in with a miner he once knew a thousand years before the strike. Before the cursed strike, it had scarred them all, but it had scarred him more than most. He had killed a man. Killed a man in cold blood, a man they told him was a scab, a traitor to his kind but was, in fact, a top Union boss.

When he found this out the day after the killing, he thought he might have been set up and used the blood money he received to move his family to Ireland, where Brodie had an uncle. There, he took a job for a while as a lorry driver. No one missed him back home; he phoned a mate and told him he'd got a job down south driving a bus, and everyone took it as fact. They all had their own problems with the strike still on.

For a while, the move worked out. The house they rented was cheap and larger than their old one in Scotland. He was making money again, and the kids were young enough not to care. Even his wife seemed content to start over in a new place. But the nightmares wouldn't stop; he could never get enough sleep, it made him moody, and they got into fights. He took sleeping pills and drank heavily to get some rest. Eventually, he got fired for drinking on the job, and the downward spiral began. His wife left. He went on the dole and frequently thought of suicide, but gradually, the dreams became less frequent.

The dreams, oh yes, those sweet dreams. There was the one where the truck had exploded on impact with McDonald's car, trapping Brodie in the truck's cab, where he slowly burned to death like Joan of Arc, only with no thought of ever going to heaven. Then there was another where the stag, watching what he'd done, walked over to Brodie standing by his truck. Brodie stood there, memorized by the magnificent animal, before the stag suddenly rammed his huge antlers into Brodie's gut, leaving him to bleed out in agony at the side of the road. In another, he got out of the truck in the Irvine warehouse and was gunned down like a 1920s mobster movie. His dreams came in many different flavors, and there were only two common themes—he died in agony and very slowly.

When the Roger Cook TV show *The Cook Report* aired in 1990, the nightmares started again more frequently. He'd been conned, lied to, and used to kill what most likely was an innocent man. The story outlined allegations against Scargill,

Windsor, Evans, and Miller but nothing about McDonald. Brodie put two and two together and he figured McDonald was on to them and that's why he was paid to kill him. The image of McDonald's head poking out the car's windshield and looking skyward haunted him. He saw it in mirrors, pictures, and the glass windows of shops he passed by.

Eventually, he moved back to Scotland, sure that if he had been framed, he would have been arrested by now. He trundled through a score of casual jobs living, yet not living. He had no hobbies, few friends, and nothing he particularly wanted to spend the money he did make on. It was a hollow life, but at least it was a life. He could still see his kids now and again, and that, if nothing else, made life worth living; it was not something McDonald could do.

CHAPTER FIFTY-SEVEN

Present Day –Data Breach at MI5

There was a rap at Prime Minister Preston's study door and a man entered without waiting for permission. None of the secretaries were in the outer office yet and he knew he'd find the PM already at his desk, in his oversized leather swivel chair.

"Morning, Jenkins," said the PM, eying him suspiciously. "To what do I owe the pleasure of the minister of defense in my office at 7:00 a.m. before I've even finished my first cup of coffee?"

"There has been a low-level data breach at MI5, sir. Russian hackers," said Jenkins solemnly.

"Fuck, how low level?" snapped the PM.

"The good news is it's nothing current. The boys detected the breach quickly and shut it down fast. All the stuff released online is from forty years ago, although some of it is a little embarrassing," stated Jenkins.

"Like what?" snapped the PM irritably.

"Like some details of the Military Reaction Force, formerly titled the Mobile Reconnaissance Force or MRF for short," said Jenkins.

"And what was that?" asked the PM.

"In essence, it was a clandestine hit squad targeting Irish Republican Army (IRA) members during the Troubles in the early seventies. It was off the books, of course, but they terminated over forty IRA members and potentially a few innocent civilians along the way. Most of the records were destroyed by the army after they disbanded the unit, but MI5 apparently kept some. The data included the names of some soldiers, a handful of whom are still living. Those names will undoubtedly be all over the internet as soon as the Russians decide how to use the information to our maximum embarrassment. Although, given the KGB's top-heavy command system, that may or may not buy us a few days."

"Good heavens," said the PM. "That will create a firestorm for the press, not to mention the possibility of reprisals."

"I have police officers visiting each of the remaining members, sir," said Jenkins. "And communications are preparing a statement from you denouncing the unit."

"I'm not sure in the circumstances at the time I would have denounced it at all," countered the PM. "The Brighton Hotel bomb meant to kill Thatcher, and the Birmingham Pub bomb alone killed what? Thirty people and injured over two hundred?"

"All the same, sir, we need to get ahead of it, and of course, you'll have the final edit," responded Jenkins.

"Okay, what else?" asked the PM with a sigh. This news was not a good start to his day, and it was about to get worse.

"Most of it was Cold War stuff that is of little importance in today's political climate, old news, really. But there is something I think you should look at." Jenkins handed him a manila folder.

"What is it?" demanded the PM.

"It's a classified file from 1984 detailing MI5's involvement in the miners' strike."

"And want's so interesting about that?" asked the PM.

"MI5 was apparently considering eliminating Arthur Scargill, which they thought would end the strike in a week," said Jenkins.

"Rubbish! That sort of thing does not go on in Britain. We do not run around killing our own citizens," exclaimed the PM indignantly. "IRA members I understand, but union leaders? Tell me it's not so. Jenkins, this isn't the United States."

Sometimes, the PM could be so naïve, thought Jenkins. "Sir, in the national interest, we can, and we do occasionally, remove people with extreme prejudice."

"And what the fuck does that mean in English?" asked the PM, no longer trying to hide his anger.

"To use 'extreme prejudice' in terminating someone means to exercise a very high level of caution in identifying the target before killing them and to ensure that there is no collateral damage," offered Jenkins.

"Well, those guys must not have sent James Bond for Scargill is alive decades later," said the PM smugly.

"You are right; the operation was botched, and—" Jenkins paused "—they might have killed someone else by mistake."

"Oh, my God, who?" exclaimed the PM.

"A man named George McDonald, the Miners' Union's number three. He was a Scot from Lanarkshire. And a real up-and-comer in the Union," said Jenkins.

"Well, what do you mean might have killed him? Either they did or they didn't," barked the PM.

"On his way to the meeting he was involved in a hit-and-run accident—a head-on collision with a large truck, based on the impact. The truck, along with the driver, was never found.

The man MI5 had heading up their Union infiltration project and the Scargill sanction was a Russian double agent. He was apparently in the same vicinity that day and disappeared that evening. They never really found out what happened. He showed up in Moscow a decade later as a KGB colonel. Only three people were involved; all the details were left up to the agent, so as few people as possible knew anything about it," said Jenkins.

"Okay, so a miner called George McDonald may or may not have been killed by a Russian agent on a country road in Scotland. Why would he kill him and not the man he was supposed to kill, who was the face of the strike?" said the PM. "What good would that do?"

"McDonald was on his way to a meeting with a reporter with details of serious corruption in the Union and the KGB's involvement in funding and manipulating state affairs. It would have seriously damaged Russia's spy network within the Union and not just the Miners' Union," said Jenkins, "other UK unions as well. McDonald looked like he might be the logical choice as the next Miners' Union boss as people were becoming tired of Scargill. He would have ended the strike, rooted out the corruption, and booted the Soviets back to Moscow."

"And how do you know all this?" asked the PM.

"Because there was a file in his car, in his briefcase," said Jenkins, reading a brief on his iPad.

"We assumed that the assassin was supposed to snatch it or torch the car but that he might have been surprised by someone and left the scene in a hurry without the info."

"And am I to believe this never came out in the news?" asked the PM.

"The police handed the briefcase to Special Branch, who gave it to MI5. They thought they could use it to their advantage by infiltrating the unions with their people rather than publicizing it and outing everyone."

"And should the name George McDonald mean anything to me?" asked the PM.

"No," said Jenkins.

"Okay," said the PM, trying to follow along. "So why are you telling me all this?"

"Because information about the proposed assassination is now online," announced Jenkins.

"Look, I know it's all very James Bond and distasteful stuff, but why would the death of a Scottish miner forty years ago be of much interest to anyone? Embarrassing, yes, but we will just deny it, say it's fake news and old fake news at that," said the PM dismissively.

"I don't think that's how Sarah McDonald will see it," said Jenkins grimly.

"That's his wife or his daughter, I assume?" asked the PM.

"Yes, sir, it's his daughter."

"Well, I don't see how some forty or fifty-year-old Scottish housewife is going to cause much trouble," said the PM, speaking dismissively again.

"If she were a housewife, I am sure you are correct, sir, but it's a little more complex. Allow me to explain," said Jenkins.

"Yes, I certainly wish you would," said the PM irritably.

"McDonald's daughter was born Sarah Margaret McDonald. Her father died when she was eleven. Her mother was convinced at the time that he had been assassinated. She drank and smoked herself into poor health from grief and died of cancer before her daughter turned twelve.

"A neighboring family adopted the daughter, also a mining family, who took good care of her until she left home for university. She took the surname of her adoptive parents, who also preferred to use her middle name, Margaret, since that name had been both their mothers' Christian name. Want to guess what her new surname was?" asked Jenkins."

No, tell me it was not Maggie McGown?" said the PM, astonished and alarmed.

"Got it in one. That's why we have had difficulty finding out more about her. In 1986, Scotch House, where all the birth records were kept, hired a third party to convert all the paper records to digital. Some of the files went missing and never made it into digital form. Hence, we never found her original birth record or adoption papers and we were all looking for the wrong name anyway."

"And how did they find this out?" asked the PM, brow furrowed.

"As soon as they knew of the data breach late yesterday afternoon, someone at MI5 had the good sense to ask where the daughter was. The Lanarkshire police held a massive emergency door-to-door campaign last night, and some old lady remembered the girl and the family that took her in. The parents are alive and well in Benidorm."

"And why did we not know this sooner?" asked the PM.

"I don't suppose it was ever important to MI5 what happened to the girl. McDonald was dead, the strike was still raging, the IRA was blowing things up all over the place, and her mother was still alive. There was no reason to keep any tabs on an eleven-year-old girl," said Jenkins.

"Did we give her mother any compensation?" asked the PM.

"McDonald had only been working for us for a few weeks and refused pay."

"Really!" said the PM.

"He was a real patriot; it was all about exposing the Union's corruption. I guess he expected a reward, but he certainly would not take our money, although it was offered. The Union paid off the widow's house, and we lost interest after that; it wasn't our problem. Anyway, I'm not sure MI5 would have done much for an operative that was only with them for a few weeks and was not on the books, so to speak," said Jenkins.

"I see," said the P.M. "Does any of this explain McGown's abject hatred of England and the Conservative government in particular or her desire to place the entire security of Europe in serious jeopardy?" asked the PM.

"It might," said Jenkins. "According to the old lady the police interviewed in Lanarkshire, she had always suspected her mother was right and that we had killed her father."

"What do you mean by us? I was only ten years old," said the PM indignantly.

"I mean u, as in the Conservative Party was in power with our own Maggie at the helm," said Jenkins.

"What I still don't understand is how the hell you cannot know if we killed a man," the PM said aggressively.

"It's complicated, sir, a perfect sequence of things going wrong that never happens in the Bond movies," said Jenkins with open palms.'

"What a fucking mess.' said the PM. "Get M or Q or whatever his letter is these days round here right now."

"The director general, sir, he's already on his way. He'll be here in ten minutes," replied Jenkins.

"And get him to send an agent in Edinburgh round to McGown 's office at once before she reads it online," ordered the PM.

"It may already be online," said Jenkins. "But I've sent a security brief to all the major news outlets asking them to delay mentioning anything for forty-eight hours on national security grounds. Most will comply, but once word leaks out, the dam will break quickly."

"Well, let's hope she's too busy to see it before she hears it from us. On second thoughts wait until I have my meeting with the director general. Maybe he will have some better ideas!" said the PM.

The director general showed up forty minutes later.

"Sorry the traffic was horrendous." The PM scowled.

"What in the name of Jesus happened?" he asked.

"It's too early to say how the data breach happened but we'll get to the bottom of it," said the director general.

"I'd bloody well hope so, this is very embarrassing," said the PM. "I understand Prime Minister," said the director general apologetically.

"All of the current IT systems were put in place before my time and have been under review," said the director general.

"What about this Military Reaction Force and plots to kill Scargill. Is this true? Is that how we operate?" asked the PM.

"Again, Sir, before my time. But yes, it's true," said the director general.

The PM sighed, "Well you'd better get a man up to Scotland immediately and explain things to Ms. McGown before she reads it in the news."

"There are currently no suitable agents in Scotland, I'm sending a man up from London. He's already on the train," said the director general. "Why the hell is he on the train and not a plane?" asked the exasperated PM.

"Because he was already on a train to Manchester when we contacted him and he is the best man for the job,' said the director general, "he's been fully briefed,"

The meeting ended and the PM tried hard to focus on dispatching routine work for the next few hours.

He was just about to leave his office for lunch when an aide buzzed him and told him the president was on the line. It would be 7:00 a.m. in Washington, and this was not a scheduled call. Whatever it was would not be good news.

CHAPTER FIFTY-EIGHT

Present Day–The PM and the President

Back in the Oval Office, President Anderson asked Admiral James "Jim" Mitchell, "What do you propose we do with this Chinese situation in Scotland?"

"Well, sir," said Mitchell thoughtfully, "we can be Maggie McGown's special friend, which will alienate our relationship with Westminster, the rest of what's left of Britain and the EU. But she's not exactly singing 'Yankee Doodle Dandy' anyway.

"Or we can aid in her demise with a rash of false stories on social media, hoping the next first minister is more to our liking. Or we can arrange for an accident on her helicopter for a quick solution. We have already placed a CIA mechanic in the aviation company that services her chopper in Aberdeen."

The president sighed. "The last option is a bit drastic, is it not?"

"Not when you look at the stakes involved, sir," said Mitchell.

"Okay, start soft but fast. Get the CIA to find her weak spots. Lesbian lover, drinking, drugs, or gambling problem, whatever will help discredit her, find it."

"We have looked, sir; she has none of those issues. It's simpler than that; she just passionately hates the English."

"Why?" asked the president.

"No one seems to know," replied Mitchell.

"Who's financing her?" asked the president.

"She is financing herself; she's the richest lady in Scotland, but she has no shortage of donors and supporters either," said Mitchell.

"Okay, get London on the line right away, and let's see what ideas they have to nip this in the bud," said the president.

"Ah, there you are. Good Morning, Mr. President," said PM Nigel Preston as they began their video call.

"Look," said the president, "I'll cut right to the chase: the USA strongly condemns the Scots' plan to lease Prestwick Airport to the Chinese government and remove your nuclear subs from their base in the Clyde. It poses a clear and present danger to our NATO allies, not to mention what's left of you Brits. Also, allowing them to invest in other infrastructure is extremely dangerous and irresponsible."

"Yes, I can understand that, Mr. President. We feel the same way and have conveyed our thoughts to her in no uncertain terms, but she's very strong-willed," said Preston.

"How the hell can she kick your nuclear subs out of Scotland and, in the same breath, lease an airport to the Chinese, which she must know they will use as a clandestine military base?" said the president loudly. "The Scottish government needs to ensure that economic interests do not constantly trump security concerns. The CIA has recently discovered that the UK is one of China's top priority targets thanks to its close relationship with the US and its perception as an opinion leader. China's global ambition is to become a technological and economic superpower on which other countries rely. That represents the greatest risk to the UK, not their missiles. They will conquer from within. This must not be allowed to happen."

"They are giving her a great deal of money, and, quite frankly, she is pissed they won't fast-track her back into the EU. Perhaps you could use your influence to help me make that happen?" said the PM. "My influence with the EU is about the same as a rabbi's influence in a mosque," he scoffed.

"Even though we are the ones protecting their ass, it pisses me off how ungrateful they all are, especially the frogs," said the president. "I'd like every meeting I have in Europe to take place in Omaha Beach so those bastards are reminded what our boys did for them and continue to do!"

"When Putin invaded Ukraine, it certainly woke them all up," said the PM.

"They are still all spending far too little on defense except for you guys, Sweden, Finland, and, believe it or not, Greece," said the president.

"What do you suggest we do?" asked the PM. "I've begged her to reconsider, but they are paying her billions, and we don't have the cash to match their offer."

"I'll tell you what we'll do," the president said sternly. "We'll make her an offer she can't refuse, but she won't like it. It's going to sound a little more palatable coming from you, but understand this—one way or another, the Chinese will not be leasing that base," said the president, his voice rising. "It's a direct challenge to the world order, and we will not stand idly by and watch it happen.

"It's the most dangerous thing to happen since the Cuban Missile Crisis," the president continued. "In the meantime, you need to get someone up there pronto and get her to change her mind by whatever means are necessary. Otherwise, we will have to consider more drastic measures."

"You mean assassinated?" asked the PM not sure he was reading him right.

"Let's just say I wouldn't be flying anywhere or staying in any place with more than one story," said the president in a non-committal tone.

The PM, not sure if the president was joking, said, "Well, given how successful your CIA was in assassinating Fidel Castro, the result might be a long time coming."

The president grunted, laughed, then said, "Don't worry; I'll send a Mossad agent!"

The PM hung up, ran his hand across his face, and called a COBRA meeting of his top advisors. What else could go wrong in one day?

CHAPTER FIFTY-NINE

Present Day —Man on a Mission

MAGGIE WAS IN HER STARK HOLYROOD OFFICE. Although it was far bigger than her first office, she had removed everything except the desk and two chairs when she became the first minister and hadn't gotten around to the task of decorating yet. Joan, Maggie's secretary, came on the phone. "There is a man here to see you. He doesn't have an appointment. He says he's from Thames House."

"Send him in," she said, curiosity in her voice.

At six-foot tall, with square jaw, piercing blue eyes, and short-cropped blond hair, he was handsome, looking more Swedish or Californian than English. With looks like that, he should have been on a movie set, Maggie thought. His suit was a custom-fitted Savile Row type. She looked him up and down as he stood in front of her desk. She was hit with the smell of his cologne—Polo.

"Good morning, Mr. Bond," she said playfully. "My husband used to wear that cologne."

"I know," he said.

"Of course you do. You're from MI5."

He nodded. "Haversham, Major John Haversham, ma'am. The director general sent me to give you a full briefing on the situation, one you should have had a long time ago, I suspect."

He put out his hand. She took it and shook it firmly. He had large, soft hands, unusual for a military man, for she could tell by his body language he was military even without his title.

"Well, Major Haversham? To what do I owe the pleasure?"

His face twitched into half a smile at the compliment. "I'll get straight to the point. There has been a data breach at MI5. Certain…." He hesitated. "Certain *information* has found its way online. No doubt it will be front-page news tomorrow. We wanted to get ahead of it and fill you in before it comes to you secondhand and without any context."

Maggie raised an eyebrow. "What kind of—" she paused "—information?"

Haversham cleared his throat. "In 1984, during the miners' strike, after the Battle of Orgreave in June of that year, foreign money from Libya and the Soviet Union poured into the striking miners' fund. The money was for the miners' relief fund, but much of it found its way into the pockets of the Union executives. At the same time, the Soviets, in particular, wanted to encourage civil unrest. A decision was made to sanction a change of leadership in the NUM."

"Arthur Scargill?" she asked with a tilt of her head. All of a sudden, she had a cold feeling in her stomach. "Let me get this straight. You are telling me there was a government-sanctioned plot to undemocratically remove a union leader?"

"Quite."

"And you would remove him how?"

"No comment."

Maggie frowned. She found it incredible she was having this conversation. "By *force majeure*?"

Haversham turned his clear blue eyes on her. "The government feared more riots and a complete breakdown of law and order. There had been several deaths, hundreds of injuries, and more than 11,000 people had been arrested. The strain on the police force was overwhelming, and contingency plans were in place to bring in the army. Not to mention the tremendous financial cost and psychological strain to the entire country."

"So you decided to 'remove' Arthur Scargill," Maggie interjected. "Obviously he lived a long life, so what went wrong?"

"We believe a KGB double agent tipped off someone in the Miners' Union. The plan never came to fruition."

"Why are you telling me this?" Maggie said with a growing sense of alarm. She felt a trail of ice run through her. "Has this got something to do with my father?"

"I'm sorry to say that we believe the same KGB agent killed your father, although we have no physical proof. His car was found at a port twenty miles from where it happened, and he disappeared on the same night as your father's death. That same day, he was due to undertake a certain matter for us, which he did not do. Of course, we had no inkling he was KGB at the time."

"My father, a Union representative, was killed by the KGB?" Maggie said. "It doesn't add up."

Haversham smiled. "Unfortunately, it does. We believe your father really did want the best for the miners. He knew the Union leadership was rife with endemic corruption. He also knew the aims of the foreign governments were not to help the miners but to tear down the fabric of British society. A society he wished to preserve. It could have been coincidence, but I don't believe in coincidence. And I can tell you categorically it was not MI5 or Westminster that killed your father, as went some of the rumors at the time."

"Why would they kill him?" Maggie felt suddenly like a small, frightened girl again. "Why?"

"The Soviets were funding the strike, and the KGB had several agents in the Union. Your father had uncovered rampant corruption in the Union and was on his way to deliver a file on the matter it to a newspaper reporter. That file would have destroyed the Union's power overnight; their leaders had played the working men for fools."

"And why tell me now?" Maggie asked. "Why not forty years ago?"

"Official Secrets Act, and you were only eleven at the time."

"So you lied about it. You lied and covered up and frustrated the police investigation."

Haversham kept a poker face. "Comes with the territory, ma'am."

Maggie stared at the man; his arrogance was astounding. Inside, she was awash with conflicting emotions. She gripped the edge of her desk. "Can you prove it?" she said.

Haversham brought his hands together and interlocked his fingers for a moment before he spoke.

"I do not have proof that the KGB killed your father. But we know he was frustrated after a particularly fractious meeting at the NUM headquarters. He was smart enough to realize that it was beyond simple corruption, beyond the reach of the local police. Russian involvement was a matter of national security, you see. He saw where the strike was heading and where the money was going and, more importantly to him, not going, and he wanted to do the right thing. That and the fact that he knew the Soviets were ultimately out to destroy the fabric of British life. They had no interest in the miners."

Maggie stared at Haversham's face. Behind the handsome façade was a ruthless mind.

"That's not all, is it?" she said. "I mean, you didn't come all this way to tell me this in person without wanting something from me, did you?" "The feeling among our allies is you have grossly underestimated the Chinese desire for world domination and our determination to stop them. That little stunt you pulled in Zurich got the Americans' attention and ours. You must not lease Prestwick to the Chinese; the nuclear subs must stay on the Clyde. There is not a better deep-water location suitable for rapid deployment with support systems in place. It is hoped that now you know the truth about your father, you will see things with a more global perspective." "Have you come to threaten me? Am I to meet my father's fate too?"

Haversham smiled. "Not to threaten. To protect. More precisely, to protect you from China. It is cold out there, Ms. McGown. Very cold outside the protection of NATO and her allies. It will never be in your best interests to get into bed with a killer. And make no mistake, China is no better than the Soviet Union, only it's service with a smile. China is on a mission to become the world's dominant superpower, by any means necessary. And I mean *any*. Neither Whitehall nor the

Pentagon will allow the Chinese to take control of military installations on the British Isles."

Maggie stood up suddenly behind her desk, scraping back the chair. "Are you suggesting, Major, that a change of leadership in Scotland has already been 'sanctioned'?"

"No comment," he said. "No Comment," repeated Maggie "Next you'll be pleading the fifth like your American puppet masters will you?"

"I'm sure it won't come to that but Panama, Granada, Iraq, Afghanistan, why would this come as a shock to you? If you don't play nice, there are always consequences. Just look at our own Falkland War. We sent troops halfway across the world to retake an island home to more penguins than people," said Haversham.

Maggie stared at those blue eyes. They were like sunshine on the arctic; they looked inviting, but they were cold and would drag you pitilessly down. She shook herself. Focused on the present crisis.

"Here's the deal," she said. "In order for me to renege on the agreement with the Chinese, I need a better offer. I need funding for infrastructure, I need jobs, and I need some trade deals pronto. Not in five or ten years when the lackeys in the corridors of power finally get around to it."

Haversham smiled again and put his hands in his pockets. "I'm sure we can come to a suitable arrangement. The general principle has already been agreed."

Maggie fixed her eyes on him. "Alright," she said, surprised by the easy victory. "What are the next steps?"

"Our people will be in touch to confirm the details and liaise with Washington on your behalf." He gave her a little bow. "I think we understand each other. Good day, and thank you for your time, ma'am."

As he turned to go, Maggie snorted out a laugh. "You're a cold bastard," she said.

Haversham turned. "I've been called worse. I shall take it as a compliment from you."

But Maggie still had one thing on her mind. "For all this to work, there's one thing you must do. You have to prove that Westminster was not involved in my father's death. Prove it, beyond doubt, and you'll have yourself a deal."

Haversham put his head to one side. "Westminster was *involved*, but certainly not in your father's death." He took out a plastic-coated security pass from his pocket. It was dated. Very dated. Tinged off white and at least forty years old. He slid it across the desk. It had a headshot of her father on it. And an address: 142 Grower Street, London W2.

"What's this?" she said. "Where did you get this?"

"It was your father's building pass. That's our old address. Don't you see? He was one of us. Your father, George McDonald, was working for MI5."

CHAPTER SIXTY

Present Day–Retreat to the Highlands

After her birth parents' death, Maggie thought about them daily but didn't talk about them; it brought back too many painful memories. After a couple of months, she had settled into her new family and buried herself in books as her father had done in his free time. Her new family was kind, and it was not long before she referred to them as ma and pa, just like the girls on *Little House on the Prairie* did on television. Not mum and dad or mother and father. She already had one of those, but Ma and Pa. Out of respect for her new parents and to kill the pain of her loss, she was mentally strong enough to compartmentalize the previous eleven years of her life into one box and start a new life with them. She had done the same again after Robbie's death. Strangely, this ability to compartmentalize her life was a great talent, even if it was one she wished she had never had to use. Now she would have to do it again.

Maggie had spent the next two hours after Haversham left thinking about how her hatred and faulty narrative had backed her into a dangerous corner, and it had all been for naught. Her father had worked for MI5 and had probably been killed by the KGB; she was incredulous but thought and suspected it all to be true. Didn't people always say the truth was stranger than fiction?

Finally, she called the US president. It was a tense twenty minutes until he could take the call.

"Good evening."

"Good afternoon to you, President Anderson," replied Maggie as pleasantly as she could make herself.

"I trust you now realize what's at stake here?" asked the president solemnly.

There was silence for a few moments.

"I'd be giving up millions of dollars in infrastructure investment if I turn down the Chinese, not to mention thousands of jobs. That might not mean much to a wealthy country like America, but it means a lot to a small country like Scotland," said Maggie.

"We'd be happy to up our game, rebuild the airport for you, increase our military spending there, and get some US operators to commit to regular flights there," said the president.

"Okay," said Maggie. That was better than she expected; she silently punched the air with her fist.

"Airports are cheaper than aircraft carriers," he added.

"What about using your influence to get us back in the EU?" Maggie asked.

"My influence there is limited, but we can put some pressure on them based on what we are calling the Scottish Security Pack, which will benefit NATO. You will have to be patient, three to five years minimum. And you will also have to adopt the euro and be reasonable in meeting their tax expectations, but it will get done."

Not what she had in mind, thought Maggie, but what alternative did she have?

"Best of all," said the president, "I am going to pressure my people to fast forward a trade deal worth millions to the Scottish economy."

That sounded better, and once Maggie gave the commitments necessary, the call ended quickly.

Next, Maggie called the PM; it was a tense call, but he was able to put on the famous rogue charm he exuded, and the call ended cordially enough, given the circumstances.

Then she called the Chinese ambassador and told him with deep and respectful regret that the deal was off. The outside pressures from London, Brussels, and Washington were just too significant. He was very unhappy, and she knew without him saying anything that the ramifications of that decision would affect all their other investments in Scotland. It was a heavy blow for Maggie and the country, made somewhat softer by the US concessions.

At noon that day, Maggie made the shock announcement on BBC Scotland. "I have an announcement that will disappoint some and excite others. Effective immediately, I am resigning as first minister." There was a collective gasp from the reporters in the media room.

Maggie waited for silence and continued. She could not say that she could not live with the thought of taking orders from the English-backed Americans. She had been bluffing about leasing the airport to the Chinese and taking their billions in investments, but she was not bluffing about removing the nuclear subs. That had been on the SNP agenda for decades and she was ready to finally deliver. It was not that she was against them in principle it was the fact that they never kept any of them in England, making Scotland a first strike target. Now Scotland was no longer part of the UK she had been even more determined to get them off Scottish soil. So, instead, she had invented an unspecified health crisis.

"I must take care of a recently diagnosed health problem at once, for I value my health over everything.

"I feel I have accomplished a great deal in my eighteen months at the helm. Scotland is already on the path to a more prosperous economic future.

"I am glad to tell you that we have had a better offer from the USA regarding the future of Prestwick Airport. In a call with President Anderson today, he also assured me that he would fast-track a new and lucrative trade deal worth millions to Scottish-based industries.

"As for getting rid of the Trident submarine base, which the SNP has promised for decades, I have decided that Scotland had better keep the subs in the Clyde. Just in case the English ever try to invade."

There was spontaneous laughter in the room. *If they only knew*, thought Maggie.

"On top of this, the US is adding a boatload of money to the sovereign wealth fund because of the decision, which will benefit all Scots.

"I made the very capable Abby St. Clair deputy first minister an hour ago, which means she will automatically take over as the next first minister."

She was young and talented and could always count on Maggie's support. She would mentor her behind the scenes to make sure none of Maggie's hard work went to waste.

Maggie would retire to her Highland castle out of public view for a while. She had always loved the Highlands. She would hike, golf, write her memoirs, and find some charity to champion. She would have loved to have finished the job she started, but the fight was gone, whooshed out of her like a burst balloon with the truth of her father's death. Whitehall was not and never had been the enemy she thought they were; it had been her motivation and now it was gone.

On the plus side, something else was gone that she didn't even realize had been there. The tremendous weight on her shoulders. The anger, hatred, and emotional drain of the narrative she had chosen to believe about her father. It was so liberating to let it all go.

Her father had done the right thing for his Union and his country. She had tried to do the same. She went downstairs to the oversized garage, walking past the Mercedes GT and Ferrari Roma, they were Robbie's of course; he loved his cars. She opted instead for the perfectly restored 1969 Beetle with a blue and white stripe down the center and a number 53 on the bonnet just like in the movie *The Love Bug*. Robbie had bought it for her as a birthday gift.

CHAPTER SIXTY-ONE

Present Day–Confession

Tom Brodie opened the wrought-iron gate and walked slowly down the short gravel path, boarded by a well-kept rose garden on either side, his feet crunching the gravel with each heavy step. He knocked loudly on the small, whitewashed cottage door with a grey slate roof and bright red door that served as the rectory for St. Mary's Catholic Church, coughing hoarsely as he did. Brodie was not a healthy man; his once large frame was now all skin and bone, the flesh loose and colorless, his eyes dead, set well back in their sockets.

Father Innes, the long-serving priest, came to the door. He was a short man in his seventies with a friendly round face, steel-rimmed glasses, a nearly bald head, and a surprised look on his face.

"It's been a long time since we have seen you at Mass, Tom," he said in his soft Irish brogue.

"Aye, Father, it is nigh on forty years, I should guess," said Tom.

"So, to what do I owe the pleasure?" asked Father Innes curiously.

"Well, since I'm about to meet my maker, there are a few things I need to get off my chest other than the cancer that is killing me," said Tom in a hoarse and serious whisper.

"But you must always have hope," said Father Innes in a soothing tone honed by years of practice with such matters.

"Cancer of the lungs, twenty-five years down the pits breathing soot and a pack-a-day habit of John Player Specials likely didn't help. I've got three to six months at most, and I want to come clean. It's been a weight on my shoulders for forty years that's only got worse the older I've got," he said flatly, his voice back to normal.

"Do you want to go to the confessional?" asked Father Innes.

"No, Father, what I have to say I can say right here or in your kitchen," said Tom.

"Well, come into the sitting room and I'll have Mrs. Granger make us some tea," said Father Innes kindly.

They sat adjacent to each other in two large leather armchairs with a small table in between for tea. They made small talk for five minutes until Mrs. Granger, Father Innes's part-time helper, appeared with the tea and biscuits. "Well, it's certainly nice to see you here, Tom," she said with a smile; without waiting for a reply, she nodded politely at both men and left.

There was a moment of silence, and then Tom came out with it. "Father, I killed a man."

The priest looked at Tom with grave concern and encouraged him to continue. "Go on...."

"It was almost forty years ago on the Dalry Road, hit him head-on with a MAN truck loaded full of coal."

"Were you drunk?" asked the priest.

"No, Father, sober as a judge," replied Tom earnestly.

"Well, it was an accident then," suggested the priest.

"No, Father, it was not an accident. I was paid a thousand pounds to do it," said Tom.

The priest frowned, not believing what he was being told. He had known this man since he was a boy. "Was there not an investigation?" he asked, trying to make some sense of what he was being told.

"No, the truck was driven to an industrial estate in Irvine. There was surprisingly little damage to the truck; the bumper and front light were replaced the same day and it was repainted a different color. The police classified it as a hit-and-run.

But if I had stuck around, I was to say a deer jumped in front of the car and it swerved head-on into the truck's path. There was nothing I could do to avoid it. You know, it all happened so fast. But I was a coward, Father; after crushing the car, I just lost my nerve and ran. It's a remote road, as you know. There was no one around."

"Who was the man?" asked the priest cautiously now, with a flicker of understanding crossing his eyes.

"George McDonald," said Brodie.

"Ah," said the priest; that was a name he recognized. It was national news at the time. "He was a big man in the Miners' Union, right?"

"Aye, he was a rising star," agreed Brodie. "A lot of people thought he would replace Scargill. The union paid me to do it."

The priest raised a worried eyebrow. "The Union," he said incredulously.

"You have to understand," said Tom in a pleading tone, now close to tears. "My whole family was starving. We had been on strike for months. We had no food, no money, and only the occasional handout from the Union—five quid here, five quid there, and a free meal if we were on the picket line.

"Also, I was a young Union radical, practically a communist, I had drunk the Union's poison; the ends justified the means, and I was desperate. They told me the man they wanted dead was a scab, a spy. I never knew who he was. They never gave me a name. They said he talked a good game but, in reality, got paid by Westminster. They said he worked for MI5 and had infiltrated the Union to destroy it. Back then, the Union was all we had, and I was daft enough to believe them."

"Why on earth would someone in the Union want him killed in the middle of the miners' strike?" asked the priest.

"He knew too much," said Brodie. "The scale of the corruption McDonald was trying to uncover came out years later, but what could I do by then? I had committed murder; I couldn't come forward without spending the rest of my life in jail. As sorry as I was, I was not willing to do that."

Finally, Brodie said, "Father, his family deserves to know the truth. I've documented my part along with a couple of Polaroid pictures I took of the crash. It also includes a rather long letter explaining my profound remorse. I'm too old and sick to go to jail, but when I pass, I was hoping you could give this envelope to Angus Frasier, formerly of the *Daily Record*; he'll know what to do with it. Will you promise you will do that?" pleaded Brodie.

"Yes," said the priest. "But why him?"

Tom got up to leave.

"Wait," said the priest. "Don't you want absolution?"

"No, Father, I do not. I'll see myself out, Father." And with that, he got up and quickly left.

Father Innes went to the liquor cabinet and poured himself a large Scotch. It was not even three o'clock. He went to his bookcase built on top of a set of four drawers, placed the envelope in the top left drawer, and closed it. Maybe it was time to think about retiring.

CHAPTER SIXTY-TWO

Present Day–A Message from the Grave

WHEN A MAN SETS HIS MIND TO DIE, NATURE RARELY prolongs his fate. Tom Brodie died three months later. Father Innes presided over his funeral, a small affair with a dozen people. He had divorced at some point and was estranged from his family, with just a few old guys from the local pub to see him off. He left all his worldly goods, including his house and car, to benefit the local orphanage. His final act of penance guessed Innes.

Angus Frasier was surprised when he got a message from a priest requesting a meeting who said he'd found him on Facebook with the help of an altar boy. Frasier had agreed, and two days later, he watched from the window of his small, well-kept, two-bedroomed bungalow in Largs. Its stone window frames and front door were painted a glossy black. A man Frasier assumed was a parishioner pulled up in a white Toyota, and the priest got out.

Frasier was now in his late seventies but was enjoying good health. He welcomed the priest at the door and invited him into a tiny hallway and the adjoining sitting room. Frasier sat down and beckoned Father Innes to sit in the large leather armchair beside him.

"It's a rather delicate situation," Father Innes said as he handed Frasier a large manila envelope, which, despite his curiosity, had remained sealed since Brodie had given it to him. Frasier looked at it carefully, reached for his folding glasses on the coffee table, and slowly opened it.

"Father, you'll forgive me for my poor manners. There is a fair amount of reading here. Would you like to help yourself to a drink? I could use a wee dram myself." Frasier pointed at a small hardwood liquor cabinet in the corner of the room.

"Yes, of course," said the priest, who got back up and opened it to see it contained three bottles of whisky from different Highland distilleries.

"Any is fine," said Frasier in his thick Glasgow accent. "But I think you'd better make it a double."

It took Frasier a little less than ten minutes to read through the file, and he did so without speaking. The document had been typed double-spaced for easy reading and notation. The bulk of it described the dire living conditions of Brodie's family nearly ten months into the miners' strike. Then there was a confession that he was paid to kill McDonald, along with a brief description of the accident and two Polaroid pictures of the wrecked car. Frasier winced when he saw them; he had taken a similar photograph once a thousand years ago, or so it seemed. And yet it also seemed like yesterday up on the lonely road.

He continued reading. It was all there. The priest woke with a loud snore, looking around to get his bearings. "Oh, sorry," said the embarrassed clergyman, "I must have dozed off for a little while."

"That's alright, Father. I do the same thing myself these days," said Frasier, pointing at the envelope. "A nasty business this, I remember it well. I followed the story for several years, trying to find out what really happened. It was one of my great unsolved mysteries. I take it you have some idea of the contents, Father?"

"Tom Brodie said he killed a man," said Father Innes. "Said he was paid by someone in the Miners' Union to do it, but beyond that, I don't need to know any of the details."

"There are still a lot of unanswered questions. I'm a little too long in the tooth to be doing all the leg work, but my son Duncan is a reporter, and I'll bet he'll be more than glad to do some digging on a story like this."

"Can anything good come out of it?" asked the priest.

"I don't know, Father, but I suspect it might tie up a lot of loose ends for a lot of people, not least of which the people who deserve to know most," said Frasier thoughtfully, rubbing his chin.

"He had a daughter, must be in her fifties by now. She was ten or eleven when the accident happened. I bet she would want to know the truth. And the detective who handled the case, David McMillan, took a lot of abuse over finding nothing. Many suspected the police washed their hands of the crash too quickly because they were pissed off at the striking miners, but I know McMillan never did."

"I think he's still alive, though many people from that time are gone," said Frasier sadly. "I played golf with McMillan years later and discussed the case. That case haunted the rest of his distinguished career." He got to his feet, signaling the end of the meeting to Father Innes. "He always said that was the one that got away."

CHAPTER SIXTY-THREE

Present Day –Costa Del Crime

Angus Frasier's son Duncan Frasier now worked for an independent news blog based in Carlisle, that focused on climate and environmental issues. At six foot two he was a couple of inches taller than his father, although he shared his father's bright blue eyes and curly black hair although his father's was now white. He stayed fit with mixed martial arts, hiking, and mountain biking plus the occasional game of golf with the old man. Not much happened in Carlisle, so he was excited by his father's call.

The editor of the blog did not have the money or the interest to follow a national murder story like this, so Frasier took a long overdue week's holiday. He had jumped at the chance to follow this story the moment his father called and took off for Scotland at once. He headed for his father's home in Largs first to review the material and his father phoned ahead to set up a meeting with Father Innes the following day.

His father had a personal archive of the events, and he brought out the original newspaper clippings from 1984. There had been interest in the story for several weeks after the crash, but there were no witnesses, and no truck was ever found, so the investigation just petered out.

The next day, Angus Frasier accompanied by Duncan met with the priest in his small cottage. After introductions, the younger Frasier got straight to the point. "Brodie gave a lot of details in his confession and took all the blame himself, yet he says someone paid him? Father Innes, do you recall the name of the man Brodie says hired him to kill McDonald?" he asked excitedly.

"Oh dear, he did mention the name once, I think. But I was so shocked by his story I did not pay much attention; it didn't seem to matter at the time. It was so long ago, and I was focused on Tom. He was struggling to get it all out, and his body was wracked with cancer by then," said the priest.

"Please try, Father," coaxed Duncan.

"It was a very common name. I remember something like Smith, or Jones, or Green."

"Was it Arthur Scargill?" prodded Angus.

"Oh no," he said with a dismissive shake of his head. "Even I would have remembered that; he was on the television every night back then."

"Ever hear the name Collins?" asked the younger Frasier.

"No, I don't think so," Innes said, shaking his head as he looked up as if for divine inspiration.

Duncan reviewed his list. "Was it Windsor?"

"No, I think I would have remembered with the royal association. I try to do that with my parishioners' names: marry the name to something else. It jogs my memory. You know, like Charlie for Chaplin, Dusty for Miller—wait, I think that was it, yes. Is there by any chance a Miller on your list?" asked the priest.

The reporter consulted his list. "Yes," he said excitedly. "Ken Miller, he was the number two in the Miners' Union."

"Well," said the priest, smiling, "That sounds right. I do hope that was helpful."

"Father, for a reporter, it was a godsend." He thanked the priest and they both left at once.

They got in Duncan's SUV and headed for Largs as he speed-dialed the office. "Frank, check if you can find a guy called Ken Miller." Frasier thought if he was still alive, he was most likely still living in Yorkshire. "And find me a recent picture of Tom Brodie deceased."

The office called back five minutes later. "Ah, the wonders of the internet," said Frank.

"We found him, and he is alive and well, or as well as you can be at seventy-eight years old, living on the Costa Del Sol in and around Marbella, where he has been in a large penthouse overlooking the marina in Puerto Banās since 1990. He resigned from the Union and moved there five years after the end of the strike, two days before the *Daily Mirror* newspaper and the *Cook Report* investigative TV show ran a two-part exposé on the missing millions from the miners' support fund."

"What a coincidence," said Frasier.

"Indeed," said the voice on the other end of the line.

"Dad, are you still doing stuff with that amateur theater group?" he asked.

"Aye, I am," he replied.

"Do you think you could pull off a Yorkshire accent?" he inquired.

"Aye, I could indeed. I spent weeks practicing last year when we put on *All Creatures Great and Small*. You know, about that vet in the Yorkshire Dales. Although it might not fool a Yorkshireman."

"Perfect," replied Duncan.

"What have you got in mind, Son?" asked Angus.

"Nothing much, just solving a murder and giving you the biggest scoop of your career," he said with a smile.

"Oh," said his father with a puzzled look, rubbing his chin.

"How do you feel about a little trip to Spain?" asked Duncan.

"When do we leave?" replied his father. "The weather here has been awful."

"First I need to see if we can get the police file, so we have the complete picture for the article," said Duncan. "I've been working on a story that ought to grab the coppers' interest."

CHAPTER SIXTY-FOUR

Present Day – Rochester, Minnesota

It was 7:00 a.m., Detective Jack Thomas sat across the table from Duncan Frasier at a small roadside café off the M8, halfway between Glasgow and Edinburgh, with a look of suspicion on his face.

"What can I do for you, Mr. Frasier?" asked Thomas coolly.

"Well, I'm hoping for a bit of quid pro quo cooperation," said Frasier.

"Go on," said Thomas.

"I need some help pulling some files on a cold case from 1984, and in return, I have an interesting item for you regarding Stephen Mackintosh," said Frasier.

"Macintosh is already convicted and in jail for life, so I don't see what I have to gain. I got my man," said Thomas with a hint of a smile.

"No, Detective, you got a man but not the man," said Frasier emphatically.

Thomas gave him a concerned look then said challengingly, "Are you trying to tell me someone put that crackpot up to it?"

"Perhaps," said Frasier.

"You have proof?" challenged Thomas.

"I have a smoking gun," said Frasier. "The proof is up to you."

Thomas considered this for a moment in silence.

"I want everything you have on a 1984 hit-and-run accident, near West Kilbride," said Frasier.

Thomas thought there could be very little harm in copying a forty-year-old unsolved traffic accident. "Okay, I'll see what I can do," he said.

"You will get me copies of the files?" Frasier asked to confirm.

"Yes," said Thomas.

"Stephen Macintosh had a daughter, Jennifer, his only child. She suffered from a rare form of cancer and was treated at the Mayo Clinic in Rochester, Minnesota, a week before the assassination attempt on Maggie McGown," said Frasier.

"So?" said Thomas.

"What do you know about Green Energy, Detective?" asked Frasier.

"They build wind farms and send SNP ministers' kids to high-end private schools if your newspaper is to be believed," said Thomas.

"And how would you say the relationship might be between the current SNP leadership and the Green Energy bigwigs?" asked Frasier.

"I should think it strained at best. Haven't the Scottish government put a hold on some hundred-million-pound contract or something?" asked Thomas.

"They have," said Frasier.

"I don't see what, if anything, this has to do with Macintosh's daughter," said Thomas dismissively.

"Desperate people do desperate things especially for the ones they love. She flew to Minnesota on one of Green Energy's private jets and I bet you a pint of Tennent's if you look into who paid the hospital bill, which would have been well over one hundred thousand dollars, it wasn't Stephen Macintosh."

Thomas's face drained of color. "And you found this out how?"

"Because I'm a reporter," said Frasier. "I've been looking closely at Green Energy ever since an old crofter died on Skye about two years ago when I worked for the Record."

"Have you indeed," said Thomas.

"Amongst other things I track their private planes on FlightAware. Let me know if I can pick up the file tomorrow, and I'll leave you a short list of other things you might want to check out." He got up and left, leaving Thomas drumming his fingers on the café table, lost in thought. Finally, he grabbed his mobile and dialed Maggie McGown's office asking for an immediate meeting.

CHAPTER SIXTY-FIVE

Present Day –Thomas and McGown

McGown was reached at her home near Inverness, and it took Thomas the best part of four hours to get there. More than a dozen cameras tracked his car's progress from the estate's gates to the doors. One of Maggie's security detail, she had kept them all on, waved a metal detecting wand over Thomas and his ID was checked before he was allowed out of the hall and shown into the study.

"Good afternoon," said Thomas.

"And hello to you, Detective, to what do I owe the pleasure of an emergency meeting?" asked McGown as ushered him from the spacious hall into a well-appointed study surrounded by books. She took a seat behind the large teak desk and he on one of the two high-backed leather chairs in front of it.

"New information has come to light regarding the attempt on your life several months ago and I wanted to tell you in person. I feel you are still in a heightened state of danger," said Thomas briskly.

"Is that so, Detective?" asked McGown with genuine curiosity. "And why would that be, now that I'm not first minister?"

"Look, I don't know. I have not verified any of the details yet, but I have what I believe to be good information that shows a direct connection between your would-be assassin and Green Energy. I understand you blocked a very large contract. Until I verify it one way or another, I'd like to offer you an additional protection detail," said Thomas.

"I think I'm protected well enough. I have my own four specialists, someone with me 24/7," said McGown. "It's like having four James Bonds on my team," she said bravely, although she felt far more vulnerable than she looked. She knew as well as anyone that if they really wanted you dead, there was always a way.

"May I ask where you got this information?" asked McGown.

"Sure, it was a reporter," said Thomas.

"Is he a trusted source?" asked McGown.

"I don't know. I've never met him before. His name is Duncan Frasier," said Thomas.

"Frasier, Duncan Frasier, yes, I've met him," said Maggie. "Quite tall, black hair?"

"Yeah, that's him," said Thomas.

"What did he want in return?" asked McGown. "Reporters always want something."

Thomas hesitated then thought, *What the heck?* It was only an accident decades ago. What harm could it do? "He wanted information on an old car crash."

Maggie froze. She had a bad feeling in the pit of her stomach. It took her several seconds to gain control of her speech before she could manage a weak "How old?"

"I don't know, 1984, I think, he said." Thomas was now concerned from the look on McGown's face. He should have said nothing.

"What is the man's name?" asked McGown, barely able to get the words out and visibly upset.

"McDonald," he said. "Common enough name up here."

"Aye, that it is," she agreed. "But I wouldn't waste your time looking for the file, Detective."

"Oh," he said, somewhat put out. "And why's that?"

"Because the file's not in the police archives anymore," said McGown. "It was the first thing I asked for when I became first minister." She opened the top drawer of her desk and held up a manila file.

Thomas looked at it, confused. "Why?"

Maggie stood up, signaling and end to their meeting, but said nothing.

"Have I done something wrong?" asked Thomas.

"Not at all. You follow up on the lead he gave you on Macintosh, and I'll hand deliver this to Frasier on your behalf if that's okay with you. It's a copy. The original is in a safe."

Thomas stood up, wanting to ask more questions, but McGown cut him off holding up a hand to silence him. "I'd love to find out more about this Green Energy connection, but I have a very pressing engagement I must attend to first." She scribbled down a number on a Post-it note and handed it to him as she walked past him. "Do me a favor and text me Frasier's mobile number. And thank you for driving all the way up here on my account."

Thomas took it and headed to his car.

CHAPTER SIXTY-SIX

Present Day–Spain

Maggie sat alone in the vast sitting room with the phone in her hand waiting in nervous anticipation for Detective Thomas to text her Frasier's mobile phone number. She should have made him give it to her then and there, but she needed rid of him, she didn't have time for his additional questions. That and the fact that she wasn't thinking straight. She thought she had hid it well in front of Thomas, but now she was an emotional wreck. Why was this reporter looking into her father's death over forty years ago? She had to know. The text came as she heard Thomas's car crunch down the gravel driveway. Finally, she felt she might get some closure on her father's death or was that just wishful thinking? It was a death she had kept well hidden from prying public eyes although it had never been far from her thoughts for four long decades. She dialed the number at once. Frasier answered on the second ring. "Hello?"

"Hi, is this Duncan Frasier?" she asked.

"Aye, it is,"

"Maggie McGown, I believe we met once," she said.

"Oh, hello," he said in a friendly tone. "You're right we did. What can I do for you?"

"It's more what we can do for each other," she said.

"Okay," came his reply, obviously curious.

"I want you to help me find whoever killed my father," she said in a rush of words. "I have the police file you asked Detective Thomas for in my possession. I'd like to bring it to you and exchange information."

"I'm not sure I'm following you. George McDonald was your father?"

"Yes, I was adopted."

'Aye, alright then," said Frasier sounding intrigued.

"Where are you?"

"I'm at the old man's place in Largs."

"Text me the address. I'll be there in an hour," said Maggie and hung up.

Maggie's helicopter touched down in a field just outside town, where a black Mercedes waited to take her to Angus Frasier's modest bungalow. The younger Frasier greeted her at the door and they sat in the small lounge, Maggie and Duncan on the small green sofa and Angus in the large leather armchair. Angus handed Maggie a folder of press clippings about the 1984 incident while she, in turn, gave Duncan the police file.

"A man called Tom Brodie has confessed to killing your father," said Angus and he handed Maggie his neatly written letter. She read it quickly, a lump in her throat as she did, memories of her father flashing through her head like a movie reel.

"Where is he?" she demanded angrily. "This man Brodie?"

"He's dead," said Angus, handing her another press clipping, this time a short obituary with a picture of the man from decades before. Maggie glanced at the younger Frasier confused for a moment, there was a definite resemblance.

"So that's it?" asked Maggie, shaking her head in disbelief at the anticlimax.

"No," said Duncan. "We believe the man who ordered the killing may still be alive. In Spain."

"Someone ordered him killed, why?"

"Your father had information that this man had a great deal to lose if it were published. He made sure it wasn't."

"And that man is still alive?"

"Yes, we believe so"

"Who is he?"

"He was a Yorkshire miner, Ken Miller, someone high up in the Union during the strike."

"Then what are we waiting for?" demanded Maggie.

"I wanted to make sure we had all the pieces together for the story," said Duncan. "That's why I asked Thomas for the police file, I wanted to get the facts straight. I wasn't even born when it happened. Also, there is something else you should know about. Your life may still be in danger."

"Thomas told me, and I don't care; right now, this is far more important to me. Let's go to Spain," said Maggie impatiently. "Whoever is after me is unlikely to be looking there."

"I was looking into flights when you called," said Duncan. "There is one early tomorrow out of Manchester into Malaga, nothing out of Glasgow until later in the week."

Maggie took her mobile phone from her handbag. "Max, call NetJets and get me a plane to Malaga, Spain, from Glasgow or Prestwick, whichever can fly first. Three passengers, plus yourself, leaving at once."

Ninety minutes later, Max drove the Mercedes sedan onto the runway and parked twenty yards from the plane, on the far side of the terminal, at Prestwick Airport. They were in the air ten minutes later, the two reporters enjoying their first taste of private flight on a Challenger 350. They all sat together in the small cabin with eight luxurious cream-colored, leather captain's chairs, in two groups of four facing each other. A pilot and a co-pilot sat upfront. The plane took off effortlessly and reached ten thousand feet rapidly whereupon the co-pilot came back to play hostess.

"Well, this beats Ryanair, eh Dad?" said the younger Frasier, toasting his father with a large glass of Scotch.

Maggie sat there pensively lost in thought. It was finally nearly over; would she now finally know the truth? Should she feel happy? Sad? Melancholy? She wasn't sure how she felt, but there was plenty of pent-up anger.

CHAPTER SIXTY-SEVEN

Present Day–Sinatra's

There was a large black SUV waiting for them on the runway on the opposite side from the main terminal in Malaga. Max took the wheel for the forty-minute drive south to Puerto Banās, the glamorous playground of the rich and famous. They checked into two two-bedroomed apartments at the Hotel Benabola, Maggie liked to keep Max close at hand since the assassination attempt. The Frasier's shared the other.

After showering and changing, all four of them dropped their belongings back in the car. Max had insisted they leave the area after meeting Miller as a precaution. He had arranged for them all to stay at small hotel in the hills run by an ex-army buddy. They left the garage and walked a short distance to a small café inland from the harbor, where they ordered four small draft beers.

Maggie looked hard at Duncan Frasier; she had to admit he had more than a passing resemblance to the pictures she had seen of Brodie. He was about the same size, with broad shoulders and had a similar smallish head, he could easily have been his brother, but she was still concerned. Did Angus look like his son when he was that age? She supposed he might have.

"Do you think Miller will fall for it?" asked Maggie. "I mean accepting you as Tom Brodie, Angus?"

"Well, that's what we are all banking on. According to Brodie's confession he came to work for Miller as a driver-cum-minder late in the strike. He'd only worked for him for a few weeks before he got a big payday and vanished. Miller must have met thousands of men during the strike," said Angus. "And it's been forty years so let hope he's not got the memory of an elephant."

"Why do you think he'll admit to anything even if he is guilty?" asked Maggie.

"Because," said Frasier, "I'm guessing he's an arrogant prick who thinks by throwing his money and weight around he can get away with anything."

"Dad will try to provoke him," said Duncan.

"You should be careful," said Max.

"I'll be fine. Duncan will be in the bar just in case," said Angus. "If we find Miller where we think he will be it will be better if you get him away somewhere quiet," said Max, "Go to the Navy bar."

"Aye I was there once many years ago," said Angus with a sly grin.

Maggie paid in cash for the beers, and they all walked a couple of hundred yards to Sinatra's bar in the harbor. They had a good idea from his social media posts that this was where Miller hung out. Maggie and Max grabbed drinks and sat inside watching the bar; it was agreed they would sit this part out, too many cooks in the kitchen. Angus ordered two beers and casually asked the small, bald Spanish bartender juggling cocktails, with a permanent smile and a constant banter, if he knew his "Old friend from Yorkshire, Ken Miller?"

"But of course I know Mr. Miller," came the smiling reply in perfect English. "You will find him here most nights around 8:00 p.m."

Both Frasier's went into the back of the bar, away from the street, and nursed bottles of Heineken while they waited.

"So, this is how the rich live," said Frasier Senior, marveling at the boats in the harbor and the constant stream of super cars that crawled along the harbor front.

At around 7:50, a board-shouldered, pug-faced man with a large beer belly and a decent head of slicked-back silver hair greeted people and slapped others on the back. He was obviously a fixture in the place. "That looks like Miller, Dad, show time," said Duncan as he slipped out of the bar across the street to the harbor wall, looking at the oversized boats while faking a phone call and watching his father from a distance.

Angus waited; patience was something you had to have to be a good reporter. He watched and waited until Miller had downed two beers and a whiskey all in forty-five minutes. Miller then left the crowded open bar at the front and walked inside the glass walled, air-conditioned premises to the bathroom in the back of the building. As he came out of the men's room Frasier walked up to him, hand outstretched. "Mr. Miller, what a surprise so good to see you after all these years."

Miller looked at him, puzzled, then smiled. "Do I know you?"

"Sure, you do. It's Tom Brodie," said Angus.

Miller looked at him and shook his head.

"We did business together," said Angus.

"We did?" said Miller, confused and studying the man intently. "When?" he asked, trying to jog his memory, which naturally was not as good as it used to be.

"November 1984, I did a job for you," said Angus. "I murdered George McDonald for you, do you remember?" said Angus.

The color drained from Miller's face and a glimmer of recognition appeared. A couple of people nearby glanced over at them.

"It's a bit crowded in here for a chat. Do you mind if we go somewhere else?" asked Angus.

Miller hesitated, looked Angus up and down; and Angus knew at once he was sizing him up. He was almost as old as he was, tall but half Miller's weight, and Angus bet Miller still fancied himself strong for his age. *What harm could this old fart do to me?* Or something like that thought Angus.

"Of course, we can stay here if you want. It won't take long," said Angus.

Miller glanced around nervously then said, "Okay, where shall we go?"

"Let's go to the Navy bar. There will be no one in there at this time of night," said Angus. If the Navy bar was anything like it used to be decades ago it would be dead, the place was a morgue until about midnight when half the hookers in Spain suddenly appeared, followed by guys to sample their wares. Angus could tell Miller was unsuccessfully trying to remember Brodie's face. Age took its toll on everyone, he guessed. He could see the wheels turning and could see the confusion on Miller's face. Angus turned and walked slowly away, and Miller trudged after him in silence.

They walked back one street from the port to the seedy second alley and entered the dark Navy bar. It was almost empty; there was a couple in the middle of the bar and one lonely guy sitting at the end nursing a bottle of Heineken. Miller greeted the bartender by name. "Hey Sten, two beers, mate."

Frasier was surprised by this gesture but guessed that Miller thought he might as well be friendly until he found out what he wanted. They took the two pints and went to a table in the farthest corner of the bar. The place smelt of stale beer and industrial-strength disinfectant. Later, it would be a battle between fifty brands of perfume and two dozen men who seemingly washed in cologne.

"So, want's all this about?" asked Miller, still sounding more curious than alarmed.

"You were a Union man, Mr. Miller," said Angus. "What I am here to talk about is fair wages for work done."

"What are you talking about?" asked Miller, his irritation clearly rising.

The lone man at the bar was Duncan who strained to hear what was being said while keeping his back to the two old men in the corner, but he couldn't hear more than the occasional word.

Angus took out his mobile phone, turned it off and placed it on the table in front of him as Miller eyed it suspiciously.

"I'm just curious. What does a hit cost today?" said Angus with no emotion in his voice.

"Puh, you are a prick, but if you must know, about five grand. In fact, it's the only thing that has gone up since the twenties. The price of a hit," Miller said smugly.

"And do you remember what you paid me?" he asked again.

"No, I fucking don't," barked Miller.

"But you do remember paying me, right?" asked Angus.

"What's your fucking game?" snapped Miller.

"I already told you," said Angus calmly. "Fair pay for a fair day's work. I took the risks. You got the reward."

Miller was getting red in his pudgy face, and he was no longer trying to conceal his rising anger.

"You paid me a grand. Does a thousand pounds sound right to you?" asked Angus, unperturbed by Miller's anger on the outside but feeling the butterflies flying in all directions inside.

"Whatever," said Miller with a sigh, obviously eager to end the conversation and return to Sinatra's bar with his buddies. Frasier could also sense Miller was still trying hard to remember precisely what Tom Brodie looked like forty years ago, but thankfully it didn't seem to come to him. So many faces, so much time.…

"Then you shortchanged me," said Angus.

"Are you trying to blackmail me?" said Miller in a harsh whisper, taken aback by this brazen statement.

"Not at all. I just want fair wages for a fair day's work," said Angus. "It looks like you did very well out of the deal."

"How much do you want?" asked Miller cautiously, unsure he was reading this guy right. Something was off with him.

"Five hundred thousand euros," said Angus.

"Fuck you. I paid you a thousand pounds in cash to get rid of that prick McDonald and you are not getting a penny more. That was good money at the time!" snarled Miller, his arrogance at boiling point.

"You told me at the time he was working for MI5; you were right about that, but you were wrong about him wanting to bring down the Union." Miller looked puzzled as Angus continued. "McDonald was a Union man through and through. He just wanted to expose the corruption of you and your mates and do the right thing by the miners. You lied to me. You just wanted him out of the way so you could keep your fingers in the piggy bank," said Angus.

"He was a self-righteous prick who put his nose where it wasn't wanted. I should've killed him sooner than I did. It would have saved us all a lot of trouble," said Miller. "Now fuck off before I have someone break your legs."

"Alright. If you want to play like that," said Angus, picking up his mobile phone.

He got up without saying anything and walked to the lone younger man sitting at the bar with his back to them. He opened his sports coat and handed him a pen. His job was done, and he walked out of the dingy bar into the bright evening light. He kept walking to the opposite end of the port, as far away from Miller as possible. He felt disgusted but vindicated too. Miller was a murderer, even if he didn't do the deed himself.

The man at the bar got up and left behind him. Miller watched them both, trying to figure out what was happening, but the bar was very dark, and his sunglasses only made it worse. He could only see a couple of dark silhouettes, but he knew he didn't like what he saw.

CHAPTER SIXTY-EIGHT

Present Day –The Navy Bar

Once outside the Navy bar, Duncan Frasier uploaded the audio file from the pen to his iPhone and sent it to the cloud for safekeeping. The signal was too weak to do it inside the bar. Mission accomplished, he turned and walked confidently back in. Miller was still fuming in the corner, trying to figure out what was going on. But a Yorkshireman was not going to leave half a pint unfinished. Frasier sat down opposite him uninvited and put a piece of paper on the table.

"Who the fuck are you?" snarled Miller.

"I'm your guardian angel," said Duncan Frasier with a smile.

"Like fuck you are," said Miller.

"Have you ever seen that movie where the sales guy holds up a pen and says, 'How much is this pen worth?'" asked Frasier. "Then he adds all kinds of value into the pen about how it's made and why it's so unique and keeps increasing the price."

"What?" said Miller. "What the fuck are you talking about?"

"Would you like to buy this pen?" asked Duncan Frasier, holding it up for him to see.

"No, I fucking wouldn't," snarled Miller and he narrowed his eyes at this latest unwelcome intrusion into his evening ritual.

"That's a shame because I reckon this pen is worth at least the five hundred thousand euros Mr. Brodie just asked you for, and maybe far more?" said Frasier.

"What is your game, son?" asked Miller, visibly confused and angry.

"You appear to be a wealthy man, Mr. Miller," said Frasier as he pushed the piece of paper forward with an account number and sort code written on it in large, easy-to-read numerals. "I'd like you to put one million pounds into this account tomorrow morning. In return, I'll give you this pen."

"And why would I want your fucking pen?" croaked Miller.

"Because on it is a recording of you admitting to hiring Tom Brodie to kill George McDonald," said Frasier.

Miller looked puzzled. "Are you guys stupid or what? If you use that audio, Tom Brodie is also going to jail. He is the one who killed McDonald, not me."

"Tom Brodie died two weeks ago," said Frasier. "Cancer."

Miller's face changed from a look of aggressive confidence to utter confusion. "Mother fuckers," he said as it clicked.

Duncan could tell that the situation was beginning to sink in, and he could see Miller didn't like it one bit. He was thinking, trying to buy himself time. "You know you can't just wire a million euros into your account and not expect the bank and the Revenue Service to ask all kinds of questions you won't be able to answer," he said.

"It's not going into my account," said Frasier.

"Well, where the hell is it going?" challenged Miller. "You can't send a wire without a name attached to the account; whatever name you put on it, there will be questions. You won't get away with it."

"Oh, I think we will," said Frasier. "The bank account is the Yorkshire Home for Retired Miners. But make the donation anonymous; I wouldn't want you to get any credit you don't deserve.

Better still, donate it in the memory of George McDonald."

Miller's eyes opened wide in disbelief. "You are not taking the money for yourself?"

"Not everyone is a crook like you," said Frasier.

"How do I know you won't copy the recording and try to get more money from me?" snarled Miller.

"What? Don't you believe in honor among thieves?"

Miller grunted.

"You'll just have to trust me, and I hope that thought keeps you awake for many years to come," said Frasier. "I'll see you back here at 8:00 p.m. in forty-eight hours to allow time for the money to clear and give you the pen." With that, Frasier got up quickly and made for the door, holding the pen high in his right hand as he walked away. He could feel Miller's eyes followed it out the door. Frasier knew what a wounded tiger like Miller would be thinking now. He'd be thinking about getting rid of him. Frasier was sure Miller would know enough dodgy Russians, Albanians, or Sicilians in Puerto Banās who would be eager for the job.

The two Frasiers met Maggie and Max back at the underground parking lot beneath the Benbola. Max got behind the wheel and eased the car out of the garage.

"How far of a drive do we have, Max?" asked Maggie.

"Rhonda is an hour away up in the hills, and Joe's little place is quiet and safe."

Maggie noticed Max check several times in his rear view that they were not being followed as he headed north on the motorway. She sat quietly lost in thoughts of long ago, her father at the wheel of a small white car as they drove north up the banks of Loch Lomond. She was at once angry, frustrated, sad and, while she hated to admit it, a little scared and excited by the prospect of confronting Miller herself.

CHAPTER SIXTY-NINE

Present Day–Nicked

Angus and Duncan Frasier sat on the balcony of a small hotel in Rhonda, it was set on a cliff with a magnificent view of the ancient bridge spanning the gorge to their right and the magnificent rolling countryside to their left. They were discussing the story they were both writing.

"I figure we could get at least ten thousand pounds for an exclusive," said Duncan.

"You'll get far more than that if you sell it to the English papers, Son," said his dad.

"I know," he replied, "but like you always say, Dad, it's not always about the money. This story is your legacy as well as mine. Call the *Record* and see what they will give us for an exclusive," said Duncan.

"What about Miller?" asked his father.

"I've contacted Scotland Yard and they are flying men out tonight once they clear it with the Spanish authorities."

"Just be careful, Son, a man like that living on the Costa del Crime for thirty years is bound to have friends you don't want to meet," said Angus.

"That is for sure," he replied.

The money from Miller was not there the next day, but at noon the following day, the Yorkshire Miners' Home called Frasier as requested, confirming that the generous donation had been received. This part he had left out of the article and in his discussions with Scotland Yard.

The two men from Scotland Yard and a Spanish officer met him at a small café a couple of streets back from the port where all the action was located. The officers wanted to take control from here, but he needed pictures of the arrest for his story, so he refused to reveal the final location until just before he entered the bar. Despite their protests and warnings that he may be in danger, he left them sitting at the café, glancing over his shoulder to ensure they were still there before darting through an ally into the second street from the port. It took him four minutes to reach the front of the Navy bar. Frasier texted them the Navy bar's location, and they confirmed they were exactly four minutes away at a brisk walk, half that if they ran; it was all the time he would need. Max and Maggie were already waiting there for him when he arrived.

Frasier entered the Navy bar, followed by Maggie and Max, allowing time for their eyes to adjust to the darkness before moving forward. Maggie wore a big floppy hat and square sunglasses making her unrecognizable. Miller was sitting at the back, where they had met before, with two local strong men seated on either side of him. One had a shock of curly hair and a thick black beard that made Miller think of a pirate; the other was tall and gaunt with a scar across his face and a look of evil in his eyes. Frasier glanced at the bar and noticed no one behind it, reasoning the bartender must have been told to disappear. Then he looked back at the three men. "I don't remember inviting anyone else to our party," he said good-naturedly but standing ten feet back from the table and feeling far more nervous than he sounded.

"Who the fuck are you pair?" asked Miller aggressively, pointing at Maggie and Max. "And where is the fucking pen?"

"It's right here," said Maggie, holding it up. Miller was obviously confused.

Frasier stepped to the side so Maggie could stand directly in front of Miller and took out his iPhone slowly as if he was about to perform a magic trick.

Maggie stared at him, a whirlwind of emotions coursing through her veins. Now fifty years old she stood face-to-face with the man who had shattered her world when she was just a child of ten. Decades had passed, yet the weight of that loss had not diminished. As she gazed into the eyes of the one responsible for her father's untimely demise, a storm of emotions churned within her. Anger, a silent ember that had smoldered through the years, blazed into an inferno. The grief, long suppressed but never forgotten, clawed at the edges of her composure. She could almost feel the echoes of her younger self, that innocent girl forever changed by the tragedy.

"I don't get it; why the fuck do any of you care about some dead fucking miner forty years ago?" asked Miller as Maggie moved the pen back and forward in front of her face as if trying to hypnotize the three men in front of her. All three men were watching the pen intently, their eyes moving ever so slightly from side to side.

"Because he was my father," said Maggie. "And I hope you rot in hell."

The color drained from Miller's face.

Suddenly, Maggie snapped and sent the pen flying at Miller's face, Frasier videoing his shocked reaction with his iPhone. Miller batted the pen away from his face with a swipe of his right hand. It slid across the wooden floor into the corner of the room, hitting the wall and stopping.

"Get that," Miller hissed to one of the men by his side. "And you," he said, pointing at the other, "make sure these sorry sons of bitches never see the light of day again."

Instead, the light of day suddenly filled the room as two men burst into the bar panting. *They were fast,* thought Frasier. "Scotland Yard," said one.

"Ken Miller, you are under arrest for the murder of George McDonald," said the uniformed Spanish policeman in passable English.

The two bodyguards looked at Miller, unsure what to do; there was a brief Mexican standoff where nobody moved, each sizing up the others. But the question was quickly answered as armed Spanish police swarmed the room behind the yard men. Frasier just stood back and got it all on camera, especially when the yard boys put the cuffs on Miller as he snarled at the three of them with primal hatred.

After brief statements to the police the three of them joined Angus at a tapas restaurant near the airport. Miller had donated one million pounds to the miners' home and would most likely die in an English jail, not in his sunny penthouse apartment in Spain. It did not make up for the life of George McDonald, but at least it was something thought Maggie. She was drained, mentally, emotionally, and physically. Somehow it felt like her father had died all over again. She sipped her wine but didn't really taste it.

The *Daily Record* promised the Frasiers' story would be front-page news the next day, the scoop of a lifetime. And for the first time in his life, TV crews and reporters were waiting for him outside his home in Largs. This was his fifteen minutes of fame, and he would milk it as long as he could.

CHAPTER SEVENTY

Present Day
–The Albanian

DETECTIVE THOMAS HAD RECEIVED AN EMAIL FROM Duncan Frasier the evening they had met suggesting he view CTV footage of the bridge leaving the Isle of Skye the night of an old crofter's death. It was a death Thomas had to research, which had been ruled a misadventure, but which Frazier was convinced was connected to Green Energy. Frazier suggested Thomas look for a large SUV, possibly with foreign number plates, witnessed by an unnamed man, perhaps an illegal. Frasier also provided details of the plane flight to Minnesota and a passenger list, although Thomas had yet to learn how he had come up with the latter.

It took 48 hours, but his team found a large SUV and tracked it to a ferry crossing from Newcastle to Amsterdam. Early the following day, Thomas called Interpol and explained that two years ago, an old crofter in Scotland had died after refusing to sell his land to Green Energy. A witness had seen a vehicle near the scene, and Thomas asked for help tracing the SUV.

In the meantime, Maggie McGown and Duncan Frasier were front page news, solving a forty-year-old mystery case in Spain, giving further credence to Frasier's tips.

Thomas had a mystery of his own to solve. He got a call from the Dutch police two days from detective Peter Van Pelt.

"Detective Thomas, we have found the SUV and the two men driving it on the night of the ferry crossing. They are both already known to Dutch police."

"That's quick work, detective. What did they say?" asked Thomas.

They say they were sightseeing in Scotland and had never seen the old man," said Van Pelt

"And do you believe them?" asked Thomas.

"Not for a minute. When I suggested that we had DNA evidence to put the old man in the back of their vehicle, their story quickly changed," said Van Pelt.

"But you don't have DNA evidence," protested Thomas.

"They don't know that; perhaps we can still get it if we need it," said Van Pelt.

"So, then what did they say?" asked Thomas.

"They said they had been taking pictures when the old man came along the cliff with a bottle of whisky and offered them a drink. He sat in the cargo space, and they had a couple of rounds in paper cups and left," said Van Pelt. "They suggested the whisky might have clouded their earlier memory."

"Still not enough evidence to get a conviction," said Thomas.

"No," said van Pelt, "I have let them go. I have nothing to keep them, but my men are watching them, and they are not so bright."

"Oh?" said Thomas.

"They left the station in a cab and went straight to Green Energy's headquarters," said Van Pelt.

"Thank you," said Thomas and hung up. All circumstantial, no case, but he was sure Frasier had been right of that.

His next stop was to re-interview Stephen Macintosh, and he set up a meeting for the following day, doubting he would get much from him even with knowledge of his daughter's cancer treatment. That door opened wide on his way to the jail the following day with a call on his mobile from a man he did not know at MI5.

"Good morning, detective. This is Major Haversham MI5. I have something interesting for you passed onto me by a colleague in Langley, Virginia."

"CIA?" asked Thomas.

"Indeed, it seems that a man called Harold Janssen tried to hire an aircraft mechanic in Inverness to sabotage Maggie McGown's private helicopter."

"Is that so?" said Thomas.

"Yes, only the man he tried to hire is a CIA operative put there to look out for Ms. McGown," said Haversham.

"Really?" said Thomas.

"Their words, not mine. Anyway, he took a fifty thousand Euro deposit from a bagman and captured it on film. He then subdued the man and called us. Our people interrogated him as a matter of national security. The bagman did not know who had hired him, but we traced calls he had made from his burner phone to a burner phone belonging to Harold Janssen. Janssen was waiting for the job to be done before getting rid of it."

"You guys can trace burner phones?" asked Thomas, a note of envy in his voice.

"I'll expect you and your boys will want to have a chat with Janssen. The evidence will be in your inbox shortly, but I wouldn't bother waiting for it to arrive. It's a rock-solid case. Good day." The line went dead.

It would take Thomas two hours to get to Aberdeen; he called the jail and canceled his interview request. It was always better to be polite. Then he called police headquarters in Aberdeen and asked for a team of officers to be ready to assist on his arrival, for a major arrest, while being evasive about the nature of the target pending incoming evidence.

Five police cars arrived at Green Energy headquarters, and officers poured into the building in front of astonished staff. Thomas and his local counterpart took the lift to the second floor, other officers took the emergency stairs, and others stayed on the ground floor. Janssen was at his desk when the two detectives and two supporting officers entered his office. He wore a look of total disbelief. "What on earth do you think you are doing?" he yelled as the officers advanced; he was grabbed by the arms and cuffed.

When Maggie returned to her estate, there was a message from Detective Thomas that told her to call him urgently. She did.

"I assume you know Harold Janssen?" asked the detective.

"I do."

"He's just been arrested for hiring someone to kill you and possibly the murder of an old crofter on Skye."

"Wow, that's interesting. How did all this come about, ace detective work?"

"That's right, only it wasn't mine. Your friend Duncan Frasier did most of the work."

"Go on."

"And a Major Haversham also offered us some help." Thomas patiently explained what had transpired while Maggie listened in silence.

"Wow, you have been a busy boy. Good work, detective."

"As I said, most of the credit goes to Duncan Frasier; The pair of you can't seem to keep out of the news. I think there might be a movie in all of this caper."

Maggie laughed.

"It's none of my business, of course, but what will you do now?" asked Thomas.

Maggie did not reply at once and then spoke slowly as if thinking it through as she spoke. "I'm going to take some me time to digest everything that has happened. I will mentor Abby St. Clair and help her however I can. And then we will see.

CHAPTER SEVENTY-ONE

Present Day–Nardini's

MAGGIE LET A COUPLE OF DAYS PASS FOR THE MEDIA frenzy to die down, although they were still camped out outside her estate hoping for a glimpse; then she called Duncan Frasier. "Duncan, I wonder if I might set up a meeting with you and your father."

"Yes, of course," said Frasier. "When?"

"How about tomorrow at say 11:00 a.m.?" "Sure. Where?"

"Do you know Nardini's Café?" she asked him.

"Everyone knows Nardini's. I've been going there for treats since I was old enough to remember," said Duncan with a laugh.

"We will see you there then."

A black Mercedes sedan waited for her at the landing spot just north of town and whisked her to Largs' most famous landmark, Nardini's Café. She had been here once with her father and mother on one of their weekend trips in the Bug. The memories came flooding back, distant yet vivid.

Frasiers young and old were sitting near the back, facing the door. It was all Maggie could do to stop herself from running to meet them. She was at the booth in twenty large paces, shook hands, and sat opposite the men; they ordered two coffees and a cappuccino while Max took up position a couple of tables away.

"Wow," she said. "I don't know where to start."

"The beginning is usually the best place," said the older Frasier with a kind smile.

"Well, I have a proposition for you, but first I was wondering. Why did you publish it in the *Daily Record*? Indeed, a scoop like this would have gotten you far more money in London from the *Mirror* or the *Mail*. Angus had long since retired and you left the paper about the time we first met."

Duncan glanced at his father. "That's true; the *Mirror* offered much more, but it was my father's story and paper. It's a Scottish paper, and like most publications these days, it is struggling to find its place in a digital world. It just didn't seem right to sell it down south. But I kept the TV rights; I think the story would make a great movie or even a mini-series."

"Did you?" Maggie said excitedly. "And how much would you want for those rights?"

"I hadn't really thought about it," said Duncan. "I just thought it was a good story."

"What if I was to offer you and your father a hundred thousand pounds to write the script plus 20% of any money the movie or mini-series makes, and I will fund the production?" she said impulsively.

Both Frasiers looked at each other in disbelief.

"This is a big story, and the public has a right to know. Plus of course I want to honor my father's legacy, and, as it happens, I don't have a job right now, so I can help in any way I can, production assistant maybe!" said Maggie as she got up. "There is one more thing I want. I want you to finish the story on Union corruption you were going to write from my father's information, update it with whatever else you can find, and publish it. Think about it; I need a quick break."

She walked to the bathroom, chatting briefly with the waitress. The two Frasiers talked in a low voice, but there was not much to say. They knew a lifetime opportunity when they saw it. Maggie returned, sat down, and smiled expectantly at the two men. The waitress appeared with three knickerbocker glories, bringing smiles all around, and they shook on the deal. "Can I bring David McMillan in as a consultant on the project? He was the detective in the case," asked the elder Frasier.

"Angus, you can bring in anyone you want!" said Maggie.

AFTERWORD

Where Did All the Money Go?

BY ANGUS AND DUNCAN FRASIER

L ANARKSHIRE UNION LEADER GEORGE MCDONALD HAS been dead for over forty years, but the questions he asked when he was murdered on his way to see me, Angus Frasier,

at the height of the miners' strike have never been answered.
"Where did all the money go?"

After the 1984 miners' strike, Arthur Scargill was elected to lifetime presidency of the National Union of Miners (NUM) by an overwhelming majority in a controversial election in which some candidates claimed they were given very little time to prepare any challenge to his candidacy. He did not step down from leadership of the NUM until the end of July 2002, when he became the honorary president. It was a presidency marred by controversy, lawsuits, and questionable accounting.

During the 1984 miners' strike, the money came in by mail in five-pound, ten-pound, and twenty-pound donations from ordinary working-class people in the street. They were often accompanied by letters of support. The cash came in suitcases carried by a courier from Libya, fifty thousand plus at a time, in bundles of twenty-pound notes. It came in wires from Russia to secret bank accounts in France, Switzerland, and Poland. The bank accounts were all controlled by one man and his French friend.

The money came from Union leaders' tours of mines in Holland, Germany, France, and many other European countries. The NUM representatives raised thousands of guilders, francs, and marks in cash and brought them back to the UK in brown paper bags, duffel bags, and briefcases. Other industries' unions in the UK donated cash collected from their members. Unions in other countries sent checks or wired money that bounced from bank account to bank account until no one was quite sure where it was.

Shortly after the end of the strike, Scargill moved from a house he had bought before the strike for £25,000 to a 200,000-pound house. The average price of a home at that time was £57,901. There is, of course, nothing wrong with wanting a bigger house, but that was a mighty big jump, especially since he claimed not to be paid during the strike.

In 1993, Scargill tried to use Thatcher's flagship Right to Buy scheme to buy a luxury three-bedroomed flat in Shakespeare Tower on the Barbican Estate in Central London. His application was refused because the flat was not Scargill's primary residence. Former Scargill loyalist Jimmy Kelly said he was astonished to learn of the attempt to buy the flat. "It's so hypocritical it's unreal," he said. "It was Thatcher's legislation, actually giving council tenants the right to buy their own houses. If it had been made public before then, there'd have been a huge outcry. I think people would be astounded if they knew that." Giving further credence to the hypocrisy label, it was a scheme that the political party Scargill founded, the Socialist Labour Party, had sought to abolish.

For years the NUM had been paying £34,000 annual rent for the flat on Scargill's instructions, without the knowledge of NUM members or many senior officials; Scargill claimed the NUM should continue funding his flat for the rest of his life and after that for any widow who survived him. Chris Kitchen, NUM leader at the time, said, "I would say it's time to walk away, Mr. Scargill. You've been found out. The NUM is not your personal bank account and never will be again." Kitchen said that Scargill "has had thirty years of decent living out of the Union, and he's got a pension that's second to none. Had he done the humble thing and walked away with what he was entitled to, his reputation would still be intact.... I've always said that if Arthur can no longer control the NUM, he'll try and destroy it. That's what I believe."

Persistent as ever, Scargill kept trying and, in 2014, bought the property under the scheme for half its estimated value of two million pounds. He claimed he would donate the flat to the Union, but no such thing has ever happened. Chris Kitchen said of Scargill, "There is his public image as a socialist and a trade unionist that Arthur likes to portray, but the reality is he is a capitalist, in that he's all out for himself. And he's done very well out of it. I honestly do believe that Arthur, in his own world, believes that the NUM is here to afford him the lifestyle that he's become accustomed to."

The Union argued that Scargill had unlawfully continued to occupy a rent-free luxury apartment in London, which was initially provided for his use during the miners' strike. The case went to court and, in 2019, a judge ruled against Scargill, ordering him to pay £576,000 in rent and legal costs.

Financial Impropriety

In 1990, the *Daily Mirror* and the Roger Cook investigative TV show accused Scargill of mishandling money donated to the striking miners during the 1984–1985 strike. Many of the sources were those who had previously worked with him in the NUM, such as Kim Howells, Jim Parker, his bodyguard, and Roger Windsor, NUM CEO. It was alleged that, of the money donated from Libya, Scargill took £29,000 for his bridging loan and £25,000 for his home in Yorkshire but gave only £10,000 to the striking Nottinghamshire miners. In addition, it was alleged that he had taken over £1,000,000 of cash donated by the Soviet Union for the Welsh miners and placed it in a Dublin bank account for the "International Miners' Organization," where it stayed until a year after the strike had finished.

There was much criticism of Scargill within the NUM from the Welsh and Scottish areas, who briefly considered splitting from the NUM. Windsor, former chief executive of the NUM, admitted on TV to taking £29,500 to pay off his mortgage. Scargill had given him the money in cash and, according to Windsor, told him to "Regard it as a gift from Libya." These allegations were verified in an audio interview with the *Daily Mail* by Steve Hudson, the NUM's accountant.

The 253-page Gavin Lightman QC report commissioned by the NUM in (1990) exonerated Scargill from taking money to pay off his mortgage as had been alleged by Windsor. However, Lightman concluded that Arthur Scargill had sought political and financial help from the Soviets and the Libyan leader Colonel Gaddafi and that there had been a number of misapplications of funds, including the operation of two separate sets of accounts, one official and the other unofficial, the latter having no supervision or control. This Lightman called a "remarkable breach of duty" and suggested that Scargill should repay the money to the NUM.

The report also charged that Scargill had channeled funds that should have gone to the Union to the international organization he set up in Paris and used it for personal projects. It alleged, for example, that he borrowed $150,000 from the organization five months after the strike to buy a new house, lent money to Heathfield, and paid for house repairs without Union knowledge.

Lightman said that in trying to trace the missing funds, he received no cooperation from the IEMO, which he described as "practically impenetrable." As for Scargill, Lightman added, "I regret it has been my strong impression that Mr. Scargill's story on a number of points has changed as it suits him throughout the conduct of this inquiry."

In July 1990, the NUM executive voted unanimously to sue Scargill and Peter Heathfield, general secretary of the NUM. This action created the unlikely scenario of a union led by Arthur Scargill suing the IEMO, another union led by Arthur Scargill. It was all getting very messy and was about to get more so.

In September 1990, the certification officer brought criminal charges against Scargill and Heathfield for willfully neglecting to perform the Union's duty to keep proper accounting records. Scargill reached an agreement to repay money to the NUM shortly after this. The prosecution brought by the certification officer was rejected in July 1991 on the grounds that it would be inappropriate to use the material provided in confidence to Lightman's inquiry.

In May 2002, the editor of the *Daily Mirror* at the time, Roy Greenslade, one of three reporters involved in the original story, wrote an article in the *Guardian* apologizing to Scargill for the false claims about paying off the mortgage and for putting too much trust in Roger Windsor, who at the time had still not repaid the £29,500 that he had taken from the Miners' Welfare Fund, money that the Lightman Report had asked that he repay. Meanwhile, the two other reporters involved in the article published articles standing by their story.

In 2010, the NUM's current general secretary Chris Kitchen stopped subscription payments of £20,000 a year from the NUM to the IEMO, which had been paid since 1985 and totaled more than £464,000. He had no idea what they were paying for, and no answer was given. In addition, there were questions about a one-off payment of £145,000 to the IEMO shortly before Mr. Scargill retired from the NUM in 2002. The Union's national executive committee was never consulted. Mr. Scargill said the payment was a grant and because an NUM trust fund made it, it did not need to be reported to the Union's national executive committee.

19 July 2019, the High Court ordered the International Energy and Miners Union IEMO (Arthur Scargill and Alan Simon) to pay the NUM the sum of £161,299.29. The Union

is also seeking to recover further sums regarding legal costs and will continue to receive additional future payments from Mr. Windsor.

The whole truth may never be known, but one thing that's sure is that Arthur Scargill became a multimillionaire while miners lost their homes, jobs, and entire industry. Rather than slow down the demise of mining, the disastrous strike helped speed up its end. The actual cost of the strike was far more devastating than the loss of jobs or the eight lives lost. Lifelong friends became lifelong enemies, pitting father against son and brother against brother when one or the other crossed the picket line, desperate for the income to save his home or feed his family. The scars ran deep and the wounds never healed. Whole communities were torn apart. Others died slowly as the mines closed and the men had to move to find employment.

Famed Scottish Union leader Jimmy Reid said, "Arthur Scargill's leadership of the miners' strike has been a disgrace. The price to be paid for his folly will be immense. He will have destroyed the NUM as an effective fighting force within British trade unionism for the next twenty years. If kamikaze pilots were to form their own union, Arthur would be an ideal choice for leader."

The strike's failure helped Thatcher revive the British economy but had significant implications for the future of labor unions and coal mining in Britain. Union membership fell from 40 percent of the nation's workforce to 22 percent. Four decades after 1984, NUM President Kitchen said, "There are many aspects of the strike and its aftermath that have yet to be thrashed out in public. I would have thought that someone who was public enemy number one (Scargill) with MI5 tapping his calls and following him, I'm very surprised he managed to live the life he did and get away with what he did without being pulled up."

There is indeed strong evidence that the government was involved in questionable tactics to undermine Scargill. There is even more evidence that the police used excessive force and trumped-up charges, hundreds of which were later dropped, to subdue Union pickets. With so many conflicting stories and shady characters involved, we will never know where all the money went or how much of it there was. One thing seems clear, however; much of it never went where it should have, to the hard-working miners and their families caught up in a strike not all of them wanted or believed in—led by a former communist, Marxist, and founder of the Socialist Labour Party who became a multimillionaire along the way. Maybe capitalism is not so bad after all, Arthur?

Notes:

UK COAL INDUSTRY

At its peak in 1913, Britain's coal industry employed 1.2 million people at nearly 3,000 collieries. The last deep coal mine in the UK, Kellingley Colliery, in North Yorkshire, was closed December 2015.

The National Union of Miners had 187,000 members in 1984, by 2002 there were only 5,000.

YVONNE FLETCHER

Although sufficient evidence existed to prosecute one of the co-conspirators, no charges were brought as some of the evidence could not be raised in court due to national security concerns. As of 2023 no one had been convicted of Fletcher's murder, although in 2021 the High Court of Justice determined that Gaddafi'sally Saleh Ibrahim Mabrouk was jointly liable for Fletcher's murder.

MI5

MI5 have admitted to tapping Union phone lines and monitoring Arthur Scargill's movements. Interestingly this started during Callaghan's Labour government preceding Thatcher. On June 26 1977, during an unrelated dispute at a London film processing company, a worried Mr. Callaghan told ministers gathered at Chequers—his official country residence—that they were "not dealing with respectable unionism but rent-a-mob and that if things continue on the present basis there could well be fatalities and circumstances which might be in danger of bringing the government down." Mr. Callaghan was particularly concerned about the activities of Mr. Scargill who was organizing thousands of miners to join the pickets. On July 5, he instructed officials, "Keep me informed about Scargill's movements. He may have to be warned off."–*Daily Mail*

ABOUT THE AUTHOR

Born in Oxford, England, and growing up in the Midlands near Shrewsbury, Andrew Wood immigrated to America in 1980 to pursue a career as a professional golfer. Unfortunately, lack of talent held him back, and he accidentally found himself running a small karate school in Southern California. After struggling to survive for 18 months, he decided to focus all his attention on increasing his sales and marketing skills by reading hundreds of books.

His interest in marketing became a passion, and he quickly turned the single school into a national chain of over 400 units. After selling out of in the late '90s, he moved to Florida, where he founded Legendary Marketing, a business designed to combine his passion for golf and travel with his marketing expertise. There he quickly built a name for himself in the golf industry with the early adoption of websites, social media, and email marketing.

Author of over 50 books on a wide range of topics including: Sales, marketing, Leadership, creativity, travel, personal development and fiction. Not bad for a kid who quit school at 15, never graduated from high school, and still can't spell a lick!

For more info visit
www.AndrewWoodInc.com

Contact:
Andrew Wood, Directly @ Andrew@Legendary-Marketing.com

Join him at
www.LifeWellLived.expert

Confessions of a Golf Pro

The story of a golf professional trying to make it through life at a private club with 521 bosses, a cougar nymphomaniac, one good member and a board president intent on his demise.

This story follows the hilarious everyday life of a golf professional through lessons, committees, PGA section meetings, club rules, demo days and golf trips. Plus, the daily grind of trying to please over 500 members who complain to him about everything from the speed of the greens to the home owners' association, along with a hundred and one other things over which he has no control. At breaking point, he starts replying to emails and requests the way he'd really like to reply, which is a far cry from what they taught him at PGA business school!

While the president's intent to remove him and install his son-in-law is relentless, our pro has more tricks up his sleeve than the assistant pros who hide his inventory or the slick suits from the big management companies that think they can waltz in and steal his job. Success is always the best revenge!

Career Change- The hilarious adventures of a middle-aged accountant who becomes a reluctant gigolo in Monaco.

After getting made redundant, watching his pension fund implode, and finding his wife has left all in 24 hours, 48-year-old accountant Peter Stevens is broke and depressed. After drowning his sorrows for two weeks he takes a friend's offer and goes to stay at his apartment in Monaco. There he meets a beautiful blonde on an elevator who gets him a job with her escort service.

Never very good at sex, according to his wife, things do not start out well as he careens through a series of disastrous dates. His efforts at online dating looking for a normal relationship are equally doomed to failure. But with practice and sex lessons, he begins to get better at his craft and starts to turn his life around. The short, punchy chapters are an easy and humorous read as our hero tries to piece back his finances, love life, and self-esteem.

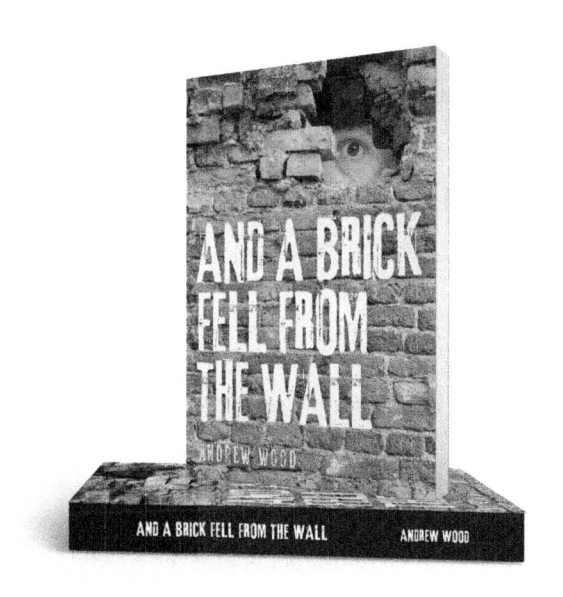

And a Brick Fell From the Wall

1979- Tettenhall College for boys was a private school near Wolverhampton. Posh though it appeared, it was a school with a dark secret. Bullying and abuse were rife, and not just among the pupils. The headmaster was a sadistic Irishman who wheeled his slipper and cane with abandon. Our class of 11- and 12-year-olds all lived in constant fear.

As a child, you are taught to trust and respect your parents, teachers, policemen, and priests. But no one ever tells you what to do when you know in your heart they can't be trusted. When you know that what the adults are doing is wrong. You are in uncharted territory, alone, making decisions you don't want to make. That you shouldn't have to make but that must be made anyway.

I knew the only way to stop the bullying was to confront it. For me that point came on November 16th, 1979. The #1 song on radio Luxem-bourg was "Another Brick in the Wall" by Pink Floyd. It gave me courage, gave me hope and told me I was not alone. It connected with me as no song ever had before or has since. It was the song in my head when I committed my first murder. I was just thirteen years old...

OTHER BOOKS BY ANDREW WOOD

Career Change

Confessions of a Golf Pro

Confessions of a Golf Pro Round Two

Desperately Seeking Members (as Harvey S. Mcklintock)

How to Unleash Your Creativity

How to Create a Life Well Lived

Fame–How to Build an Iconic Personal Brand The Restaurant Marketing Bible

The Author's Marketing Bible

Legendary Advice—101 Proven Strategies to Increase Your Income, Wealth & Lifestyle

Legendary Achievement—How to Maximize Your True Potential & Live the Life of Your Dreams

Cunningly Clever Marketing

Cunningly Clever Entrepreneur

Legendary Selling

Legendary Leadership

Making Your Business the One They Choose

The Traits of Champions (with Brian Tracy)

The Joy of Golf

The Golf Marketing Manual

The Golf Marketing Bible

The Hotel & Resort Marketing Bible

The Golf Sales Bible

Golf Marketing Strategy

How to Make $150,000 a Year Teaching Golf

And a Brick Fell From the Wall!

Available at

www.AndrewWoodInc.com

Printed in Great Britain
by Amazon